A Son Called Gabriel

A Son Called
Gabriel

A
NOVEL

DAMIAN McNICHOLL

PEGASUS BOOKS
NEW YORK LONDON

Pegasus Books Ltd.
148 W 37th Street, 13th Floor
New York, NY 10018

First Pegasus Books edition September 2017

Interior design by Maria Fernandez

Library of Congress Cataloging-in-Publication Data is available.

ISBN: 978-1-68177-504-3

10 9 8 7 6 5 4 3 2 1

Printed in the United States of America
Distributed by W. W. Norton & Company, Inc.
www.pegasusbooks.us

To Larry Caban,
for all the encouragement, belief, and unwavering love.

A Son Called Gabriel

PART ONE

September 1964–August 1970

One

The choices were school or the big stick, and the decision seemed easy to make. My younger sister, Caroline, and any other boy in the whole of Ireland would choose school, but I knew I was right in refusing to go. I was six and had been going to school for almost a year. I was tired of being picked on, spat at, and just wanted to leave. I glanced down the road one more time and saw that my friend Fergal was now sandwiched between Jennifer and her twin brother, Noel. They stopped and looked back for a moment before disappearing over the brow of the hill.

"I'm definitely not going," I shouted at Mammy.

The idea of staying at home with my sister and James, my four-year-old brother, seemed far more sensible. Mother stood at the front gate with an angry look on her round face, hands pressed against her hips.

"Get to school this instant or I'll fetch a sally rod and beat the living daylights out of you."

I stared at the birdshite on the tarmac for a few moments before starting toward the house. "It's all right for you to say I must go, but you don't have to deal with Henry Lynch every day. He makes the others gang up on me and you won't listen."

"You must go to school, or you'll just be a stupid Harkin." She always said my father's family was stupid when she got angry.

"I don't care."

"Last year, you wanted to go so much, I went and got permission for you to start school very young. I did that for you, Gabriel, and if you don't go now, I'll be a laughingstock."

That part was true. Fergal was more than a year older than me and, when he started school last year, I cried and demanded to go along with him. I cried so hard for two days that my mother took me to the primary school and spoke to Mrs. Bradley, the headmistress. She tested my thinking and speech and said I could start, because I was bright and way ahead of my years.

"That was before I knew Henry Lynch would be in my class," I said.

"You must try harder to get him to like you. Talk to him instead of shying away . . . and don't take his name-calling to heart. You must be a man, Gabriel. Nobody likes a boy who's too sensitive."

That wasn't the reason Henry hated me. He hated me because I wasn't interested in playing football with him and the other boys. Where was the fun in chasing a ball around a mucky field? I wondered. I preferred playing stuck-in-the-muck with the senior girls. Even though they were eight, nine, and ten, I was every bit as fast as them. And stuck-in-the-muck wasn't just a girl's game like Henry kept saying. You had to be every bit as fast and skillful as footballers in order to avoid the person playing the jailer. Otherwise, she tagged you and sent you into the jail corner.

"I'm still not going," I said, as I walked toward my mother.

She wagged her finger before she ran up to a nearby hedge, broke off a sally rod, and started charging at me.

"I'm not putting up with this nonsense. Your sister's starting after the summer holidays, and I'm not going to tolerate you showing her a bad example."

Mammy seized my arm and I watched the rod, with its baby green shoots just like kitten claws, rise until it became a thin, dark line against the sky. It fell and rose, fell and rose. Hot stings spread out over my bare legs. One thump hit the exact same spot as the first and I started to dance about the road. I tasted the salt of my tears as I tried to dig my heels into the tarmac, but she was much stronger and dragged me down the road.

A car came from behind us as we reached the brow of the hill. The driver honked as it passed and stopped five yards ahead. It was old Mr. O'Kane. Quickly, I wiped my eyes and cleaned my nose on my pullover sleeve as we walked up to the window of the car.

"Howdy, Eileen," he said. "Do you want a lift?"

"This one's decided he doesn't like school and is refusing to go this morning." She laughed. "If I don't teach him who's boss, he'll end up in Borstal."

Borstal was not a place I wanted to go. Declan Keefrey was in Borstal, had been sent there for stealing, but boys didn't get sent there simply for refusing to go to school.

"I was never one for school or the books myself." Mr. O'Kane winked at me. "Son, you have to go to school to learn, because a body can't get anywhere nowadays without an education behind him." As he smiled, the gaps between the tiny purple veins that looked like spiderwebs on his cheeks stretched and widened. "I dare say if you're anything like your uncle Brendan, you'll be a smart fella."

Uncle Brendan was a priest in the foreign missions whom I'd never met. He didn't ever come home for visits. My grandmother wanted him home, but he never came.

"Hop in and I'll take you to school," he said.

I knew I'd have to go now, as I couldn't refuse in front of a neighbor, but Mr. O'Kane's car was the joke of Knockburn. It was shaped like an egg at the back, was also the same color as an egg, and had tires as narrow as stroller wheels. All the boys laughed at it when it passed by on the road, and now Henry Lynch would see me getting out of it at school.

"I'll walk, thanks," I said.

"You're now late," said Mammy. Her lips stretched horribly thin again. "Get in the car at once."

Ancient and very small, the school had a slate roof and thick walls with three large windows on either side, each with sixteen small glass panes. It stood perched on a hill at the end of a long, winding lane and was surrounded by a dry moat ringed by beech trees with smooth-barked trunks. Coal-black crows nested in their silvery branches and ten of them rose into the air cawing as we drove along the driveway. Fergal and the others were climbing the hill, a shortcut everyone took to reach the school building, and I crouched down in the seat as we passed by so he wouldn't see me. Luckily, Henry wasn't by the main door as Mr. O'Kane pulled up, and I bounded out of the car and disappeared inside.

At my desk, I thought about what my mother had said about trying harder with Henry. An idea jumped into my head just before lunch. Every day, we ate at our desks under the supervision of Miss Murray, our teacher, and I'd noticed Henry always had the same food to eat. It was always strawberry jam on bright yellow Indian meal scones. He never had ham or a chocolate bar like me, because his father was on the dole and couldn't afford it.

Henry shared the desk immediately behind me with Simple Brian, a much older boy who was a spastic and blew spittle bubbles through his rubbery lips that always dribbled down his chin. I turned around, forced a smile, and said, "Henry, would you like one of my ham sandwiches?"

Henry had wiry hair that reminded me of the scrubbing pads Mammy used to clean saucepans, and his sneaky, bright eyes stared at me under his lashes. Mammy said he had bad hair, not good hair like mine, which was straight and glossy brown. She also said he wasn't good-looking like me, because I had my father's "black Irish" coloring and looked brown and healthy all year.

"Why would you give me one of your sandwiches, Harkin?" he asked.

I made sure to meet Henry's stare and tried to control my shaking legs. "I thought you might like to try something different."

"Have you spit on it?"

"I have *not* indeed."

His eyes darted to the sandwich in my damp hand. Simple Brian watched, slimy dribbles trailing from his mouth, and I knew I wouldn't want to eat my chocolate bar now, either.

"I'll also give you my chocolate today."

"I'll take the chocolate bar, but I won't have the sandwich unless you eat a piece of my Indian scone."

Henry's family lived in government housing and I was sure his house wasn't clean like mine. I glanced at the horrible-looking yellow scone and saw where the red jam had seeped out and dried around its edges. It looked like blood.

"I'm not so very hungry today."

"Is my scone not good enough for you to eat? Is that what this is about?"

"I just thought you'd like some ham for a change, that's all."

"Harkin, are you saying my ma can't afford to buy ham?"

Of course they couldn't afford it. I laid my sandwich on the desk before him. "I'll have a tiny, tiny piece, then."

He broke off a huge piece and watched as I took a bite. It was dry as straw and I saw a black hair on it as I raised it to my lips. I wanted to hurl it away. Henry took a bite of the ham sandwich and we watched each other chew.

"How do you like my ma's scone?"

"Delicious." My belly flipped.

"In that case, you can have the rest and I'll take another ham sandwich."

"You're sharing each other's lunches, boys," Miss Murray said. "Look, girls and boys! Look at the example Henry and Gabriel are setting. They're sharing. Sharing is so good to do. Now, who can raise their hand and tell me another person who shared a feast?"

No one raised a hand.

"I'll give you a hint. His name begins with a 'J.'"

Still, no one raised a hand.

"*Jesus*, boys and girls," she said. "Remember . . . remember I told you Jesus gave his body to the apostles to eat?" The teacher looked at Henry. "Goodness! Henry, quick, quick. Clean Brian's mouth this instant. He's dribbling badly."

Henry hated sitting beside Simple Brian, because the teacher always made him wipe his mouth. The corn in the scone felt like cement powder in my mouth. I wanted to vomit.

My plan worked. Henry stopped calling me a sissy and getting the others to gang up on me. So long as I gave him a sandwich and half of my chocolate bar every day, he didn't bother me. Then, one afternoon after school a few weeks later, he came up to me, prodded my chest, and told me I had to hand over every chocolate bar or whatever other treat I had for lunch from the next day onward. Although it didn't seem right, I did it—until I grew angry with myself. Every time I gave up the chocolate, I was reminded of how I was completely in his power.

"I can't give it to you anymore," I said at the beginning of the second week. My voice shook. I could hardly hold his stare.

"I'm going to make it very rough for you again, cunt," he said.

"What you're doing is wrong, Henry."

"Don't tell me what to do, you fucking sissy boy." He poked my chest with his finger like a jackhammer. "I'll give you a good thrashing if you don't give me the stuff."

Still I refused, but he didn't hit me. Instead, the name-calling and spitting returned, much worse than before.

After the summer holidays, at least once a week, Henry and some other boys started to come around to where I played with the girls to cause me trouble. They'd trip me up as I ran about releasing girls from jail. They'd call me nasty names that cut my mind to ribbons. I tried to ignore them, but I could not block the words. They darted inside my head. They felt like my mother's sharp carving knife slicing my brain to pieces. I'd try to go on with the stuck-in-the-muck game, but I felt so ashamed in front of the girls. They tried to stop Henry, often sending him away, but minutes later he and the others would return. Eventually, Jennifer and the others gave up.

I also started getting it bad from Daddy. My friend Fergal and I had had an argument walking home from school one afternoon. My father was weeding in the garden and, as we drew up to the gate, he asked Fergal jokingly which one of us was the better footballer. Fergal told him I didn't play because I preferred being with girls. I knew it was only Fergal's anger talking, but it set my father off and he demanded I play with the boys. To please him, I decided to make an effort. All the boys had a favorite English football team, so I studied the teams and picked one, to make sure I had a name ready for the next time I was teased about not having a favorite.

"Hey, Harkin, haven't you picked a soccer team to support yet?" Henry said at lunch a few weeks later, after Miss Murray had disappeared behind the pink curtain. The curtain ran along the width of the room, dividing it into the senior and junior sections, and she always went into the senior section to drink black tea with the headmistress after we finished eating lunch.

"I quite like Chelsea."

His eyes widened with surprise as the other boys crowded around.

"Why?" Henry's sneaky eyes moved slowly from face to face to make sure everyone was listening.

"I like the color of their outfits . . . and Chelsea is a nicer part of England."

"The color of their kit doesn't matter a fuck." Henry stood and smacked the top of my head with his palm.

This was the first time he'd smacked me and I needed to tell him to stop, but I couldn't bring myself to say anything. He wasn't fooled by my answer, either. I'd picked Chelsea because I liked the photographs of the players in their blue shorts, not because of their skills.

"Seeing as you have a team now, I think you should play with us today," Henry said, and he looked at the other boys real sneakily. "You can't support a team properly until you understand the game."

"Yes, come on, Gabriel," said another boy.

The sun was shining when we got outside, and the girls had started their game. My sister, Caroline, was running about the yard in her purple-and-white pinafore, a matching ribbon in her long dark hair. The jailer wasn't at all interested in her, though. She was only five years old, a small fry, too small to play with them. They allowed her to be there only because of me. They should've just put her in jail, like I was forever telling them, and she'd be happy.

Caroline's eyes locked on mine as she waved. The girls' happy shrieks filled the playground and I wanted badly to join in. But Henry had a point. I should give football another try.

"Gabriel, come and free me," Jennifer said. She was Noel's twin, but didn't have yellow-green teeth like him. She brushed hers.

"I'm going to give football another go."

"Ach, why, Gabriel? Don't play with them. I *must* be released."

I turned to Henry. "I'll come and play with you in a minute." Running over to the jailer, I whispered, "Put our Caroline in jail."

"If you promise to release me before anyone else when I'm next in jail," she said.

"I promise."

"Before freckle-faced Jennifer?"

"I'll release you first."

She ran over and tagged my sister.

"I'm catched, Gabriel. Look, she catched me," Caroline said, and she ran joyfully into the shady, damp corner that was our jail.

I ran to the other side of the school. Some boys and girls were lining up to slide down the hill to the bottom of the dry moat.

Their trousers and skirts were streaked brown and gray from cinders and ashes dumped there from Mrs. Bradley's fireplace. Henry was picking the football teams as I drew up.

"You're on the other team, because you're useless," he said.

He was picking for both teams even though he had no right to do so, but the other boys were obeying him. A few minutes later, the game started. Every time the ball rolled in my direction, I prayed it would stop, or someone would reach it before it came to me. Boys swarmed around me, pulled at my sweater, cursed, kicked my shins. Twice, Henry came over and smacked my head in the middle of the tackling.

"Stop hitting me, Henry," I said, after he smacked me much harder a third time. "That's not allowed in the rules."

"How the fuck would you know the rules?" He hit me again on the side of my face. "Come on, Harkin, fight me. Or are you a yellabelly?"

I just looked at him.

"Let's see you fight him," another boy said.

The game was forgotten as the boys huddled close. Tears welled in my eyes. I wanted to hit him, but I knew fighting was wrong. I turned away.

"Le-le-leave him be, Hen-Henry," said stuttering Anthony. "You-you-you asked him t-to play ball and-and-and he did."

"Shut up, Stuttery-mouth," Henry said.

Fergal watched, but said nothing. He was my friend, my best friend, but he also liked the other boys. When I met his eye, he quickly looked down at the ground. Henry was king.

Suddenly, Henry lifted his foot and kicked my arse. He stuck up his fists like Cassius Clay and began to dance around me. It looked silly. The boys cheered. Fergal laughed with them. Seeing him laugh gave me a much sharper pain than the one in my arse.

Henry's fist hit my nose. I heard the crack inside my head. I put my hand up and felt my nose. When I brought it down, there was blood on my fingers. The boys saw my blood and cheered.

"Hit him back, Harkin," one of them cried. "Let's see the color of his blood."

Older boys gathered around now; my blood excited them as well. They ordered me to floor Henry. My head was sore. I raised my hands and formed fists, but still I could not hit him.

"Gabriel, kill him," said Noel. "Don't let us down. Don't let a boy from the other side of Knockburn beat the shite out of you."

"I don't want to fight."

"Coward! Coward!" the boys cawed.

"Fighting's for animals. They don't know better." I dropped my fists to my sides and started to leave. Henry pushed me hard in the back and shoved me out of the loosening ring of boys.

"Gabriel is a coward! He's a big sissy!" the older boys yelled. "Gabriel Harkin's a sissy boy!"

I ran back to the girls to get away from their teasing. Caroline was hunkered down in the jail corner, but I didn't feel like releasing her. Standing near a pile of twigs and split logs alongside the school wall, I waited for Fergal to come to me. The coal-black crows shrieked. I waited. The boys' yells mixed with the girls' laughter and the crows' shrieks. Still, he didn't come. A fiery tear slid down my cheek.

"Oh, stop your damned crying," I said aloud, and gritted my teeth until they hurt.

A few minutes later, the headmistress came out and rang the brass bell, and I went inside. Another lunchtime was over, but something had changed forever. I really hadn't known I would never fight. But now I knew, and the boys did, too. Henry knew he could hit me and I would not fight back.

That night, I told my mother I'd been in a fight and walked away from Henry.

"That was the right thing to do," she said. "You won the fight because you did that, Gabriel. You're the winner and a real man as a result."

I did not feel like a real man. Nor did my mother have the power to make me the winner. Only the boys had that power.

"It's come to fighting now," she said to Daddy later. "Should we speak to Henry's mother, or the teacher?"

"Quit your talking. This'll toughen the lad up. He can't run to teachers about things like that. It'll only make it worse. He's got to learn to hold his own." Daddy rubbed his large nose for a moment with a finger blackened by the oily grease of the truck he drove, then said to me, "You've got to stand up for yourself and not let that Henry Lynch push you around. Fight back like a man. Real men stand their ground, Gabriel. They don't run away under any circumstances."

I looked over at my mother, but her eyes stayed fixed on the TV screen.

Two

After Granda Harkin died in May, there was a huge rumpus because Uncle Brendan didn't come home for the funeral. Granny Harkin was heart-sore for weeks afterward because he hadn't come, which made Auntie Celia even angrier with him. I overheard Mammy say to Daddy that Brendan was a priest, should know what was proper, and wasn't he the right bad article? When I asked why Uncle Brendan was a "right bad article," she got angry and told me to mind my own business.

In the middle of all the tears and anger, Uncle Tommy, Daddy's other brother, got married. Mammy said the neighbors would talk, as he was marrying so soon after Granda's funeral, but Uncle Tommy decided to go ahead, because the priest was booked and "good money" had been paid for the hotel reception.

After their honeymoon in Wexford, Uncle Tommy and his new wife moved into our house, and I didn't understand why. Nor did I like it, because James and I had to leave our bedroom and share Caroline's. When I asked my mother, whose stomach was growing very big, she said they were staying until their new house was built.

"When it's finished, they'll leave and things will get back to normal 'round here, thank God," she said. "Until then, you'll be extremely nice to your new Auntie Bernie."

Pleasant for the most part, our home was a one-story bungalow with three small bedrooms, a living room where we watched TV, and a kitchen with tan-colored tiles, sky-blue cupboards, and a square table that could be opened and made larger when needed. One sky-blue cupboard was a larder where two plastic buckets stood on a concrete shelf on one side: a faded red one to keep the milk bottles cool and a blue one for our drinking water. It was my job every Saturday and Sunday to fetch water in the blue bucket from the spring in our fields. We also had a sitting room, the prettiest room in the house. It had shiny white bird ornaments that Uncle Brendan had given my parents as a wedding gift, a round brass mirror above the fireplace, and a dark red sofa and armchairs that felt, but didn't smell, like leather.

"Give your auntie a hug," Daddy said to me, as we were watching TV on their second night in our home.

"I don't want to give her a hug."

I was still cross about her moving in and, what's more, I had sneaked into my bedroom that morning and found her sleeping on my side of the bed.

"Luksee, Gabriel, do it," he said.

Caroline was on my aunt's knee, fingering the white beads Auntie Bernie wore around her neck. They had once belonged to her dead mother and Auntie Bernie used them to hide a raised brown mole with a hair in its middle. She was always asking Mammy if the mole was changing color, until Mammy was black in the face. Auntie Bernie always put Caroline and James on her lap. She never asked me to sit there; not that I wanted her to, because her perfume was fierce bad.

"Gabriel thinks he's too old for hugs, don't you?" Auntie Bernie said. She began to straighten Caroline's hair ribbon.

"When will you be leaving our house, Auntie Bernie?" I asked.

Her fingers froze on the ribbon.

"That's very rude," my father said. He winked at Uncle Tommy.

"This house is too small and Mammy said she'll be very happy when your new house is finished and things can get back to normal 'round here."

Auntie giggled, high as a flying kite, as she pushed Caroline off her lap.

"I said no such thing," said Mammy. "Honestly, the lies children dream up." She looked at me sharply. "Don't tell lies."

"We'll be leaving in a few months," Uncle Tommy said, and smiled as he played with his dark ginger sideburns, which ended near the bottom of his cheeks. Uncle Tommy was forever twisting and playing with them and Auntie Bernie was forever telling him to stop. I liked his sideburns, and also liked feeling the hard bump when he bent his arm and told me to feel his muscles. His lower arms had reddish hairs just like the Chelsea players. They felt silky under my fingers when he grabbed my arms and swung me 'round and 'round in the garden until my head spun. I liked him to do that, even though I was now seven years old: my shoes would fly off and the cool air would rush into my striped socks, right between my toes, and when he set me down, I'd be drunk with dizziness. That made him laugh. I'd clown about and pretend to be really drunk, until my father would start talking to him and he'd forget about me.

Uncle Tommy and Daddy were Granny Harkin's sons. Caroline, James, and I were powerful scared of Granny Neeson, our other grandmother, because she never smiled and was so sour-faced. Her face was almost square and she had a red sty in the corner of her right eye that I hated looking at, yet saw every time she asked me a question because it would be rude not to look at her. We had to be very quiet when we visited her, too. She liked neither noise nor children.

Even my father didn't like visiting Granny Neeson. When we had to visit, he always made excuses to go places with Joe, his best friend, and that always caused enormous arguments. Mammy would shout at him in the scullery, he'd roar back an answer, and then she'd say he didn't want to visit because her family wasn't good enough for the Harkins. When she got really cross, she screamed. She'd scream that Granda Harkin had never liked her, even when he'd come to her, cap in hand, to ask for the big favor and she agreed to help the Harkins out.

"Who the hell are the Harkins but a bunch of damned sheep farmers with bad land at the end of the day?" she'd always say during a fight. Daddy always told her to shut her mouth, because she'd promised never to repeat anything about the "big favor," and then he'd grab pots and bang them against the draining board of the sink. Caroline, James, and I hated the banging and we'd gather in a ring in the middle of the scullery. At these times, my father would never pick Caroline up and hug her when she started crying. She was forgotten. I'd pray for it to stop, which always worked, even though it took a while. Then my mother would come to me.

"I'm sorry, Gabriel," she'd say. "I don't know what I'm saying when your daddy makes me this mad."

I didn't know what she was talking about, either. I asked about the "big favor" once, but her voice sharpened and she warned me not to be nosy. She'd only been getting back at my father, she'd say, and my granda had been "a holy man, may God have mercy on his soul."

Visiting Granny Harkin was much easier. She lived only two miles away and James, Caroline, and I were allowed to go there when we pleased. Her home lay at the end of a long gravel lane winding through purple heather and looked like a white shoebox with a thatched roof. Pink, sweet-smelling roses as big as men's fists grew on one side of the front door. Uncle John, my godfather, lived with her because he wasn't married.

Though we didn't like to talk about it too much, Caroline and I agreed Granny Harkin's house wasn't as tidy as Granny Neeson's. Uncle John's sheepdog had fleas, stank quite a bit, and slept under the kitchen table. Also, her ragged sofa cushions were never straight, the cream range was never shiny, and the top of the walls and white ceiling were black with turf soot. Uncle John didn't do any housework because he was a man, and Auntie Celia, my favorite cousin's mother who had a shop in Duncarlow, was far too grand to come out and help Granny, whose leg was bad.

When I visited alone, I liked to sit at the green Formica table and watch Granny take off her elastic hairnet and undo her bun. Her hair was long and shiny and looked like Caroline's, except that the ropes were silver, not black. Sometimes she allowed me to brush it, if I promised not to do it hard.

"Gabriel, you and Caroline are the picture of your uncle Brendan when he was your age," she said as I brushed. "He was the handsomest man in Knockburn. Aye, your granda had to hunt the girls away. When he was a teenager, they were forever trying to kiss him." My grandmother looked out over the fields for so long her eyes watered. "Oh, it's hard, Gabriel. Nobody but your poor old granny knows how hard it is."

"But when you look at me or Caroline, then you can still see him, Granny," I said.

It was stupid to say that. I didn't have black wavy hair like Uncle Brendan or Daddy. Mine was dark brown and straight, I had a cowlick for a fringe, and my eyes were hazel, not gray like my father's.

"Even if I don't have the wavy Harkin hair."

"It doesn't have to be wavy to be Harkin hair."

"Mammy says it's too soft and corn-stalk straight to be Harkin—"

"Your mammy's arse and parsley. Jesus, you have the Harkin hair . . . and you and Caroline have Brendan's and your daddy's brains, as well. So that mother of yours needn't be going about the country saying that you haven't got Harkin hair."

I always said something like this if we were alone when she talked sadly about Uncle Brendan. It made her stop crying. She'd forget to be sad and her face would redden and tiny balls of spittle would fly from her mouth and spark on the table as she spoke. Granny was very kind and holy, but liked Caroline and me better than James because he had the square face and shortness of the Neesons. Sometimes, she gave Caroline and me a half-crown apiece, but only gave him a shilling. That made Mammy mad, but my father would only laugh.

"I hope he's happy in Kenya, Gabriel," Granny said, and she sighed hard. "Ouch! Jesus, Gabriel, don't brush my hair so damned hard or you'll leave me with none."

"Sorry." I brushed in silence, because Granny was thinking about Uncle Brendan in Kenya again.

"Yes, he's been away long enough," she said. "He should come home where he belongs. The whole thing's forgotten. He can get a parish here. Sure, they're crying out for priests in Ireland. I don't know why the hell he has to stay in that godforsaken place when there's a loch full of souls in need of saving here. Aye, he should just come home to his mammy."

"What's forgotten, Granny?"

She said these things when she talked about Uncle Brendan, but every time I asked about the forgotten thing, she wouldn't say what it was. She'd say "all's well" or "my dotage is starting, Gabriel," and all I could get was Uncle Brendan wouldn't come home and she wanted him home. Not even Cousin Martin could find out what she was talking about, if he happened to be around when she said these things.

Once, Granny had cried really sorely, because it was Uncle Brendan's birthday and she couldn't see him. I'd never seen her crying so hard. As soon as I'd gotten home that afternoon, I'd told Mammy and asked why Brendan didn't come to see Granny and what thing was forgotten. After sitting on an armchair and drawing me in front of her, she'd made me repeat word for word what Granny and I had been talking about.

"Your grandmother is starting to lose it," Mammy had said after I'd finished, "and I want you to promise me you'll ask no more questions about this ever again. If you don't promise, I'm stopping you from going up to visit her alone." She'd also made me cross my heart never to bother Granny with that sort of question.

I came out of my thoughts about Mammy and the forgotten thing when Granny cleared her throat. "Your godfather's taking my lambs to the market this afternoon," she said. "Yours will be also be going, so I'm going to give you your wee fiver today."

Every year she gave me a lamb—this year I'd named it Bonny—and when market time came 'round, she gave me five pounds. Of course, I always wanted to take the lamb home and make it my pet, but she'd only allow me to see it a few times throughout the summer.

"I'm old now and don't wish my lamb to go to the market this year," I said. "So I won't take the fiver, if you don't mind."

She took the brush from me and laid it on the table. "That's not possible."

Granny made a plait, swirled it into a bun, and put on the hairnet again. It was silly that she brushed her hair only to tie it up the same way again. She hummed as she pushed the sticking-out bits underneath the net. I waited until she'd finished and looked at me again.

"Why not?" I gave her my biggest Harkin smile.

"It'll go to the market and you'll get the money."

"What will it do at the market?"

"It'll be sold and taken to another place."

"Why not let it stay in Uncle John's fields?"

"Who's saying they're your uncle's fields?" My grandmother hobbled toward the door. "Aye, I'm not dead and buried yet." She stopped after she'd opened it. "I'm just going outside for a minute. Put on the kettle for tea."

I peeped out the side window. The cream-colored paint on the dusty sill was cracked and bulged in the corner where rain had leaked in. Granny stood in the little garden and fumbled underneath her long skirt. She hunkered down in front of the blood-red-and-green stalks of her rhubarb patch. Granny always peed there during the daylight, which was a reason I pretended I didn't like rhubarb jam when she wanted to make me a sandwich. As she was pulling up her knickers, I put the dented kettle on the hob and, meeting her at the door, told her I was going up to the mountain to see Uncle John. I ran off in case she tried to make me eat.

Granda's old carthorse with the star and three white socks was grazing in the meadow and I stopped to watch him. "Hello, aul Rory," I shouted, but he was deaf. Uncle John didn't put him inside the shafts of the blue and orange cart and let me ride with him like Granda had done. He'd bought a tractor with the armfuls of money he'd got in Granda's will. Rory wasn't needed anymore.

I thought about Granda for a moment. I thought about him sitting in his favorite chair near the range, watching me watching him from the other chair as he puffed on his pipe. I could see his gray hair, his hazel eyes, the brown spots on his hands, and his curly pipe now lying on top of the window pelmet. His pipe lay dusty and forgotten on top of the pelmet and his overalls and Sunday suit were on hangers in the storage room. They didn't have his smell anymore. His suit now smelt damp, the cloth cold and limp between my fingers.

When I reached Half-Mile Hill, I saw Uncle John near the sheep-dipping pen. A helper—wearing dungarees that must have been too big, because he'd tied a hay bale rope around his waist—was with him. As I drew closer, I could smell the sheep shite. The ewes were running about with bulged and rolling eyes, glistening round marbles dropping from their dirty arses because Uncle John was grabbing their lambs and shoving them into a smaller pen. Uncle John dragged an ewe roughly by its small horns up to a pot of bright red paint and jammed its head between his legs. His fat tummy almost touched the sheep's back as he bent over and grabbed a stick from the paint pot with his crooked fingers, broken years ago in a Gaelic football game.

"Where's my lamb, Uncle John?" I asked.

He continued to form the "J" of his "JH" mark on the sheep's side. "Over in the other pen."

The sheep bucked, and he cursed and yanked its fleece. I ran over to the smaller pen and, grasping the smooth metal side rails, jumped up on the narrow concrete ledge and looked about for her. Lambs bleated in every corner. Two were scared witless, many had horn buds popping from their heads, but all the ones with black-and-white faces looked the same. The helper came over with another, fumbled open the narrow gate to the pen with one hand, and dragged it inside where it skidded on the shite after he set it free.

"Which is my lamb?" I asked.

"What are ye on about?"

"Where is the one my grandmother gave me?" I looked behind to see if Uncle John was still marking the sheep before turning back to the man. "There's so many of them. How do they get to the market?"

"We take them in that trailer over there. Do you want to come? We're leaving in an hour or so."

The trailer was small, about twice the size of a horsebox, with slatted sides. I couldn't see how all the lambs could fit into such a tiny space.

"All the lambs fit in there?"

"Aye."

"How long do they stay at the market?"

"Until they're sold and taken to the abattoir."

I loved the sound of that name. "Will the lambs run as free in the aba . . . abavar as on this mountain?"

The man's eyes narrowed, and creases as puffy as the wrinkles on my school shirt formed at their sides. "You're quite the joker."

"What do you mean?"

Uncle laughed.

"What do you mean?"

"Sure you know as well as I do they're shot and sliced up nice as pie so your mother can buy a chop or two for your Sunday dinner."

My legs buckled. I watched Uncle John mark another ewe with the blood-colored paint. Charging from the pens, I hurtled down the hill and over the meadow, not stopping until I reached the last gate before my grandmother's house. My chest was as tight as the skin on an onion. I couldn't breathe. I forced myself to take a gulp of air before climbing the gate. A stitch started up in my side as I ran across the final pasture. Auntie Celia's car was parked alongside the rhubarb patch. I wondered if Cousin Martin had come with her, then heard his younger brother, Connor, asking Granny for a glass of orangeade as I opened the door. Even though Martin was nine and Connor only a year older than me, I liked Martin better. We loved to read adventure books and talk about them afterward. Connor didn't like reading and was sneaky: if Granny said he couldn't have juice, he'd take it behind her back anyway.

Martin was in the living room. While happy to see him, it made things tricky on account of Granny had warned me not to tell my cousins she gave me a lamb every year. I sat on the sofa beside Martin and waited for a chance to speak to her alone. The clock's big black hands jerked and moved, jerked and moved. At last, Connor said we should go to the river and poison some trout with disinfectant.

"What a good idea," I said.

Martin's eyes widened. We hated killing trout.

"You can go, provided you don't go near the deep part," Auntie Celia said. "Go and make your dam. By that time, I'll have measured out the disinfectant and one of you can come back and fetch it."

"Go on to the river and I'll wait for Auntie Celia to measure out the stuff," I said, as soon as we got outside. "That way, I'll make sure she gives us plenty."

"I'll wait, too," said Martin.

"Go and help Connor make the dam."

Martin's fair skin, usually white as my pillowcase, turned patchy red. It turned like that when he was either angry or telling lies, the last thing being something Connor was better than Martin at doing. Connor never looked you in the eye when he talked, which made it hard to judge if he was telling the truth.

After turning away sharply, Martin started marching down the lane, his arms swinging like a soldier and his stumpy legs moving even faster to keep up with them.

"Why are you here, Gabriel?" Auntie Celia said, as I came inside.

"I need to ask Granny something."

"Off you go with your cousins."

The skin in the middle part of Auntie Celia's upper lip was cracked and must have been dry all the time, because she was always wetting it with her tongue. Auntie was thin, but had the widest bottom Caroline and I had ever seen. She wore a gold gate bracelet that looked nothing like a gate. It was loose and forever moved up and down her wrist, because she talked with her hands as well as her mouth.

"It's important I speak to Granny."

Auntie Celia's nose wrinkled like I'd farted. "Hurry up, then run along and catch up with the boys. She and I wish to talk."

I went to my grandmother and put my lips to her ears.

"No whispering," said Auntie Celia. "Didn't your mother tell you that's extremely rude?"

"It's only for her ears."

Her tongue paused on her dry cracked lip. "My, but he's a sneaky one, isn't he? Wants to keep secrets from his Auntie Celia who's so good, she's invited him to stay at her house for part of the summer holiday. I wonder where he gets his sneaky streak. Certainly not from the Harkins, that's for sure."

The big clock's hour hand was on the twelve.

"I shan't have you staying in my house if you're sneaky. I shan't, because I don't want Martin or Connor learning to keep things from their mother like you country boys do."

"Say what you need to say in front of your auntie."

"It's okay to say, Granny?"

She fixed her hairnet as she nodded.

"Uncle John's taking my lamb to the aba—to the killing place, to be turned into chops, and he must be stopped."

Grandmother's hands dropped to her lap like a falling hatchet.

"And what might this be about?" Auntie Celia said. Her smile flew off her face and she stood up like she'd been whacked across the back of the head. She walked up to the range and rested her wide arse on the shiny metal bar running across its front. "You gave him a lamb. Why did you not give Martin a lamb? They're best friends. Is there a reason only *he* gets a lamb that escapes me?" She shifted, the metal bar turned, and a tea towel with a brown stain fell to the floor. Auntie Celia stared but didn't pick it up. "Why don't you think to give my son—your grandson, I might also add—a wee lamb to go to the abattoir?"

"I don't want any more fivers if this is what happens to the lambs you give me each year," I said. I tightened my mouth and looked at my grandmother. "Please stop Uncle John from taking—"

"A fiver!" Auntie Celia exclaimed. "You're spoiling this boy rotten. Sweet Jesus and his mother, a fiver." As Auntie pointed at me, her bracelet slid to where her thumb joined with her hand. "He's special, is that it? Just because he's . . . well . . . just because Harry's children live out here in the country, you tend to them hand and foot and give them fivers. Mine get nothing. Not a single sausage."

"Please save my lamb."

"Not a sausage do my boys get from you, from one end of the year to the—"

"The trailer will soon be leaving with my lamb—"

"They get enough to do them," said Granny. "Sure, you've got a shop that's making you cartloads of money."

"And I work myself to the bone for every—"

"Granny, I'm begging you not to let my lamb go to the killing place."

"You go now to your cousins," said Auntie Celia.

"Stop being so hard on him, Celia." My grandmother hobbled over to me. "Uncle John will come in for his tea before he leaves for the market. I'll get him to take your lamb out and put her back in the field."

"And take the whole damned can of disinfectant to Martin," said Auntie Celia.

I raced to my cousins and told them why I'd wanted them to leave for the river. Martin forgave my slyness and the three of us ran back to the house and hid behind the high ditch by the rhubarb patch. Uncle John and the helper came, parked the trailer, and went inside for tea. The lambs bleated, but I could see only wool puffing out from between the narrow slats.

I tried opening the door, but the bolt wouldn't budge. Connor tried, then Martin, but we could not make it move. When Uncle came out, I ordered him to take my lamb out of the trailer.

"She's right in at the back." Uncle didn't even check. "Don't worry. I'll bring her home."

"You're lying, Uncle John. First, you took it away from its parents and now you're taking it to be killed."

"Stop this silly talk, Gabriel. That wee lamb doesn't know who its parents are."

Three

My mother was still screaming in the bedroom as Nurse Noonan drove into the driveway. She got out quickly, opened the back door of her car, and leaned inside. She took out a chunky black case and ran into the house without closing the car door. We'd been told she was delivering our new baby, though I didn't think it could be in Nurse's case; it looked far too small. Twenty minutes later, Auntie Bernie came into the garage, where Jennifer had set up a pretend school, and told us God had appeared in the bedroom and brought us a sister.

Nuala was trouble from the beginning. She never wanted to sleep. When she did, it was only for small stretches at a time, and Mammy's heart was broken. She hadn't had a good night's rest for weeks. Everyone was given orders to be very quiet when the baby was asleep. We had to be especially quiet in our bed-rooms and, because we had no indoor lavatory, if we needed to do more than pee, we had to creep down the hall. Nuala heard the smallest noises.

Early one morning, I woke up needing to go outside. As I passed Uncle Tommy and Auntie Bernie's bedroom, I heard a great deal of noise, which meant Auntie was disobeying orders and would waken the baby.

I opened their bedroom door and couldn't make heads or tails of what they were talking about. My bed's springs were squeaking louder than James and I could make them squeak. The room was dim, a tiny slice of morning light squeezed past the crack in the curtain, and my top sheet, the one I liked with the pattern of yellow flowers, was half-bunched on the floor. Uncle Tommy was on top of Auntie Bernie, who had her legs wrapped tightly around his very white backside. He was pumping her like a bull I'd once seen pumping a cow in a field. She was also talking as if she was out of breath and whimpering like a puppy badly in need of petting.

"Why are you pumping Auntie Bernie?"

They stopped. Everything went in slow motion before my eyes, as their arms and legs moved and they separated from each other. Uncle Tommy rose and walked down the bed, his long dokey jerking up and down. Auntie Bernie had red hair in her private place. She stuck her arm out and tried to grab the sheet, but missed. She tried again, raising her back and turning a bit, and I could see her hanging tummies with brown red knobs. They were exactly like a sow's tummies, only there were two, not twenty.

"You're not supposed to be in here," she said.

The slow motion stopped. Uncle Tommy swiped his under-pants off the top of the vanity and fell against it as he raised a leg and tried to hop into them.

"Nuala will wake up because of this noise," I said.

"Thank you for reminding us," Uncle Tommy said. "You just go back to bed now."

I turned to leave, but looked back. "Why were you pumping her like a bull?"

"Don't ask cheeky questions that only concern grown-ups," Auntie Bernie said.

"Why is it cheeky?"

"Your auntie had a wee puncture." Uncle Tommy smiled at Auntie Bernie, who looked at him crossly.

"Does Daddy fix Mammy's punctures?"

"Yes."

"Who fixes yours?"

Uncle Tommy laughed. "Men don't get punctures."

"Why not?"

"Leave my bedroom," said Auntie Bernie.

"It's *my* bedroom," I said, and left.

Later, I overheard Auntie Bernie talking about me in the kitchen.

"He saw my breasts, but I don't think he saw anything else. And he saw Tommy's thing . . . you know . . . a bit stirred up."

Mammy giggled.

"Do you think it could hurt him at his age?" I could tell by her voice that Auntie was worried. "I don't want him to be damaged by what he saw us doing."

"Gabriel's more sensitive than Caroline or James, but it'll do him no harm. He's not the first youngster to have walked in on shenanigans and he'll not be the last."

"All the same, I wish I could be sure."

"We'll watch and see what happens."

"I read somewhere that it's good to give a child a wee shock if they witness anything out of the ordinary and appear troubled by it," said Auntie Bernie. "It's supposed to distract or something. Do you think we should try it, if we think he's troubled?"

"We could."

On the way to school next day, I said to Fergal, "Auntie Bernie wants to give me a 'wee shock' to make me forget something I saw."

"That's bad, Gabriel," he said, after I'd told him what I'd seen. "My brother caught Daddy doing that to my mother, too. He dragged him out to the byre and thrashed him for watching. He was beaten so hard, the marks turned blue. *That's* the 'wee shock.'"

For the following two days, every time Auntie Bernie came into the living room, I went outside to play or sat as far away from her as I could. I tried not to even speak to her, not until she'd forget I'd seen her getting pumped.

"Gabriel, why are you always looking under your eyes at me these days?" she asked when I was in the living room with Mammy and her early one evening.

"I didn't know I was looking at you under my eyes."

"Why do you always sit so far away from me?"

They were watching *Crossroads*, their favorite TV program, during which we were never allowed to talk. My mother turned from the screen to look at me. I knew I couldn't tell a large lie, because I was making my First Confession soon.

"I'm not staying out of your way."

"Why are you lying?" Auntie said.

My palms were sweaty and I rubbed them against my pant legs.

"Tell the truth, Gabriel," my mother said. "First Confession's coming up."

"Because Uncle Tommy pumped you and you're trying to shock me."

Auntie nodded at my mother and they rose from their chairs together. Mammy switched off the TV, told me that she and Auntie were going to the generator shed and I was to knock on its door in exactly one minute. After counting to sixty, I went out. Mammy opened the door. Above the generator, light streamed though tiny holes in the zinc roof that Daddy had been asked to fix but hadn't. The stink of diesel mixed with Auntie Bernie's fierce bad perfume and there was a black oily stain on the concrete platform on which the generator sat. My mother stepped out into the sunlight as Auntie came to the door opening.

"Put out your hands and close your eyes until I say you can open them," she said. "Don't even peek."

"I don't want to be hit."

"You won't. I have a present for you, that's all."

"Do as you're told," Mammy said.

I stretched out my hands and felt something light placed in them.

"Okay, you may open your eyes," Auntie Bernie said.

It was a very long, white-pink thing with an angry face, black eyes, and small brown-red horns like knobs. The face was so angry that I was frightened, until I realized it was just a stupid balloon.

"Aren't those little horns just like the little horns you saw on Auntie Bernie's chest a few days ago? She was wearing balloons, and Uncle Tommy was pumping them up that morning. Isn't that so, Bernie?"

"Aha."

It wasn't the same, though, and their "wee shock" was just a balloon with an angry face. Why were they trying to frighten me with a worm balloon with tiny brown-red horns and saying Auntie had been wearing one?

My mother picked up a twig and dug its jagged end into the balloon. It burst into a piece of wet rubber with the brown-red horns still sticking out.

"Now that you know why Uncle Tommy was helping me in the bedroom, you can forget all about what you saw," said Auntie Bernie. "Let your mind think about First Confession, instead."

"You won't go into her bedroom again, will you?" said Mammy.

"No way."

"Do you promise?"

"Yes."

"Give your auntie a kiss to say you're sorry and you may leave."

I was supposed to be sorry? I didn't want to kiss her, but I wouldn't be excused until I did. I put my tightly pursed lips to her cheek and made sure not to breathe in any of her perfume.

"That's my best nephew," Auntie Bernie said. She swept my hair from my eyes. "It's all out of your mind now, isn't it?"

"Can I tell what I saw as a sin when the priest hears my confession?"

"You cannot indeed."

"Say nothing about this to the priest," my mother added.

"But if I do, then I'll really be able to forget, because it'll be truly forgiven."

"Jesus, you will *not* tell such a thing to the priest," said Auntie Bernie. "He won't, will he, Eileen?"

"He won't."

"Will you be telling him what you were doing when you go to confession?" I asked.

Auntie looked at my mother. "Yes, that's it exactly. I'll tell him. Now remember, Gabriel, if you tell him about my sin, the priest will know . . . and God will not take away the large stain on your soul. In fact, he will add another, larger—"

"Bernie!" said Mammy. She turned to me. "Just tell him you've disobeyed me, Gabriel . . . or tell him you stole a chocolate bar behind my back, if you can't come up with a proper sin before then."

"But I haven't."

"Just tell him anyway, son."

First Holy Communion took place a week after first confession. The headmistress and Father McAtamney had been giving us catechism classes every lunchtime for months and we'd been told we'd receive beautiful white prayer books and rosary beads after the Communion Mass. One day before, the priest visited the school and made the catechism class sit in the front three rows while Miss Murray sat behind us and kept Simple Brian and the infants on their best behavior.

Father McAtamney sat at the teacher's desk, removed a circular, silver box from his pocket and took out a large wafer and held it up. "Children, this is a piece of bread which represents the body of Christ. Now, today is just a practice. Our Lord will not be so big tomorrow. I will break pieces of this and after I say 'Corpus Christi,' you must respond, 'Amen.'" He looked at Henry Lynch. "What will you say?"

"Amen, Father."

"That's correct. Jesus will look after you and guide you after you've received Him. One last thing: you must not chew Our Lord. He must be swallowed whole. Why must He be swallowed whole, Gabriel?"

"Because, Father, our teeth would likely hurt Him."

Father McAtamney smiled. "That's not correct."

The boys and girls laughed. My cheeks were on fire. Henry got his question right, I got mine wrong, and now I mightn't be allowed to receive Our Lord.

"Your Uncle Brendan is a priest, isn't he?" Father asked.

"Yes, Father."

"Ask him next time he's home for a visit and he'll tell you why it's forbidden. Will you remember to ask?"

"I won't be asking, Father."

"Why?"

"He never wants to come home."

Father looked over at the teacher sitting near the blackboard. "Why doesn't he want to come home, do you think?"

"Mammy won't tell me." My face was blazing now.

"Don't tell fibs, Gabriel," Father McAtamney said. "Fibs are venial sins and stain the soul only a little bit less than mortal ones."

He asked if anyone else had committed any venial or mortal sins since their confession. Everyone shook their heads, just as our teacher had warned us to do, and then he asked the final catechism questions. I got everything right. Fergal did, as well, and we would now sit together in the pew nearest the altar rails at the Communion Mass.

Henry got two questions wrong, and I was surprised when the priest said he could still make his Communion. He'd got his catechism wrong, plus he was in a state of mortal sin, because he'd told Fergal he'd stolen a shilling from his mammy's purse, bought sweets, and not confessed it. As God was all-knowing, Fergal and I believed Our Lord would be furious and race up Henry's throat as soon as he received Him at Mass.

At First Communion, Our Lord tasted no different from the practice bread Father had given us at school. I'd expected it to taste like blood. Fergal and I watched as Henry knelt at the rails and received. He chewed Him three times and looked at us with his sneaky eyes as he walked by. Any minute, I expected choking and vomiting to begin.

Nothing happened. Henry was in a state of mortal sin, he had chewed Our Lord, and nothing happened. His soul was black with sin, yet Our Lord had stayed inside him, just as if he'd been as spotless as Fergal and me. It made no sense.

After Mass, Father McAtamney came up to Mammy as we stood outside the church. He patted my head and told her the strange thing I'd said about Uncle Brendan not wanting to come home.

"Come to think of it," he said, and stopped speaking as he looked around the graveyard for a moment. "Brendan hasn't been home for a long while. Any word of a visit in the offing?"

"Not in the immediate future, Father. The missions are so very busy, as I'm sure you understand?" Mammy laughed falsely as she laid her hands on my shoulders. "It's so funny you should bring this up when I was just thinking the other day how lovely it would be to have him visit." Her fingernails dug into my skin, so hard I almost cried out.

"That is a coincidence, indeed," he said, and looked at her without blinking.

"We can't be selfish." Mammy coughed. "Much as the family wants him home, the mission comes first, doesn't it?"

"Indeed."

My mother was silent the entire journey home. No sooner had we got into the kitchen than she fetched the wooden spoon and attacked my arse. "Don't let me *ever* . . . don't you *ever* . . ." She breathed heavy as she whacked, " . . . don't let me ever hear that you've told any news you've heard within these four walls to the priest or anyone. And don't make up stories, either. Your uncle Brendan will be home when he can get away from the missions, do you hear?" She stopped hitting me. "If I hear another story like that from the priest's mouth, it'll be the last story out of yours. I'll cut your tongue out. Now, get to your room this instant."

Instead of collecting money and praise for First Communion from visiting relatives, I found myself alone in my room, punished for lying when it wasn't me who'd lied. I listened to everyone laughing, grew angry, and decided my mother needed to be punished, too. Taking a pencil, I drew animals, houses, and figures on the wallpaper, but it still wasn't punishment enough; they could be erased. I took my pen and drew ten more, though just below the headboard, where she couldn't see them. I knew the damage was there. That was enough.

Later, she came in and told me I could come out to the living room again if I apologized and promised never to tell lies about Uncle Brendan. I said I was sorry without meaning a word. But the matter wasn't forgotten on her part, either. She wouldn't look at me, nor did she even speak to me, until Uncle Tommy came home from working on his new house that evening. After giving me ten shillings for being a real Catholic now I'd tasted Our Lord, he told Mammy that he and Auntie Bernie would be moving out. Their new furniture had arrived that afternoon. *Then*, Mammy's stony face changed. *Then*, I was the greatest son. I was the first of her children to receive Our Lord and now nothing bad would ever happen to me because He was inside my body.

Four

On one side of our house was a small garden with a high tree. Its rough, reddish trunk was thick and curved up from the bottom like a bow. After Uncle Tommy and Auntie Bernie left, James and I moved back to our bedroom and I could look out the window again and hear the tree's branches creak as they swayed in the wind. I would watch for ages and wonder how my tree could stay up in the driving winds, despite its sharply bowed trunk. Noel, whose two front teeth now shared a brownish spot where they met, had taught me to climb it. The best way was to sprint up to it, stick your fingers into the scaled, corky bark as you raced up the trunk, and grab its lowest branch to hoist yourself into it.

Partway up, the tree split into two smaller limbs. It was tight to squeeze past the upper branches because there were so many, but the limbs were bendable at the top. I would pull them toward me and peer out to the rusty tin roof of the long outbuilding stretching all the way across the bottom of the garden and beyond, to where sheep and cows grazed in the Knockburn fields that were ten shades of green.

One Saturday afternoon, Noel and I were perched in my tree and he asked me to go into the outbuilding with him because he wanted to show me something. We climbed down the tree quickly. On the outbuilding's gable overlooking the road was a scarlet mailbox and, as we climbed the gate next to it, Mr. Smith, our bald Protestant postman with bandy legs, drew up in his Royal Mail van. He removed letters from the mailbox and laid them in a wire basket.

"Noel, do you want to take your mother's bills and a letter from England?" Mr. Smith asked.

"I'm not going home to the aul doll yet."

Noel called his mother "the aul doll" behind her back. His father called her that and Noel liked to talk like him, though my mother said it was naughty and if he were her son, she'd break his back.

After Mr. Smith left, we hopped over the crumbling white-washed wall and ran up to the empty pigsty, where Mammy had once bred pigs until she'd grown tired of the smelly work.

Noel drew back the bolt of the door, which had a broken hinge and ragged holes at the bottom that rats had gnawed. Inside, it was silent, and the dim space smelled of stale hay and dust. The sty was divided into two pens. A dented trough and a long metal pigging crate with a wide base that narrowed at one side like a capital "A" stood in one of them, and broken hay bales, yellowing newspapers, and a bundle of clothes were in the other.

A thick concrete wall separated the pens. Eight feet above them was a narrow wooden beam running into the blackness at one end of the loft.

"Jump up on the pillar and walk across the beam," Noel said. "The surprise is in the dark part of the loft."

"Rats are up there." It was also high. I didn't like heights and I feared I'd slip and fall to the concrete floor.

"Don't be an eejit. Follow me."

Noel jumped up on the beam like a monkey, spread his arms to help keep his balance, and ran across. I jumped up on the wall and hoisted myself very slowly on the beam. Where the tin roof met the top of the stone walls, thin wooden planks jutted out at two-foot intervals and were nailed to the underside of the beam. Three broken planks dipped like lopsided seesaws toward the floor of the pen containing the pigging crate.

My stomach lurched. "I don't want to go over there, Noel."

"Don't be a coward like you are with Henry Lynch."

I narrowed my eyes but still couldn't see him.

"It's easy. I'll come back over and fetch you." Suddenly, a light shot out from the darkness and Noel walked across, shining a flashlight at the beam. "Stretch out your arms and walk fast like this." He spun around and crossed the beam again.

"What do you want to show me?" I said, instead of moving. "Why don't you bring it over here?"

"It's a big secret. You'll like it. Once I show it to you, it'll become our secret . . . just yours and mine."

Stretching out my hands, not daring to blink or take my eyes off the beam, I started across. I felt as if I was losing my balance near the end and ran the final five steps.

I found Noel sitting inside a nest of hay. It reminded me of the nests Granny Neeson's laying hens had in their coop, only it was much bigger and smelled dead musty. A thin line of bright light streamed in from a small hole in the roof where it had rusted away. I could hear Caroline and James playing in our backyard.

"Is this it? A nest of hay."

"No."

Noel fumbled within the hay on the far side of the nest. Dust rose into the air. I sneezed. He brought something out and set it before me.

"What is it?"

"Dirty magazines." Noel laid the flashlight on the side of the nest so it shone on the magazines, opened one, and pushed it toward me. The flashlight made two fuzzy rings and the white-hot circle fixed on a picture of a naked woman with black hair lying on a bale of hay. I stared at her for just half a second, but I saw everything. She had the same knobs as Auntie Bernie and her tongue was pointed and curled up over her upper lip. Her fingers dipped inside her private place.

"Auntie Bernie has hair down there, too."

"That's her fanny. And these are her tits." Noel kissed all over the page as he made slurping noises. "You have to do it now."

"I don't want to do that . . . the rats . . ."

"Kiss her tits, *now*."

"No."

"Do it, or I'll push you off the beam when we leave."

As I stared at the picture, my knees and arms shook at the thought of crossing the beam again. "I want to get out of here. You shouldn't have brought me here."

"Shut up, shut your mouth." Noel leaned over and pressed his moist hand with tiny, sharp bits of hay on it hard against my mouth. He pushed until I tasted his salty skin. "Shut up or I'll hit you something fierce."

I nodded and he took away his hand. I wiped my tongue with the sleeve of my sweater.

"Kiss her tits and then we'll go," he said. "You must do this to make it our secret."

"If I do it, can we go home?"

"Yes."

I took the magazine in my hands. The paper was glossy and some pages were bubbled and stuck together where the magazine had once been wet. It smelled old, dirty. I closed my eyes and kissed the page fast.

Noel snatched the magazine and tucked it back into the side of the nest. "Let's go."

I didn't trust my shaking legs so I crawled across the beam slowly, slid down the concrete wall, and then ran into the sunshine where my eyes hurt sharply at first. At the mailbox, Noel put his face close to mine, half-closing his eyes the way he always did when he was going to give me a warning.

"Those magazines are our secret. Just yours and mine. If you tell your aul doll about them, I'll have to tell her that you kissed a woman's tits. And don't tell it as a sin at confession, either. Father McAtamney will leap out of his box and yell at you in front of everybody."

Most nights in bed, I concocted funny stories about our neighbors to entertain James before he went to sleep. Often, Caroline would sneak into our bedroom to listen. To keep them interesting, I watched people, noticing how our Knockburn neighbors talked or the funny ways they moved their heads or hands, and included them in the stories. Caroline and James's favorite ones were about Jennifer, but I'd used her so often, it was becoming difficult to make up new things to say about her.

One evening, Caroline stopped a story about the priest five minutes into its telling.

"It's not funny, Gabriel. Plus, it's like one we heard before." She looked at James. "Do you think it's funny?"

He shook his head.

"Tell us one about Jennifer," she said.

James also wanted a Jennifer story, though not another about her stealing from our mother's kitchen cupboards behind her back, nor the one where she made us play school and slapped us on our hands for making spelling mistakes. I thought for a minute and then began a story about her and me out riding horses in the fields and how she came upon a wallet full of money on the ground and stole fifteen pounds.

About halfway through, the police gave chase, Jennifer saw a barn, and we ran inside to hide. The police passed by and we were safe, but then Jennifer spied a hay bale, lay on it, and asked me to kiss her tits.

"What are tits?" asked James.

"The things Auntie Bernie and Mammy have . . . I'll draw what they look like underneath their bras." I fetched a school exercise book and drew a woman with long hair lying on a hay bale. Then I drew the tits with their knobs. "Auntie Bernie's hair is ginger down there." I drew squiggly lines between her legs.

"On her bottom?" Caroline asked.

"That's not her bottom. It's her fanny. Take off your pajamas and show James yours."

Caroline didn't want to take them off, but James kept asking until she did. Her fanny looked like the hay woman's, except Caroline's was bald. It looked like the mouth of a mailbox. I whispered in James's ear to ask if she would let us touch it. When he did ask, she shook her head and ordered us to take off our pajamas and show her ours. James pulled down his pants.

"I think you could put a very tiny envelope inside yours," I said to Caroline.

James giggled.

Caroline shook her head so quickly, her fringe swept to the side. "James and you are made of slugs and snails . . . and your things are the puppy dog's tail." She pulled up her pajamas. "I would never want a tail."

"Well, you'll get tits and you won't be able to wear an undershirt anymore," I said. "You'll have to wear a bra *and* your fanny will get ugly hair."

"Don't *say* that."

"It'll be like Auntie Bernie's."

Caroline started to cry. James laid his hand on her shoulder but she shook it off with a jerk.

"I'll ask Mammy and that'll sort it out once and for all," James said, and he climbed out of the bed.

I leaped up and slammed the bedroom door shut, almost squashing the tips of my brother's fingers, and winked at him as I told Caroline I was only joking. She peeked through her fingers and then her tears changed to huffy sniffs.

"We mustn't tell Mammy we know words like tits or she'll be very angry," I said. "Nor can either of you mention to Noel that I taught you these words."

"Why not?" Caroline said.

My sister always asked questions that got to the bottom of things.

"Because they're grown-up words that we're not supposed to know yet."

"I see . . . very good."

Her *I see*s and *very good*s were annoying. She liked to behave like Mammy, acting as if the answer to her question was to her liking and the matter was now at an end. But I needed to be surer. I fetched Mammy's Sunday missal and made them swear upon it that they wouldn't repeat it to anyone, Caroline agreeing only after I promised to tell a story about Jennifer at the seaside.

The seaside was on our minds because it was summer and our parents took us there on Sunday outings. I loved to walk along the high harbor walls and look down at the boats bobbing in the dark green water. Everything was so colorful, the brightly painted boats and the large white-and-pale-gray seagulls flying and squealing in the sun. Some of the gulls swam like ducks with puffy chests, while others walked on their bright orange legs on wet rocks covered with slime and rubbery seaweed.

"The people who own those yachts are rotten rich," Daddy said to James and me at the harbor one afternoon.

I followed the direction of his pointed finger to a pale blue boat with a silvery sail. "Yacht" was as lovely a word as the thing itself. I whispered it four times to make sure I'd remember it, so I could put Jennifer in one during a bedtime story.

"Can we get a yacht?" I asked.

"They're very expensive and I'm not rotten rich. Not yet."

A large yacht with two rotten rich people on it began to move. It sailed out of the narrow mouth of gleaming rocks and headed toward the blue-gray distance where a ship was crossing. How I wished we could be rotten rich and sail into the misty distance.

"We'd best return to the others," said my father.

To get to the beach, we had to cross a wooden bridge with two- or three-inch spaces between the old planks, and I could see bobbing rotten wood and seaweed in the water below. It didn't have any handrails and I feared a plank might suddenly break and we'd fall into the water.

James wasn't afraid. Slipping his hand from our father's, he skipped into the middle of the bridge, stooped to his knees, and peered beneath. I hung back.

"Oh, come on, Gabriel. James did it no problem and you're older than him." Daddy looked down at my brother. "You're a brave man, aren't you, James? Brave like your daddy."

"That makes me bigger than him," my brother said.

My father liked to compare James and me, and say my brother was just like him. He said that because my brother loved football and played with toy lorries. He said it because their favorite color was red, almost the same red as the lorry he drove to take excavators to demonstrate for possible customers at shows. James always wanted Santa to bring him lorries, while I wanted pencil cases or cows and horses for my farmyard set. Being older, I knew Santa didn't exist and the idea to tell my brother this came into my head before I walked across the bridge, but I didn't.

Caroline, baby Nuala, and my mother were sitting on a red-and-black checked rug my mother had laid out on the soft, warm sand. Most people sat on rugs, though there were also people who'd rented striped deckchairs from a man in a small hut farther along the beach. My father slipped on a pair of maroon swimming shorts with a moth hole on the right side and ran toward the sea.

"I want to go in the water today," I said.

"You've got no swimming trunks. Just put on some sun cream and tan," said Mammy. She didn't want us going near the water, as she feared we'd drown. My lack of swimming trunks was her handy excuse.

A band of men and women walked slowly up the beach. The men wore navy blue pants with stripes almost the same color as my father's swimming trunks and their jackets had small cloth pieces of the same color on their shoulders. A few carried horns and trumpets. Rays of sunshine caught on their instruments and they flashed like cameras. As they drew nearer, an old woman with seagull-white hair gathered in a bun stopped, raised her hand to shield her eyes, and then pointed to an empty spot about twenty feet away from us.

"Who are those people, Mammy?" I asked.

She peered at them for a moment. "It's the Salvation Army."

"What do they do?" asked James.

"They're the *other* sort," Mammy said, in a low voice. She clicked her tongue against the roof of her mouth. "The nerve, coming to try and convert us on the beach. I don't know why they can't just leave people alone." She said all of this out of the side of her mouth, as she didn't want anyone sitting nearby to overhear her.

Caroline nudged me in the arm to show me that the old woman was stepping up on a wooden fruit box. After she'd climbed up, she waved a thin rod slowly and the band began to play. The other band members started singing "The Lord Is My Shepherd," the same hymn we sang at Benediction.

"Why are the Protestants playing our hymn?" Caroline said.

"Shush. It's a hymn for all religious denominations."

"I see . . . very good."

"But they change the words a bit, of course," Mammy said.

"Do they change the words of all our hymns when they sing them?" I asked.

"I think so, but not the ones about the Blessed Virgin. They never sing hymns about Our Lady, because they don't believe in Her."

Her quiet voice was dead silly because I didn't think anybody was listening. A woman lying nearby was reading, her husband was asleep, and their children were building sandcastles.

"Why do they change our hymns?" Caroline said.

"Because *they* think their words are better."

The woman glanced over as she turned a page.

"I see . . . very good," said Caroline.

Protestants are really damned, I thought.

"But they're not, of course," Mammy concluded.

The singing stopped and the old woman started preaching. "Better not to have been born than to sin and close your hearts to Jesus. Yes, I say, better not to have been born than not to be saved." Her voice grew louder and she thrashed her arms about every which way. "Sinners among you, sunning and cavorting on this golden beach, hear my words. Listen to my words and repent. Accept Jesus and be saved. Accept and be saved, because only God's kingdom is golden and sunny." The woman went on and on for what seemed like hours, talking about repenting and getting saved. When she finally stopped, she looked about the beach as she wiped her brow with a hanky.

"Can we be saved even though we're Catholics, Mammy?" I asked.

"Stop listening to that gibberish, Gabriel." Mammy looked about quickly as if she'd just remembered we were on the beach. "Those words are not for our ears," she said more gently. "We have a better system for saving the soul."

"She's talking about Our Lord, too, so why is their system different?"

"It's about how *they* adore Jesus."

"So their Jesus is a different man?"

Mammy smiled widely at the woman who'd been reading, as she was now watching us closely. After she hurriedly returned to her book, my mother bared her teeth at me.

"James and Caroline, when your father comes back, I just might ask him to take you for ice cream," she said. "I might do that, if you're all very quiet."

"But Mammy, is their Jesus a—"

"Shut up, Gabriel," said Caroline.

It was the last week of school and I was in big trouble with Mrs. Bradley, the headmistress. It had nothing to do with Protestants or hymns, and nothing to do with me, either. It was Henry Lynch's fault. I'd known it as soon as he'd told the lie.

I'd heard Mrs. Bradley's shrieks from the other side of the pink curtain that ran across the middle of the room and separated the junior and senior classes. A rumpus then broke out as the senior girls began screaming. At first, the headmistress blamed the older boys for putting the mice in her drawer. I heard her shouting at them, but then she ordered Noel and another boy to lower the separating curtain a few minutes later. As soon as it was lowered, she asked the juniors to stand and asked us one by one if we'd done the deed. The idea of her hand touching a mouse was very funny until she came to Henry. He blamed me.

"Are you sure it was him?" she said.

"Yes, miss. I saw him go into the senior room with his hands in his pockets this morning. He definitely went in there and I knew he had no business being in your part of the schoolroom."

Three more of Henry's friends swore they'd seen me go behind the curtain, too. Henry's older brother, sitting in front of Mrs.

Bradley's table, raised his hand and said he also remembered seeing me near her desk.

"Gabriel Harkin, come and see me this very minute." Mrs. Bradley looked at Noel and nodded. "Raise the curtain again . . . but do it so it doesn't sag in the middle so much."

I had no choice but to obey.

"I can't believe you put mice in my drawer," the teacher said. "Gabriel Harkin, you of all people." She leaned toward me until her clear blue eyes were level with mine. "Confess, and I may not punish you as hard as I intend to."

Mrs. Bradley's mouth was small and tight, her face purplish, and little lines were gathered just above her upper lip. She didn't blink.

"I didn't do it, miss. I don't know why they're blaming me."

"The words I want to hear are, 'I'm sorry.'" She sighed. "Well, they say still waters run deep and now I know they most certainly do." Her mouth turned down. "You'll be trying to tell me the mice chewed their way inside of their own accord."

The senior girls and boys laughed. I lifted my head a little and peeked under my eyebrows, until I came to Jennifer's freckled face. She was laughing.

Mrs. Bradley looked at the other students before she rose and fetched a stick propped against the fireplace. "Hold out one hand and then the other."

She gave me two slaps on each hand, then said, "Now, say you're sorry and the matter will be closed."

My eyes and hands stung.

"I'm very sorry, Mrs. Bradley."

"You'll never scare a teacher again?"

"No."

She slapped me on each hand another time before dismissing me. Everyone stared as I lifted up the curtain and walked in. Miss Murray looked sad.

I wanted to point and shout at Henry. Instead, I sat at my desk and tried to go on as if nothing had happened, but I couldn't concentrate. I turned back to Henry and saw his evil smile. A tear ran down my cheek. I turned away and wiped it off. Another tear followed. I wiped it off, too. Miss Murray didn't ask me a single question, not even the multiplication ones the others didn't know. She asked Henry the hard ones and I put up my hand when he got them wrong. Still, she ignored me. I was dead to her.

"Did it hurt?" Fergal said at lunchtime.

I'd just finished my sandwiches and found him waiting outside the school door when I came out. I was surprised to see him. He always played with Henry and the others.

"Of course, it hurt."

"That Henry's a bad article. He shouldn't have done that. I feel bad you got punished for something you didn't do."

"Why didn't you stand up and say I didn't do it?"

He looked into my eyes before allowing his gaze to drop to the ground, the way he always did when he knew he was in the wrong.

"Thanks for asking," I said. "You'd better go before the football teams are picked and Henry starts wondering where you are."

Five

Granny finished reading the blue airmail envelope, which the postman had asked me to give her when he saw me turning into her lane. Her eyes shone misty.

"You're going to meet your uncle Brendan," she said. "He's coming to visit."

I looked at the sky-blue page Granny laid on the table. I'd seen the backward writing when I held the envelope up to the sun as I'd walked up the lane, but hadn't understood how the pages of a letter could be inside because it was so thin and light. Granny had known, though, because she hadn't ripped it open like she normally did envelopes, instead pulling back its gummy flap carefully and unfolding it into a one-page letter.

A family get-together took place at her house the following evening. As soon as Auntie Bernie arrived, the stink from Uncle John's dog surrendered to her nasty perfume. Uncle John sat in my grandfather's old chair, dressed in a Sunday suit that was far too tight, his belly bulging over the narrow trouser belt.

"Children, the grown-ups wish to discuss Uncle Brendan's visit, and you must go outside and play," said Auntie Celia.

She signaled Uncle Frank, her Scottish husband who some-times wore his kilt to Mass on Sundays, to give up his armchair to her with a number of small, quick waves of her hand. Auntie Celia disliked small chairs on account of her very wide hips. As he rose, Uncle Frank glared at her with the same sunken, black eyes as Connor's, the only difference between them being my uncle looked into your eyes when he spoke to you.

"Don't come back for an hour, if you know what's good for you," Auntie Celia said as we filed out.

Outside, before we started our game of piggy-in-the-middle, Martin said, "Mammy doesn't really want Uncle Brendan to come home."

"Why not?" asked Caroline. She pushed a rope of hair behind her ear.

"Because he disgraced the family. Mammy says he shouldn't stir the pot and should just stay out among his Africans at the missions. That's all I could get. When I asked some more, she slapped my ear and said I shouldn't be listening to other people's conversations . . . and you know she always beats Connor, never me."

After a while, Martin and I got bored with the game and decided to sneak inside, but Uncle John's smelly dog came out from under the table wagging its tail. Auntie Celia looked over her shoulder and stopped talking. She called Martin over and made him sit at her feet. My grandmother, Auntie Celia, and Mammy had puffy eyes. As I sat on the sofa beside my mother, Uncle John and Granny watched me.

"Tell everyone what you won in the big GAA raffle last week, Martin," Auntie Celia said, running her fingers through his wavy, dark blond hair, which she lightened in summer with lemon juice. She peered down at Martin, her mouth slightly open, ready to move her lips in time to his words, something she always did when she asked him to tell his good news.

Martin had flat feet, was only an inch taller than me, and had skin the color of white china that turned red when he was in the sun, even when the sun was as weak as the tea Auntie Bernie liked to drink. He was also very careful about his teeth and brushed after every meal, although I didn't think they looked any whiter than mine. Behind his back, Connor said his brother was touched in the head, because he'd once caught him brushing after eating an apple. "Anyone with an ounce of sense knows apples are good for you," he'd told me, but I stopped him saying anything bad. Martin was the same as God to me.

"I won a two-foot doll in a scarlet flamenco dress and her eyes open and close when she sleeps," said Martin. "She's *very, very* expensive."

Auntie's cracked lips stilled at the same time Martin stopped talking. She leaned toward my mother slightly. "My Martin's lucky in the raffles, Eileen, eh?"

"It appears so."

I was a little hurt Martin hadn't mentioned the doll to me. I thought we told each other everything.

"What does he want wey a damned doll at his age, Celia?" Uncle Frank said. "Give it tey Harry and Eileen's wee lass."

Martin's lips changed to a thin line as he regarded his father.

"What good is a prize like that tey a boy?" said Uncle Frank. "You know I'm right. They should have given him its value in money instead."

"Seeing as the Scots are tight as a duck's behind, it's expected you'd make a remark like that, Frank," said Auntie Celia.

Uncle John and Daddy laughed.

Auntie Celia passed one hand over her long fingers as she explained that Martin had asked her to keep it safe for him so he could give it to his future wife one day. "I've stored it away in the attic, where it'll remain." Without stopping for a breath, she told Uncle John he needed to lose weight fast, because his stomach was a disgrace, and a new argument began.

"Big Sunday," the official closing of the summer season, was very hot for a September day. We arrived at the beach earlier than usual, because my father said there would be more people in attendance. He changed quickly into his swimming trunks and went to the water. His snow-white arms flashed and cut into the water as he swam against glassy waves that lifted him up and then set him down like a floating cork. The water looked so pretty, so inviting, and I was determined to get into it, even if my need caused a hissed argument between my parents in public. I waited 'til Daddy came out but, before he could dry himself, I asked nicely if he'd teach me to swim.

"It's my last chance this summer," I added.

"You've no swimming trunks, so that's that," said Mammy, her words coming out faster than a gobbling turkey. "Next year, maybe."

"A boy of eight should know how to swim," said my father. "He can wear his underpants."

"He will *not*, Harry." She looked about her. "No swimming trunks means no swimming, simple as that."

Daddy seized my hand and we marched to the man in the green hut who rented out the deckchairs to see if he sold swimming trunks. The old man wore a grubby white handkerchief tied in a knot at each end on his bald head and had a tattoo of an anchor with some rope on his leathery upper arm. He eyed me up and down a few times, then shook his head.

"I don't sell them, but I've a pair I found the other week on the beach that you're welcome to. I don't think they'll fit, though."

Even before I saw the mustard-colored trunks, I decided they'd fit.

After my mother learned they were secondhand, she snatched them from me. Her eyes and nose crinkled in strict examination. "They need to be washed. You don't know who was last in them. That all adds up to no swimming today."

"Nonsense," said my father, "the saltwater will sanitize them."

Mammy seemed to agree. I slipped into them hurriedly, for fear she'd change her mind.

"They're a little big, but they were free, so they'll do," she said. "You make sure Gabriel doesn't go under, Harry."

"I'll keep them safe, Eileen," Daddy said.

Caroline said she wanted to swim as well and started to huff. As she always did, Mammy gave in and allowed my sister to wear her stripy pink knickers. James arrived bare-arsed just as we reached the point where the raggedy edge of the foamy water disappears into the sand, before it returns to the sea.

My father held me and tried to show me how to float. In all honesty, when he held me in his arms, *that* was more magical than learning to swim. He put his hands under my tummy—I was dead surprised it didn't tickle, but supposed that was because of the cold water—and told me to paddle like a dog. The sight of my paddling made him laugh, just like Uncle Tommy laughed when I used to act drunk after he'd swung me around in the garden. I'd never heard Daddy laugh so loudly about anything I'd ever done. Suddenly, everything was beautiful: the sparkling water, the laughing people, Caroline pushing back her glistening hair, James scooping handfuls of water and hurling it at us. Each time my father took away his arms, I'd sink and swallow mouthfuls of the salty water. But he'd just pick me up and tell me to try again. I kept trying, trying, trying.

"Well done, Gabriel," he said, after I swam five feet. I had to stop when my arms and legs got heavy. "I knew you could do it, son."

Even the cold waves gently brushing my sides as they moved toward the shore felt warm as I stood licking the salty water dribbling over my upper lip. Everything inside me glowed hotter than the sun's rays cutting through the water to the golden floor beneath.

"Next year, you'll be able to swim better than me," he said. The four of us began horsing about and hurling water at one another.

After we came out, Daddy left to go and change. We played at the water's edge until I got bored and said we should walk up to the curving concrete seawall. The wall was ten feet high and shaped like a cresting wave. Its uppermost part cast a band of black shadow on the sand where we sat and dug our feet into the coolness. Farther along the beach, the Protestant Salvation Army band played hymns.

A man in jet-black swimming trunks walked toward us. He stopped beside a woman sitting a few feet in front of me and talked to her as he picked up a towel, rubbed his wet hair a little, and then flipped it over his head to dry his back. His body was a healthy brown and water droplets glittered like tiny diamonds over his legs and chest.

I could not stop looking at him; I took in every inch. His ice-blue eyes looked over the woman's head and caught me watching. He smiled.

My heart skipped a beat and I looked away quickly. I pretended to play around with a handful of sand and stole another peek when I thought it might be safe. As my gaze reached his face and our eyes touched again, my heart skipped another beat. I couldn't understand what was happening.

Taking a pair of underpants and red shorts from a bag, he placed them on the sand, turned his back on me and put the wet towel loosely around his waist. I crawled closer and watched as he wriggled out of his swimming trunks. He kicked them toward the girl and began drying his private parts. After he'd finished, he picked up his underpants, stood on one foot, and put the other through its leg hole. I crawled over, stuck my head beneath the towel, and looked up. I needed to see him there.

"Shoo, you naughty boy," the woman said, in the same kind of voice Auntie Bernie had used when I'd seen her privates.

I pulled my head away fast.

"You shouldn't do such naughty things."

My face felt hotter than the sand beneath my fingertips. Caroline and James watched, still as shop window dummies. The man looked down at me and laughed.

"I'm very sorry I looked at you while you changed, mister." I lowered my gaze to his legs.

"That's quite all right, young fella."

"Go to your mother at once," the woman said.

The three of us raced like frightened dogs over the sand. Caroline told Mammy what I'd done and she scolded me.

That night, my sister sneaked in to hear a bedtime story. I pretended to be angry with her and ordered her to leave. But my anger was fake, an excuse. I didn't want to tell a story. I wanted to fall asleep remembering the beautiful man's face. I wanted to relive the water droplets glittering like diamonds on his brown back and legs.

⁂

Auntie Celia placed a large bundle of notes beside the canvas bag full of coins and put on the kettle. Martin and I followed her into the living room, where she settled into an armchair. She'd invited my parents to tea and closed her shop half an hour early without counting the day's takings or writing out her banking slips.

"You know my feelings about Brendan," she said. "I just don't know how I'll react until I see him in the flesh. But since he's coming, we'll have to decorate and clean up Mother's house. People will want to visit and we can't have the neighbors seeing how shabby it looks in daylight." Her lips pursed. "She's no longer fit to keep the place tidy . . . and that stinky dog of John's will have to stay outside—where it belongs, anyway."

Auntie turned to Mammy. "I'm sure I can count on you to help with the decorating. And it goes without saying that we'll all chip in to buy wallpaper and anything else."

"Chip in," Mammy repeated. "John will be getting the house when she dies. He should pay for the bits and bobs that's needed." Her mouth snapped firmly shut.

"Oh, I don't know if our John will be getting the house and contents," said Auntie Celia. "What do you say, Harry?" She leaned forward in her chair. "Sure she hasn't made a will yet. Or has she, and I'm not privy . . . just like some other things I haven't been made privy to these last few years?"

"What are you talking about?" my mother asked.

"Well, I didn't want to raise this indelicacy but . . . well, seeing as you've touched on things, there's the giving of a lamb, for starters."

"Jasus, don't you know John will get everything?" said Daddy. "He's the eldest and none of us are interested in farming."

"The lamb-giving has nothing to do with us," added Mammy. "Besides, I don't like to go up to your mother's to clean and paper and do things a *daughter's* supposed to do." There was a short silence, then she said, "She treats me enough as an outsider as things stand."

"Hmm." Auntie Celia's tongue flicked up and rested on her upper lip.

My mother said, "Children, clear the room. The adults need to talk about your uncle Brendan's arrival."

"Well, I certainly can't be expected to do everything, given my sentiments about Brendan," Auntie Celia said. "Harry, is there or is there not a will?"

"What are you talking about?" he asked. "Your sentiments, my bloody arse. If anybody's entitled to sentiments, it's me and Eileen, and we don't have any."

Auntie Celia took a handkerchief from her cardigan sleeve and sniffed as she dabbed each nostril. "Aye, I suppose it's sentiments that explains the lamb-giving, too."

"Wanes," said Mammy, "leave this room."

"Does Granny have a will, Mammy?" said Martin.

"Get out, you nosy thing," said Auntie Celia.

After we went upstairs, Martin said to Caroline and me, "Would you like to see the doll? I found it the other day."

"Yes," said Caroline.

The attic was crammed with schoolbooks, old chairs, and a huge TV set. It was almost as dusty as Noel's nest in the pigsty. In one corner stood a large wooden horse that Martin and I had played with years ago. He went into the opposite corner, cast off an old towel covering a cardboard box about twice the size of a shoebox, and brought it over to us. Inside was a doll in a gown like a foaming sea of frills. After taking it out of the box, Martin nursed the thing like it was a baby.

"Let me hold it," Caroline said.

He made no move to pass it to her. Caroline watched him rock it for a few moments before giving me a look that said I must tell him to hand it over immediately. In truth, it wasn't right he wouldn't give it to her, but I also couldn't scold him. Martin was just like me: the town boys hated him as Henry hated me. They called him a pansy because he was forever readjusting his heavy bangs. The difference between us was Martin didn't care what the boys called him. They were dirt in his eyes—although he did warn Connor often that he wasn't to tell them he owned a doll.

My sister's look turned sour, but still I said nothing. I picked up a bundle of old photographs lying on the seat of a dusty chair. The top ones were brown and white and contained people I didn't know. There were black and white photos at the bottom of the pile.

"I asked nicely if I could hold the doll, Martin, and you must give her to me because I'm the girl."

"This photo's got Auntie Celia in it," I said. She wore a wedding dress and stood with a large crowd of people on the steps of a church. "And here's one of her beside our uncles and aunts. Daddy mustn't have known Mammy when Auntie Celia and Uncle Frank got married. She's not there."

"Let me see that," said Caroline, forgetting the doll. "Uncle Brendan's not in priest's clothes, either."

I studied my father's and Uncle Brendan's faces and saw they were alike, except Uncle's hair was wavier.

"Mammy doesn't even keep photographs of Uncle Brendan on the walls," said Martin, as he put the doll back in its box quickly. "Not even the ones of his ordination that he sent her. Those are stuck in her chest of drawers."

"Why?" I said.

"She won't tell me."

Carnival week in Knockburn brought the football season to a close. Football teams from surrounding areas competed during the week to reach the final, which was played early on Sunday evening, and a silver cup was presented to the winners following a guest tea and concert that night. Everyone in Knockburn came to the carnival. It was the highlight of the year, a chance for neighbors to chat in a place other than the churchyard after Mass on Sundays.

James went to the carnival because of the football, and Caroline because she could walk around the perimeter of the field eating ice cream with her friends. I went for the amusements. There was hoopla, an air gun target practice area, and a set of five swing boats that looked like real rowing boats, painted in bright pinks and apple greens with gold trim. The boats hung inside a wooden frame, like a huge swing, and you made them arc through the air by pulling on a rope attached to the crossbar above.

Jennifer was best to take up in a boat. Though eleven and bossy, she screamed louder than the other girls when she was frightened.

We climbed inside. After the boat swung pretty high, Jennifer let go of the rope and gripped the metal bars. When she closed her eyes and screamed, I tugged the rope with all my power, pulling until I felt my arse rise off the bench and my body grew weightless as the boat arced and almost passed over the crossbar in a complete circle.

"That's enough, you scamp," the owner shouted. "You're scaring the life out of your girlfriend. Stop pulling on the rope."

I closed my eyes to enjoy the last arcs.

"I've got one more shilling," I said to Jennifer, when the boat came to a stop. "Do you want to go again?"

She climbed out. "Let's go meet the others at the fire on the other side of the field."

It was the hour when day was under attack by millions of tiny spots of the night's darkness, and its silvery light was squeezed to blackness. Here and there, around the edge of the field, people had lit fires to make smoke and stop the gnats from feasting on their blood.

"Over here, Jennifer," said her friend Kathleen as we drew near.

Ten girls and five boys were there, some of whom I didn't know because they weren't from Knockburn. Kathleen broke away from a boy she'd been standing beside and ran up to us.

"Jennifer, that tall boy I was standing beside comes from Craigban. He says he's twelve and fancies you something rotten. He asked me to ask you if you'd like to go on the swing boats."

The sweetish smell of burning grass was very strong as the fire was getting started. As Jennifer looked the boy over, her nose crinkled like she'd smelled something dead. "He's very skinny. I'll think about it."

The boy kept grinning and Jennifer pretended to ignore him as we stood holding our hands out to the flameless fire. As the players ran up and down the field, their shouts to pass the ball mingled with insults from some of the adult spectators. The boy edged closer and closer until he was at Jennifer's side. Soon, their quick glances became smiles, then low talking and giggles.

A few minutes later, she turned to Kathleen and me. "I'm taking a quick spin on the boat with Mickey. Don't go away; I'll definitely be back."

While they ran off toward the swing boats, I saw four figures step from the sideline of the field and walk toward the fire. As they neared, the smoldering grass burst into flames. A band of nose-to-stumpy-tail dogs ran across the chest of one boy's crimson sweater. I knew the sweater. I didn't need to see his face. I wanted to run.

"Where have you been hiding all week?" asked Henry.

"I've been about." I scratched behind my ear to kill a gnat and felt a great surge of warmth in my armpits.

"Gnats eating at you, are they?"

"Hey, Henry, we sure whipped you in the under-twelve game yesterday," said one of the boys I didn't know, as he heaped grass on the fire. The others laughed. "We beat you solidly . . . and on your home ground, too."

"You were lucky, that's all," said Henry. He turned his sneaky eyes away from me and took a step toward the boy.

"Luck had nothing to do with it. We won fair and square."

I started to back away, slowly, but Henry spotted me.

"Where do you think you're going?" he asked.

I looked away.

"Let's ask sissy boy here what he thinks. Were they lucky or not?"

Everything fell quiet. All eyes raked my face.

"Well?"

My mouth was dry as fluffy cotton. "I didn't see the game."

"Why didn't you?"

He didn't give my tongue time to free itself from the roof of my mouth.

"Because you're a pansy, that's why. A pansy who'd rather sit in a swing boat."

The others laughed.

Henry took the step toward me. "Am I right?"

I stared at the nose-to-tail dogs and didn't answer. There were eight dogs, all the same size, all with the same heads and tails.

He jabbed my chest with his finger. "Are you a sissy or a pansy?"

It was a beautiful sweater. I couldn't decide if the dogs were Labradors; they had the right outline, but Labradors were honey-colored, not black. And they didn't have stumpy tails, or did they?

"Speak up, Harkin."

I met Henry's eyes. I looked into his dark pupils, now grown large because the flames had gone out again. They held no pity. My gaze fell to the Labradors again. I wished I could say I was a sissy, let him have his laugh. Then it would all be over. But my tongue refused to form the words.

Henry grabbed my shirt and I heard a tear. A button popped and spun to the ground.

"You only have to look at his fucking jeans," he said. "Hey, everybody, look at Harkin's jeans. They're purple, for fuck's sake."

It was true. They were purple with white stitching on the seams, so different from any jeans I'd ever seen before. I'd begged my mother to let me have them. Now, I wished she'd put down her foot and bought me blue ones, just like the other boys wore.

"Henry, I want to go. I haven't done anything to you."

"Admit you're a sissy as loud as you can so everyone can hear. *Then* I'll let you go."

I prayed Jennifer was on her way back. "You know I can't say that."

He threw me on the ground and fell upon me. "Help me take off Harkin's jeans," he said to the other boys.

His friends pinned me down. No one tried to stop them. I struggled and jerked to push them off, even tried to scratch their faces like a girl. I didn't care. They seized my arms and pulled down my trousers. Henry gripped the elastic band of my underpants on both sides of my waist and with a sharp tug made me naked from the waist down.

I felt everyone's eyes on my thing. A girl's high-pitched giggle arced across the smoke. The boys held me fast.

"Admit you're a sissy and I'll give back your pants." Henry rose and stood over me, my bunched jeans in his hands. "Come on, Harkin. It's very easy. Just say, 'I'm a sissy.'"

Strangers knew every inch of my body. I didn't want them staring at my thing anymore. "Please give me back my jeans because . . . because—"

"What's going on?"

Henry's friends let go of my arms and rose as Jennifer marched up. I pulled up my underpants.

"Why aren't you and Mickey on the swing boats?" Kathleen asked Jennifer.

"There's was a long line . . . and you, Henry Lynch, give Gabriel back his trousers or I'll order the girls to take yours off. Then we'll see how big you act when everybody has a gawk at your smelly wee thing." She nodded at Kathleen and the other girls. "Get his knickers off."

Henry dropped my jeans and fled. Some of the girls gave chase into the darkness.

"Thanks, Jennifer," I said, after I'd put on my pants.

She'd also seen everything. I couldn't bring myself to look her in the eye.

"You don't have to hang your head like that. I've seen Noel's many times and yours is no different."

Six

We sat cross-legged on the rug in front of the fire at Granny Neeson's house. James and Nuala were outside teasing her hens, and Caroline and I had come inside after growing tired of climbing the neat turf stack. We had pretty much wrecked it, anyway. My family, including my father, which was very rare, was visiting Granny to invite her and Aunt Peggy to a station Mass to be celebrated by Father Brendan at our house in two weeks' time.

"Pull off Sinead's head and give it to me," I said to Caroline.

Sinead was her doll and she didn't like boys touching it, but my sister also knew I created fantastic hairstyles for it when I was in the mood.

"What will you do this time?" she asked, as she popped off its head and handed it to me.

"Plaits, I think."

Her doll had long, shiny hair that felt real between my fingers. I undid the bun my sister had tried to make, laid out pieces of green and purple wool that I'd brought with me, and set to work. Aunt Peggy's eyes bore into me as I plaited. She was Mammy's older sister and still wore her hair in a beehive, even though my mother kept telling her that she was too old for the style. A lazy eyelid made her left eye look as if it was almost closed and she insisted we call her "Aunt" because she didn't like "Auntie."

"He's good at doing hair, isn't he, Peggy?" said my mother.

Aunt Peggy's eyes met mine. "Eileen, should he really be playing with a doll, do you think?"

"For Pete's sake, he's *not* playing with the thing. He's artistic. And besides, Caroline likes him to work on its hair."

"All the same, it's not good to encourage him to play with it," said Aunt Peggy, not having listened to a word Mammy said.

"I'm *not* playing with the damned doll," I said. "I don't play with dolls. Can't you tell it's only the head, for Pete's sake?" I held it up by a plait and shook it at Aunt Peggy. "I'm doing its hair, just like I do Granny Harkin's hair."

"Don't dare raise your voice to your auntie Peggy." My mother couldn't get used to the fact she preferred to be called "aunt," either. "You mustn't talk back to your elders."

"If it's not playing, what would you call it then, Gabriel?" Aunt Peggy asked.

"I'm teaching myself to be a hairdresser. That's what I'm going to be when I grow up."

"If that's the case, what's your mother sending you to school for? Hairdressers don't need to know how to write . . . and hairdressing's a woman's job, anyway."

"It's not. I saw men clipping women's hair on TV."

"Those aren't men."

I turned to my mother. "What does she mean?"

She didn't answer.

"Those people are effeminate." Aunt Peggy glanced at Mammy before bending toward me. "I'll wager *those* people played with dolls when they were young. Oh yes, you can be mighty sure those sort of men played with dolls."

I didn't understand the word "effeminate," but it was clearly something terrible. Daddy looked up from his paper and ordered me to give the doll back to Caroline.

"Look, Peggy, our Gabriel's very artistic and this is a part of that," Mammy said. "Go on, Gabriel, finish the hairdo . . . but make it quick, okay? And another thing, Peggy, remind me to show you the artwork he brings home from school when you come to the Mass. His teacher says he's a great drawer. And he can sing *The Black Velvet Band* totally in tune. Come on, Gabriel, sing for your auntie." My mother slid forward in her chair. "Sing it for her."

"No."

"Sing *at once.*"

I cleared my throat before starting. *"Her eyes are shining like diamonds, sure you'd think she was queen of—"*

"Aye, drawing and singing's one thing," said Aunt Peggy. "But this other business needs curtailing. He'll turn out fey if he plays with dolls."

"Fey?" said my mother. "What the hell does that mean?"

"Strange," said Aunt Peggy. There was a little silence. "I mean, it's not as if he plays a bit of football for balance."

I saw myself standing in the middle of a swaying seesaw, trying to keep it level.

"It's high time you played a bit of Gaelic football instead of doing hair, boy," said Daddy.

"I don't want to."

"Mark my words, it's balance that's needed," Aunt Peggy insisted.

"You'll do as I say," Daddy said. "Knockburn has a junior team, and you'll be on it. Every one of your uncles was on the Knockburn football team when they were boys. Luksee, the Harkins were always good footballers. You can be, as well."

"Brendan wasn't much of a footballer," said my mother.

"He can't be used as an example in this instance," he said. "Besides Brendan, the rest of us played."

"Sure, you didn't even make the official team, Harry," Mammy said. "Not really . . . at least that's what your mother told me. She said you were just a substitute. In any event, Gabriel's not interested in football, so that's that. Not everyone needs to be chasing after a leather ball."

"He's not interested in machinery, either," said my father.

"He's got his farmyard set," my mother said. "There's your balance, Peggy."

"He shouldn't be given a choice, not at his age," said Aunt Peggy.

"Aye, you're right about that," Daddy said. "Now you're talking sense, Peggy."

My mother rose off her chair. "Let my bit of a boy alone." She pursed her lips at my father, then glared at Aunt Peggy. I was sure they were going to argue. Granny was in the kitchen, and I wished she'd come in and stop them. "Listen, Peggy, when you drop that dandy who won't marry you and meet someone who will and have children of your own, then, and only then, can you start to lecture me on what mine should or shouldn't play."

She was talking about Aunt Peggy's boyfriend, who wore cream-colored trousers in winter and had shoes with thin leather soles that Daddy said came from Italy. My aunt's lazy eyelid popped wide open so both eyes were now perfectly balanced.

"It's not my fault he doesn't want to get married yet! You are all against him because he dresses nicely and takes a bit of a drink now and then."

She covered her face with her hands and her shoulders heaved. Now I hoped my grandmother would stay in the kitchen until Mammy finished.

"A drink now and then?" said Granny Neeson as she swooped into the room, holding an unwrapped currant cake in one hand and a bread knife in the other. "He reeks of it sometimes. It's so strong, I could ask him to breathe on my wettest pieces of coal in the fire and they'd burn with no trouble."

"So Mammy's right, Aunt Peggy," I said. "I'm artistic and can do the doll's hair if I want and you shouldn't interfere."

My mother pounced and whacked both my ears. "Don't you ever talk back to your Auntie Peggy like that, you bad article." Her words grew loud, then soft, as they bounced against a wall of high-pitched ringing in my head. "When I get you home, I'll beat the living day-lights out of you. Give that damned doll back to Caroline. *Now!*"

The half-finished plait unwound as I passed the head back to my sister.

"Let him be, Eileen," Aunt Peggy said. She wiped her eyes with her finger. "He's only a child and doesn't know any better. I shouldn't have spoken."

They were friends again. I was in a complete muddle. I couldn't leave, or even speak.

Lightning flashed across the pencil-lead-gray sky, and it thundered and rained heavily on the afternoon Uncle Brendan flew into Belfast airport. Granny Harkin, wearing her new navy blue dress and white cardigan, wound her rosary beads between her fingers, praying as fast as the crazy woman I saw every Sunday at the chapel. She was scared the plane to Belfast would fall from the sky, as she couldn't understand how such heavy things stayed in the air even in good weather. She interrupted her prayers with a "Jesus Christ, what the hell was that?" after every thunderclap.

By four o'clock, everyone was gathered for Uncle Brendan's arrival. Our house had been picked because it was larger than Granny's. The sweet smell of roast beef drifted in from the kitchen.

"Oh, sweet Jesus . . . sweet Jesus and His mother, would you look who's driving in," said Auntie Celia from where she stood by the window.

I ran over to see Mr. O'Kane's eggshell-colored car with the pram-like wheels pass over the cattle grid at our main gate.

"Even worse," said Auntie Celia, "I've just seen Kate the nun's head gawking out the back window."

The nun's name was Kathleen and her religious name was Sister Pious. She was also Mr. O'Kane's eldest daughter. She lived in a convent in England and had been over visiting her parents and collecting pots of money for charity from everyone only two weeks ago.

"Eileen . . . Eileen, you'll have to get rid of that nun fast or she'll find out all about our Brendan's going away," said Auntie Celia, and she wrung her hands. "Harry, you know how emotional Mammy gets. She'll be asking Brendan why the hell he went away so quick and why he didn't come home for Daddy's funeral in front of that bloody nun." Auntie Celia said all of this, even though Granny was in the room with us. "Oh, sweet, sweet Jesus, get rid of them. Somebody get them away from here."

"I'll not talk like that, Celia," Granny said. "Sure, Kate went to school with Brendan. It's good she's here."

"You answer the door, Celia," said Mammy.

"I can't send the nun packing. I went to school with her. Harry, tell Eileen to answer the door and get rid of her. Eileen, just keep them standing on the doorstep and they'll take the hint . . . oh, please, Eileen, please do it—for my sake, if not your own."

My mother let out a great sigh as she left. I went out to watch. After saying what a pleasant surprise it was to see her again so soon, Mammy said in her fake friendly voice that it was a bit of a bad time to call as Uncle Brendan was arriving after being so long abroad and the family were gathered to greet him.

"I know," said the nun. "He phoned last week and asked that I be here. That's why I flew in from Coventry last night. I'm sure you don't mind."

Uncle Tommy's car arrived between heavy rain showers a little time later. Martin and I spilled out the door in front of Daddy, Granny, and Uncle John. Auntie Celia stayed with Kate the nun and her parents. They wouldn't come out to greet him as Mr. O'Kane said only immediate family should have the honor.

Uncle Brendan climbed out of the car wearing a cream brimmed hat with a narrow brown band. He looked like my father, except he was thinner and his skin was the same healthy brown as the beautiful man I'd seen on the beach. As he smiled, two lines in his forehead opened wider and I saw pure white skin between the cracks.

"I feel like I'm really home with all this rain," he said, and looked at the sky.

"Oh, son! Son, you're home," Granny said.

Silence followed her proclamation, broken only when a passing crow cawed. Granny let out another cry as she limped toward Brendan.

"Ah, Brendan, son, you've come back to me," she said, in a croaky voice I'd never heard before. "Why did you go away so sudden, darlin'?"

Daddy's mouth was slightly open and he exchanged glances with Uncles John and Tommy. Uncle Brendan put his head over her shoulder as they hugged, eyes closed tighter than a newborn calf's. After a moment, he stopped patting Granny's back and pulled his head back to look at her. He wiped the corners of her eyes with his finger and kissed her right cheek.

"Mother, I've missed you. I've missed you, but it had to be . . . but now I'm home."

My eyes watered.

Uncle John and my father walked up to Brendan. They shook hands, Uncle John said, "You're welcome home," and Brendan stretched out his arms and pulled them into a huge hug. My father didn't know what to do, his hand hovering an inch away from Uncle Brendan's waist for a second or two before he gripped him firmly.

"Where's our Celia?" Uncle Brendan asked, after they separated.

Granny looked about. "Kate the nun's here. She must have stayed inside with her."

"I'm here, Brendan," Auntie Celia said, in a voice that was as high as Caroline's. She pushed past Auntie Bernie and me. Her face was sweaty as she started toward him. "You got bad weather for coming home, but you're looking grand, thank God . . . well, maybe a bit on the thin side and . . . have they . . . have they not been feeding . . . ?"

Auntie didn't finish the sentence. She started shaking and her hands flew to her face. Uncle Brendan rushed up and wrapped his arms around her, which made my grandmother cry again.

"It's all right, Celia," he said. "It's been too long." Gently, he took her hands away from her face. She looked up at him like Caroline sometimes looked at me when she wanted something.

"I'm making a fool of myself in front of Kate the nun. She'll be gawking out the window and wondering why the hell I'm behaving so silly."

"The black sheep's home, Celia."

"Brendan, she doesn't know anything . . . I hope?"

My grandmother stopped a loud nose blow halfway through. "Gabriel, come over here," she said.

After I was over beside her, I gathered my shoulders small, placed one foot on top of the other, and dropped my eyes to the ground.

"Say hello to Brendan," she said, and pushed me forward.

"Hello, Uncle-Father Brendan," I said. I peeked up at him.

He held out his brown hand, the palm white as frost. His fingers were thick like Daddy's and my hand disappeared as the brown fingers closed around it. I'd wanted to shake his hand like a grown-up, but as my hand was lost inside his, all I could feel was his lovely warmth.

"You can just call me Uncle Brendan." He winked at Daddy. "I don't stand on formality here. Besides, it's far too long to say it the other way."

"Okay."

"Isn't he a handsome fellow, Brendan?" my grandmother said. "And look at Caroline, too." She called my sister over. "They look just like you did at that age. They've also got Harry's and your brains."

My father laughed and said it was Brendan who had the brains. James came up carrying Nuala, who looked too heavy for him to hold, but Granny didn't introduce them until Uncle Brendan asked who they were, as he picked Nuala up and grinned at her.

"Oh, Brendan, I wish you'd have come home and made up with your father on his deathbed," Granny said. "Why couldn't you just have come?"

"These children are so pretty," Uncle Brendan said, ignoring her. He looked into my eyes. "Did you know Grandmother says I was one of the best-looking men in Knockburn? Why, I was so handsome, she had to stop the girls from wanting to kiss me."

"And what about me?" said Uncle Tommy.

Everyone laughed. I was dead surprised Uncle Brendan would talk about kissing girls. He was a priest and priests weren't supposed to think about women that way. As soon as my mother approached, he set Nuala down and shook Mammy's hand and then, gripping both of her forearms, he looked into her eyes for a long moment before kissing her cheek. She blushed dead high. Mammy hated kissing.

"Gabriel's good at his books," Granny said.

"You like school?" Uncle Brendan asked.

I couldn't stop my eyes from falling to my feet again. "It's okay, except for Henry Lynch."

"Who's he?"

His voice was so deep and musical, not sharp or rough like the Knockburn men's voices. His laughter rose from the pit of his belly like Daddy's.

"He tries to fight me all the time."

"Look at your uncle Brendan when he speaks to you," said Mammy. "Henry's one of those hooligan Lynch's from the other side of Knockburn. But I'm sure my Gabriel's no angel, either. He's also a bit shy, so Henry takes advantage."

"Are you shy?" Uncle Brendan asked.

"Damn the 'bit shy,'" said Auntie Celia. "He and my Martin are not shy when they want to go out and poison trout like we used to do, Brendan." She beckoned Martin and Connor over.

"I was shy, too," Uncle Brendan said. "Your father fought my battles. He always had to protect me." His eyes swept away to watch Martin and Connor walking toward us.

"Oh, many's a scrape I got into on account of you, Brendan," Daddy said.

As Auntie Celia introduced Martin and Connor, she ran her hand through Martin's bangs so the hair stood up crisp.

"Take those Scots eyes off the ground and look at your uncle when you meet him for the first time, Connor," Auntie Celia said. "You and Gabriel, the pair of you are so alike."

I was nothing like Connor. He never looked at you when talking, ever.

I saw Kate the nun glide over the gravel toward my uncle, the tip of her wooden crucifix bouncing against her beige habit. She took Uncle Brendan's hands in her marble-white hands, but he didn't remove them as fast as possible.

"My, but it's good to see you in the flesh at last," she said. "It's blessing enough from the good Lord to receive your letters, but there's nothing like meeting our brothers on the old sod." She looked at Auntie Celia and her lips turned up a little, exactly like the Blessed Virgin's weak smile in any picture of the Holy Family. "Sure there's nothing better than having all your family together, is there, Celia? It's just such a terrific blessing."

"A blessing indeed, Sister Pious," said Auntie Celia. "The Lord is most gracious."

Later, when we went into the sitting room, Mr. O'Kane, who now had a glass of whiskey, told yarns about the Harkin boys when they were young. Kate the nun kept looking at me. Every time I looked at her, she was staring. I shifted in my seat and looked to Uncle Brendan. The more I studied his face, the more I knew Granny was wrong. Caroline and I didn't look anything like him. He was brown; his nose was bigger and straighter than mine. I put it down to the fact she might have forgotten what he looked like, because he'd been away for so long.

Kate the nun finally stopped staring and looked over at Uncle Brendan when he began a story about bringing frogs' spawn into my primary school when he and she were young. This led to the grown-ups talking about children and education.

"I teach little black boys and girls arithmetic and English in a bush school with a tin roof," said Uncle Brendan. He'd looked only at me when he said that. "It's much poorer than your school."

I didn't know if I was supposed to feel sorry about his bad school, so kept quiet.

"What stage are you at in English?" he asked me. "Are you doing joined-up writing yet?"

"Yes."

"Martin's cursive penmanship is gorgeous," said Auntie Celia. "Absolutely gorgeous."

She asked Martin to fetch a pen and paper and write a long sentence with large words to show Brendan. Immediately, my mother also made me write a sentence. Even though I tried my best, my writing was definitely bigger and less pretty than Martin's.

It was even more fun visiting Granny now that Uncle Brendan was staying with her. Visitors dropped in to see him. I enjoyed listening to the stories about the old days, and there were apple tarts and delicious currant cakes for tea. He and my grandmother also visited neighbors' houses. One evening, he asked my mother if I could come along and she agreed.

"Uncle Brendan, when will you be going away again?" I said in the car.

He was sitting shotgun with Uncle John. We were on our way to visit an old woman with cancer whose daughter had asked Uncle Brendan to give her mother a blessing before she died.

"He's only just arrived, so we don't talk about that," Granny said, so sharply my cheeks burned. It must have shocked Uncle Brendan, as well, because he turned around to look at her.

"I'm here for a while yet," he said to me, "and then I'll stay in London for a week or so before I fly back to Kenya."

"Why are you going to London?" she asked. "Fit you better if you went to see our bishop before you leave and see if he can get you into a parish or a school in Ireland."

Granny had ordered me not to talk about his leaving, but here she was, breaking her own rule.

"It's as little as the church could do for all the money I throw into its plate on Sunday," she continued.

Uncle John laughed.

"Can I go back with you?" I said. "I could teach the boys over there how to do joined-up writing."

"I don't think your teacher would let you," Uncle Brendan said.

"He should come home where he belongs, shouldn't he, John?" Granny said. "The Lord knows you shouldn't have gone away in the first place. You should have gone to the seminary in Maynooth, instead of running off to Rome . . . nor did you need to run to the missions in the arse of beyond, either."

"Why did you not come home when Granda was dying?" I asked my uncle. "And why won't Auntie Celia hang your ordination photograph on her wall?"

"Who said she doesn't hang it up?" Granny asked.

"Martin."

"Your cousin's telling tall stories," she said. "He'll get a good ear boxing the next time I see him . . . I'll straighten that out with Celia the next time I see her, Brendan."

Things went quiet until Uncle Brendan began humming. "Listen, Mother," he said at last. "You'll say nothing to her." He started humming again.

"Why did you not come home to see Granda?" I asked.

"Your grandfather and I were pigheaded and disagreed about something that happened a long time ago. It's something that only concerns grown-ups and is forgotten now."

"Granda wasn't pigheaded."

"Adults have different sides to them, Gabriel," he said. "They can be bad to some people and nice to others, all at the same time."

Granny tut-tutted and said, "He was your father, Brendan."

"I had to stay to help the poor people," Uncle Brendan said. "I couldn't come home because they needed me more than Granda did. Your granda always wanted me to be a priest. He wanted that and he got his wish. He knew I'd have to stay and help people if I were needed in Kenya, even if he was dying." Uncle Brendan looked out the side window for a moment. "You'll be able to help them, as well, if you feel the need when you're older." He turned back to me. "Do you think you'd like to help the poor and needy?"

Lights from an oncoming car shone inside as I thought about the question. Making new hairstyles was what I really enjoyed. But if I became a priest, I could fly in airplanes to Africa and convert souls.

"If I can be a hairdresser *and* a priest," I decided.

Uncle stared out at the road.

"You can't be both," said Granny. "People must choose in life."

"Don't you want to be a farmer, like me?" asked Uncle John.

"Gabriel, you don't have to choose between things like that," said Uncle Brendan. "Besides, you've got plenty of time to decide. You mustn't rush into things like the priesthood. It's a very hard life and . . ."

He didn't finish. He stared out the window, his lower lip quivering.

"And what, Brendan?" Granny prompted, watching the back of his head without blinking.

"I've forgotten what I wanted to say, so it can't have been too important." Uncle Brendan laughed, but the sound didn't come from his belly like it normally did.

My grandmother lowered her head to look at her hands. Uncle Brendan watched her in the front mirror. She didn't see him, but he was watching. The car was silent until Uncle John started whistling.

As soon as I stepped into the old woman's bedroom, a terrible smell filled my nose. She was lying in bed, her skin the color of wet newspaper, staring up at the ceiling with watery eyes. A vase of bright pink roses stood just inside the door. It was nighttime and flowers were always taken out of the sick room before the person went to sleep. A bottle of Lucozade stood beside her dark, cut-glass rosary beads, light from the bedside lamp making them glitter like rat's eyes. A missal with a curled-up cover was also on the bedside table. One curtain with big flowers and slim, curling leaves puffed out into the room due to the breeze sweeping in from the open window.

"She's riddled with cancer, Father Brendan," said Mrs. McCloskey, the woman's daughter. "It won't be long now. She'll pass soon, please God. The doctor put her on morphine a few days ago. She's stuffed to the gills, but it's making the passage easier."

The heavy stink I'd noticed was morphine, though it smelled more like rotten meat. The breeze couldn't help in a room so stuffy with sickness. No one seemed to notice the stench. I couldn't understand why the daughter was saying such terrible things in front of her mother, who was probably listening as she stared at the ceiling.

Uncle Brendan took a thin purple scarf like Father McAtamney's from his pocket and hung it around his neck. He opened a tiny bottle of Holy Water and began praying as he sprinkled the woman.

"I won't give your mother any Eucharist, as she can't swallow," he said, and he laid his hand gently on her shoulder. "Let yourself go," he added. "Have a good cry."

Mrs. McCloskey turned to me instead. "Son, would you take a sip of Lucozade?" She nodded at the bottle on the table. "The good Lord knows Mammy won't see this bottle empty."

I didn't want to drink a dying woman's juice. "That's okay, Mrs. McCloskey. Don't trouble yourself."

"Such manners," she said to Granny. "Isn't he the fine wee gentleman?" She started toward the bedside table. "It's no trouble, son."

"*No*, thank you."

"Don't be rude and take a glass of juice when it's offered," said Granny.

I looked at the bottle. Visitors always brought it when they visited sick people, because it had glucose in it and was supposed to make people feel better. The bottle was wrapped in the crinkly gold-orange plastic paper and I loved to peer through when someone was sick at our home and had been given a bottle. Its color was brighter than any sunglasses and turned the world instantly happy, making the trees brassy-green and the sky brassy-blue, no matter what its actual color.

"I'm not thirsty, Granny."

"Nonsense."

"I don't like Lucozade, anyway."

"Since when?" she asked. "*You*, who's always sneaking it when I'm sick. You don't think I know that?"

Mrs. McCloskey laughed as she poured some into the only glass on the table and gave it to me. I didn't want to catch this woman's cancer. I thanked her and pretended to sip, watching the threads of tiny bubbles float to the top. I tilted the glass so they'd think I'd drank a lot.

"Don't spill it, pet," Mrs. McCloskey said.

As soon as they looked back at the old woman, I edged closer to the pink, velvety roses, pretended to smell them and chucked the juice into the vase.

Uncle Brendan caught me. He looked at the glass, at me, back at the glass, and then nodded toward my feet a couple of times. I glanced down and saw juice had spilled onto the lino. Quickly, I wiped it away in a great curving streak with my shoe.

"Goodness, you must have been thirsty," Mrs. McCloskey said. "Have another. You're a growing boy."

"I'm full to bursting, thank you."

"One's enough for him," said Uncle Brendan, and he came over and put a hand on my head.

We went into the parlor, where my grandmother and Mrs. McCloskey joined us a few minutes later. I was sure I smelled the morphine there, as well. Mrs. McCloskey's next-door neighbor was helping to serve visitors with refreshments and the woman gave me a cup of milky tea and a slice of cherry and raisin fruit-cake. I didn't even nibble it.

Father McAtamney arrived and went in to see the old woman, staying only a minute before coming out to chat to Uncle Brendan.

"His headmistress tells me he's a smart young fella, though not above the odd trick or two," the priest said, turning the conversation to me after they'd finished discussing the old woman as if she were already dead.

Granny looked surprised.

"Yet another Harkin with brains, as well as a few tricks to boot," Father McAtamney said, and winked.

"He says he might go to Africa and cut hair and help in the missions when he's older, Father," said Granny.

"Is it a priest like his uncle Brendan he wants to be?" Father McAtamney asked. "Sure, he's young enough yet. It'll be a while before you know if there's a call for you." He chuckled. "By then, you'll have discovered the lasses and will want to be out gallivanting with them."

"What's the call?" I asked.

"God calls some boys to be priests when they're older," the priest said. "Just like your uncle got a call. Isn't that right, Father Brendan?"

"I suppose."

Father McAtamney paused with his teacup before his lips and looked at him for a second.

"How does the call come, Father McAtamney?" I asked.

"Into your head."

In two months, I would be an altar boy, wearing a black soutane and white surplice with lace crosses on its sleeves that my great-great-grandmother had embroidered. Uncle Brendan had worn the same surplice as a boy.

"Will being an altar boy help me get it?"

"It will." Father McAtamney tapped Uncle Brendan's knee. "What do you say, Brendan?"

Uncle stood. "I say it's time for us to leave."

"Father McAtamney says I'll get a call to be a priest but it won't be for a while yet," I said to my mother, as I threw open the door and barged into our kitchen an hour later.

She was stacking a milk bottle to cool in the red bucket of cold water inside the larder. "I'm praying ever so hard you will get a call one day," said Mammy.

"You know about the call?"

"Yes."

My grandmother and uncles entered the kitchen.

"The only thing that might stop God calling me is if I discover girls."

Mammy took the teapot and walked up to the stove, but Uncle Brendan told her not to bother because he was "tea'd out."

"You won't be interested in girls or let them stand between you and the call if it comes, will you?" my mother asked.

"I won't."

"Take time to choose what you want to do, Gabriel," said Uncle Brendan. "Remember, only you must decide this. Being a priest is a lonely life, though it's full of people."

Mammy's eyes narrowed at Uncle Brendan. A strange quiet began, exactly the same kind as had happened earlier in the car.

Seven

On the night of the station Mass, I insisted on wearing the surplice with the hand-stitched lace crosses. Uncle Brendan had asked me to be his altar boy. As he unpacked the bread and wine, he told me to light two candles already placed on the altar, which was actually our kitchen table. Mammy had taken it into the sitting room and draped in her best white Irish linen tablecloth.

"Put the bread, water, and wine on the side table and I'll tell you when to bring it to me during Mass," he said. He watched to make sure I didn't spill it.

Martin was allowed to kneel beside me during the Mass. I warned him he wasn't to touch the brass bell with the mahogany handle standing between us. Only I was allowed to ring the bell and only when Uncle Brendan nodded. Unfortunately, during Mass, I thought he was nodding when he wasn't and I rang the bell so loudly and often that my mother took it away, muttering that no one could hear the priest during the consecration.

Afterward, Uncle Brendan walked around the house with a silver bowl and a rattle with tiny holes and blessed every room with Holy Water. The stuff kept splashing on my face every time he sprinkled, which meant I had to bless myself and say the same prayer over and over until he was finished. Following the blessing, all the women went to the kitchen to prepare the food while the men and Kate the nun sat in the living room.

Martin fingered the embroidery on my surplice. "Let's put on a fashion show."

"Good idea."

While Caroline went outside to fetch James and Connor, Martin and I went into my parents' room and searched in my mother's wardrobe for the best things. By the time the others arrived, I'd put on a lilac dress with tiny sycamore leaves underneath my surplice. Martin chose a black petticoat and rolled stockings up his thighs. Connor and James refused to wear women's clothes, not even when Caroline begged them to do it for a laugh. Instead, they raked through Daddy's side of the wardrobe for his nicest shirts and ties. Caroline put on a skirt and blouse while I slipped into a pair of high heel shoes to finish my look.

"I'm going to do my face," said Martin. He sat before the vanity and opened my mother's makeup bag. "Are you as well, Gabriel?"

"Certainly not."

"Suit yourself." He patted on face powder and put on lipstick, looked in the mirror as he smacked his lips, and finally kissed a tissue, just like women do. "I still don't feel quite dressed for our show." His eyes darted around the room and then he went to the chest of drawers, searched about until he found the knickers drawer, and fished out a bra.

"Strap me into this, Gabriel."

After I fastened the metal eyelets, he stuffed two pairs of my father's socks into each cup. "Perfect," he said. He fixed at the petticoat's thin straps as he looked in the mirror. "I'll take first place with this get-up."

"Jesus, Martin, you are like a woman," said Connor, and he wolf-whistled.

We took turns strutting up and down the hallway. As each person walked up and down, the others gave marks out of ten and wrote their scores on sheets of paper. My high heels clicked as I walked and Mammy's handbag swung back and forth on my forearm like I'd seen her do at weddings, though the surplice's sleeves kept getting in the way. My right foot slipped out of the shoe as I tried to do a perfect turn at the end of the hall.

"Falling out of the shoe doesn't lower my score," I said.

Martin walked down the hallway in bare feet, sweeping his fingers through his hair and pouting as he held his head at many odd angles. He looked so realistic because of the false tits. James and Connor agreed, but, when the marks were counted and he won, Caroline refused to accept the decision.

"I must win. I'm the real girl here."

"I'm the only one with diddies," Martin shouted. His face colored and he pointed at the bra angrily. "You didn't even have the gumption to do that and *you* call yourself a woman. The judges' decision is final. *I* won."

Caroline's mouth opened. She closed it quickly and pushed her ropes of hair behind both ears. "I see. . . . Very good, Martin. You win, hands down." She took off the skirt and patted down her clothes. "Let's have another competition. But first, I'll go check if the sandwiches are ready."

"I'm starving," said Connor.

My sister left the room.

"That showed her," Martin said.

"I think we'd better change quickly," I said.

"Rubbish," Martin said. "We'll do another show and tell Caroline she's excluded. She'll just complain when I win again." He looked me up and down and added, "You should take off that bloody surplice. It looks ridiculous over a dress. That's why I marked you down, severely."

"Why are you rude boys teasing the life out of poor Caroline? Can't you play nicely together?" Aunt Peggy called. Her heels clicked faster than mine had done as she came down the tiled hall. When she came upon us, her mouth went goldfish-like. "Your mother's frocks." She turned to James. "What's going on here?"

"We're playing dressing up and Caroline's angry because Martin made tits from socks to make a better woman and won."

Caroline smirked from the doorway.

"James, what did you say?"

"Sorry, I meant to say diddies, Aunt Peggy."

"You boys have minds dirtier than public lavatories." She glared at Martin, whose fingers worked furiously behind his back. But he couldn't do it himself and needed my help. Aunt Peggy grabbed his arm and ordered us to go to the sitting room. Martin struggled and dug his fingers into her beehive, loosening a long piece of hair at the top that she didn't notice. It looked like a horse's tail as she swung her head back and forth.

"Let me get out of this bra first, Aunt Peggy."

"*No.*"

"You've no right to hold me so tightly."

She yanked him powerful hard. We scampered down the hall like lambs. I could hear the low hum of conversation behind the closed sitting room door as we drew near.

"Caroline, open the door and go inside," Aunt Peggy said.

As we spilled in, Kate the nun put her white hands to her face. Auntie Celia was the first to laugh, followed by the nun, then Uncle Brendan.

Aunt Peggy let go of Martin, crossed the room to the other door, and called into the kitchen, "Eileen, come in here and get an education about the need for balance."

"What are you going on about now, Peggy?" Mammy shouted.

"Gabriel's dressed in your second-best frock and Martin's in one of your bras and wearing makeup." Her loose hair drifted back and forth as her head moved. "Caroline, it seems Gabriel and his cousin want to be little girls." Aunt Peggy snorted. "Shall we send Martin and Gabriel to school in pinafores and bobby socks?"

"Aunt Peggy, this is all a game," I said. "I don't like wearing women's clothes. We're doing a fashion show."

"Why isn't James in a frock?"

I didn't have a good answer and looked from adult face to adult face until I came to my father's. His lips were clamped and his eyes drilled into Martin. Mammy looked surprised when she came in, but only for an instant. Then she laughed.

"James also knows a very bad word, Eileen," said Aunt Peggy. She shook her head again. "A very bad word." Mammy's eyes followed the swishing horsetail. "You'll have to wash his mouth out with soap. Tell your mammy the bad word."

"Fart."

The adults laughed.

"I'm forever telling him not to use that word." Mammy smiled. "James, you must use the word 'wind' instead."

"No, no, no," said Aunt Peggy. "That wasn't the bad word." As Aunt Peggy's head shook, Kate the nun burst out laughing. "James, tell the truth and shame the devil in front of Sister Pious."

I caught Caroline's eye and bared my teeth.

"Tell your uncle Brendan the disgusting word and he'll ask God to forgive you," Aunt Peggy said.

"I said 'tits.'" James bit his lip as he glanced over at me.

Daddy threw back his head, laughing from his belly.

"Where did you hear such a word?" my mother said. "I want the truth now, or your uncle Brendan won't ask God to forgive you." She looked at Kate the nun, then at Uncle Brendan. "He certainly hasn't heard it around here. They've picked it up from that Noel and Jennifer living across the fields." She turned back to James. "One last chance or you've got a date with a very big stick, my lad."

James flinched. "Gabriel told a story with that word in it . . . but he used it only once."

"What was the story about?"

"I don't remember."

"Gabriel, tell your story to Uncle Brendan and Sister Pious right now."

"I can't remember it, either, Mammy."

"I don't believe you. You've got the memory of the taxman."

"I don't remember. Honest to God, I don't."

"Where did you hear the word?"

My mind flashed to the dirty magazines in the loft. "At school."

"Boys-a-boys, they learn quicker and quicker at school these days," Mr. O'Kane said.

All the adults agreed, and the men began talking among themselves again.

But when it was something bad, my mother never let go. She kept on and on until she got to the bottom of the matter. "Who said it at school?"

"It's so long ago and—"

"You're a sneak, Gabriel." Instantly, she seized my arm, pulled me toward the door, and ordered me to my room.

"Don't be so hard on him, Eileen," said Uncle Brendan. "Boys of his age are rascals. He did no harm. If that's all the bad words he learns, you'll have little to worry about."

I didn't want my uncle to think of me as a rascal.

"You're away and don't know him like I know him, Brendan." Mammy's high pitch caused the room to quiet. Everyone stared at her. "Well, he has to be shown what's right and wrong," she continued. "And lying is wrong."

Uncle Brendan's eyes moved from her face to the sofa leg.

"Oh, I remember now," I said. "It was Henry Lynch. *He* wanted me to say that word in front of the girls. That's why he and his friends pinned me to the ground and tore off my shirt button at the carnival that time."

Mammy always said the Lynch's had filthy mouths and she disliked Henry because he caused me trouble. And what I'd said wasn't a full lie.

"That's not the story you told me at the time. You said Henry hit you for no good reason. So, you're a liar as well as a sneak. I'm glad I listened to your father and didn't make a fool of myself running to complain to his mother." She pointed her finger at the door. "To bed, you sneaky liar!"

"I've told you where I heard the word."

"Bed." She pointed at the door again.

Uncle Brendan stared at the leg of the sofa and Kate the nun was biting her lower lip as she watched him. I started out of the room, making sure I banged the door as I left.

As I lay on the bed, I could hear Caroline and the others talking. A surge of pure hate rose up inside me. I hated Caroline. I hated Mammy. I hated Aunt Peggy. I hated Henry Lynch. And I hated my father for stopping Mammy complaining about Henry to his mother. My head tightened and began to ache. I knelt by the side of the bed and slammed my fists into the mattress over and over. When I finished, the tightness was gone, but I remained on my knees.

"Please, God, please help me. Please kill Henry Lynch in a car crash. Please kill him and I promise I'll say my rosary properly every night. I'll even think about each mystery like I'm supposed to." I didn't care if anyone heard me. Finally, I said one Our Father, three Hail Marys, and a Glory Be to the Father, just to be one hundred percent sure, in case my own made-up prayers didn't reach His holy ears. As I was getting up, Caroline came in the room carrying almost half of a fruitcake.

"I'm sorry," she said. "I was angry at Martin and I didn't think James would say the word." She turned down her lips. Her chin crinkled as she gave me the cake. "I didn't mean for you to get punished."

"Well, I did, didn't I?"

My sister looked at the cake. "I brought you a big slice."

Fruitcake was my favorite and I knew what she was doing. I pretended to be angry still. "So, I see."

"Shall I get the others to sneak in and see you?"

I nodded.

Caroline walked up to the open door and stopped. "So I'm forgiven, completely?"

"Only this once."

Eight

My parents had gone to a wedding in Belfast early in the morning and left Jennifer and Noel in charge of us. They were due to sit the eleven-plus examination in a few weeks. The exam was important. If they passed it, Jennifer could go to Saint Veronica's Convent and Noel to Saint Malachy's College.

Saint Malachy's was a boys' day school in Desertvale and Mammy said I would be going there. When my turn to sit the exam came, she planned to make me practice eleven-plus questions until they were second nature. She also said Noel and Jennifer wouldn't pass and they'd have to settle for attending the intermediate school, because their mother preferred talking about people behind their backs to helping her children learn.

That was fine with Noel. He didn't want to go to grammar school; he wanted to leave school as soon as he was sixteen and join the Merchant Navy, just like his father had done.

Noel stopped humming, licked a postage stamp, and pressed it onto an envelope. "Do you want to see the girls in the dirty magazine again?" he asked, as Jennifer called James up to the kitchen table to correct his sums.

We were playing make-believe school. That's all Jennifer ever played. Noel had been writing to his pen pal from County Carlow in the Irish Free State. He'd found her address in the pen-friends corner of the *Saint Martin de Porres* magazine and also hoped to visit and feel her tits one day. I didn't think it would happen. She'd asked for his photograph in her last two letters and Noel kept pretending to forget to send it. He told me he needed to have better ones taken, but I knew the honest reason was he was afraid she wouldn't write back after she saw his rotted front teeth.

"It's raining fierce," I said, "and Jennifer will wonder why we're going out in it."

"I have to post my letter and she'll do what I say."

Jennifer had given me geography questions to study. They were about different types of rocks, things Jennifer and Noel were supposed to know and I wasn't, even though I was now in the senior side of the schoolroom, too.

Noel hadn't mentioned the dirty magazines for a long time. Since our first trip, I'd always refused to go to the hay nest when he asked. Now, the idea of looking at a naked girl lying on hay bales seemed more interesting than learning about something I didn't have to know yet, especially with Jennifer punishing me for answering the questions incorrectly. That was another thing about her: she loved to whack us, so no matter how well you did, nothing was ever done to her satisfaction.

"Okay, let's go."

Noel informed Jennifer it was his turn to be in charge of me and he was taking me with him to the mailbox, and then we were going to play something else. As Jennifer peered over James's book, her thick eyebrows moved closer together until a tiny gully formed. "I need to test him first."

"Afterwards, if Eileen and Harry aren't back from the wedding when we get back."

James said he wanted to go, too, but Jennifer said he'd gotten two sums wrong and she needed to speak to him about the mistakes. We left James bawling and ran to the pigsty. Because I was now nine years old and taller, I found it much easier to climb up on the beam. Nor was I frightened of heights anymore.

"Where did you get these magazines, Noel?"

"Somebody gave them to me."

"Who?"

"Somebody . . . stop asking so many damned questions."

Noel passed a magazine to me and I flicked through the pictures of women taking off their clothes.

"This magazine's best," said Noel, "because it has letters from men who say what they'd like to do with women they see walking along the streets."

Noel read a letter from a plumber who described what he'd done to a man's wife while on a house call to mend a leak. After he finished reading, Noel spread the magazine on the hay so I could also see another story unfold in pictures. Two dark-haired girls in frilly white knickers and a man in a dark pin-striped suit were sitting on a brass bed. As Noel turned the pages, the girls' clothes came off, until they were nude. Then, they undressed the man and got on the bed with him.

As I stared at the pictures, I remembered the beautiful man I'd seen at the beach with the water droplets glittering like diamonds on his tanned legs. I hadn't thought about him since Uncle

Brendan's visit, but now I saw every detail of his face as if I'd seen it yesterday. I wondered what he was doing at this very moment, right now, as I was reading dirty magazines in a stale nest of hay.

"That man's giving her a good pumping," I said.

"He's riding her. That's what your thing's really for." Noel looked at me. "Do you want to see mine?"

"Why?"

Noel unzipped and arched his body as he lifted up off the hay and wriggled down his jeans and underwear. I saw the white of his arse glowing in the torchlight. His thing appeared.

"Touch my cock and see what happens," he said.

"What happens?"

"Touch it."

I laid my hand on it and it began to grow. The growing stiffness surprised me and I pulled my hand away.

Noel began to stroke it fast. "Take off your clothes."

"I don't want to, Noel."

"Do what I say."

"*No.*"

"Look, it's just to compare," he said more softly. "Come on . . . just for me."

As I did, Noel undressed, as well.

"I want you to do to me what the woman is doing to the man in the photo," Noel said.

"Yuck. I don't want to do that."

"I'll do it to you next and you'll see how nice it is. That's why other boys do it to one another. It's just so good."

Noel lay back and placed his hands under his head. The rain crashed upon the zinc roof like a hundred beating drums in the darkness. Way back in one corner, a steady stream of drops leaked through a hole and fell into something hollow. Slowly, I moved my lips closer and closer until they touched his thing.

HIGHLAND PARK PUBLIC LIBRARY

"That's it, Gabriel."

His voice was croaky. As he raised his upper body to watch, I got a whiff of his sweaty underarms and began to heave. Quickly, I leaned over the edge of the nest and vomited.

"What's the matter with you?"

"I want to go home."

I sat up and shivered. The hot sourness in my nose and throat stung, my eyes watered and the smell of my sick made me want to vomit again.

"Keep doing me."

"I want to go home and do Jennifer's test."

"Keep doing me."

"You didn't wash under your arms and you stink and that's what made me sick."

Noel sprang up as if stung by a wasp. "Put on your clothes and let's go. We'll come back another time and I'll teach you to play the doctors and nurses game instead. Would you prefer to do that?"

"What is it?"

"You take off your clothes and I'll be the doctor and examine you and then you do the same to me. Loads of boys play that game, as well. Would you like to play that?"

"I'll do that game."

"But this is a secret between us. You must keep it as much of a secret as the magazines." He stared at me fiercely. "If you tell, I'll have a word with Henry Lynch, and then both of us will gang up on you."

As Mammy had predicted, Noel and Jennifer failed their exams and had to go to the intermediate school where the pupils wore gorgeous burgundy blazers.

After Noel did the other kind of examination on me, I found I liked it a lot. We played doctors and nurses every time he asked. We always began by looking at the magazines. As the months passed, Noel got me to do new things to him. After I'd done him, he did the same to me, so we'd be even. I didn't vomit anymore, because Noel washed himself and his skin now smelled of soap.

The nasty part of our game was thinking about Noel's rotten teeth touching me there and the beautiful part was the lovely pains. I enjoyed the lovely pains. They came after Noel had been playing with my thing for a bit. The pains were powerful strong and not like any other pain I'd ever had. They built up slowly inside until they took over and I felt like a prisoner in my own body. The lovely pains overcame all my thoughts and made me forget about everything. But after they ended, I didn't want Noel to touch me anymore. Then, my thing would be sore and not sore at the same time. That's the best way I can explain it. Sore and not sore at the same time.

Other feelings would also come, feelings that made me whip my clothes on, make excuses, and leave, because I needed to get away from Noel. I couldn't bring myself to talk to him about these lovely pains. All I knew was I enjoyed them, but I couldn't understand why I was having them—or why they changed quickly into bad feelings that made me need to leave until the next time.

༜

Rain had fallen for two days and the river was black and flowing angrily. It had burst its banks in low places. Many of the fields were waterlogged and cows stood sadly in matted groups underneath dripping branches, their shins deep in mud, steam spewing from their nostrils like smoke.

The chugging snorts of the old generator at the back of our house made me very nervous. Mammy was worried that rain would pour through the leaking roof and mix with the diesel and snuff it out. Sometimes, the lights flickered and solid black lines rolled up the TV screen. Each time it happened, my mother leaped from her chair and cursed Daddy because he hadn't fixed the leak. Finally, she lit two pearly candles she had waiting on the windowsill.

My sister, brother, and I hated the heavy rain and spluttering generator because it led to arguments after Daddy lost his temper. Nuala was three and didn't understand, so she just watched them with huge eyes. I wished I could fix leaks. They weren't massive—but the arguments were. They always reached a point where Mammy wanted away from the "wilderness"—her word for Knockburn. She'd threaten to take us away and live in a town, where there was proper electricity and flush toilets. That sort of chat would make my father even angrier, until he'd curse furiously and tell her to clear the fuck away with the bunch of us.

Just after the lights flickered really badly and Mammy rose again, someone banged on the front door. Though only five-thirty in the evening, it was pitch-dark outside.

"Who the hell can that be in this weather?" Daddy said, as he rose to answer the door.

"Maybe somebody come to fix the roof," my mother said. She turned to me. "Gabriel, go and see who it is. I'm in no mood for company. If it's visitors, come in quickly and tell me so I can clear off to the bedroom."

I went, my father trailing after me. Mr. O'Kane stood at the door as sheets of rain swept past the overhead lamp like the fast-turning pages of a book, the streaky drops changing to liquid silver as they caught the light. The tiny veins in his cheeks were turned blue-black by the driving wind, and water dripped like a leaking faucet from the tip of his nose.

"Harry, the Lynch boys went fishing after school and they haven't come home, and the mother's beside herself wey worry," he said to my father, his voice out of breath as he reached the end. He swallowed hard. "I've never seen the likes of the river since I was your lad's age." He nodded in my direction. "We've found a fishing rod, but there's no sign of them. They've already got people combing the banks, but more are needed."

"Fetch my wellies, Gabriel."

"May they be spared and found safe," Mammy said. She paused and watched my father squeeze one foot into a Wellington. "Harry, be careful at the river. We don't need you to get drowned."

I'd been saying my Henry prayers for almost a year now and wanted them immediately undone. I'd really tried to avoid Henry, but it wasn't possible; the school playground was small and I'd also see him at concerts and other Knockburn events.

But he didn't annoy me every single day. Some mornings, his seat would be empty and I'd wait, sizzling with electricity, for fifteen minutes after the bell rang and class began. No one was ever later than fifteen minutes to school. I'd watch the clock until the big hand passed the quarter after and if he hadn't come by then, I'd be fine. There were also days when he was at school and left me alone, but even those days were filled with worry, because I didn't know if he would eventually pick on me. Every time I saw him come toward me, my stomach turned into a jumble of living knots.

I'd learned not to look him in the eyes. The thing was to stare at his chest until he finished prodding and pushing me about. Standing still made me feel ashamed, because I knew I was afraid of him. But later, in the quiet of my bed, I was king, as I recited my Henry prayers for him to die.

Now that it might have happened, I realized I didn't want it to. I didn't want anyone to die. Wanting Henry dead had been a way of releasing my anger. Also, I had only one more year of primary school to go and then Henry would be history. I'd pass my exam and go to grammar school, where everything would be different. Henry wasn't smart; he was bound to fail. He'd end up going to the intermediate school like Noel had and I'd be at Saint Malachy's with no more fears, surrounded by boys who really liked me.

I felt sweaty cold now. My heart leaped at the very thought of the word "dead." I tried to swallow, but couldn't. As I watched my father put on his anorak, my mind screamed to God, begging Him not to have listened, begging Him to spare Henry and his brother. After Daddy left, my mother suggested we say another rosary. I fell on my knees.

"We'll say the sorrowful mysteries on account of poor Henry and his brother, Gerald."

"I don't want to say another rosary," Caroline said. "We've said one, so we'll just tell God right now it was for Henry. He'll know. They were already in the river at the time we were saying it."

"Shut your mouth, Caroline," I said. Her thinking was dead dumb at times. "Don't you want them to find him alive?"

Mammy looked at me as she blessed herself.

I prayed harder than I'd ever prayed. I didn't allow my mind to wander as I concentrated on Jesus's agony in the garden and His long Crucifixion. I even said the decade my father would have said if he'd been present.

Afterward, we waited for two hours, but Daddy didn't come home. Mammy sent me to bed. I couldn't sleep. I kept tossing and thinking of Henry in the swirling water, the black-eyed trout gaping like they did when we took them from the river after my cousins and I poisoned them. I prayed until the wheels of a car passed over the cattle grid at the main gate and then I got up and raced into the living room.

As Mammy poked the fire, golden flames sprang up and began to dance. "You didn't hate Henry as much as you led me to believe, did you?"

I searched my father's eyes as he entered.

"They're gone," he said.

"It can't be." Mammy dropped the poker and it continued to rattle on the tiles as she sank into her chair. "Tragedies like this don't happen in Knockburn."

A silence arose, broken only by the sucking noise of trapped water as my father shuffled out of his Wellingtons, his wrinkled trouser bottoms soaked black.

"That means the funerals will be on Friday," she said. "I feel so sorry for that poor woman. A drunk for a husband, not a penny to bless herself with, and now this catastrophe to deal with."

I heard, but my brain couldn't take it in. Henry was dead. He was dead in real life. Dead meant no tomorrow. Dead meant polished coffins with shiny handles that no one wanted. It meant heavy clay and darkness. His coffin was made and lay waiting for him. *Dead*. It had been made while he'd eaten his breakfast this morning. It had been made and lain waiting while he'd read his composition this afternoon in class.

"Where did they find the bodies?" Mammy asked.

"They found the wee boy . . . the one who's at school with Gabriel—"

"Henry," Mammy said.

"Aye, they found his body in a very deep part of the river with his brother on top of him."

His body. Daddy said "his body." Henry was no longer a person. He and his body had been a whole person, but were now separate.

"The water carried him under and his sweater was badly snagged in the open door of an old car wreck," Daddy said. "I think the brother must have been trying to save him and got exhausted." Another short silence started up. "They've taken the bodies to the morgue."

"Was he wearing a red sweater with dogs on it, Daddy?"

"Aye, it was red."

I saw every Labrador on his sweater. It was Henry's favorite, though it was too small for him now. He'd stretched it until it was thin and very wide at the bottom.

"Thank God it's none of our children," Mammy said.

"I don't want Henry dead!"

Mammy jumped and clutched her chest.

"He can't be dead," I insisted. "His coffin can't be made yet."

"God wanted Henry and Gerald to come home," she said.

"No, that's not it. I prayed to God that He'd take Henry in a car crash, but He drowned him instead. God listened. That's why he's dead. He's dead because of my Henry prayers."

The curls of Mammy's auburn hair were loose, because she hadn't put rollers in her hair for a few days; her eyes had little red lines in their whites. She looked old. *Dead.* I stared at Mammy's eyes, saw how the jagged red lines looked like tiny forks of lightning crossing the whites. *Henry is dead. is He is not in his body anymore. He is no longer a person.*

"It's not your fault," Mammy said. "God doesn't grant requests like that. He doesn't listen to boys who ask such things."

"How do you know?"

"He knows because boys and girls are always asking for things like that." She nodded at my father. "Tell him that's the case, Harry."

"Henry had a great big smile on his face when we found him," said Daddy. "It was terrific. That definitely means he was happy to go home."

Because Henry had been in my class, Mammy said I had to go to the wake, even though I was young. Henry's parents didn't own their home like we did. They rented a council house and paid monthly rent to the government. The walls didn't even have wallpaper. They were painted pale blue. The net curtains were dirty with smoke and there wasn't a picture on the wall, not even one of the Sacred Heart or the Virgin Mary.

The grown-ups sat with long faces in the living room. Old and young men were together, some with flat caps with grimy peaks perched on their knees. They spoke in low voices as the women served tea and sandwiches or passed around silver trays filled with cigarettes. The air was heavy with sadness.

Their bodies were in a bedroom. As I approached, my heart started beating so fast, I thought it was going to burst from my chest. Sweat broke out all over my body. My hands felt clammy. Two gleaming coffins lay on the twin beds, a white one with bronze handles for Henry and a brown grown-up one with silver handles for his brother, who was almost a man. A thick yellow candle burned on a table between the beds. Its golden flame flickered back and forth in a draft caused by people as they walked about and peered at the bodies. Mr. and Mrs. Lynch sat in rickety chairs before the candle.

"Sorry for your troubles," said my father. He shook Mrs. Lynch's hand and then her husband's.

"Harry, my men have been taken from me," said Mrs. Lynch, her voice just a croaky whisper.

"It's God's will, but it's hard," Mr. Lynch said. His fingers were orange-brown from smoking, a thing he shouldn't have been doing, because he was poor and on the dole.

Mrs. Lynch was dressed in a black frock and stockings, her eyes swollen with dark rings around them, her face and hands as white as Henry's coffin lid. Soon, that lid would be wet and mucky. Soon worms would crawl over it.

"Come and have a last look at your wee school friend," Mrs. Lynch said.

"Sorry for your trouble, Mrs. Lynch."

I offered my hand, but she didn't take it. The coffin was lined in pale yellow frilly cloth and looked cozy. Henry's face was smooth, but paler than I remembered, and his hair was still frizzy and swept away from his closed eyes. He wore clothing that was also pale yellow. A white, glossy-backed Holy Communion book was tucked beneath his clasped hands and his rosary beads were wound like a rope between his joined fingers.

I stared at his fingers, at the hangnails and lines in their skin. I was surprised his fingernails had been cleaned. I couldn't believe they were the same hateful fingers that had tightened to fists and often smacked me. Nor was Henry smiling, as my father had said. His lips were thin and closed tightly and a piece of cotton wool peeped from one shiny nostril. *What's cotton wool doing in his nose?* I wondered. Had drowning made his nose bleed? Had he bled in the morgue? His eyebrows were still dark and curly. I wondered why I hadn't before noticed the very thin scar running through his right eyebrow.

I could not take my eyes off Henry's death face—it was the same and also not the same. Henry was not a person anymore. He and his body were separated. I looked at the face, spotting a mole I'd never seen before, and I wondered what he'd say if he saw me looking at him so closely. I was looking at Henry's death face, at the little white scar in his eyebrow he'd have known about and the cotton wool stuck in his nostril, and he'd never know. Henry would never know what his last face looked like.

Suddenly, I felt an urge to reach inside and touch his stilled fingers. I grasped the one he'd jabbed my chest with so often. It was cold and felt like a chicken foot. I whipped out my hand.

"Will you remember Henry in your prayers?" Mrs. Lynch said.

I didn't speak.

"Will you miss your little friend?"

Again, I didn't speak.

"Gabriel, will you never forget your friend?"

My father coughed twice and narrowed his eyes when I looked up at him.

"I won't, Mrs. Lynch. I won't forget him."

Nine

One Saturday afternoon, it felt like Henry had reached out from his grave to attack me one last time. His death created a vacancy in the Knockburn under-twelve Gaelic football team. It was late in the season and the team was doing well in the league. The boys were driven to their games in an old dented minibus and James was first to see it pass through our main gate. He ran into the kitchen to tell our father that Ciaran Bradley, the team manager, was walking to the door.

"Hiya, Harry," Ciaran said to Daddy. He entered without knocking. "I've just picked up Fergal. We have a game at three o'clock and I'm in a tight jam. I wonder if you'd see your way to letting your eldest boy act as a substitute for us."

"This one's got two left feet and can't play football," said Mammy.

Ciaran had a face in the shape of a triangle with a bulging forehead and pointy chin. He always wore the same moss green sports coat that rode up at the back because he carried so much loose change in its front pockets.

"A bit of running about will be good for the boy," Ciaran said, nodding at me as if he were my best friend.

My father ran his fingers slowly through his hair.

"To tell you the God's truth, Harry and Eileen," Ciaran continued, "if you could let him come, I'd be eternally grateful, like. We have two players off sick and the Kelly twins, our real substitutes, are having extra tuition on account they're not doing so good on their eleven-plus tests. So I'm in a tight spot, like, and can't find anybody else at such short notice."

"I don't have any football shoes, do I, Mammy?"

"We'll kit out with shoes, shorts, and a sweater," Ciaran said to me.

"Get your bag," said Daddy.

"I've also got to work for my eleven-plus, just like the twins."

"Get your things and out you go to the bus," he said. "You need toughening up and a bit of rough fun will do the job."

Matters had now gone beyond the point where huffing could help. I fetched my dusty sports bag from the wardrobe and wiped it off, not that I needed to take it because I'd nothing to put into it. As I walked toward the minibus, the boys peered, their heads tilted sideways like a bunch of hens examining dirt that they'd just raked for bugs.

"I'm glad you could come," said Fergal. "You'll be able to say you helped us win the cup if we get to the finals."

The boys were already kitted out in black, white, and gold Knockburn jerseys. Phelem Welsh was sitting next to Fergal, so

I sat beside Stuttering Anthony. They were very civil and, after a few minutes of teasing me good-naturedly, forgot I was among them and discussed football tactics.

Throughout the journey, I remained quiet and stared into the passing fields. It was as if the boys were talking from a great distance and I was a spectator. My mind flipped between the moment when I might have to step onto the field and my father's last remark. Thinking of that helped lessen my fear. My father just didn't know or understand me.

It was as if a heavy curtain suddenly parted and I saw how differently he treated James and me. He treated Caroline far better, too, though she was a girl and fathers had a soft spot for daughters. But James was a boy. And yet it was me who had to do all the hard work about the house. In winter, I split logs that were too thick with a hatchet whose handle was too long. He made me weed lawn borders in summer and cut grass with a push mower that wouldn't cut lard because he wouldn't sharpen it, just like he never mended the roof of the generator shed. I had to wash his car in freezing weather using water so icy, my hands turned red and cold. And not once did he say, "Well done, Gabriel," when I'd finished. James was now almost seven, the very age I'd been when Daddy'd first given me these jobs, yet he didn't order him to help me. Nor was my brother scolded when he refused to do his own chores.

The football game was every bit as horrid as I thought it would be. Sitting beside Ciaran on a damp bench in a borrowed Knockburn jersey that smelled of stale sweat, I watched boys race like clowns up the field after a sodden leather ball. Now and again, as they reached the opposing team's goal, Ciaran would leap off the bench and urge one or another of the players to sink it into the net for a goal or over the H bar for a point.

Twenty minutes into the second half, Ciaran decided to try me out, because they were winning by such a wide margin. The ball felt cold and slick as it mashed into my chest. I seized it with my hands but, before I decided what to do with it, an opponent smacked hard into my shoulder and tore the oily thing from me as I tumbled to the grass. The ball passed quickly up the field from player to player and was finally lobbed into our goalmouth. Even though we were winning, two of my teammates shook their fists and cursed me out.

It didn't help that Ciaran watched my every move. I felt I had to keep running about like a frisky puppy even when the ball was nowhere around, otherwise he'd think I was just plain lazy. His eyes watched as I fumbled my hand-to-toe moves when I did have the ball, and it never went in the direction I aimed when I kicked it. It spun off to the side or, worse, landed in the hands of an opponent. The piercing shriek of the referee's final whistle was sweet music. I walked off the mucky field determined never to be on one again.

"That wasn't half bad, Gabriel," Ciaran said, his downward-pointed jacket pockets jingling as he ran up to me. "You're a nifty wee runner. We'll work on the kicking and ball handling skills."

"If he knew how to kick straight, it would help," Phelem Walsh said. "He's good for nothing, right Fergal?"

"That's enough, Phelem," said Fergal. "He's never played before. You need to give him a chance."

Phelem looked hurt and I was happy. I was happy because it was the first time Fergal had stood up for me.

⁂

The following Saturday, I waited by the window in the living room until I caught sight of the minibus and then I dashed out and went to the hay nest in the pigsty. I pulled down my pants and tried to read one of Noel's magazines, but I couldn't concentrate. For what seemed like hours, my father, James, and even Nuala called out for me. James called my name once from near the curved tree I liked to climb. I feared he'd come and look in the pigsty. After their calls stopped, I waited five minutes more in the dark quietness interrupted only by the throaty chirps of a curlew in the far-off bog.

"Where the hell were you?" my father said, when I walked into the house. "You've embarrassed your mother and me. You've embarrassed the hell out of all of us. I was so badly done, I offered James to go, but Ciaran said he's too young."

"You don't get it, Daddy. You don't understand me."

"Caroline, fetch me the fucking sally rod. I'm not going to stand idle while the likes of this answers me back." His eyes flashed like headlights turned on high beam.

As the last one had been broken over James's arse the week before, he sent Caroline to the hedge to pluck a fresh one. I waited with Mammy and James in the tense silence. It was one of those horrible silences you never want to end because you know something worse is coming. I kept playing out the scene about to take place in my head as I looked over at my mother and tried to reach deep into her eyes. She looked everywhere except in my direction.

A few minutes later, Caroline arrived holding the thickest brute of a stick I'd ever seen. It was thumb thick. I looked at it and then I looked at her. Mammy called her a wicked hussy and ordered her to fetch a proper sally rod or she'd also get beaten.

My father thrashed me soundly. He thrashed for so long, my mother jumped up and grabbed his arm as he and I spun about the room. Still, he wouldn't stop. He continued thrashing and cursing and thrashing while she tried to get him off me and accused him of being possessed. I screamed above the din. My legs, lower back, and arse had purplish streaks after he'd finished. I hated him. Every time my trousers touched burning skin, I hated him.

Studying in earnest for my eleven-plus exam started after the summer holidays. I was now in my final year at primary school. I was to sit the exam in November, at age ten, as I'd started school a year earlier than everyone else. Cousin Martin was now a pupil at Saint Malachy's.

Every afternoon, Mammy sat me at the kitchen table and made me answer questions from hundreds of mock tests within a limited time period, so I'd be used to the pressure on the day of the actual exam. After each test, she marked my work and explained the mistakes I'd made. Questions about train distances traveling at certain speeds especially tormented me, because I could never calculate the correct answer. I was just no good at them.

"I want you to take the rest of the day off," Mammy said one afternoon after a very bad score. "You're not getting one bit better at these train questions. You need some time off to clear your head. Your father and James are about to leave for Larne. Go with them."

"Let's do another type of question instead."

"It'll do you good to spend time with your father and brother in the lorry."

The trip to Larne was long and uncomfortable. We drove for miles along narrow country roads that wound through fog-covered mountains, stopping just once at a lorry driver's café that had filthy toilets and stunk of engine oil. During the trip, I sat on top of the hard, plastic hump dividing the driver and passenger's seat and watched the great wipers sweep across the greasy windshield. The throb of the engine beneath vibrated my arse.

The interior of the cabin disgusted me with its cream-colored, grimy ceiling and its floor covered in oil-smeared wrenches and blackened rags. Equally as nasty were the scratched dials and the dust-caked dashboard that I was forced to lay my hands upon each time my father braked sharply. I wondered why he made me wash his car in all kinds of weather, yet couldn't keep his own truck clean. James didn't mind any of it. The fog lifted as we reached the flatlands surrounding Larne. The view of the faraway harbor was miserable, the water lifeless gray and the ferries crossing to Scotland dull and tiny.

James adored Daddy and was very interested in the truck. He asked questions 'til I wanted to scream at him to stop. His contentment widened the distance between my father and me. With James, he talked and laughed in an adult way about diggers and English and Irish football teams. My father never asked about my schoolwork or the books I read. He never approached when I played with my farm set. He never straightened my tie when I dressed for church.

As I listened above the throaty roar of the engine, I felt sad I couldn't be more like my brother. I had once tried to talk to my father about these things, but my interest wasn't there. My knowledge of lorries wasn't deep and it showed. Our conversations always stopped quickly.

Of course, my father didn't know I felt this way. He would tease me about not wanting to drive machines. "Every house has to have a gentleman who doesn't like getting his hands dirty, so you'll be ours," he said often. I'd laugh and hurt all at once. And ever since the thrashing, I felt angry. I felt so angry that he didn't try to understand me. And I just couldn't make the feeling go away.

While our father went into the administration offices to sign papers for the new diggers he'd come to collect, James and I walked past a long row of ships. Two had strange names that we couldn't pronounce. I asked a man about them and he said they were Soviet commie ships.

The dark green water smelled of stale pee and a greasy film of slime, cardboard, and small planks of wood floated between the ships. An old man sat smoking a pipe at the end of a jetty, the tip of his long fishing rod hovering inches above the water. Out of the distant grayness, a ship loaded with blue and rust-red metal containers sailed toward the harbor mouth.

"Maybe the digger Daddy's picking up is in one of those containers," James said.

"It probably arrived yesterday."

I paused and looked at my brother. He was shorter than I had been when I was seven but he was much more confident. James was popular with his friends—they chose him to captain his football team at school—and he was usually kind. Only when he was very angry with me did he tease me about not doing things boys were supposed to do.

"James, why do you think we do so many things differently?" I asked him. "I don't like doing the things you like, like playing football and reading adventure books. And why is it I always want to play the Indian when we play cowboys and Indians even when I know they always lose in the films?"

James tossed a stone at the water and counted the number of skims it made. "They don't lose when we play, because you're far stronger than me."

He picked up another smooth stone, passing it from palm to palm before fitting it between his thumb and forefinger. The ship was closer now and its movement made the water lap against the pilings. James stooped and hurled the stone. It popped in and out of the water four times and hopped over a floating piece of wood. Skimming was something we both enjoyed, so I searched and found three flat stones. We skimmed and James won, because I couldn't get one to bounce more than three times.

"Hey, boys, you're scaring away my bloody dinner," the old man shouted. "Get away o' that." He spat into the water and began to rise from his seat.

We ran back to the lorry, where Daddy had already loaded one bright yellow digger with a white roof and scarlet wheels onto the flatbed and was driving another up the skids. The digger's cheerful colors stood out against the dirty tarmac, dull brown harbor buildings, and the rusted commie ships. After we'd climbed into the cabin, James slid into the driver's seat, grabbed hold of the huge steering wheel and began to make lorry sounds, pretending to drive us home. When my father finished securing the last digger, he came and stood beside the cabin door while he talked to the harbor clerk.

After ten minutes, anger welled up inside me. I burned and wondered how my father could be so selfish as to make us wait like this. Winding down the window, I listened, but already knew he would be telling silly stories about people and stuff that had nothing to do with diggers, stuff that meant nothing to this clerk. The clerk looked bored, kept looking toward the office every few moments, but Daddy kept nudging his arm as if the two were best friends. This habit of his annoyed me. I simply couldn't understand why he nudged strangers while talking to them, or why he had to talk a pile of shite with them in the first place.

"We need to get home," I said down to him. "Mammy wants to take me shopping for new shoes." I struggled to hide my burning. "Let's go."

He looked up for a second before turning back to the clerk, who was glancing at his watch again. "These young ones have no patience," said my father. "I'll 'new shoes' him."

"I have to be getting back to work myself," the clerk said. "Take care until I see you next time."

After he'd climbed into the cab and started the engine, Daddy said, "Gabriel, you see that wee man I was talking to just now?" He curled the tip of his tongue over his upper lip while he turned the steering wheel, glancing often in the long side mirrors and out the front window as he reversed. He'd always start a sentence like this and then go quiet when he was doing something tricky, keeping a person guessing until he'd finished the job—another habit that drove me crazy.

"What about him?" I said, fighting to stop my voice from rising. I hated having to dig an answer out of him, but that's what was expected.

"Aye, you see that wee man, there." The tongue curled again. "Well, that wee man would buy and sell his mother. He's also as black as tar. Oh, Jasus, aye, black as tar. That wee man would shoot a Catholic between the eyes as quick as he would look at him. You can't trust the Protestants."

Politics was big in our house at that time. The Catholics were marching in the streets to complain that Protestants were discriminating against us in housing and government jobs. We were also demanding the right to vote. Daddy liked only a few Protestants. He hated Paisley, one of the Protestant leaders, most of all. But he also didn't like the clerk, because he was a Protestant who would shoot a Catholic between the eyes, and yet he'd talk rivers of shite with him.

"Why did you talk to him so long, then?" I asked.

James picked up on my sharpness and gave me a *shut up* look.

"I have to speak civil to the Protestants because I have to do business with them," said Daddy. "You'll find that out when you're working. Oh, Jasus, aye, my boy. You have to be civil to them, because they have all the power. That wee man was only civil because I work for a Protestant firm and he thinks I'm a Protestant. Aye, he thinks it's safe to talk to me. These Larne boys are a black crowd and wouldn't allow the likes of you and me to live in their town. Jasus, no, they'd burn us out . . . and shoot us in the back as we ran away." He laughed. "Oh, the dirty Protestants have their day of reckoning coming and I can't wait to see it. We're marching in the streets to get the vote and sit in the government. And if they don't let us sit, well then, sons of mine, the IRA will start a civil war and shoot the whole lot of them."

"But killing Protestants is wrong," I said. "You told me once, I wasn't to pray for anyone to die. You told me it was wrong. Isn't shooting a Protestant dead just as wrong?"

He didn't answer. He started whistling "On Top of Old Smokey," instead.

"Do you like sailing about with your daddy?" he asked after a bit. "I know James does, but do you?"

My father always moved to another subject whenever he didn't want to answer. He did it every time Mammy asked him a question he didn't like. She said that was exactly how he tried to change a subject.

The taking of my eleven-plus was exciting and panicky. Boys and girls sat two seats apart from one another and we were not allowed to turn over the exam paper until told to begin, at nine o'clock exactly. After the page rustlings stopped, the room became cough-quiet. Despite hours and hours of mock tests, my hands shook. The clock's tick sounded fast and loud, fast and loud. I looked at Fergal, sitting a row in front of me, and saw that he was already writing.

A bolt of panic slammed through my body and I charged through the first question, desperate to answer it even before I'd read it fully. "Cow is to herd as sheep is to . . . " Two of the choices were "flock" and "frock." I entered a cross in a box and moved on to the next question.

What I'd done didn't hit me until after the exam was over, when people were talking about the questions and one girl joked about the ridiculous "frock" choice. The word circled and circled in my brain. I was sure I remembered putting the cross in the box beside it. I couldn't believe I'd been so stupid. Beside myself with fear that I'd done the same thing with a lot of other questions, I hurtled down the corridor to the headmistress's room and told her what I thought I'd done.

To my surprise, she only laughed and said it was just a bit of nerves, that everyone made a mistake or two under pressure and I was one of the boys whom she expected to "pass with flying colors."

My mother wasn't so happy. She said I'd be a sorry boy if Fergal got a fat envelope in the mail—crammed full of grant information, travel pass applications, and other stuff about grammar school—and I got a thin one when the results came out.

One Saturday in February, around the time when the results were due, our bandy-legged, Protestant postman walked up the garden path clutching a bunch of envelopes of all sizes and thicknesses. Convinced she saw a small brown envelope in his hands and unable to bear it, Mammy ordered Caroline to open all the letters and fled to her bedroom. The first fat envelope was *The Far East*, Mammy's mission magazine; the next, her new family allowance booklet. The third bore the Education Board's red stamp.

Seizing the envelope from my sister, I tore it open and took out a bundle of pink, pale green, and white application forms. I ran to my mother's room where she sat with her fingers stuffed in her ears on the edge of the bed. Her eyes searched mine. I looked at the floor.

"Jesus, you've failed. You've failed, and I thought you'd get into grammar school like Brendan and go on to be a priest." She paced between the bed and vanity twice. "What will he think of you, after being told you're so brainy?" Her voice was shriller than a barn cat's at night. "I knew you'd failed as soon as you came home and told me you'd got that frock and flock question wrong. You're stupid, that's what you are. Well, there's nothing for it now. It's off you go to intermediate school with Noel and Jennifer and the rest of the failures."

Unable to keep a straight face, I told her the truth. "I passed, Mammy."

She touched her heart and sat on the bed again. "You cheeky nab. You almost gave me a heart attack." She reached out for the forms. "All my novenas have been answered. You're a good boy, Gabriel. I knew you had the brains."

She glanced at Caroline, who had followed me into the bedroom. "And you, my lady, you'll have to follow your brother's lead and pass when your turn comes." She paused as she riffled through the sheaf. "Did you ask the postman what thickness of envelope he had for Fergal?"

"I did, but he said it wouldn't be right to say," said Caroline.

Mammy's lips thinned. "Sure it's as little as he could do to tell a body whether it was fat or thin."

As it turned out, Fergal and Cousin Connor passed, too.

My father was very proud of my achievement and told everyone who visited that I was going to grammar school. It was great to hear him boast—so great, that I forgave him everything and promised myself never to be angry with him again. Uncle Brendan wrote after he learned the news, saying how proud he was of me, and inquiring if I still wanted to be a hairdresser like I'd told him once. He added "ha ha ha" at the end of the question. That made me laugh. I wondered why the hell I'd ever thought to be a hairdresser in the first place.

Granny Harkin, who always said "plus-eleven" instead of "eleven-plus" no matter how many times I corrected her, slipped me five pounds, but my mother took it from me as soon as she left.

"We'll use that to help pay for your uniform."

She allowed me to keep the ten shillings that Granny Neeson had given me, an amount that made her furious on account of the fact that my grandmother had pots of money, I was the first grandchild of hers to pass the exam, and Granny Harkin had given me more. She complained about it to Aunt Peggy, who nodded but gave me nothing but advice on how best to study hard.

The last few weeks of August were a whirl of activity as I prepared for Saint Malachy's. Because entry was automatic upon passing the exam, the school didn't interview me. My first contact with the school came by way of a welcome letter from the headmaster, in which he included a copy of the school rules. My mother was not happy to read she had to buy me two pairs of sneakers: one pair for sports and another for wearing in class, because outdoor shoe soles scuffed the polished floor tiles.

We visited the outfitters who supplied the uniforms. The assistant was as polished as his dark wooden counter at selling clothing, but Mammy knew all his tricks. He watched her face as he stated the prices and offered other choices when she shook her head and pretended she'd buy the shirts and charcoal pants at a factory shop. He was also full of fake praise when I tried on the cheaper type of permitted blazer. It had no slits at the back like Martin's.

"I don't think it will do," I said. "Martin's has slits."

"You can get one with panels next time," said the shop assistant. He emitted a horse-like whinny as he winked at my mother.

"You're going there to learn, *not* for a fashion parade," Mammy said.

That wasn't exactly true. Martin, who was now in his second year, had told me I must on all accounts get pants with flared bottoms. He'd told me that he and his friends were the school's trendsetters and he'd managed to persuade Auntie Celia to buy him a pair with fifteen-inch flares.

"What can Celia be thinking?" Mammy said, after I fished out a pair of the fifteen-inch ones from the rack and held them up for her to examine. "They look like curtains."

Things grew even worse for me when the assistant informed her that two items she was inspecting, a gorgeous black-and-royal-blue scarf with a thin white stripe and a peaked blue cap, weren't compulsory attire.

Other things occurred as a result of my having passed the exam that I didn't expect. Now that I was starting grammar school, my mother began treating me as if I were already eleven. I was allowed to wear long trousers anytime I chose, even during the hot summer days. Mammy also told me she would no longer barge into the kitchen when I was sitting in the tin bath on Saturday wash nights.

Neighbors treated me differently, too. They didn't just think I was brainy, they knew it now. I had passed a government exam. *That* was the proof. Old people told me I was definitely as brainy as my uncle Brendan, that I'd go just as far if I kept on the straight and narrow like him. All I had to do was follow Uncle Brendan's example and my life would be "charmed" like his.

PART TWO

September 1970–October 1978

Ten

I saw the beautiful gray stucco building with its churchlike
windows, green copper roof, and large brass cross rising into
the early morning sky as I stepped off the bus. Adjacent to
it was another double-story structure of salmon-colored brick,
with windows trimmed in moss green and a flat roof that looked
far too modern in comparison. Attached to the highest gable of
the older building was the Saint Malachy's crest, a white bird
with outstretched wings symbolizing the Holy Ghost hovering
above an open book containing Latin words, the same crest as
the one sewn on the breast pocket of my blazer. The other new
pupils and I followed the older boys up a long driveway flanked
by slender arborvitae, behind which were three tennis courts
on one side and a football field with H goal posts on the other.

"Old Quackers is already here," said Pearse, a fifteen-year-old boy walking with his friend just ahead of Fergal and me. "His car's here."

Quackers was their nickname for Father Rafferty, the head-master. I could see his orange-red car parked beside the glass main entrance doors.

"Why's he called Quackers?" asked Fergal.

Pearse threw back his head and laughed, the ends of his thick hair catching on the dandruff-flaked collar of his blazer. "Because he's a priest and crazy about ancient Greek and religion. But he's most crazy about using his tickler."

"Tickler?" I said.

"His strap," said Pearse. "It's got a piece of steel sandwiched between the upper and lower leather strips, so your hand gets an extra tickle for free."

I couldn't believe Pearse was saying such terrible things about a priest.

"You'll be meeting him and the tickler soon enough, now you're officially prisoners in this shithole for the next seven years." Pearse looked at his friend. "Right, Mickey?"

"Dead right," said Mickey, a boy of about five foot six with an oval face. His eyes were so hard they could drill holes in mahogany. Though his legs were bowed like our postman's and he had hands almost down to his knees, he walked tough with his chest puffed out. He was also wearing his indoor white sneakers outside, which the school rules forbade.

"I wonder which of these motley runts will be the first to get acquainted with the tickler's bite?" Pearse asked. He looked at Fergal and me.

Pearse was from Ballynure, a small Protestant town four miles from Knockburn where the Protestants and Catholics rarely socialized. Eight Catholic families lived in the black stone, two-story houses in the upper part of Main Street, the unofficial Catholic end of Ballynure, though some Protestants didn't want any living in the town at all. Just before the Twelfth of July every year, a day when the Protestants marched in the streets of towns with drums and fifes to celebrate King William of Orange's victory over the Catholic King James in 1690, unknown persons in Ballynure painted Union Jacks on the walls of the Catholic houses to upset them.

After it was certain I would attend Saint Malachy's, my mother had taken me to Ballynure to speak to Pearse about the school. Pearse's father owned a pub—three rooms on the ground floor of their home that only Catholics frequented. Protestants who weren't "saved" had their own pub. While we waited for Mrs. Brennan in the gloomy hallway decorated in chocolate brown paisley wallpaper, the stink of beer and cigarette smoke wafting in from the public bar, Mammy kept tut-tutting because she hated alcohol.

Pearse had been very friendly when we met for the first time in the parlor, with its velvet curtains and heavy chairs with carved claw feet. He'd even made my spirits rise by telling me what a great place Saint Malachy's was, that I'd learn German, Irish, and a host of other fascinating subjects.

"You'll also play loads of sports as well," he said. "There's tennis, basketball, track and field, and rugby."

"Rugby?" said Mammy, frowning at Pearse's mother. "I can't believe they play a Protestant game at Saint Malachy's."

Before we'd left, Pearse had promised her that he'd watch out for me. He'd even put his arm around my shoulders as we stood outside the front door of the pub. But he'd behaved so differently on the bus this morning, grunting only a greeting when he got in and then ignoring me, even after I moved seats to sit beside him. He'd also embarrassed me in front of the other boys when the bus stopped to pick up Mickey and he'd ordered me out of the seat so that his friend could sit. I didn't know what I'd done wrong or how to fix it.

Fergal and I stood with about a hundred other boys at the front of a huge gym with a knotted pine ceiling and a stage framed in gray velvet curtains at one end. Honey-colored climbing bars ran up the two longest sides of the gym and the wall opposite the stage was painted dark blue and had a basketball net affixed to it. Behind one set of bars, a wall of large windows overlooked a handball court.

"I hope they'll put us into the same class," Fergal said. "I don't want us to be split up."

"Me, neither."

A priest entered with his shoulders thrown back and his head tilted toward the ceiling and the teachers went quiet. He clutched a clipboard in one hand and lifted the bottom of his flowing soutane as he ascended the short flight of steps to the stage, like a woman does when wearing a long dress. After adjusting his spectacles, he peered out at us for a moment without smiling. This, I knew, was Father Rafferty.

Within five minutes, he welcomed us to the school and informed us that we were a privileged bunch of boys. He reminded us of the rules about hair length, proper uniform, and wearing sneakers indoors at all times. After calling out boys' names, he ordered them to stand in line across the width of the gymnasium to form classes. Fergal's name was called out first and he took his place in Class 1B. More names were announced and the class grew. Fergal kept popping out of the line to check if there was still room left for me. The class grew larger and larger.

Just as I'd about given up, my name was called and I walked past Fergal to squeeze into the narrow space between the last boy who'd been called and the wall.

After I heard Connor's name called for Class 1A, I didn't hear another thing. I was too busy deciding whether I should be glad I was in the same class as Fergal or jealous my cousin had been put into an "A" class—1A sounded superior to 1B and, if that were the case, my mother would not be pleased.

As I was trying to decide, a woman in a short pleated skirt with the fattest legs I'd ever seen told us to follow her. Her skirt was far too short. The class filed in silence along the corridor, passing closed doors with little side windows through which I could see boys seated at desks, the only noise coming from our creaking sneakers and the teacher's stockings rubbing where her thighs kissed.

"My name is Miss Brown and I'm your form mistress," she said, after we'd seated ourselves behind box desks with hinges running across the top. Graffiti covered the sides of the desks. Fergal sat beside me and neither of us could believe graffiti existed at Saint Malachy's.

Miss Brown's nostrils flared. "You're my little men and I intend to see you all do well under my tutelage."

Her shining, pale brown eyes met mine and she smiled again, a smile so warm and special I knew from that instant I'd do everything in my power to please her. She took us to the stationery store and walked us throughout the school, pointing out the different classrooms and laboratories, teachers' staff room, and the headmaster's office. We came to a cloakroom that smelled of dirty feet. A sneaker with a broken sole lay on one of ten highly varnished benches running its length. Each boy was allocated a peg with a number written beneath and told to hang on it his shoe bag (bags sewn from old curtains or bed sheets), which contained the outdoor shoes we'd been carrying with us. Again, she told us about the rule not to wear our indoor shoes out-of-doors.

Back in the classroom, we were shown how to make a time-table and also told a bell would ring every forty minutes to signal the end of a class. As I stared at the timetable I'd made, I was amazed I'd learn nine subjects every day and still have time to take two breaks.

Introductions were next. Miss Brown told us to stand in turn, announce our names and where we came from in a "loud Saint Malachy's voice," and ask one question. When my turn came, as the words tripped out, my voice was alive with trembles that wouldn't stop. I could not lift my head or halt the damned trembling.

"Speak up, Gabriel, and look at the other boys when you speak," Miss Brown said. "Remember, I said in a confident Saint Malachy's voice."

I took a deep breath and looked up just like she'd said. Twenty-one heads of all shapes and sizes watched and waited for my words. It felt like a thousand boys watched. I gripped the sides of the desk until I thought it would splinter. I said, "I'm Gabriel Harkin and I come from Knockburn."

"Very good, Gabriel, but you forgot your question," Miss Brown said.

My form teacher had just praised me and no one had laughed. This was going to be far different from my previous schooling.

"Miss Brown, are the boys in class 1A smarter than us in 1B?" I asked. I held my breath.

"An excellent question, Gabriel. Boys, I want you to know that 1A and 1B are one and the same with regard to intelligence. One and the same."

The bell rang soon thereafter and we were led to a room called Group Activities 1 for Latin class, where Miss Brown left us in the hands of Mr. Carmichael.

The Saturday after my first school week was very hot. House martins swarmed about the house and garage, their high-pitched twitters filling the sky as they prepared to leave for warmer countries. As I watched their darting flights, I wondered if some of these same birds would go to Kenya and build their nests on the eaves of Uncle Brendan's school, because he'd once told me they had house martins there as well. Thoughts like that made me feel close to him, despite his being so far away in a country that I knew nothing about. A week previous, he'd sent me a lovely letter wishing me well at Saint Malachy's and had also enclosed a photograph of his new school extension. I'd pinned it to my bedroom wall.

"Gabriel! Gabriel!" Nuala ran into the backyard, where I was tossing a rubber ball against the wall. "Mammy says you and Caroline must take James and me for our last summer bath in the river before tea. You must do it now."

During the summer months, if it was warm, our mother liked us to bathe at the river because it saved her having to do it. I always picked the same spot for us to bathe, right where a high bank of rust-red clay reared up on one side. Prickly rings of gorse carpeted the other side and the shimmering river water sang as it trickled over the smooth stones. No one but cows chewing cud on the lip of the high bank could see us naked. When we got to the river, it was always Caroline's job to shampoo and rinse James's and Nuala's hair and mine to make sure they washed their arses, necks, and inside their ears.

I placed my arms on Nuala's shoulders. Her front teeth criss-crossed slightly and made her smile impish. Her every request always began with a "must."

"We must, must we, Nuala?"

I fetched some towels and we went to the river. After we'd bathed Nuala, she got out of the water and disappeared among the gorse clumps, returning a few minutes later clutching a hen's egg. She gave it to me. The egg was yellowish and peppered with tiny white spots, and I wondered how a hen had managed to escape its coop and make its way down to the river to lay it.

"Were there any bones nearby?" I asked, thinking a fox had caught the thing and it had laid the egg in fright before it died.

Nuala shook her head so vigorously her curly hair flew away from her face.

"Take me to the spot where you found it."

We toweled ourselves quickly and dressed. As she and I searched the area, Noel appeared from behind a dense gorse bush. He took the egg and smashed it against a mossy stone. A terrible stink lifted from the runny mess. Nuala jumped back, pinching her nostrils.

"I was looking for you and your aul doll said you were here," he said. "How'd the first week at school go?"

"I've got a really gorgeous form mistress."

Noel looked at my sister. "Go back to the others and tell them Gabriel's coming with me. We'll be back in a minute."

I watched Nuala scurry across the clearing and disappear just as Caroline called out she'd caught a fish with her hands and wanted me to see it. I started toward the river, but Noel seized my arm.

"Let's go to the bridge."

"Let's go and see the fish."

"It's only a bloody trout she's tickled. You've seen a trout before, haven't you?"

I shrugged and followed him. As we walked along the riverbank, Noel and I compared timetables. Even though he was over twelve, he didn't study German or Irish, because his school was only an intermediate, not a grammar one like mine. He had to study nasty subjects like woodwork and metalwork.

We came to a deep part of the river where the water was pitch-black, and rusty-colored froth clung like soapsuds to the trailing brambles and grass. Near the edge, a sack peeped out of the water's still surface. Noel bent over and pulled it toward him. Water rushed from its loose weave as he held it up. After the trickles became a steady drip, he laid the sack on the grass and opened it. "Just as I figured."

I peered inside and thought it was a pile of black and white rags until my eyes focused. Inside were five Border collie pups curled around a glistening black stone, their eyes closed as if asleep.

"Some farmer's bitch had a litter and the bastard's drowned them," Noel said.

He drew the twine around the neck of the sack and tossed it into the water again. I watched the bag float and then sink silently beneath the blackness. The rusty froth rocked back and forth until the last ring of ripples vanished and the water stilled again.

"We should find out who did this and report him to the RSPCA," I said.

"What good would that do? Sure, the river's full of bags of dead kittens and pups."

On the way to the bridge, I couldn't stop thinking about the pups. As we drew near, I could see Fergal's house through gaps in the trees, about two hundred yards farther up the brae. I heard his voice and saw him playing ball with three other boys on the road. I wanted to show him the sack of pups and called out his name as I waved. He didn't look at us. Only the smallest, a fry of a boy acting as goalie, looked back for a moment before turning back to the game.

"Shut your fucking mouth. We don't want them coming down here." Noel checked to see if the boys were coming. "We'll go to the pigsty, instead."

"I can't. We're expected home for tea soon."

The bridge had two arches whose stone ceilings stood five feet above the riverbed. Water flowed entirely through the far arch but only partly through the nearest one, leaving a two-foot strip of stones and grainy sand where people could walk to the other side without getting their feet wet.

"We'll go under the arch," he said.

After climbing over a fence of sagging barbed wire running across the mouths of the arches, we walked into the cool, dim shade. Noel stopped halfway inside. A car passed overhead with a whoosh of wheels and the rising whine of its engine as it picked up speed to climb the hill. The noise faded, replaced by the babbling of the cheerful water. Without speaking, Noel unzipped his jeans and pulled down his underpants to just above his knees.

"Quick, do me."

His voice sounded hollow underneath the bridge. I couldn't believe what he'd asked. We always started our play with doctors and nurses. Now, he was skipping that bit and wanted the last part first.

"We can't play here." I watched in scared fascination as his thing grew. "It's not dark enough . . . and we haven't done our doctors and nurses examination."

"I want you to suck me now. Nobody will see us. Only this one time in daylight, Gabriel. I'll do it to you, too. Take down your trousers and kneel before me."

I sank to my knees. Noel's white legs and jutting thing looked so out of place among the crumbling lime and moss on the bridge's walls.

"I don't want to do this, Noel. I'm feeling so sad about the pups."

It wasn't right to do this here, especially since my brother and sisters were playing farther up the river and a bag of murdered puppies lay in the water. Noel put his hand around the back of my head and pulled my face toward his middle. Moments later, his hands left my head at the same time a loud gasp came from the entrance.

I turned, expecting to see James. But Fergal stood there. He stared at me kneeling in front of Noel's thing, His bangs were clumped with sweat. It all seemed unreal; I thought I was dreaming.

I sprang to my feet and looked again. Fergal wasn't there, but I heard grunting as he scrambled up the ditch. As fast as my thoughts, I whipped up my jeans and spilled over the barbed wire fence. I grabbed the back of Fergal's pants before he plunged through a hole in the hedge.

"Wait a minute." My heart knocked so loudly, I thought he'd hear it. "Noel and I play doctors and nurses. We examine each other for fun." My lips were dry. "You caught us doing the last bit first and . . . come and play with us, if you want."

Fergal shook his head. "My cousin said you were calling out for me, that's why I came. But I'm not playing any game like that."

"Why not?"

He shrugged. "I'm going back to my cousins. I'll see you on Monday morning."

I don't know why—I think it was his gaze and voice—but I was scared of him for the first time in my life. I needed to make things right.

"Noel found a sack of drowned pups and I'll show you where they are."

Fergal looked into my eyes for a long time. He didn't blink once. I met his stare, though it was powerful hard to do it.

"I've got to go. Another time."

I watched as he passed through the hole in the hedge and then stood staring at the empty space for a long moment. When I returned underneath the bridge, Noel was gone. Just his footprints, my footprints, and the hollows where my knees had sunk into the grainy soil before him remained.

Eleven

Fergal said no more to me about what he'd seen. As the days passed, I convinced myself he'd seen very little, though part of me kept asking why he hadn't wanted to join in the game. His words had had a hard edge, too, which troubled me.

I was so troubled, I asked Noel the following Saturday, while we were in our nest, if boys really did play this game together.

Noel switched on the flashlight and propped himself up on one elbow. "Of course, they do."

"Why did he say he didn't want to play 'any game like that'? That's exactly the words he used, Noel."

He didn't respond for a moment. "Lots of boys do it," he said finally. "You needn't worry. Some do it only with girls. Others do it with boys and girls, both."

"So there's nothing wrong with it, then?"

"Not one single thing." He switched off the flashlight. "Fergal just doesn't want to do it."

I felt so happy about this that I forced myself to stay after the lovely pains passed and the other feelings, the ones that always made me jump up and leave, came over me. I ignored them and forced myself to stay, because I wanted to continue pleasing Noel.

After a while, he began making weird noises. Soft noises like cries. Cries that grew louder and deeper. His body trembled and he called out, "I'm coming, I'm coming."

I pulled away, fumbled about until I found the flashlight, and switched it on.

"First time you've been able to make me do that," he said.

"Do what?"

"Come." There was creamy liquid on his stomach.

"What's that on your belly?"

"Spunk. Only older boys make it. You can't yet."

"What is it?"

"A man rides a woman until his spunk comes out and it mixes with her egg to make a baby."

"Why did you make it come out?"

"You can't stop it. It's a feeling that comes over your body and won't stop."

Everything clicked instantly in my brain. I knew exactly what he was describing. "Is it like a lovely pain?"

His face scrunched. "That's a good way to describe it . . . and your aul doll will explain it when she gets 'round to telling you about sexual intercourse."

⁂

I waited for my chance to ask my mother about sexual intercourse. It came on bath night four days later, after I'd washed and was sitting in front of the fire while she read a magazine. Two hours earlier, they'd argued and Daddy had left the house. The disagreement had started because he was going out to the pub with his friends. She hadn't been out for a long time and was fed up, she said, and she told him that he was a married man and should be taking her, as well, because she was his wife, not his slave. She said also he had to change his ways, because I was at grammar school now and beginning to understand more about the nature of adult relationships.

"Exactly what did you mean when you said to Daddy I'd be understanding more about adult relationships now that I'm at Saint Malachy's?"

"Oh, I meant all sorts of things." She flipped a page crisply.

"Would it include things like . . ." I paused and looked at Caroline, but pressed on. "How a man's spunk mixes with the woman's egg to make a baby?"

Caroline was brushing Nuala's wet hair and pushed her away at my words. She'd dared me twice to ask Mammy after I'd told her what Noel had said.

My mother closed the magazine slowly. "Spunk is a filthy word, Gabriel." Her nostrils widened. "Filthy."

"Why's it filthy?" Caroline asked.

"Shut up, you, or I'll send you off to bed." She turned back to me. "Don't ever use that word again."

Mammy ordered James and Nuala to bed. She peered into the fire until they'd left the room, watching its orange-and-mustard-colored tongues flutter and lick the crackling coals.

"Caroline, check and make sure James isn't listening in the hallway."

After Caroline returned to say he wasn't, Mammy said, "The pair of you, go sit on the sofa."

We sat rigid at opposite ends of the couch as our mother studied the dancing flames again. Her lower face glowed in the light and muscles on the side of her mouth twitched. Something big was coming.

"It's time to tell you the facts of life, because you're at Saint Malachy's now, Gabriel." She rose and switched off the television. "Caroline, you're smart and will be experiencing little changes to your body shortly, so I'm going to tell you also."

Mammy took a deep but slow breath. "Son, you may hear a lot of awful words to describe the private parts of your body from the boys at school. They use words like that because they haven't been told the facts of life properly. Those boys have learned about the sacred act of sexual intercourse the wrong way. Never forget that sexual intercourse is sacred. It's a gift given by God for the purpose of bringing new life into the world."

My mother sat stiffly as she explained about the changes that would occur to my penis and Caroline's vagina. She explained the actual doing of the sacred act. She used words like "engorged" and "spermatozoa."

"God also allows sexual intercourse at times other than when the woman is trying to conceive. He allows it when a woman isn't ovulating, but she *must* use the rhythm method. If she uses that method, then the Catholic Church says it's okay *not* to produce a baby."

"Isn't there another way a woman could avoid conception?" I asked.

"How might that be?" Mammy's voice had risen at the end of her question.

"Well, if the man lies flat on the bed and the girl climbs up and sits on his engorged penis, then that would stop the spermatozoa coming out, wouldn't it?"

Her jaw slackened for a split second. "I'll wash that dirty mouth of yours out with soap. How on Jesus's good earth did you come up with such a filthy idea?"

"It's a law of physics that things don't flow upward."

"Physics doesn't apply here."

"Can a blind man's penis get engorged?" Caroline asked.

"Yes, and that'll be all the questions for today."

"How can a blind man get engorged if he can't see his wife?" I asked.

"You'll understand the mystery if you get married . . . though, of course, I'm still hoping you'll be the priest in our family."

"Are you going to get Daddy to explain the other part to me?" I said.

"Other part?" Mammy cocked her head.

"About men doing it together?"

"Jesus, Mary, and Joseph, what are you saying? Haven't you been listening? Men don't do the sacred act with other men. That's unnatural."

Icy tingles passed instantly from my hipbones to the top of my spine. The hairs on the back of my neck rose. My ears exploded in bells.

"It's only the women that have eggs . . . forbidden . . . abomination . . . eyes of the Church . . ." Her lips moved faster and faster. "Unnatural . . . mortal, mortal sin . . . abomination . . . hear such a thing?" She stared at me as if expecting an answer. "I asked where did you hear of such a thing, Gabriel?"

My mind raced faster than the tumbling pieces of James's kaleidoscope.

Abomination. "I don't remember, Mammy." *Forbidden.*

My voice was weak and false, as weak and false as my lie.

Unnatural. Forbidden. Abomination.

I couldn't say I heard boys talking about it at school, because it was unnatural. I realized then that no boy did talk about this at school. How could I have been so stupid?

Mortal sin. Abomination.

An image of the man at the beach popped into my mind. I saw myself crawling underneath his towel. I'd wanted to see all of him. It was unnatural to have wanted to see him naked. Another image flashed, the one of Fergal watching me kneel before Noel at the bridge.

"Tell me the truth, Gabriel. Who told you about this wickedness?"

I met her gaze. It was as hard to look at her as it had been to look at Fergal at the bridge. Noel had lied to me. God forbade it. I would go to hell if I died. Fergal had known it was an abomination. Was this why he looked at me strangely in class sometimes, or was I imagining it?

Chills raced up my spine again, yet inside I was frying. My mind leaped from Fergal to the polished altar rails where I knelt to receive Holy Communion every Sunday. I was a sinner receiving Our Lord's body. It was hell for me when I died. Roasting flames and bodies that never cooked. Another surge of sweat came as soon as I realized I could never confess such wickedness to Father McAtamney. Not even in the pitch-dark of the confessional could I whisper this evil. Even more terrifying, I'd have to go on receiving Our Lord's flesh in a state of sin, because I was too young to refuse. Mortal sin would pile upon mortal sin. I couldn't breathe.

Clawing every ounce of my strength together, I raised my eyes to her face. I felt transparent as glass. I was sure she saw my every thought. But I had to continue as if everything were normal.

"Mammy, I made a stupid mistake. I just thought sexual intercourse was such a wonderful gift from God that it was for all kinds of people to enjoy together."

"Now you know better," she said.

Twelve

Next time I saw Fergal, I could barely look him in the eyes. I felt like my cousin Connor. My new knowledge changed everything. I felt such shame, I was sure I reeked of it and he could smell it. And I was sure the other boys could smell my shame, too.

School and the classroom became a living hell. If I thought Fergal was acting coldly toward me, I suffered a thousand agonies. I would check constantly to see if he was upset with me about anything, to see if he was still my friend. If he chose to sit beside another boy in the classroom, I was convinced it was because I was an abomination. If I saw him and the boy he was sitting with snickering in class, I was sure I was the reason. I was certain he'd told him about what he'd caught me doing to Noel. I'd brace for odd looks and the teasing to begin. I couldn't talk to anyone about it and felt so alone in the crowded classroom. Instead of concentrating on my lessons, I'd try to count the number of times Noel and I had done it, asking myself why I'd allowed it to occur in the first place.

It got so bad that I began to avoid Martin and his gang of three friends. I'd fallen into the habit of meeting them by the handball court where we'd play. If the court was already taken, we'd usually go to an empty classroom and eat our sandwiches while we chatted. It didn't matter to them that I was only a first-year or that I wasn't in the House of Cork. (Our school used a four-house system for competitive purposes at sports and examinations. The house that accumulated the most points won a trip abroad at the end of the year. I was a member of the House of Belfast.)

It didn't matter to his gang what House I belonged to because I was Martin's cousin and he was their leader. The other members were Giles, Niall, and David. Giles was the most colorful and, until I'd learned about my wickedness, I really enjoyed him. Although only thirteen, he was already six-foot, skinny, and extremely funny. He refused to trim his patchy sideburns or wear his hair regulation length and was forever hiding from Father Rafferty.

But he was also girly. Some of the other boys had nicknamed him "Pansy" before I came to Saint Malachy's. He didn't care. He'd even given Martin and the gang permission to call him that name, telling them the more it was used, the less ammunition it gave the other boys. They'd see it wasn't hurting him and the joke would be on them. The gang hadn't been able to bring themselves to say "Pansy," but had compromised. They called him "Pani" instead.

As gang leader, Martin had us make our school ties in loose, exaggerated knots, roll up our blazer sleeves, and strut about the corridors and around the edge of the football field as if we were doing a fashion parade. Until I found out about my mortal sin, I'd loved to strut with them. Until then, I hadn't cared much about Pani's girlishness or the name-calling.

For the first time, I was glad I didn't have fifteen-inch flares in my pants. They looked ridiculous and made Martin and his friends stand out from the rest of the boys. I began to think the name-calling and wolf whistles were directed at me as much as at Pani. The boys could smell I was different, in the same way a healthy dog can smell another is sick and snaps at it to get the sick one to leave.

I didn't strut with the boys for six days. On the seventh, Martin stood outside my history classroom when the lunch bell rang, the top of his indigo toothbrush peeping from his breast pocket, because he always brushed after eating.

"What's the matter, Gabriel? The others say you don't want to associate with us anymore."

"That's not true." I looked at the wall instead of his rolled-up blazer sleeves and exaggerated tie knot, both of which annoyed me.

"What gives, then?"

"I just don't like all the name-calling. It's got under my skin. I can't hack it."

"*Please*. I've told you before you shouldn't give a hoot what these heather-goons say."

Heather-goon was Martin's name for country boys—a name that hurt, because I was from the country, too.

"I *care*, Martin."

"You know as well as I do that the insults are directed at Pani, *not* you and me."

Martin paused as Fergal and two other boys came out of the history room. Fergal's eyes locked on Martin's indigo toothbrush. One of the boys had his arm around Fergal's shoulders, which made me instantly icy inside because of what I'd done to Eamonn Convery, a quiet boy who'd tried to be my friend in chemistry class two days ago. As we were sitting on our stools at the lab desks, Eamonn had put his head near mine and rubbed his hair playfully against the side of my ear. I'd wondered why the hell he'd done it and warned him not to do it again in front of two other boys. He'd turned scarlet and I'd felt dead sorry as soon as I'd seen his mortification, but I hadn't apologized.

"You simply must stop being so sensitive, Gabriel," said Martin. "I'm always telling you this."

"Put that toothbrush in your inside pocket."

My cousin looked puzzled.

"I don't think—"

Two more boys came out of the room and I stopped talking until they'd passed by.

"I don't think it's only Pani they're calling a pansy," I said. "It could . . . it might be some of the rest of us, as well."

"I don't give a damn about the heather-goons." Martin's face puckered. "Half of them can't even speak proper English, for Christ's sake. It's what you believe about yourself that matters. You mustn't allow these people to control your life." He swept his bangs, which he bleached with lemon juice, off his forehead. "For Christ's sake, let them call us any name they want. They'll be the idiots when they see it doesn't bother us."

I liked Martin when he acted like a big brother. In fact, I was jealous of Connor in this regard. Often, I thought how wonderful it would be to have an older brother to act as my protector, just as Uncle Brendan had told me Daddy had protected him.

"These farm boys are jealous of us, Gabriel. Look how some of the seniors roll up their blazer sleeves as soon as school is finished and they're walking out the gate to the buses. Who do you think started that? *We* did. That's who. Our group started the whole thing.

They want to look so hip when they chat up the Saint Mary's Convent girls. But never forget, *we* started the craze." Martin pointed a finger at his chest. "The heather-goons follow us when it matters."

It made sense, but I still needed time to think and told him so. I needed time to analyze, just like I analyzed everything, turning it over and over in my mind until all angles were examined.

For the next few days, I thought and analyzed. The more I did, the more I realized he was dead right. Martin didn't give a damn if the boys called us names. Pani didn't give a damn, either. Neither did David or Niall. So why should I? Martin was also right about me—I was far too sensitive and that needed to change.

Another amazing thing happened over the course of the next few days. My mind stretched Martin's opinion to apply to the terrible thing I'd done with Noel. I was being far too damned sensitive about that, too. Yes, I had committed a sin. But I hadn't known it was a sin. I hadn't known it was an abomination when I'd been doing the acts. God would understand if I asked Him to. What had happened was unnatural, but God knew I wasn't evil.

The hardest part to analyze and overcome was the confessing aspect. I could never tell a priest. The very thought of confessing always brought Uncle Brendan to mind, which set me back every time because it whipped up the shame again. I thought about how clean living and holy he was. I could never tell him, or any other priest. As I analyzed that problem, it popped into my head that God was all about forgiveness, too. God would forgive what I couldn't tell a priest. I would talk to Him directly and ask for forgiveness. No priest was required here.

At my bedside, for the next ten nights, I got down on my knees and chanted the Act of Contrition. I did it faithfully. I did it swiftly, too, before James came into the room and asked what the hell I was doing. I also talked in my own words to God, told Him how sorry I was and that I'd never do it again.

An astonishing thing happened as I was doing this one evening. He came to me. He came and spoke inside my head in a beautiful, fatherly voice. He told me I was completely forgiven. I heard Him clearly, as clearly as the pealing bells of Derry City.

He asked only one price: I had to stop avoiding Noel and tell him it was over.

⌘

"Your aul doll said you were down here," said Noel. He walked toward me with his hands in his pocket. "Do you want to go to the hay nest?"

I was fetching drinking water from the well. "I won't be doing the caper with you ever again, Noel." Lifting the buckets, I started quickly across the field.

Noel looked surprised as I hurried past him. "What are you talking about?"

"You heard."

He followed me. "Why?"

"You know why."

"I don't."

I put down the buckets so hard, water sloshed over the sides. I looked him in the face. It wasn't hard, because I despised his ugly face now. Everything about Noel was ugly. He was a thin body of ugliness and filth and I wished he were sixteen and leaving to join the Merchant Navy, like he wanted to do.

"I know the facts of life. What we've been doing is unnatural, a mortal sin. Men don't do that sort of thing. It's an abomination. You'd best drop to your knees and ask His forgiveness. I did."

His yellow front teeth flashed as he smiled.

"Sexual intercourse is sacred and for making babies," I insisted.

"Lots of men do it together. *That's* the God's truth."

"It's a mortal sin and I'm *not* doing it again."

Noel's face contorted into a hideous mask. "You tell your aul doll about us?"

I picked up the buckets and started walking. Water sloshed over the rims and soaked my jeans. "I didn't."

"Make sure you don't. If you do, I'm going to tell her exactly what you did to me . . . and more importantly, what you got me to do to you." He came in front of me and started to run in reverse as we advanced across the field. "I'll tell her every detail and she'll believe me because I'm older than you." His eyes pierced mine. "Do you understand?"

I didn't respond.

"Do you understand?"

He was the one who'd offered to do it to me. But I'd permitted him. Did my permitting him make me as guilty as him? I wasn't sure. I really wanted him out of my sight.

"I understand. Leave me alone."

"I'm glad we see eye to eye."

He started quickly across the field. He lit a cigarette, its blue smoke whipping behind his head as he slouched toward an arching gap in the ragged hedge. His camel-colored jacket merged with the turning leaves as he passed under the narrow arch. My shoulders and arms throbbed from carrying the buckets, but the pain was lovely. Never would Noel touch me again. Not so much as a finger of his would touch my clothes, and this lovely pain would bear witness to my promise to God.

My first school examinations occurred in mid-December. I sat with two hundred boys in the huge gymnasium with its wall of windows that let in the bleak gray light. No two members of the same class were allowed to sit within ten feet of each other, in case they were tempted to cheat. Teachers stalked the narrow aisles with folded arms and slowly swiveling heads, hoping to catch a boy or two succumbing to temptation. Trust was taught but not practiced at Saint Malachy's.

Toward the end of the term, the results flooded back and it became quickly apparent that I hadn't done well. With the announcement of each result, clusters of boys sat tallying averages during class breaks and then compared their scores with one another to ascertain who was in the lead. Latin, Irish, and mathematics were my downfall. I'd failed them miserably. My other results were average and I ended up in sixteenth place out of a class of twenty-two. I finished ten places behind Fergal, which ensured I had my first terrible Christmas.

The report card arrived on a snowy late Saturday afternoon at the end of January and gave rise to fresh misery when Mammy resurrected her scalding comparisons to Fergal. I stared at the list of results, already embedded in my brain, and my class position in each subject. They were written immaculately in black ink. Only one other thing appeared in the report card. It was written in blue: "Only a mediocre student," was Father Rafferty's comment in dusty blue fountain pen ink.

"What the hell does 'mediocre' mean?" my father asked.

"Nothing good," Mammy said. "Fetch me your school dictionary, Gabriel."

I fetched it and gave it to her, though not before checking in my bedroom.

"It means average or inferior." She looked aghast at my father.

"Jasus, you're making a fool of us," Daddy said. "You're no good with your hands and now you're proving you're no good at the books, either." He picked up his newspaper and the pages crackled fiercely as he opened it. "Aye, that Fergal's a far smarter pup than you."

The very mention of Fergal's name made my mother go ballistic. "You won't get your nose out of the bedroom if you don't swear to improve," she threatened.

"What are we going to do with you?" Daddy added. "Luksee, if you can't learn your books, you're neither good to man nor beast."

"I'll do better next time," I said in a low voice, my mind's voice screaming at him to shut his fucking mouth. I turned to my mother and froze Daddy out. "Mammy, I will do better, I promise. I'll pass all my subjects. I'll beat Fergal and end up in the top ten of the class."

"See that you do," said Daddy.

"May I be excused?" I said to Mammy.

"That's all your father and I want, Gabriel. We want you to be in the top section of your class. You've got the brains."

She paused and ran her eyes over the report card again as if it might somehow have changed for the better. "I'm going to see Father Rafferty and have a wee chat with him. Maybe there's something we can do to help you." She glanced at my father. "We'll go see the priest."

"I've no intention in this world of going to see any priest."

"He's your son, too."

"Luksee, I'm not going near that priest and that's that. Gabriel's got to pass the books on his own."

She went alone. Unfortunately, Father Rafferty couldn't put a face to my name and told her she should have brought me along. But his not being able to place me was the way I wanted things. Boys avoided him as he walked along the corridors. We darted into classrooms or under staircases, speaking to him only when summoned or when he couldn't be avoided.

Mother explained to me that he went through my report card line by line before he consulted a big burgundy book in which teachers had written detailed comments. Miss Brown had written I had tremendous potential. Father Rafferty told my mother he'd "watch my progress with much interest." As she repeated his words with emphasis on "interest," a new fear entered my heart.

Thirteen

I was grateful for my form mistress's comments. They dispelled my mother's fears that I might be removed from the college in disgrace.

And Miss Brown was magnificent. She smiled and joked with me more than she did with the other boys and I was more lighthearted and relaxed in her English and history classes than I was in any other class. She was also lenient when she caught me talking, rendering halfhearted scoldings and calling me a chatterbox.

The other boys didn't care for her as much and I took it personally if I overheard them muttering she was a "damned Protestant." That she was Protestant was true, but that mattered nothing to me and certainly didn't lessen her ability to teach

Catholic boys history and English. I also disliked it intensely when they called her cruel names like "Thunderthighs" because of her fat legs.

Martin had her for second-year history and she was partial to him, too. At lunchtime, if our gang happened to be passing the staff room and she was exiting with her friend Miss Quinn, she'd chat about us.

"Gabriel and Martin and these boys are excellent young men," she'd say. I felt so grown up.

By unspoken agreement, Fergal and I didn't sit together much in Miss Brown's class—or any other—in the second term. Suspicion and jealously stalked the friendship. He was now the yardstick of success in my parents' eyes. Each time I informed my mother that I'd done well in a class test, I wasn't congratulated until she learned if I'd trounced Fergal. Competition between us was fierce, concealed by smiles and little jokes with jags. I didn't care that he was more popular with the other boys. I was fully prepared to yield superiority in sports, but academic superiority was an entirely different affair.

Fortunately, I didn't have to yield to Fergal on the sports arena, either. Mr. O'Dowds, the head of physical education, discovered how fast I could run around the bases during a game of rounders and recruited me to the track and field department. Thus, whereas Fergal trained for the junior football team, I spent two lunchtimes a week with other athletes practicing the one and two hundred meters under Mr. O'Dowds's watchful eye.

It was wonderful to be decent at sport. I spent part of Saturdays practicing at home with James as my competition. Even my father seemed pleased I was good at one sport, though he also admitted to knowing next to nothing about sprinting.

I began winning races at inter-school athletic meets and brought back glittering medals. For the first time in my life, I had boys slapping me on the back. "Go, Dynamite! Go, Dynamite!" they'd yell when they saw me in the corridors. I acknowledged their admiration very coolly, as boasters were detested at Saint Malachy's. But inside I shivered with pride, lapping up every word and wanting more.

Among this newfound recognition, Fergal and I continued to battle in quiet ferocity when it came to schoolwork. When test results or homework essays were graded and handed out, I made a point to ask him how he'd done and what comments the teachers had written in the margins. If he wouldn't tell me, I figured it couldn't be good. But I had to be certain. More than once, I persuaded Martin and the gang to keep watch while I sneaked into the classroom at lunchtime and rummaged quickly through his schoolbag to find out exactly what had been written.

For the most part, I did better. Only in useless subjects like Latin and Irish did he do better. Still, I'd rage about it quietly, hardly able to bring myself to talk to him.

Of course, I hid my anger behind smiles. Because lurking deep within my brain was the fear of him remembering and revealing what he'd seen beneath the arch of the bridge.

Just as my athletic wins attracted the magnificent nickname and welcome attention, so, unfortunately, did my soaring grades eventually attract unwelcome attention. I found myself a target of verbal attacks. At first, the insults were plain dumb, silly taunts like "Harkin is a sneaky stew" or "Harkin's a dynamite stew," stew being Saint Malachy's slang for someone who studied too much. But the insults escalated. Soon, stuff about Miss Brown and me began to appear on desks and other places. Nasty things, like "Harkin tries to ride fat Miss Brown but can't because his cock's too small" appeared beside the anonymous Shithouse Poet's latest verses on lavatory walls. I tried to wipe them off, only to discover they'd been written in permanent ink. I also tried to block out the comments, using Pani's practice of not allowing their sting to affect me. I told myself over and over that my decent nickname countered their words. It proved impossible. Pani must have had abilities I didn't possess, because the comments still hurt.

Calling a boy horrible names gives better mileage than calling him good ones. Quickly, the taunting started up on the bus ride home, too.

Journeying by bus had never been a good experience due to the complicated travel arrangements. I was one of fourteen boys living in Knockburn, which, because it was a rural, mountainous area, wasn't well served by public transportation. Around seven-thirty every morning, four other Upper Knockburn boys and I gathered in rain or sunshine at the corner of the Ballynure main road to catch a bus carrying factory girls to their work as machinists in the village of Muckamoney.

The homebound journey was even more chaotic. A fleet of old and new buses, caked mud on their sides and "Wash Me Please" scrawled on their dusty back windows, collected us from the town square, where boys purchased candy and single cigarettes from a nearby shop. It was Belfast Zoo at feeding time: sixth-formers flirted with convent girls while fourth- and fifth-years taunted Protestant schoolboys who wore dark uniforms much like our own, except their crests weren't religious and the ties had red, not blue, diagonal stripes.

Our bus terminated in Ballynure, where Pearse's father had his pub. Because it was too early to then connect with the evening bus taking the factory girls home, the Education Board organized a taxi to transport those who lived in Knockburn. On top of all that, my bus had the questionable honor of being known as the rowdiest bus leaving Saint Malachy's front gates. No less than four times since my arrival, Father Rafferty had kept us behind after morning assembly to lecture and threaten us due to complaints from bus drivers and the traveling public.

"Gabriel Harkin's a big lick-my-arse," Paddy Flannagan, a fellow in my class, shouted down the bus one afternoon. "He wants to screw Thunderthighs but isn't man enough."

I was chatting to Aidan, a thirteen-year-old with whom I'd struck up a bus friendship, but my mouth shut automatically and the rest of my sentence backed up behind my front teeth.

"Ignore him," Aidan said. "Mickey's put him up to it."

I glanced down the bus and saw Paddy sitting two rows from the long back seat where Mickey sat. A short, wiry boy with an elfin face and squirrel eyes, he was allowed to sit near Mickey and Pearse at the back of the bus. Mickey was fifteen, mean, and I'd been wary of him ever since my first day at Saint Malachy's, when he'd turned and drilled his mahogany-hard eyes into my face as we'd walked along the school driveway. Even some upper-sixth boys, eighteen and in their final school year, were scared of him. Mickey loved to fight and give powerful head butts that a person could hear. They also drew gallons of blood.

"Gabriel Harkin's a mammy's boy and wants to be a priest like his Uncle Brendan," said Paddy, in a singsong voice. "Got any priests you can get to give us a vocations talk, Father Gabriel?"

Laughter rushed down the bus. He was making fun of the fact I attended vocation meetings. I loved to talk to the priests from different religious orders who visited the school to tell us about the religious life. Saint Malachy's had a strong tradition of producing priests and Father Rafferty liked junior boys to attend these meetings on the grounds they might receive an early call.

Even Paddy went sometimes, though only because he hadn't done his homework and needed to cut class.

Now, I wished I'd kept my mouth shut and not boasted that Uncle Brendan would give a vocations talk when he came home from Kenya in a month. As soon as my parents had received his letter, I had told a few of the boys I'd ask him. I'd said it without writing to ask Uncle Brendan because I figured I'd be able to convince him when I saw him. I'd only said it to impress the boys in my class and also to make Fergal jealous, as his family had no missionaries. But then somebody informed Father Cornelius, the vice-headmaster and head of vocations, who was always looking for priests to discuss missionary work, and he asked for Uncle's address so he could write and make arrangements. Then came the letter from Uncle Brendan saying he wasn't coming as he had to go to San Francisco instead. It was a nightmare: I had to tell Father Cornelius before he wrote to tell my uncle what a marvelous idea it was and I had to tell the boys it had been a mistake and he wasn't coming after all. Finally, Mickey and the others got wind of the whole thing and began to tease me about priests and vocations.

"Hey, Gabriel, why do you really want to be a priest?" said Dermot Hagan, a sixth-former, in his uncouth voice. "You'll not be able to put your hand up Thunderthighs's skirt and cop a good feel if you become clergy."

"Gabriel would rather put his hand up Father Cornelius's soutane," someone else said.

It was a joke among the senior boys that Father Cornelius was a poof. I heard them joking about it, though they said he liked blond-haired boys and I was dark.

More ignorant laughter broke out. I tried to block out the whole thing by focusing on hundreds of small, impressed diamond shapes on the back of the bus seat ahead. I willed the boys to lose interest in me, to move on to somebody else.

I didn't even hate Paddy. He was only mean when Mickey was around. Otherwise, he was a decent chap when you talked to him one-on-one. He was the class clown. He was also a natural at sports due to his wiriness, which was why Mickey and the others liked him. They used him. They put him on their team when they played indoor football before classes commenced in the mornings.

Senior boys intimidated me. From my first-ever sight of them, they'd looked like grown men. They were old, seventeen and eighteen; the backs of their hands were hairy; they had long sideburns and manly voices. I was deferential because that's what they expected. They made sure juniors feared them and showed them respect, shouldering us aside in the corridors as they thundered by. They ignored us in favor of older boys when we tried to buy goodies at the tuck shop. My deference was one difference between Paddy and me. He didn't fear them.

"Hey, Mickey wants to know if you'll give Father Cornelius a feel," Paddy said to me.

Paddy, I could handle. But Mickey was different. Now he was in on the baiting, the teasing wouldn't end until we got off the bus at Ballynure. My eyes burned. I'd been staring at the diamonds so long, I'd forgotten to blink.

Paddy laughed again. So did Dermot Hagan, and Pearse, and Jim Hegarty, a senior with a donkey's bray for a laugh. I hadn't liked him since he'd drawn the boys' attention to my schoolbag, which was made of dark brown leather and twice as large and wide as the satchels the other boys carried. On the first morning I'd taken it to school, he'd come up to me as we waited for the connecting bus outside the factory gate.

"What the fuck is this?" he'd asked.

"My new schoolbag."

"Hey, fellas, come and take a gawk at this fucking spectacle." Ha ha ha. "Harkin's carrying his brains in a fucking mobile library." Ha ha ha.

After the boys had formed a circle to gape at my bag, he'd seized the strap and affected straining noises as he tried to lift it. The boys had roared. Fergal had laughed, too.

"Mickey thinks you want to be a priest to hide the fact you're a poof," Paddy called down the bus.

My ears rang like a tuning fork. Bad scenes whizzed before me: Noel and I in the pigsty; Fergal seeing me on my knees at the bridge; Henry pointing and calling me a sissy; my knee prints on the sand.

"Ignore them," Aidan said. "If you react, you've lost. They're baiting you. They want you to react and won't let up if you do."

But Aidan didn't know what Fergal knew. Then his eyes flicked suddenly upward and I turned to see Mickey standing in the aisle beside me.

"Move over," he said to the two second-year boys in the seat across the aisle. They obeyed instantly, squeezing into the wall of the bus as if trying to become part of its lining. Mickey sat sideways, leaned toward me with a hand on each knee, and smiled like he was my best friend.

"Pearse and me think you shouldn't let that wee cunt treat you like that," he said out of the side of his mouth, indicating Paddy. He took a quick drag of his cigarette and expelled the smoke brutally. "Sure, he's that short, his arse is barely above the ground. Come back with me and beat the shite o' him."

Mickey's tone was one of silky compassion, his face ruthless calculation. All he wanted was a scrap of flying fists and blood.

As I regarded his dry, cracked lips, I wanted to slap his mouth hard enough to draw blood. Another thought instantly replaced that one: I wanted him dead. I wished he'd drop dead right on the filthy bus floor so I could dance on him. A murderous thought came next: If I had a knife, right here, right in front of all the boys, I'd stick it in his gullet and kill him.

The viciousness of my thoughts made me lightheaded. But I couldn't control them. They were as insistent as other thoughts I often had, thoughts I did put into action, like stepping on every third flagstone as I walked down the street. Or reaching a certain tree or gate before the count of ten. I acted on those because, if I stepped on every third flagstone or reached the tree before the count ended, I'd get the grade I wanted on an exam, or whatever it was I needed at the time. Those thoughts were insistent and wouldn't leave my mind until I did what they demanded. They compelled me.

The thoughts about killing Mickey circled in my mind in the same way. They terrified me, because I feared I'd turn them into acts. Sweat broke out over my chest and back and I felt my shirt stick to my skin.

"Come on, Gabriel," Mickey said. "Let's whip the runt's arse."

His voice brought me back into control.

"I don't think that's a good idea," I said. "Thanks for the advice, but I don't want to get into any trouble with the busman for fighting." My voice would not stop trembling.

"We'll form a wall to shield both of you." Mickey narrowed his mahogany eyes and curled his lips so the cigarette dipped from one side of his mouth. "The bus driver will never see yous and yous can go at it 'til your heart's content."

"I'll leave it all the same, Mickey."

Mickey's eyes bore into mine. Disgust mixed in with the hardness.

"Get back to your seat, Mickey, and leave Gabriel alone," a voice said. "Pick on someone your own age."

It was Finbar, the bus prefect, and I could have wrapped my arms around his waist at that moment. A boy of quiet authority, Finbar had facial scars from old acne. Some boys called him "Colander Head" behind his back. He was in the upper-sixth, expected to do very well in his final exams and go on to Oxford University.

"I'm not fucking well doing anything to him," Mickey said, rising with alacrity. "We were only chatting, Gabriel, weren't we?"

I remained quiet.

"And what might be the nature of your chat?" Finbar pressed.

"This and that."

"It wouldn't have anything to do with trying to get a fight going, would it?"

"No way."

"I'm glad to hear it, because I'd be exceptionally disappointed if it did."

As Mickey turned his head with a defiant jerk, a vein in his bull neck stood out. He stared sullenly at Finbar, just long enough to show defiance but not arouse anger. He strutted down the bus, pushing back his shoulders to show the other boys what a hard man he was because he'd stood his ground.

"Don't let him get to you," said Finbar.

My eyes rested on the apricot prefect's badge the size of a thumbnail on his lapel. Shaped like a shield, it had the word "Prefect" embossed in gold on its shiny face. The quiet power of that sweet apricot badge!

"How many more points have you won for our house since I last spoke to you?" Finbar asked me.

"Thirty."

"Naw, Harkin's a fucking yellowbelly," Mickey said aloud. "He's too fucking scared to fight."

"Well, keep it up," said Finbar, and he winked. "I want to go on another trip before I leave school."

Fourteen

As I fell to the ground, I tried to protect myself with my hands. But I didn't succeed and landed hard on my arse. The senior boy was to blame. He'd emerged from the doorway next to the school oratory at high speed, saw I was in his way, and shoved me aside. Some of the seniors were behaving more boisterously than normal. There were only a few weeks to the end of the school year and I think they sensed the teachers' grips on authority slackening. It certainly seemed that way: exams were over and teachers arrived later in the classrooms after lunchtime because many of them had strolled into town on account of the beautiful weather.

"Ugly pig," I said.

"What did you say?" the senior boy replied. "I'm going to teach you a lesson you won't forget."

He seized the lapels of my blazer, spun me around, kicked my arse, and finally sent me slamming into the rough plaster façade of the building. He put his face near mine, until our noses touched. I smelled his fetid breath. Sharp pains radiated from the bones of my arse like shunting railway carriages.

"I'm sorry, I'm very sorry," I said.

He flung me away from him. I doubled over in pain for a moment before composing myself under the inquisitive stares of boys crossing the paved yard between the old school building and the salmon-colored brick extension.

Later, after I'd explained to the gang what the senior boy did to me, Pani said, "Some sort of punishment's in order. Enough is enough." As he shook his head to underscore his contempt, Pani's curtain of long hair swept away from his face and exposed unruly sideburns and too large ears.

It was lunchtime and we were all in the art room, except Martin who'd gone to brush his teeth. We'd been trying for ten minutes to come up with a good means of revenge, but couldn't settle on anything decent.

"He's a fifth-year," said Niall. His upper lip quivered as he pondered. "Let's watch and see if he leaves the school grounds at lunchtime. Only sixth-formers have permission to do that, but we know others do it, too. If he tries to leave, we'll locate the teacher on duty and report him."

"That's chicken-brained, that is," said Pani. He put a piece of driftwood back on the table among the rest of the still-life objects the boys used to practice drawing. "Teachers are animals. They hate snitches as much as they hate boys who give them trouble. It's *us* who'll get our heads knocked about." He rolled his eyes at Niall. "Wise up, for Christ's sake."

Niall's eyes fell to his hands. He was very self-conscious about the warts there and was forever picking at them. He was also the most thoughtful member of the gang and this had been his first suggestion. Pani was out of line, but I didn't say so because, I knew he loved to act the boss when Martin wasn't present.

The door opened and my cousin entered. Once I'd told him what had happened, Martin said, "I've got the perfect plan. We'll give him a scare. We'll tell him to report to Father Rafferty for kicking you."

"That's bloody brilliant," said Pani. "Let's find the arsehole and tell him." He rolled up his blazer sleeves in preparation for our strut around the school to look for the senior boy. "That'll scare him shiteless."

We didn't find the fifth-former until next day. He was playing football in the all-weather pitch during the lunch break. David accompanied me while Martin, Pani, and Niall watched intently from a corner of the school building.

"Hey, you," I said, as I drew up to him with my chest out and shoulders pushed back so much they ached.

The fellow looked at David and I before nudging his friend.

"How's your arse?" he said. "First-years have to show respect for their betters." He glanced at David. "So do second-years, for that matter. And if you don't, well then, you have to be taught the hard way. Simple as that." A smart-arse grin painted his face.

"You can tell that to Father Rafferty at three o'clock tomorrow in his office," I said.

"Yes, he'll tell you if he thinks your plans to teach juniors respect are sound or not," David added.

The fellow's smart-arse grin disappeared and his pink cheeks went pale. "Ach, you chaps are joking me, aren't you?"

"Do I look like the type who'd joke about a thing like that?" I asked. "He told us to tell you he needs a word."

Our plan executed, David and I walked away, leaving the two boys conferring in the middle of the pitch as the two teams continued the game and the ball moved back and forth. The next stage of Martin's plan required me to find the boy before three o'clock next day and inform him I had indeed been joking. However, as gloating knows no limits, I decided to keep him in suspense until the two-fifteen bell rang for change of classes. This was my last opportunity to see him before three o'clock.

I'd even done my homework and found out 5B, his class, would be assembling in Room 12 at that time. As the bell rang, I stood in front of Mr. Kelly's desk while he explained to Barry Shaw and me why our crystal-growing experiment had been a miserable failure. With one eye on the teacher and the other on the door, I watched the rest of the physics class leave.

"Sir, may I be excused? We have German next and Miss Devine asked me to see her before class begins."

"This'll only take a few more minutes."

I didn't hear another word about how to successfully grow crystals. Five minutes later, I hurtled along the empty corridor, the only noise the grating screech of my rubber soles as I negotiated corners. I arrived at Room 12 with a roaring stitch in my side. Peering discreetly through the side window, I scanned inside. He wasn't there. I loitered for as long as I dared, hoping he was perhaps late for class, but he didn't arrive.

Throughout German, I shifted about in my wooden chair so much, it irritated my arse and made it itch like mad. I dashed out at the first peal of the three o'clock bell. My class had taken place in the salmon-colored extension while the headmaster's office lay in the older section of the school. The corridors teemed with boys whose faces I scoured as I threaded my way through. As I reached the gymnasium doors, I saw the fellow enter the headmaster's office.

Throughout geography and the following class, I watched the door, waiting for Father Rafferty to peer through the side window as he always did before entering a room. He didn't come.

On Friday morning, just as I was beginning to relax, someone tapped the door during religious education. The headmaster's birdlike secretary entered and I was told to present myself at Father Rafferty's office at lunchtime on Monday.

As the gang decided moral support was in order, they accompanied me along the corridor at the appointed hour, then melted into the shadow of the trophy cabinet in the vestibule adjacent to Father Rafferty's office. I walked the final five yards to his door. Pani, owing to his unlawful long curtain of hair, opted to view from an even more discreet distance and planted himself by the gymnasium doors some twenty-five feet away.

The headmaster was an expert in torture. He kept me squirming for exactly seven minutes before I heard, "Enter."

He looked me up and down as I closed the door and then he inquired as to the reason for my visit. He knew exactly why I was here; he was torturing me further by obliging me to explain it to him. After I'd finished, he ordered me to stand with clasped hands before his desk. He read a letter while I waited to prolong my discomfort and then rose and left the office without saying a word. He returned a minute later with the Burgundy Book.

"I note you've made some good progress since the Christmas term examinations." The priest pushed his shiny spectacles up his nose. "I expect your summer exam results are also reflecting this."

"So far, Father."

"Young man, look at me when I'm addressing you. Saint Malachy's boys exhibit leadership qualities. They do *not* glance at the floor like beggars receiving alms when addressed."

"Yes, Father."

I looked at the priest and had to admit that, while he had an overall cold demeanor, now that I was really close, I saw a flicker of kindness in his crinkly face. As his attention returned to the Burgundy Book, the chicken scratch words, "Only a mediocre student," thundered in my mind. This thought was followed swiftly by another: where, exactly, did he kept his leather tickler with its piece of sandwiched cold steel?

"Young man, do you hope to be successful here?"

"I do."

"Pardon?" His salt and pepper eyebrows arched behind his gold-rimmed glasses.

"I do, Father."

"What might success constitute in your mind, exactly?"

"That I will do excellently in all my examinations, Father."

His eyebrows went higher. "Is that all, young man?"

The way he said "young man" was most off-putting.

"And to be consistently good at sports, too."

His right brow lifted,

"And to be consistently good at sports, too, Father."

"And that is *all* success means to you?"

I couldn't think what else he needed me to say. The silence grew excruciatingly.

"What about character and integrity?"

"Character and integrity are very important."

"And they're lacking in your case, are they not?"

There ensued a lecture about liars and lying and the virtues he expected Saint Malachy's boys to consistently demonstrate. I only half heard, because my mind was still preoccupied with the tickler. A few minutes later, he came around to my side of his boxy desk, slipped his hand into a slit in his soutane and pulled out a limp piece of ancient leather. Within the space of sixty seconds, he'd administered three powerful whacks on each palm, their echoes chasing the little silences between each slap as they bounced off his varnished pine door. I was then curtly dismissed.

As I started toward the gymnasium where the gang now stood, Pani propelled himself out from within the shadow of its recessed doors.

"How'd it go?" he asked.

Martin's and Niall's eyes focused on my hands. Before I could reply, Father Rafferty's door opened again. Pani streaked across the vestibule in three gigantic leaps and barged out the main door, the rest of us following in his wake. I emerged into the brilliant sunlight feeling very dark.

"The pain will pass quickly," Martin said.

The ultimate authority had punished me. No one in our gang had been punished by him. Not even Pani with his illegal hair. My cousin laid an arm gently around my shoulder, but the lump in my throat would brook no acknowledgment of his kindness.

Fifteen

The rest of the summer holidays passed quickly. In the middle of August, Martin and I spent a week touring towns in Donegal with Uncle Tommy, Auntie Bernie, and their two children. They wanted to investigate renting a summer holiday cottage near the seaside. On our first day at the beach, Philip, my five-year-old cousin, begged Uncle Tommy to swing him 'round and 'round, to relive a carousel ride that he'd been on the day before. While pretending to read my book, I listened to Philip's joyful screams as he was swung in the air ever faster and it reminded me of my own pleasure when Uncle Tommy had swung me this way so long ago.

Shortly before my return to school, my mother summoned my siblings and I to the kitchen table for a family discussion, a most peculiar event as she'd never before done such a thing. As we settled around the table, Daddy came in and sat opposite us. My mother stood behind him and laid her hand upon his shoulder. The scene reminded me of those sepia photographs that I'd seen of wanly smiling husbands and wives dressed up in their Sunday best, except my father was the one who was sitting.

"Children, your father and I have made a decision that is going to affect all our lives forever. It will involve a great deal of sacrifice. There will be a lot of hardship for a time. We won't have a lot of meat on our dinner table, not even stewing steak on Sundays. We'll also have to go without new clothes for a while."

The stewing steak I wouldn't miss. It was tasteless and felt like I was chewing string.

"Your father's leaving his job," Mammy continued. "He's buying a digger and starting up a business. We have some money saved, but it isn't enough and we'll need to borrow more from the bank. That means we'll need to cut back on our expenses."

"What sort of digger, Daddy?" asked James, his voice lilting with anticipation.

"A JCB."

"Can I drive it?"

"We'll see." My father glanced at me and smiled, but I looked away.

He outlined his plan to work for the local farmers, saying he'd apply to do government jobs, too, when he had enough money to purchase newer equipment. He finished by stating we'd be millionaires in a very short time. Mammy scoffed at that, though it was clear she was delighted.

The digger, a rusty, tractor-like machine with a cab and wide front bucket, the uneven edge of which glinted in the sunlight, arrived two months after the start of my new school term. Daddy was proud, so proud that when I arrived home from school the next day I found he'd even repainted the digger. He'd done a brilliant job. It gleamed like it was brand new in the low autumn sun.

It didn't stay that way for long. He began working the thing mercilessly. He worked for hours enlarging the farmers' tiny fields, removing trees, stone fences, hedges, and ditches so they could use hay balers and combine harvesters instead of doing the harvest manually.

In my second year at school, I'd been put into class 2B and Miss Brown was still our form mistress. Connor moved from the A stream to join my class. Saint Malachy's required boys to choose a second European language in addition to German in year two and, choosing French over Spanish, he ended up in 2B. Throughout that year, I continued to excel at track and field and my schoolwork, even finishing first in my class after the Christmas examinations.

I had to endure taunts from the other boys on the bus ride home for my successes. Mickey and Pearse continued to gang up on me, in addition to a few other boys, but they earmarked me for the elephant's share. It didn't happen every day. Some days they forgot about me, or they got caught up in other mischief. There were also days when they had to stay late for sports training and I could breathe easy. But on the other days, when Mickey appeared to be in a bad mood as he boarded the bus, I'd sink down in my seat so that even the top of my head wouldn't be visible to provoke him. The ploy usually didn't work and there was no one to protect me anymore—Finbar had left for Oxford and the new bus prefect was as useful as a spare head. He was just as frightened of Mickey as I was, so he turned a blind eye to his bullying.

One afternoon, toward the end of that year, I was summoned to the back of the bus, where Mickey sat. I was immediately suspicious and didn't want to obey until Paddy came up to me, crossed his heart, and swore it wasn't for anything bad.

"He needs to ask you a question," he said, "and if I were you, I wouldn't risk annoying the senior boys by refusing to come."

No sooner was I before them than Pearse and two other boys grabbed my arms and legs and held me while Mickey poured something on my clothes. Instantly, the bus stank to Zeus's throne. People pinched their noses and thrust the upper windows of the bus wide open.

"HARKIN'S SHIT HIMSELF," a voice roared, above the furor.

The driver stopped the vehicle and stomped down the aisle, demanding to know who'd released the stink bomb. No one owned up and he was at a loss about what to do. Finally, he ordered me to come with him and made me stand by the open door for the rest of the ride to Ballynure.

"The boys got you good," Fergal said, as we started up the road.

"You call that animal behavior 'good'?"

"Don't take it so seriously."

"How would you like it?"

"All the same, you have to admit it's amazing how Mickey was able to concoct a stink bomb in chemistry class."

"Remind me to check and see if he passes his chemistry exam at the end of the year."

Fergal laughed. "You're too touchy."

"How would you like to be picked on constantly?"

He didn't reply.

After that incident, I began to sit in the front seat of the bus. I did for the rest of that year and throughout my third year, also. I didn't care if a bunch of first-years surrounded me. My bus friend, Aidan, and a few other boys who liked me sat beside me sometimes; so did Paddy, but only when he needed to copy homework from me.

In my third year, sixth-formers like Jim Hegarty, who'd teased me about my large school bag, left for university. But it didn't help my situation. The teasing continued—though a new group of boys became sixth-formers, they were either scared of or friendly with Mickey and Pearse, who were sixteen and even more powerful now.

"They threw bricks through Brennan's pub windows the other night and it serves them right, Ruth," someone said at the delicatessen, which lay on the other side of the high supermarket shelving.

The woman was referring to an attack on Pearse's father's bar, an event that was also big news in Knockburn. My mother and I were in the canned fruit and vegetable aisle and the shelving prevented Mammy from discovering the identity of the customer. Examining a can of pineapple chunks, she narrowed her eyes even more and shook her head.

"I quite agree," the other woman said. "Did you also say you wanted a pound of streaky bacon?"

"Provided it's lean." A brief pause ensued. "Ruth, my poor Trevor's scared witless. I'm frightened to death for him. They're so scared, they're erecting a higher fence around the police station and festooning it with sharp wire, just to make sure those IRA savages don't lob bombs over it." She tut-tutted. "What's this place coming to, I ask you? It's not right in a civilized society. We're living amid savages who know no bounds . . . oh, Ruth, that bacon doesn't look too fresh. It's more tan than pink."

"The bacon underneath came in this morning and I'll give you that instead." Another silence arose, fractured intermittently by the sound of metal clinking against metal. "Every last one of those IRA scum should be shot on sight. Yes, sir, shot on sight. *Then* there'd be no need to intern them."

My mother, who'd moved across the aisle to baked beans, dropped a can on the floor. I picked it up and handed it to her.

"Jesus, listen to that bitch's badness," she said and put the can, a very expensive brand, into her basket. "These are wicked women. Listen, pretend to be searching for something in case somebody comes into the aisle while we listen to the rest of her badness."

"I'll tell you something else for free," said the clerk. "A prison officer friend of my Sammy says they're learning Irish in prison. Aye, *Irish*, if you don't mind. They gabble to one another in it, just so the guards won't understand what murderous plots their other IRA scum friends on the outside are planning. And you know what else Sammy says?" She laughed shrilly. "He says the British government told some of the prison officers to learn it. Imagine that? He also says the sounds that come out of the mouths of those IRA thugs when they're speaking Irish are nothing short of primitive. Aye, my Sammy told his boss in no uncertain terms that the flames of hell will be mighty cool before he'll agree to learn that excuse for a language."

My mother accidentally felled part of a stack of spinach cans.

"Let's leave now," I said.

"That bitch is evil personified," my mother replied.

"I'm a slice or two over the weight," the clerk said. "Do you want me to take it off?"

"No, that's grand."

"How can we be expected to share power with Catholics? It's not right. The British government's out of its mind if they think they can foist this new initiative on us. Sammy says there should be an Ulster-wide protest strike. 'Close down the roads and power stations and remind the British who's in control,' he says. My Sammy's dead right, you know?"

"Oh, Ruth, wouldn't it be a grand lesson for those Knockburn people if they couldn't get down here to shop," said the customer. "That would teach them a lesson, wouldn't it?"

The clerk laughed. "It would be worth it just to see the look on their faces."

Ballynure was a Protestant town and Hamilton's was its only supermarket. It employed one Catholic, their coal deliveryman, out of a staff of twenty.

Relations between Protestants and Catholics had been strained in the province for a while. We were incensed because internment without trial had been introduced in 1971, and the only people imprisoned had been Catholics. A year later, the British army had shot thirteen innocent people dead at an internment protest rally in Derry, a rally that my parents had attended. The government in London had since been condemned internationally for their poor handling of Ulster's affairs. In reaction, the British imposed an initiative to share power with moderate Catholics. This, in turn, incensed the Protestants. The hard-liners, secure in their privileged Protestant birthright to rule, didn't want Catholics to have any say in the province's affairs. Their anger, which had previously been confined to the cities, was spreading to smaller towns and villages and, judging by the broken pub windows, Ballynure would not be an exception.

"Oh my, but it would be great fun to be at the roadblocks to see their faces when they're turned away and can't get down here for their milk and eggs," the clerk said.

Mammy's face was as purple as the label on the can of kidney beans she was examining. She never bought such beans.

"Many of those Knockburn men are in the IRA and those that are too old are offering shelter to them that's on the run," said the customer. "I can tell you exactly how their faces would look. My Trevor says if looks could kill, he'd be a goner ten times over. He sets up the police roadblocks to search their cars for guns and he says they'd shoot bullets through their eyes if they could when they're stopped." Her voice lowered. "Between you and me, though it doesn't do to say, Trevor would love to give some of them a damned good hiding. But he can't, of course. I mean he wears the Queen's uniform, doesn't he?"

"Since when has wearing a uniform ever stopped police brutality against us?" Mammy said, and she laid down the can of kidney beans. "I've listened to quite enough of this."

She emerged from the aisle like a battleship at full throttle.

"Hello there, Mrs. *Harkin*," the clerk said. She'd emphasized the surname so the other customer, a too bony woman who looked like she had cancer, would know at once we were Catholics. "It's such a gloomy day. Do you think this rain will ever stop?"

"It is so very gloomy out, isn't it?" the bony customer said.

"It's not rain makes this day gloomy," Mammy said, as the clerk handed the customer her package of bacon. "I'll have four rashers of streaky bacon and a soup bone with plenty of meat on it."

"I'll see you soon, Ruth," said the customer, and she walked quickly away.

The clerk picked up the first slice of bacon with her tongs.

"No, no. I don't want from the top," said Mammy. "I want the fresh bacon. Good, pink rashers like you gave your previous customer."

The clerk became so flustered she gave her five rashers instead of four.

"I asked for four," Mammy said, after the bacon was nicely wrapped and laid upon the counter.

"That's all right, Mrs. Harkin. My mistake. I'll only charge for four." She took the money, whisked the change out of the till, and handed it to Mammy. "Have a lovely day, now?" she said, and walked into the back room.

After Mammy told my father what we'd overheard at the supermarket, he said, "I can smell the Protestants' fear. They're scared because they know this is only the beginning." He slapped the arm of his chair. "The British will force them to share power, and then they'll withdraw from the place in two or three years. Sure, Ulster's no good to England anymore. She's made her money off the paddies. She doesn't need us now she's in the European Common Market."

"I think we're better off under Britain than we'd be under that useless bunch in Dublin," said Mammy. "Those people can't run a country. Everybody's out of work down there."

"Aye, we'll show these Ballynure people a thing or two. We'll push them and all the Protestants into a united Ireland . . . and those that don't want to live in a free Ireland can pack up and clear off to England."

"Though you've got to admit that not all the Protestants are like those women, Harry. We'd have to be fair to the good ones if we do get a united Ireland."

"I'm in a suck about what's fair or not fair for them. Have the Protestants worried about what's fair for us since 1690?"

"If we respected our differences, then Ulster would be a far better place," I said.

"Gabriel, shut up," said Mammy. "You're too young to be politicking."

"Politics, my arse," said Daddy. "It's the IRA who'll solve our problems. Mark my words, it'll take more IRA bombs and less words before the Protestants see the error of their ways."

Sixteen

The hardships we'd been warned to expect after my father started his business had not been exaggerated. He'd been working for farmers for over a year and there wasn't much cash to show for his efforts. We didn't have better meat on the table and I needed a new school blazer because I was now five-foot-eight. More than a handful of farmers pleaded poverty and settled their bills in dribs and drabs while the craftier ones didn't pay at all, figuring my father would be too embarrassed about having to constantly ask them for money and just write it off. Among the latter were several farmers from Knockburn who were always first in line for Communion at Sunday Mass.

Of course, my father was also partly to blame. He was slow to learn what Mammy had been forever telling him, namely not to perform work for farmer friends because friends and business didn't mix well. He drained their bogs, ordered quarry stone by the ton at his own expense, dug manually when the soil was too soft and the digger couldn't be used, and then accepted their excuses—or nothing—when it was time for them to pay. Daddy was a social person, loved talking and laughing with people, but useless at ferreting out money. Not even Mammy's sharpest rebukes could change him. He preferred resending bills with *Now 90 days overdue, please remit* or *Now 110 days overdue, please remit immediately* written on them in red ink. He'd even ordered a rubber stamp with the "please remit" shite on it.

Unfortunately, red-inked stamps, empty promises, and dishonest excuses didn't help pay the bills. Mammy told him repeatedly that the business wasn't breaking even, after expenses and the monthly payment to the bank was deducted. One month, there wasn't even money to cover the loan and my father, either because he was too proud or too scared, wouldn't go speak to the bank manager. Mammy went, after scraping together six pounds to show good faith.

"I can't believe how decent some Protestants can be," she said after she returned. "He was as refreshing as an ice cream on a scorching day. It's a pity there aren't more Protestants like him in this country. He understands farmers are slow payers. He also said the bank's taking a long-term view of your business . . . which, of course, is more than I am."

"It's a pity the bank doesn't have a Catholic bank manager," Daddy said. "It's easier dealing with your own kind than having to deal with Protestants."

"You don't want to talk to anybody, neither Catholic nor Protestant," said Mammy. "And let me tell you, there are many of our own kind who'd sink us faster than some of the Protestants. If we had more Protestants like your bank manager working in the government, there'd be no need for the bombings and killings taking place in Belfast. That man can see we're facing discrimination. He wants to give Catholics a fair shake. He's caught up in the spirit of this new power-sharing initiative the British started."

"He's covering his arse. Behind our backs, he wants it to fail, just like all the Protestants want it to fail. They're all the same as Paisley at the end of the day. They know it's the first installment in a united Ireland scheme."

"You and your united Ireland. We need money, not a united Ireland. It would fit you better to press those useless farmers to pay up. And don't expect me to be going to the bank manager again. If you can't speak to the bank about your debts, then it's high time you went back to driving a lorry."

Mammy was thrifty, but she still couldn't make ends meet on his earnings some months. Behind my father's back, because she knew he'd be livid about it, she approached Granny Harkin for small loans to buy essentials. She swore me to secrecy when I caught her in the act of asking and I promised, provided she told me what was really going on.

Borrowing pained her something fierce. And then came the month when she had to miss a repayment to Granny Harkin. She couldn't bring herself to ask for more money, so her next approaches were to tight-fisted Granny Neeson and Aunt Peggy. She always got a few pounds, but not before much sermonizing about how she shouldn't have allowed my father to give up his real job. Every time Aunt Peggy said "real job," I could smell Mammy smoldering as she blithely regarded Aunt's starchy beehive.

The strain cast great shadows over the table at mealtimes and I resented my father as a consequence. I resented his inability to badger the farmers for his dues and his ability to find a pound or two to go out for a drink with some of them on Saturday nights, even if he did drink only sodas.

"I can't take this anymore," Mammy said, after I refused to eat the sloppy yellow eggs she'd prepared to go with the mashed potatoes one evening.

I had to eat eggs every Friday because Catholics weren't allowed to eat meat and I hated the bony smoked fish she served. Now I was expected to eat eggs on Saturday nights, too. I pushed my plate aside, turning up my nose exaggeratedly.

What had precipitated this particular outburst was that Caroline had followed my example. In addition, Mammy was annoyed with my sister because she wasn't doing well in her eleven-plus mock exams. My sister's breasts had also grown large almost overnight, which necessitated the purchase of bras. Money had to be found for her new school uniform, too, though the jury was still out on whether that would be a convent or intermediate school. On top of all that, Nuala was now six, tall for her age, and in need of new shoes.

"Why can't you get off your backside and go collect what's due you?" she said to Daddy.

His eyes ignited, but he continued eating.

"I'm harried trying to scrape money together to clothe every one of you," she added. "I don't dare buy a new stitch for myself."

I retrieved my plate and pretended to eat the putrid slop. Caroline took my cue and did the same. Nuala bounded off her chair.

"This useless man of a father of yours," Mammy said. "All he does on a Saturday evening is preen to go out when he should be staying home."

Still, my father continued eating.

"What do you need to be going out to a pub for? I don't get out to enjoy myself, so why the hell should you? If it's out you want to go, then pay a visit to those bloody farmers."

"Why the fuck don't *you* ask them? That's all you fucking well do is complain. *That's* why I want out of the fucking house of a Saturday night. To give my head a bit of peace and get away from you." He slammed his fists into the table and it shook with the force.

Caroline's chair scraped loudly as she vacated the table in a mass of swaying ringlets. Even though I was now older, these angry moments still upset me greatly because they instantly transported me back to childhood. I felt defenseless and weak, and all my school accomplishments seemed insignificant. My stomach churned with tension, when all I desired was cozy security.

The more I watched my parents argue, the more I swore I'd never marry. It was beyond comprehension how they'd fallen in love, married, and had children, only to spend their lives insulting and threatening one another. Though I was always on my mother's side, as I watched her pace prior to her inevitable stampede to the bedroom, I swore to myself that no woman would ever possess me. I would have no millstones like women and marriage, so I wouldn't have to deal with constant arguments.

"You're not looking after your children, Harry," Mammy yelled. "They're not being properly fed. Your responsibility is to us, not to go out spending."

My father leaped up, chin, lips, and temples twitching, hands clenched into fists. He snatched his dinner plate up and hurled it onto the floor.

"Why don't you go out and get a job like other Knockburn women? You gave up your bookkeeping job because you wanted children, but there are plenty of women who had as many as you and they're *still* working in the shirt factory." A twisted smile formed fleetingly on his face. "Oh, that's right, I forgot. You're too stinking with pride for things like that . . . just like the rest of the fucking Neesons."

Caroline and I scuttled into a corner where we formed a feeble barrier between our parents and James and Nuala. I wanted to run, but Nuala was watching me, her tiny, crisscrossed front teeth exacerbating her vulnerability. I pulled her toward me.

"Count the number of geese and goslings on the wallpaper pattern and tune everything else out," I said.

She gripped my forearms. Her cupid lips moved quickly as she counted. My parents didn't usually notice us when they were this angry and we, as if driven by animal instinct or habit, didn't dare move a muscle. I scarcely permitted myself to breathe, waiting, waiting for the moment when one of them might decide to use my siblings or I to score a low point.

"I'm bookkeeper enough to know you're making no money," Mammy said. "And I'm bookkeeper enough to know we'll be listed in the *Gazette* if you don't do something about it fast."

To have your name listed in that paper meant you were a failure. You were a bankrupt, an unmentionable disgrace. All the neighbors would read about your debts.

"And for your information, I'd have a job if you had books worth keeping . . . and don't you dare bring the Neesons into this, either. You owe the Neesons more than you think, if you want to know." Mother paused to let her truthful words sink in. "If your mother had reared you right, you'd stay at home with your children. But she didn't raise you right. You're that useless, you can't even wash a dish or make a cup of tea."

Nuala abandoned her count. "Mammy! Daddy! Be friends."

My father glanced at her for a split second before focusing on my arm draped around her. "Him. You've turned him into one useless chap. He's just another Brendan. He can't even use a fucking shovel."

"Shut your trap," Mammy said.

"He can't even come out on a Saturday afternoon when I ask for help. He used to help me, but now he does nothing. Every time I ask him, he runs to you and you come to me saying he's only a boy and he has his books to study. Books, my arse. He's fucking useless. He's for nothing, if you want to know. He can't even mix with the other Knockburn lads. All he wants to do is run about with that fancy boy Martin and learn his affected ways."

"Leave Gabriel alone."

"I was out working when I was his age."

"Where has it got you?"

Sometimes I wished Mammy wasn't so quick. Daddy's facial muscles twitched rapidly. I thought he was going to hit her. He'd never hit her, but sometimes I thought it must definitely come when she said things like that.

Daddy stood rock still. Nuala's fingers pinched into my flesh.

"Well, I'm sick of the whole damned lot of you. I wish I could do what other men in my situation do and clear off for good." He yanked the door open. "Eileen, you can go to hell. You can go to hell and take him with you."

He slammed the door as he left. Its ringing echo engulfed the kitchen. I remained frozen as his footsteps receded. Seconds later, the car engine revved and was followed by a ferocious screech of gears.

"I'm not going to be like him when I grow up," I said, stooping to help pick up shards of the broken plate. "All he does is rant and go out to pubs."

"*Don't* say a word against your father."

"He's always picking on me. Always wanting me to do dirty work I don't want to do. And you heard what he said about me just now."

He would get no more love from me. To me, he was Daddy no longer. The word "Father" was a better way to address him. Used in England but not so much in Ireland, at least not in Knockburn, it was ideally remote. I was removed from him and this was the perfect word. I resolved to think of him only as "Father" in my mind from now on. Of course, I realized I'd still have to call him Daddy to his face. I'd have to use it when he spoke to me directly, otherwise my mother would notice and pass remarks after a time. Nor could I address him as "Father" in front of Caroline and James, because they'd die laughing at its ridiculous formality. I couldn't avoid calling him Daddy to his face, but he was only Father in my mind from now on.

Mammy looked at the jagged piece of plate in her hand. "He's got a point, Gabriel. You should offer to help him. Your father works like a dog. You could pick up stones and do a bit of shoveling some Saturdays." She looked at me. "He's never refused you anything when you've asked and we could afford it."

To be perfectly honest, avoiding going out to help Father had become one of my priorities. I was definitely work-shy when it came to doing manual labor. The priests at Saint Malachy's said *all* work had dignity and pleased God, and that it wasn't only Protestants who possessed a work ethic. But I couldn't buy that load of junk about all work being dignified. I couldn't see what was so damned dignified about breaking your back. I couldn't see what was supposed to be so dignified about digging drains and ditches with a shovel and pick. Nobody would do it if they didn't have to. Manual work was hard and demeaning, and I felt people should just be honest, admit it, and stop saying ridiculously good things about it.

"It's true, Gabriel. You *should* offer to help. Your daddy's a decent man. He doesn't drink. He attends Mass. While it's true he can't make himself a cup of tea, I hope you turn out to be as good a man."

Her ability to reverse herself and stand up for Father was truly astonishing. Just when I thought she hated him, just when she was threatening to walk out and take us with her, she'd turn on a penny and praise him. Jesus, this was such a source of bafflement.

I'd noticed that Caroline could change that way, too. One moment a thing was black, the next it was white, and you didn't know where the hell you stood.

Seventeen

Tiny scarlet nets were etched into the whites of my sister's eyes as she stood before my mother in a disheveled state. She'd just got in from school and the two uppermost buttons of her blue-and-white-checked blouse were missing and a long ladder ran from the knee of her right stocking to disappear beneath the bottom of her tunic. Her hair was also uncharacteristically tangled. She was now a teenager and in her third year at Saint Veronica's Convent in Carntower.

"I'm telling you, I didn't provoke them," Caroline said. "None of the girls ever speak to those horrible boys when we're waiting for the taxi home."

"You definitely didn't smile and give him a wrong idea?" said my mother.

"They called us 'Fenian whores.' They're always calling us names. But they've never touched me until this afternoon. Those Ballynure school pupils hate us because we're Catholics. That's exactly what it's about. Even the girls swear at us, and they egg the boys on, too. That's why the brute lunged and tried to grab me."

"It's disgraceful," said Mammy.

"His hand was partway inside my blouse, Mammy. I had to get away. That's why my buttons came off." Caroline started crying. "Honest to God, Mammy. It wasn't my fault."

"I believe you, pet." Mammy patted Caroline's head and laid her hand on her shoulder.

"I'm sorry about the blouse," Caroline said, amid sniffs. "I'll sew on the buttons and mend my stocking tonight."

"We'll get it sorted," my mother said. "They're a bunch of scum. Something needs to be done. You must tell Sister Margaret-Mary about this tomorrow. She'll contact the police."

"What can the headmistress do?" my sister said. "The police won't listen to a nun. Sure the police *hate* the Catholics, too."

Every evening, Caroline had to catch a connecting bus near the steps of the Ballynure clock tower. Her uniform, a royal blue tunic and blazer with a crest comprised of a cross on its breast pocket, was the giveaway she was Catholic.

Arguments between Protestant school and Saint Malachy's pupils were forever breaking out, too. Sometimes, it was the Protestants who started it; sometimes, it was Saint Malachy's boys. The whole thing was dumb.

It offended me because I was now a fourth-year and had befriended a Protestant schoolboy. Nigel lived in the Protestant fringe surrounding Knockburn and traveled the last part of the morning journey, a ten-minute ride into Ballynure, with us to catch the same bus as Caroline to Carntower. A ram of a chap with a thick neck, round face, and ginger hair (the latter unusual for a Protestant, I thought), Nigel was also in his fourth year and played rugby at Carntower Academy, a brilliant Protestant school. One morning, he chanced to sit beside me on the bus. We nodded and smiled, got talking, and I learned in the course of our first sit-together that Protestant schoolboys could be very mannerly.

I hoped he'd sit beside me the next day, and he did. I began reserving the seat for him, albeit very discreetly. I never said a word to him about what I was doing, but Nigel knew I was keeping the seat. I knew by the way he grinned as he walked down the aisle. The more we talked, the more we got to like each other. Even our mothers, who'd seen one another in Hamilton's supermarket but never spoken, began chatting when they met on account of our friendship.

Nigel fast became a source of fantasy to me. In bed, after I'd said my prayers, I'd imagine us entering into a lasting friendship where I'd visit his house, he'd visit mine, and we'd talk about every subject under the sun. I imagined us talking about the real differences between Catholics and Protestants. Not obvious stuff like religion, but rather about what made us dislike one another and what could be done to improve relations. Of course, he and I never discussed such a prickly subject on the short bus ride, but nevertheless, sitting beside him every morning talking about school stuff was one of the highlights of my day.

Another fascinating thing about Nigel was his uniform. The blazer was stunning: red and white stripes on a purplish-blue background. He also wore a matching cap and scarf that were compulsory wear. Everything was so classy and made my uniform look drab in comparison. The Saint Malachy's boys took offense to the Carntower Academy uniform, grumbling its colors were the same as those of the Union Jack, which only Protestants recognized in Ireland. It didn't matter to them that the school and its uniform colors were hundreds of years old.

Over time, some boys noticed I reserved a seat for Nigel and the pathetic nonsense commenced. Nigel and his uniform provided new fodder for Pearse, Mickey, and, of late, Mickey's younger brother, Willie, who was a third-year and fast becoming a bully in his own right. They didn't bother me during the morning commute because they were too busy copying homework from one another. It was always during the evening ride home when Mickey would send Willie down to bat me on the head for sitting beside a Protestant. I couldn't do a thing about it, because I knew Mickey was behind it.

After the bus dropped us off in Ballynure every evening, a taxi took us up to Knockburn. Six of us had to arrange ourselves in the backseat of the vehicle. It was so packed inside, I could hardly breathe, let alone move. Eventually, somebody got it into his head to torment me during this ride as well. Within five minutes of starting the journey, I'd experience small, sharp stabs in my thigh that made my eyes water. No matter how many fractions of an inch I tried to shift my leg away, I soon felt the stabs again as something sharp pierced my flesh. It was impossible to ascertain who was doing it. I complained one evening and more than one boy laughed. That's when I realized the attack had been planned.

The stabbing was all the more painful because I didn't know what to do about it. I couldn't appeal to my parents or teachers: Father would just turn a deaf ear, as he always did; Mammy always agreed with him whenever he told her not to interfere because I had to fight my own battles; and appeals to the teachers who mattered at Saint Malachy's would be most unwelcome.

Saint Malachy's was an Irish Catholic boys' school down to its consecrated foundations. Boys were expected to be tough and assertive and to show no feminine qualities, as they would be inexcusable signs of weakness. Yet, naturally, we had to respect such feminine qualities in women, as such qualities in women weren't weaknesses. They had to be respected because women were our mothers and would eventually become our wives.

Saint Malachy's boys dared not worry about facial spots, dared not show affection for one another, dared not giggle too shrilly. Most of our senior male teachers had come through this system and now behaved as gentlemen in front of women. Yet, some of them took pleasure in punishing boys in ways that bordered on perverse. So, I couldn't approach the teachers who held real power with my problem, because I was fourteen now and unyielding manliness was demanded. Not all the Saint Malachy's teachers behaved this way, of course. There were decent teachers, too—but they were low in the pecking order.

I had to find my own solution. I couldn't tune it out like I did with the verbal abuse. Trouble was, just when I'd narrowed it down to a particular suspect and observed his movements carefully, I'd find out I was wrong.

"You know damned well who's jabbing me in the leg, don't you?" I said to Fergal, after the taxi dropped us off at the crossroads one afternoon.

The ride had been particularly painful and the gloomy weather compounded my frustration. It was damp and the silent hedgerows, interspersed with middling-sized, ragged hawthorns, seemed otherworldly because of the mist.

"I do not, indeed," he said.

I cast my satchel down on the road. "How can you lie to me when you know someone is sticking something sharp into my leg?"

Though Fergal and I talked every day, we were actually estranged. Our boyhood friendship was as tattered as a tinker's clothing. We knew it, denied it, and chose instead to fill the walks home with phony conversation. Fergal was a ruddy complexioned, very average pupil, one of those jovial schoolboys one sees peering from an old class photograph whose face is familiar but whose name is always forgotten. Competitiveness and parental jealousies had distanced us to chasm proportions over the years. We lied to each other habitually about the silliest things: whether or not we were studying for a class test, or whether we were doing research or not for some project. Both of us knew we lied, and yet we went through the motions and asked the questions, anyway.

More than once, Fergal had called me a "poof" on the bus when it was noisy and he probably figured I wouldn't hear his voice. But I heard him. I'd know his voice anywhere. His voice had been around me since awareness began and you never forget a voice that's been around that long. He'd always apologize when he guessed by my frostiness I'd heard him. I always forgave him, on account of we did go back to awareness. But trust was an entirely different matter. Circumstances had rendered trust between us irrevocably dead. We were in a schoolboy's dilemma. We couldn't terminate the friendship. We couldn't do what adults do when a friendship's over and simply stop speaking, because we had to walk home together and go through the charade daily.

"How would you like someone to do that to you every day, Fergal?" I said. "It's sore as hell. My leg's full of tiny red holes."

Fergal looked at me for an instant before shifting his gaze up the road, even though he could see nothing. The clinging fog lent a ghostly appearance to his body, made him appear so different, like someone from another time.

"It's Kevin McDermott," Fergal admitted. "He says you're a big stew and you deserve it for talking to that black Protestant from Carntower Academy. He sticks you with a compass."

That Kevin thought I was a nerd surprised me. He was a very civil fellow. It was also ironic he called me a stew. McDermott, with his long teeth and Cheshire Cat smile, looked as devious as God ever intended sneaks to appear. He was in the same year as me and consistently first in his class. All the boys complained it was easier to pull wisdom teeth with chopsticks than to ever get him to share his homework.

"How do you think Kevin manages to always come first in his class?" I said.

"Because he's a stew as well," Fergal said. "It's actually more to do with the Protestant thing."

I let the fact Fergal said "stew as well" slide. "Nigel's not a black Protestant. He should get to know him before he makes judgments."

"I don't think you should be reserving seats for Prods, if you want my opinion. They're all the same. Nice to your face and stab you in the back when it suits them."

"Like Kevin's doing, you mean?"

He sighed. "You know what I'm saying, Gabriel."

"You fancy Cathy Simpson who waits near our bus line in the evenings?"

"That's different. She's a girl . . . and I only like her because I'd like to ride her, so it's okay."

Fergal was unfazed by the glaring hypocrisy. It had to do with the fact he was completely oversexed. Sex was what he and many other boys in our class talked about most of the time now. They talked tits, hard-ons, riding girls, homework complaints, latest soccer results, more tits and hard-ons. It was all big talk. If a girl approached Fergal, he'd bolt.

Though only one year younger than him, I wasn't obsessed with girls or their body parts. I liked looking at a girl overall, not just at her tits and arse. And the way they talked about hard-ons was ridiculous, about how this girl or that one made them get really stiff. I woke up stiff as well, sometimes, but I didn't go on about it as if it was the only thing in life that mattered.

Cathy Simpson was one of the really pretty girls and wouldn't give Fergal a second glance. She didn't look Irish Protestant in the slightest, either. Her silky blonde hair fell to the small of her back. She tossed it beautifully as she got out of the school bus, just like a horse does its mane in full gallop.

"I don't think you should say that sort of thing about Cathy, either," I said. "If you like a girl, what does her religion matter?"

"I would never go steady with her. You only ride the Prod girls."

Kevin liked to play chess at lunchtime. The next day, I went to the physics laboratory where the players met, took him aside before he began a game, and asked point-blank why he was stabbing me with a compass.

At first, he denied it vigorously. "How could you even think I'd do such a thing?" he kept protesting, as he tried to look me in the eye.

I told him I knew it was him because someone had informed on him. He looked away, pretending to watch an upper-sixth fellow wiggling his index finger against the tip of his nose as he pondered a move. Finally, he turned back to me and mumbled an apology.

"I won't do it again," he said, and flashed me his cheesy smile. "I promise."

Two days later, the stabbing recommenced. Three gentle, probing stabs the first day and then back to the old intensity and frequency the next. The following evening, I made sure to be in Kevin's vicinity as we bundled into the taxi. At the first stab, I took my compass out of my pocket. On the second prick, I negotiated my hand toward his leg, sank the entire point into him and withdrew it quickly. His cry shriveled to a gasp when the other boys complained about his shifting about in the packed car.

I didn't feel any pity. Not a sliver. Yes, it was a savage act, but I had to protect my body. I had to make him stop. If I didn't protect myself, who else would?

It worked. Kevin stopped the attacks. And even more astonishingly, he began respecting me. It was a slow-built respect, beginning with chats about homework that moved on to include other stuff. It felt pretty good.

Father's big break came around this time. He'd applied six months previously to be entered on a government "Select List" for subcontract work. A new business contact who was a Protestant like Father's bank manager had recommended Father's company to the government department and a letter arrived unexpectedly advising him that the company was required to assist in a multimillion-pound road building project. The job involved the construction of a bypass around a large Ulster town and Father was to be one of ten subcontractors working for the main firm, a large company with its head office in London.

After signing the contract, which would pay about two hundred and fifteen thousand pounds throughout its duration, Father took a copy of it, as well as the letter of appointment, to our bank manager and requested a massive working capital loan. Mr. Frazer was delighted, Father said, and persuaded his head office in Belfast to approve it. Six weeks later, two brand-new lime green excavators with Japanese names and metal tracks, two trucks, and a rubber-wheeled JCB digger stood in our backyard. Father had the dump trucks sprayed royal blue and gray and the words "Harkin Construction Ltd, Knockburn" written in black lettering on all the cabin and excavator doors.

No more poverty-pleading farmers had to be dealt with; we were on our way. In our familial euphoria, it didn't matter one iota that the power-sharing experiment brokered by the British government between the Protestants and Catholics was close to collapse. The hardline Protestant majority had called for a province-wide strike and they had the muscle to carry it out. They threatened to bring Ulster to her knees, closing ports and roads and disrupting the national power supply if Britain didn't back down and kill the plan. But that didn't matter to us. What mattered was our juicy British government contract.

Eighteen

Classroom six was large and had a matte white ceiling, six overhead sphere lights, and dark gray walls. Despite four windows, it remained dingy, even on sunny days, because a five-foot cypress hedge flanked an abutting narrow strip of paved yard. A blackboard ran the entire width of the front of the room. Just two steps away from it was the teacher's desk. The only other furniture was thirty box desks arranged in three-row pairs running down its length. Plump Mr. Smith, whose sloe-black hair highlighted his acute dandruff, always sat during our lesson, rising only lethargically when obliged to write new French verbs on the blackboard. French was also the only class where Connor and I sat together at the back of the room.

"Do you know what I'm doing this weekend?" he asked, one Friday near the beginning of May.

"What?" I said.

"I'm getting the feel. Rosellen McKeever's going to let me feel them."

Connor, like Fergal, talked a great deal about sex and was prone to exaggeration. I looked up from my textbook and gave him a lingering, dubious glance before resuming my reading. It was a waste of time, because my cousin didn't see it. He never looked at a person directly.

"I am. Honest to God."

Connor was as unlike Martin as a brother could be. His heavy, dark eyebrows, sunken eyes, and very large nose put him on the poorer side of handsomeness. He also loved the IRA, said he knew some of the boys in town who were in it, and was forever telling Martin and I that he was going to join them.

I knew Rosellen (as youngsters, Martin and I had played mud-pie baking and tennis with her and her friends), and the idea he'd be feeling the tits of someone I knew intrigued me greatly. I gave him the benefit of the doubt and listened as he explained how she'd asked one of her friends to tell him she had a crush on him and wanted to meet at three o'clock Sunday in the plantation running behind Connor's house.

"It doesn't mean you'll get to feel her," I said.

"That's where she took other boys to get the feel."

That, and his specificity about time and place, convinced me it wasn't a lie.

On Monday, just before lunch, we had French again and I could hardly wait. Connor had been playing matters close to his chest all morning. He'd smiled knowingly in math and English every time he noticed me looking in his direction, which made me determined not to ask and let him see how much I needed to know. Connor loved you to pry news from him because it allowed him to feel he was doing you a big favor when he did eventually get around to telling his story. I knew his game. If you pretended you didn't care, he'd trip over himself to tell you. But it nearly killed me not to ask.

"Aren't you going to ask about it?" he finally said in French class. Paddy Flanagan was ten minutes into murdering a translation of Madame Pompadour's visit to the hairdresser.

I continued moving the pencil on each word of my own translation as Paddy haltingly advanced three words, reversed ten, and advanced two. It was sad to hear it.

"I got the feel," Connor said.

"Oh, my." I stole a look at Mr. Smith, who had his nose stuck in the textbook, his head shaking slowly.

"We went deep into the plantation and lay on a bed of pine needles."

"Very comfy."

"She lay back and made it obvious straight away I could undo her bra. God, Gabriel, I got so bloody stiff." He paused for a moment. "Do you want to know the details?"

"Suit yourself."

A little while into his description, Connor's hand touched my thigh.

At first, I thought it was an accident. But it happened again, and then he stroked my leg. Every cell in my body pulsated. My thing rose instantly. While I didn't pull my leg away, I knew I ought to make some kind of protest. I glanced up at Mr. Smith and scanned the room, though it was perfectly safe, because of the wide box desks and our position at the back of the class.

Connor's stroking ceased. I made sure not to flinch as his hand moved to my fly. He rubbed and pressed tenuously for a moment and then began to unzip my trousers as he continued talking about Rosellen. I didn't hear one more word of Paddy's hideous French translation.

"You can touch me, as well," he said, out of the side of his mouth.

I reached over hesitantly, our wrists crisscrossing. I tugged his fly down. As soon as I felt him, I was mortified—his seemed so much longer than mine.

A few minutes later, Mr. Smith's chair scraped the floor as he rose and approached the blackboard. Our hands retreated and I fumbled crazily to put myself in order as the new verbs and nouns of the day appeared.

As soon as class ended, Connor told me to follow him. He took me into an end cubicle in the lavatory, where we masturbated as urinals flushed rhythmically in the background and boys rushed in and out. After we'd finished, I couldn't wait to get away from him. For the rest of the day, guilt lingered like a bitter aftertaste. I remembered the promise I'd made to God. Now I'd broken my promise at the very first temptation. I'd committed the abomination again and enjoyed it. I loathed myself. In my bedroom that night, I sank to my knees and said a slow Act of Contrition and vowed never to do it again.

Next day, Connor and I pretended nothing had happened. But that night in bed, a thousand thoughts overwhelmed me. I relived the whole event, remembered Connor's every squeeze and touch. No matter which way I turned in the bed, I couldn't stop the fizzy excitement and finally surrendered. As soon as James started breathing deeply, I took tissues I'd already placed under my pillow and put them by my thigh, made a little tent under the bedclothes with one hand and stroked myself senseless with the other.

The guilt rushed back after I finished. Once more, I recited a slow Act of Contrition and promised Him I'd never do it again.

Two days later, in French class, Connor began talking about what he'd done to Rosellen and his hand moved to my fly. I raised no objection.

Later, when I spotted him as we were changing classes, I pulled him aside.

"Don't you agree that it's an abomination what we did?" I said.

"No."

"Don't you feel guilty and sinful because we're boys?"

"I don't think there's any problem so long as we think about feeling girls up while we're doing it."

"Look me in the eye and say you truly believe there's nothing wrong with it."

He met my stare. "So long as we're thinking about girls while we do it, it's fine."

His reasoning made a lot of sense. So I continued doing it with him. I told myself this wasn't the same thing Noel and I had done, because Connor and I were thinking of girls as we touched each other. It was more difficult to push aside the mortal sin aspect, and the fact that I was also breaking my promise to God. But eventually, I managed to reconcile the dilemma by concluding that everyone breaks a promise to God at some point. It's a weakness of being human. That, together with my slow recital of the Act of Contrition, entitled me to unquestioned absolution.

Granny Harkin visited Auntie Celia every weekend and I started to go there with her. The purpose of my visits was now to see Connor as much as Martin, and he and I went upstairs to the bedroom on the pretext of discussing schoolwork.

One Sunday afternoon, I arrived to learn that Auntie Celia wouldn't permit Martin to come out of his bedroom. In June, he was to sit his O levels (the "O" being an accepted abbreviation for "ordinary") and he'd done extremely badly in the mock examinations.

O levels were a set of major exams given by the Northern Ireland examination board. The courses were of two-year duration and they were vital for two reasons. First, if passed, one could proceed into the sixth form to begin advanced level (A level) courses, successful completion of which guaranteed a place at a university. Second, the universities you applied to during the final year of school looked at your O level grades, together with the headmaster's report, in deciding whether to accept or reject your application.

Connor and I were studying nine O levels apiece and had another year of preparation before taking them. Martin was studying five because he wasn't as bright, and both he and Pani were lazy. They'd passed only three mocks each and Martin's teachers were concerned. Apparently, at a parent-teacher meeting that week, they'd informed Auntie Celia he'd most likely fail, which was why she had confined him to his bedroom and warned him he'd have to make extra efforts at his studies if he wished to continue attending the Saturday night dances every week.

Her strategy was inconvenient for me, as Connor and I couldn't do anything upstairs out of fear of Martin walking into the bedroom and discovering us. We had to go off to the forest where he'd first felt Rosellen.

On one trip there, Connor took me to the bank of the meandering stream, pulled a rock aside, and showed me a revolver and two black masks with penny-sized holes cut out for eyes.

"Don't touch the gun or your fingerprints will be on it," he said. "The IRA chaps use these when they do jobs—which are called operations, by the way."

"How'd you know the IRA hides things in the woods?"

He laughed. "I know the right fellas, don't I?" Connor's eyes narrowed and he formed a gun with his forefinger and thumb, pointing it at my right knee. "They've got me keeping an eye out for police informers. It's bye-bye to their fucking kneecaps after they're caught."

Shrieks erupted from a sycamore tree leaning over the stream and a crow flew out, its ragged wings beating furiously as it lifted into the air above my head.

"Me and the boys know how to treat informers," Connor added.

After putting the rock back in place, we continued into the woods until we came to a tree with a massive trunk. I made sure never to initiate things between my cousin and me. I'd allow Connor to make the first move, which he always did by beginning a story about what he'd recently done with Rosellen. So long as he talked about her, everything was fine. We couldn't possibly be poofs.

Uncle John came into our kitchen and Auntie Bernie, face as white as her bead necklace, followed behind him. Father Pascal, the head of the missions in Kenya, had called Uncle Tommy's home to tell him Uncle Brendan had had a bit of a turn. Unfortunately, Uncle Tommy had been away and Auntie Bernie, phobic about medical problems and continually checking her raised facial mole, had panicked as soon as she'd heard the word "turn" and came to tell Uncle John.

"I told Bernie we ought to consult with you, because you'd know what to do," Uncle John said.

Mammy pulled a chair from under the table. "Sit and calm yourself, John."

"What'll we do?" he asked. Uncle looked up at her like a little boy awaiting an answer while Auntie fingered her necklace, a thing she always did when she felt out of her depth.

"Exactly what kind of a turn, Bernie?" my mother asked.

"All I know is Father Pascal used that word." Auntie Bernie tugged at her necklace. "You know what I'm like. My ears buzzed and I could hear nothing else. When I did come to my senses, he was saying Brendan was in Nairobi and the only thing I managed to glean is Brendan's been acting strange. He ordered Father Pascal not to tell the family because he didn't want to cause us any more trouble." She paused. "Well, Father Pascal didn't agree, which is why he tried to call Tommy."

The emergent creases of displeasure in my mother's forehead were faint, but unmistakable, as Auntie Bernie uttered these last words. Electricity and the telephone had arrived in Knockburn—we'd had the latter for six months now—and Mammy had called Uncle Brendan's mission, as well as the Order's main house in Nairobi, to give them our number as the primary contact.

Picking up the phone, Mammy dialed the Order's house and demanded to speak with Father Pascal. It transpired that Uncle Brendan had been broody and withdrawn from the community for months, but started behaving erratically one morning when another priest caught him tossing the Bible and other religious paraphernalia about the sacristy of their little church. The community doctor diagnosed nervous strain and prescribed rest, and Uncle Brendan was advised to recuperate at the Order's Nairobi home. Uncle had agreed, on condition the Order wouldn't inform his family about the event or illness.

My mother insisted on talking with Uncle Brendan. When he came on the phone, their conversation was stilted. Replacing the receiver in its cradle after she'd finished and double-checking to make sure it was set down properly, as she was terrified the call might not have terminated and she'd incur huge charges, Mammy rolled her eyes.

"I'm sure you got the gist of that," she said to Uncle John. "You're not to tell your mother under any circumstances. He doesn't want anyone flying out to see him, either."

"Did he say what caused the breakdown?" asked Auntie Bernie.

"No."

"These turns don't happen to a body out of the blue, do they, Eileen? I mean normal people can't just—"

"All he said was he's been under pressure and flipped. That's all I know. He made no attempt to elaborate on what caused the flipping."

Nineteen

My parents and I stood in the display section of Auntie Celia's grocery-cum-gift shop. Mammy wanted a wedding present for a neighbor's daughter.

"It's a lovely piece," my mother said. "How much?"

"Thirty pounds. It is a lovely wee piece of Belleek china, isn't it?" said Auntie Celia. She set the nine-inch Celtic cross down on the shelf again, rested the tip of her index finger on her lips, and smiled at the ornament glittering in the overhead light. "One of the nicest pieces I've seen for a long, long time."

As she was showing her stuff, Auntie Celia informed my parents that she was allowing Connor to go with Martin to his first dance at the Fortress Inn. The dance hall was literally an old fort at the north end of Duncarlow Main Street, and the Indians, a popular band whose music I loved, were playing. Martin had told me all that at school, and we'd hatched a plan for me to bring my parents into the shop so he could get Auntie Celia to soften them up and let me go to the dance, too.

"And it's such a bargain," Auntie Celia said.

"I don't know her so well to be buying a Belleek cross of such intricacy," my mother said. Her eyes darted along the rows of ornaments. "What about that glass cat up there? How much for that?"

Auntie Celia glanced at Father before reaching for the item. "Harry, you were out at the dances when you were Gabriel's age."

"Aye."

"That *definitely* means I should be allowed to go," I said.

Auntie checked a price tag beneath the ornament before handing it to my mother. "Eight pounds and fifty-five pence?" She smiled. "Sure, let Gabriel go. After all, it is *the* Indians."

"Eight pounds and change for a glass cat."

"He can go, as far as I'm concerned," said Father. He winked at me.

"That's not glass," said Auntie Celia. "That's best Irish crystal, that is."

"Would those wee glass bubbles I see inside its head make it any cheaper, do you think?" Mammy asked.

"Bubbles?" Auntie Celia snatched the ornament from Mammy and began examining it.

"Gabriel's too young for dances," said Mammy. "Next year, maybe."

A bell rang as the shop door opened and a short woman entered with a panting spaniel on a leash. Auntie Celia greeted her as she walked behind the shop counter. My mother picked up a china vase, squinted to read the tiny price tag on its base, and then vigorously shook her head as she laid it quickly down again.

"Harry, what do you think of that china toast holder with the red and yellow rose pattern?"

"Nice."

"What do you mean 'nice'? Will it suffice or not?"

"For God's sake, woman, pick something."

Recognizing Martin's assistance was urgently required, I took advantage of their skirmish to walk quickly to the back of the shop and mount the narrow staircase leading to Auntie's upstairs flat.

I found him blow-drying his hair in the bedroom. An opened bottle of peroxide stood upon the vanity beside a tortoiseshell comb. Scarcely before I sat on the edge of the bed, the hair dryer was whirling full blast on the carpet and Martin whipped the towel from around his neck and tossed it over the bottle. What's more, his neck had turned splotchy pink, the way it always did when he was dead embarrassed. So, it wasn't just lemon juice he used on his fringe to make it blonde, like he swore to us it was. Old Pani was right—he accused Martin of using bleach every time my cousin arrived at school with his bangs blonder than usual.

"You're too early, Gabriel."

I crinkled my nose. "What's that chemical smell?"

"Has Mother asked Auntie Eileen if you can go?" he asked.

I explained that they were at an impasse, allowing my eye to travel pointedly toward the crumpled towel concealing the peroxide bottle.

He shot a glance at the towel, part of which was now damp. "Go back and keep them on the subject. I'll be down in a jiffy." He nearly ripped my arm out of its socket as he escorted me out of the room. "Quick, or they'll have made up their minds *not* to let you go."

He arrived downstairs within minutes, just as Mammy was expressing a fear that if she let me go out to this dance, it might open the sluice gates and become a regular occurrence. Martin's bangs were the brightest I'd ever seen. They were platinum. He'd tried to tone it down by splicing the strands with his normal dark blond hair.

"I'm tired of this," I said. "I'll be a fifth-former soon and you're treating me like a child. Connor's allowed to go. I'm tired of never getting to do anything."

Auntie Celia approached. "Martin, you've kept the lemon juice on your hair far too long. I keep warning you about that."

Father stared at Martin as if he were an alien.

"Auntie Eileen, anyone who's anyone is going to see the Indians," said Martin. "Let him go."

Mammy hemmed and hawed, but finally relented, though she emphasized twice that it was just for this one occasion.

With that settled, Martin whisked me upstairs to show me his new jacket. It was made of royal blue and canary yellow plaid and was gorgeous.

Connor came into the room as I was trying it on and Martin readjusted his bangs, checking every few seconds in the mirror and moving his head from side to side.

"I really think I might have overdone the lemon juice this time. What do you think, Gabriel?"

"You definitely have," said Connor.

"Shut the *fuck* up, you," Martin said.

"It matches the yellow panel in your jacket nicely," I said.

Connor laughed as I walked up to the vanity and peered in the mirror. The jacket was dead slimming; my backside didn't show at all. But it made my plum button-down shirt look extremely dowdy. In fact, it looked depressing.

"I can't go tonight," I said. "I'm wearing rags."

Connor jerked his head rapidly at me behind Martin's back to signal I should follow him. He left, and I waited a few seconds before following.

"My room's got the double bed, so you'll be sleeping in my room after the dance, dummy," he said.

I decided my depressing shirt would suffice.

Entry to the Fortress Inn ballroom was an adventure. After crossing a pebbled courtyard surrounded by thick, crumbling walls, we arrived before a massive arched Gothic-style door and passed through into a room with gilt ceilings and a creaky wooden floor. Maybe a formal drawing room in its day, the space had been regal once, but now looked scruffy and reeked of stale smoke. At its east end, we passed through a pay kiosk and turnstile and went down a flight of concrete steps, which jarred my sense of romance about the place further, and then we entered a cellar containing the cloakrooms, juice bar, and a snack area. Another flight of concrete steps swept up to the ballroom.

Martin wouldn't take off his jacket, even though the place was boiling and packed with people. Overhead lights struck a great revolving glitter ball comprised of hundreds of tiny mirror squares in the center of the ceiling. Condensation trickled down large mirrors running along the two longest sides of the room. At the front of the ballroom was the stage where the band, clad in brightly colored Indian outfits and trailing head feathers, was singing, "*Son, don't go near the Indians*," as they whooped and danced about with tomahawks.

Parallel to one set of long mirrors ran a three-deep wall of women with highly glossed lips and perfect hairdos. On the adjacent dance floor, a line of men jostled one another as they filed past the women. After observing for a while, I saw how the system worked: if a man spied a woman he fancied, he'd extend his hand toward her and she either clutched it or continued chewing gum and ignored him. Jealousies broke out among the men now and again, when two extended hands to the same woman, though this was always resolved by just a dirty look or a shove or two.

"I want to dance," Martin said. "Let's ask some women."

Connor declined, because he was waiting for Rosellen to arrive and was afraid she might see him in the line and get mad. Martin and I got in the line of men, which moved in fits and starts. About a quarter way up the room, Martin asked someone to dance and was accepted.

I struggled to both stay in formation and scrutinize the women as I continued my advance. The women scrutinized each man's face, some whispering behind their cupped hands amongst themselves. The whole scene would have been comical if I hadn't been so anxious to find a partner and prove to Martin I was as successful as him. Finding myself near the end of the queue, I grew desperate. I spied a young girl smiling and extended my hand. To my cringing dismay, her smile vanished and she regarded me brazenly for an instant before lolling back her head to look up at the ceiling. Utterly jellified inside, I closed my eyes and allowed my body to be propelled forward by the hard, jutting stomach of the man behind me.

Near the stage, I stood watching the band but heard not a note as I analyzed what had gone wrong. I didn't know whether to blame my horrid shirt, the two yellow pimples on my face, or the ugly goose down sprouting above my upper lip. One thing was for certain: I had to get a bright plaid jacket. And fast.

I managed only to recover fully from the embarrassment when, later in bed, Connor began telling me what he'd done with Rosellen in the secrecy of the car park.

A week later, I pleaded with my mother to be allowed to go to the Fortress Inn again. She complained vociferously, but gave in. With some anxiety, I walked the gauntlet to the strums and croons of Philomena Begley and her Rambling Men. I spied a good-looking girl halfway along the line and, after a quick look about to make sure no one I knew was watching in case I got rejected, extended my quivering hand. She accepted and I floated onto the dance floor with her.

Dressed in a flared lemon skirt and black nylon blouse that highlighted her ivory skin, her short dark hair glistening as if dipped in oil, a cloud of pale freckles on either side of an impish nose, she was the most beautiful girl I'd ever seen. We smiled at one another politely as we danced, looked about the room a little, smiled again, looked about some more. The music stopped. When another number didn't commence, I realized the previous song had been the end of a set and the band was taking a breather.

Gritting my teeth, I slid my arm gingerly around her waist. Martin had told me the end of the set was a critical moment: if a girl liked you, she didn't flinch and everything stayed good; if she hadn't yet made up her mind, she behaved like a nervous filly, shuffling a little but staying; and if she hoped to catch something better during the next set, she'd flee back to assume her position in the three-deep wall of women.

"I'm Lizzie," she said. "How old are you?"

I was prepared for this question. Martin had told me this was another critical moment—too young, and they walked. Lizzie stopped chewing her gum as she awaited my response. A girl's age was so damned difficult to guess.

"I'm sixteen, going on seventeen."

"You are? Me, too."

She slipped her arm around my waist. My eyes darted about, scanning the crowd for Martin, Connor, anyone from school, but there was no one to witness my victory.

The next set was slow and we started waltzing about the dance hall. It was really more of a shuffle. Presently, I spied Connor dancing with Rosellen and winked. He nodded only slightly. My cousin liked to act cool when with his girlfriend. Minutes later, I saw two fifth-year boys at the back of the room and steered Lizzie toward them, taking pains to ensure I wasn't acting too obvious. As we danced by, I rested my chin on her shoulder, stroked her glistening hair and gave them a cursory nod. One boy stopped chewing his gum. They watched like bemused cattle. As I ran my hand slowly up and down Lizzie's back, she pulled back her head and smiled. She was the same age as these boys, I only a little over fourteen, yet it was me who had her in my arms. After the set, I asked if she'd like a cola. She said she would and we walked down the concrete steps to the café hand-in-hand. Every follicle in my scalp tingled.

"I'm dying for a fag," she said, after we'd finished our drinks. "My brother's got some in his car. Do you want to come out with me?"

We went outside and searched for the car, walking up and down between rows of vehicles whose roofs glinted in the moonlight. Finally, we drew up to a rusty contraption with a piece of hay bale twine holding its hood shut.

"What do you want?" her brother said. He was snogging in the backseat.

"Give me a fag or I'm getting into the front seat to court my new boyfriend."

"Like hell, you are."

Grumbling, he fumbled in his pocket, then handed an entire packet and a box of matches to her. She took out two cigarettes. After lighting one, she placed the other carefully into her skirt pocket and led me to the other side of the fort, where couples were leaning in embrace against its thick stone walls. Above, the upper branches of two massive sycamores stretched over its battlements, while the mottled trunks of others glowed dimly within the dusky park stretching down to the river.

"God, what I wouldn't give to know the histories of the chieftains who stood behind these battlements in its heyday," I said.

"What's a battlement?" she asked.

"The notched walls above us." I pointed upward.

Her eyes drifted up. "Oh, those. I hate old forts and castles. They should just knock down this pile of shite and make a bigger dance hall." She took a long drag of the cigarette and looked up at the stars as she expelled its smoke. "You want a puff?"

To decline didn't seem manly. I took the cigarette, trying to hold it skillfully between thumb and forefinger and pointing its lighted end toward my palm like I'd seen boys doing at school. As she observed, I took a massive drag, threw back my head and inhaled deeply as I looked at the stars. Suddenly, they blurred. My chest felt as if a car had driven over it. I couldn't breathe. I coughed like an old consumptive, so much that I doubled over to catch my breath.

She stooped and picked the smoldering cigarette off the ground. "You've never smoked before?"

I tried to answer, but the smoke snagged in my lungs made me cough violently again. I shook my head. After a few moments, the coughing stopped, but the sour aftertaste remained.

"You've got to take it slowly. Like this." She demonstrated.

I tried again and this time it was a little easier. It still tasted vile, but I didn't cough. We chatted, sharing the cigarette until it was finished, and then Lizzie leaned into the wall and looked at me expectantly. Nervously, I slung my arms around her shoulders. She put her arms around my waist and drew me closer. I put my lips to hers and we kissed as the percussion from the drums throbbed through the walls. Her lips were dry and thin.

She forced my lips apart with her tongue and wiggled it about inside until she found mine. I opened my eyes and saw hers were firmly closed, which made me feel peculiar, as if I was a voyeur drinking in the planes of her face while she stood unaware. I wished to withdraw my mouth, though instinctively knew it would be rude. Closing my eyes, I pushed my tongue against hers, all the while thinking about the smoke and warm saliva exchanged between us. The kiss was nasty and I was relieved when she withdrew her mouth.

"You've French-kissed before, haven't you?"

"Yes."

Another French kiss ensued, which proved no less horrid. By the fourth one, however, I'd acclimatized, but by then, she wanted to return to the dance hall.

We'd danced only two sets when the band stopped playing and asked everyone to stand for "The Soldier's Song." (The Fortress Inn was a Catholic dance hall, so the Irish national anthem was played.) The custom was to stand rigid and not talk during its rendition, but I turned to Lizzie and asked if I could see her again, though I didn't know if I'd be allowed to attend another dance. After she agreed and the Anthem ended, we left for the juice bar, where I borrowed a pen to exchange addresses, though I had to be vague when she pushed me for an exact date.

As my mother had feared, those initial nights at the Fortress Inn proved indeed to be the opening of the sluice gates. As it was now summer vacation, it proved not as difficult to persuade her to let me attend and we reached an agreement whereby I was permitted to go on alternate Saturdays and stay overnight at Auntie Celia's.

Despite the dismal Ulster economy, worsened by a successful militant Protestant strike that destroyed the power-sharing experiment and resulted in the British re-imposing direct rule, Father's business grew. Consequently, he had money, and he always gave me three or four pounds to spend at the dances.

Caroline grew annoyed that I was permitted to attend dances regularly. Although just thirteen, her large breasts made her look much older and, thus, she felt she should be allowed to go, as well.

But Mammy wouldn't hear of it. She was scared the older boys, or even grown men, might take advantage, which infuriated my sister. She accused our mother of hypocrisy. When our parents visited relatives at night, they left both Caroline and I jointly in charge of James and Nuala, signifying that Caroline was old enough for that large responsibility. So why couldn't she go to the dance?

On one occasion after this argument, when my parents were out, Caroline kept picking on Nuala and I told her to stop. It spun out of control when she called me "fat arse." I was extremely sensitive about my backside. Boys at school teased me about its size and Caroline knew it. I hit her sharply across the face before fully realizing what I'd done. Later, I apologized profusely and she took full advantage of my remorse by insisting the only way to forgive the attack was for me to ask Mammy to let her attend a dance.

The following Saturday, I asked, promising Mammy I'd not let Caroline out of my sight. To my amazement, she agreed. Because Caroline would attend the dance, Father decided to pick us up afterwards, which was a terrible downside. I couldn't stay at Auntie Celia's. I grew extremely nervous that the sluice gates had opened permanently for my sister, too.

Caroline and Lizzie liked each other instantly. The three of us danced together the entire evening, except for the slow dances when Caroline was obliged to join the three-deep wall of glossy-lipped women. Toward the end of the night, Caroline insisted we join Martin and Sabina, his new girlfriend who worked in a factory shop, for a cola. A few minutes later, I signaled to my sister that we had to leave because I didn't want Lizzie to witness the spectacle of Father picking us up and he was already parked in front of the dance hall's main gates.

Caroline climbed into the front seat. I was glad—I didn't wish to sit shotgun with him.

"Did you enjoy your first dance?" Father asked my sister.

"I'm definitely going again, Daddy."

Father made no attempt to drive off. "I don't know about that, my girl." He peered over his shoulder and winked at me. "Did your big brother look after you well, or was he too busy consorting with the ladies?"

I looked at him dourly. Father winked and acted jovial only when it suited him. His jokes angered me. They were always on his terms. I was finding it impossible to talk to him about anything. Any conversation between us was plastic as hell. Sometimes, I had to ride in the car with him alone and we'd travel for miles in a smothering silence, the occasional rattles of the car my only amelioration because the radio was broken. I'd close my eyes and will the journey to end.

The driver of a car behind us who was waiting to exit honked his horn.

"I looked after her," I said, "and you're blocking the gate."

Unfortunately for Caroline, that night proved to be her only outing. I was back to spending alternate Saturday nights at Auntie Celia's, where Connor and I would discuss his exploits with Rosellen in the warmth of his cozy double bed.

One evening, a few weeks before the new school year was due to begin, Connor suggested at the dance that we take the girls for a stroll to the river at the bottom of the sycamore-pocked park. The idea appealed greatly, because it was such a warm night, but Martin wasn't interested. This didn't please Sabina, who repeatedly hinted how fun a walk along the river would be. Martin wouldn't renege and told us to scram.

The moon was almost full and lit up the mottled tree trunks as we made our way to the river. Couples murmured from where they lay on the grass behind trees with the widest girths. At the bottom of the park, we helped the girls climb over the barbed-wire fence and then followed the bank until we came to a quiet clearing, through which I could see the river's shining blackness. Its rippled water had been transformed into a blanket of sparkling diamonds. Here, we separated without any exchange of words, Connor and Rosellen taking one corner, where they sank to the grass, and Lizzie and I to the other.

Following Connor's example, I pulled my girlfriend closer after we lay down. The grass was soft and cool, and all was perfect save a cluster of gnats that began to feast on my neck and face. Our first kiss was noticeably different. Lizzie thrust her tongue into my mouth as before, but there was an added urgency now. Her hands slipped down the back of my jeans and fished out my shirttail.

"Isn't it nice to be outside?" she said, as her nails crossed my bare back and scraped its flesh.

"It is lovely, isn't it?"

"You can stroke me, too . . . if you like."

Connor and Rosellen were locked in an embrace and he was on top of her now. I pushed Lizzie gently on her back and eased myself on top of her. Her legs spread open quicker than a well-oiled barn door. As Lizzie's eyes were closed, I stole another glance at Connor and saw one of his hands was dipped inside Rosellen's blouse. I kissed Lizzie and allowed my hand to travel along her neck and down to her right breast, which I squeezed, immediately feeling the coarse fabric of her bra beneath her satin blouse. She emitted a low sigh and thrust her hips gently upward. Her fingernails dug into my scalp.

I was on fire as she raked my roots. I French-kissed her deeply while unbuttoning her blouse, slipping my hand inside and cupping her sheathed, full breast. Its corseted firmness was immediately off-putting. Perfume wafted from her exposed cleavage, its sweetness stronger than I'd ever noticed before. It evoked a memory of Auntie Bernie's perfumed stink from childhood.

Suddenly, Lizzie's body felt delicate and weak beneath me. I felt every quiver of her soft limbs, felt the restrained thrusts of her urgency. I needed to get away. I wanted to rise and run, but couldn't. I was the man, with the man's duty to see things through. All about me, her sweet stink, which repelled even the gnats because they no longer swarmed; all about me, her sweet stink that was at once of flowers and not of flowers. I wanted to rise and run, and yet my fingers reached behind her back and fumbled to release her bra as she arched her back.

Lizzie's eyes opened slightly. "Easy, you randy sod."

I tried again and still couldn't undo the catches. Her arms were thin as a heron's legs. Moans drifted over from Rosellen and Connor. Lizzie's painted lips stretched to coyness. Her rouged cheeks and over-curled eyelashes clotted with mascara looked bizarre now. My spongy thing wouldn't stir or rise. Not even a tiny bit.

"I think we should go back to Martin and Sabina."

Her hand froze on my back.

"We must go back."

"What's the matter, Gabriel?"

"I don't want to lose control."

Her mouth gathered for an instant and then she rose.

"We're going back to the dance," I said to Connor and Rosellen, as Lizzie brushed her skirt.

They didn't respond.

In bed later, as soon as Connor discussed his sexual exploits by the river, my thing stiffened faster than a flat bicycle tube pumped up with air. Its impertinence stunned me. After Connor and I finished and I'd recited my customary Act of Contrition, I lay with my eyes wide open, listening to the calm rise and fall of Connor's sleeping breath. I lay bewildered. Utterly bewildered.

Twenty

lmost from the beginning of the new term, circumstances improved for me at school. I was now a fifth-
year and the taunting in the bus stopped because
Mickey and Pearse had left and Willie, Mickey's aggressive
younger brother, focused on other boys and didn't confront
me now that his protector was gone.

As their teachers had predicted, Pani and Martin failed their
O levels, though Father Rafferty allowed them to come back and
repeat the year. This was an added bonus for me—it was terrific
to have them in some of my classes.

Early one Sunday afternoon, a few weeks into the term, Father
came home from second Mass and announced at the lunch table
that an IRA man was coming to stay with us for a few weeks.

"I *don't* want an IRA volunteer staying under my roof," my mother said. She slammed the gravy boat down in front of Father. "It's far too dangerous. Besides, the house renovations aren't finished yet, so where would we put him?"

Her excuse was weak. The construction was done, giving us a larger living room, another bedroom and bathroom and large kitchen with the latest German equipment. Only a few weeks of decorating remained.

"The fellas asked me at the chapel gate and I couldn't refuse," said Father. He sliced his thick T-bone steak and red blood and oily water oozed and pooled beside the boiled cabbage.

"I support the cause as much as the next person, but we have our children to think about, Harry. What if the army launches a raid in the middle of the night and finds an IRA man here? They'll intern you in Long Kesh. What'll happen to the business? What'll happen to us?"

"Luksee, they won't raid our house precisely *because* we've children in the house." Father looked at each of us in turn as he chewed his meat. "They're our cover."

"I don't want a strange man under my roof." Mammy paused and stared at her dinner plate. "Just when we're making a bit of money and beginning to have a life, along comes this business. We don't know what terrible things this man might have done. He could be one of those men who blew up the soldiers a few weeks ago, for all we know."

A month previously, the IRA had placed a bomb under a road culvert in lower Knockburn that blew five British soldiers to bits. The Protestant customer at the Hamilton's supermarket delicatessen had been dead right when she'd said Knockburn was nationalist, but dead wrong when she'd accused most men of being IRA volunteers. Knockburn people were decent and didn't support the use of violence in the main, but they were also angered by the Protestant hardliners' refusal to give Catholics any say in the running of the province's affairs.

Some young men were so frustrated, they had turned to the Provos, a group which had split from the more peaceful Official IRA, as a last resort. The Provos believed violence was justified to banish British rule and, in addition to bombings and shootings in the largest towns and cities, had stepped up their campaign in rural areas. Because of this, many IRA volunteers were on the run, and there was an unspoken code that every home in Knockburn was expected to provide refuge for volunteers if asked.

"Harry, I don't want anyone ruthless sleeping under my roof," Mammy said quickly, the rapidity of her speech underscoring her panic. "He'll be a bad influence on Gabriel and James. He might try to recruit them into that way of life. And Gabriel needs peace to study for his O levels. As it is, he's had to contend with all the noise generated by the renovations."

"I wouldn't worry about him getting recruited for the cause," Father said. "James, maybe." He looked at my brother and winked. "Aye, definitely not Gabriel."

"What about those English people you sometimes bring here to discuss business?" Mammy said. "If he hears their accents, he'll spread the word, maybe arrange to have them kidnapped . . . or even worse." She shivered.

"Luksee, a fella by the name of Seamus Regan's coming to stay, *end* of discussion. He'll be here in a few weeks' time and I don't want to hear another chirp from anyone."

"He can sleep in the damned outhouse," Mammy said, clearly stung that such a major decision had already been made without discussion.

"Deed by Jasus, he'll not. He's out fighting for his country, so he can sleep with Gabriel or James."

I was looking forward to having my own room after the decorating was done and had no desire to share my bed with a strange man. The thought of his legs and arms touching any part of my body during sleep made me wince.

"I'm *not* sleeping with him," I said. "He can share with James. I don't care if my room's not painted yet. I'm moving a cot in there tonight."

"I'm almost as big as you," James said. His face darkened, like it always did when he was put upon. "I'll take the cot and sleep in your unfinished room."

"I don't want a stranger in my house," Caroline said.

Now in the mid-throes of puberty, Caroline was self-conscious about a new spurt of growth that had left her gangly in appearance. She had the full breasts and hips of a woman and the forehead pimples and greasy skin of a girl.

"Gabriel shouldn't have to sleep with him," Nuala said. My little sister took my side in everything, even when I was wrong.

"What the hell's the matter with you?" said Father. "You should be proud to help a man who's fighting so you'll have decent jobs in a free Ireland."

"A fat lot of good the fighting has done us thus far," said my mother. "The Protestants just dig in their heels and it's we who suffer."

"I don't agree with the IRA's bombing and shooting," I said. "They're killing innocent people, as well as the soldiers. They give Catholics a bad name. As it is, most Protestants think we're all a bunch of savages and murderers."

"The Provos are very bad and Gabriel shouldn't have to sleep with one of them," Nuala said.

Mother looked at her absentmindedly. "A body can't go into a shop in Belfast or Derry without the army and police pawing at us, searching our bags for incendiary devices."

"We shouldn't really invite him here, Daddy," I said, pushing the word "Daddy" out of my mouth. "Let them find him another safe house."

"Shut your mouth," Father snapped. "Sure, you're no Irishman. You'd rather have English rule than a free Ireland."

His rabid speech wasn't even slightly true. I wanted justice and equality, too. Justice and equality were as important in life as eating and breathing. I just didn't see the sense of hating every Protestant in order to obtain it. Father and James believed Protestants who didn't want to live in a united Ireland should leave, but that was absurd. The Protestants were now every bit as entitled to live in Ireland as we were. They'd been living there since 1690.

"You don't want a united Ireland," Father continued. "You're the enemy every bit as much as them."

Father was right and wrong. Certainly, I didn't want a united Ireland.

I said, "How dare you accuse me of being the enemy? That's below the belt, that is. The Southern Irish government can't look after their own people properly, so how the hell could they manage us? They'd make a sow's ear of the North. They can't even build motorways, or provide free university education for their citizens. And the Catholic Church controls everything down there. I hate Paisley every bit as much as you, but you have to realize that other, decent Protestants can't accept an Ireland where the Catholic Church pokes its nose into political affairs."

"That's enough, Gabriel," said Mammy. "Your Uncle Brendan's a priest."

"Don't dare say anything bad about the Irish Republic," James said.

"It's ridiculous that we can't criticize what's rotten and useless down there out of fear we're acting disloyal," I said. "That makes no sense to me, and—"

"You're too fucking English," Father said. "Always backing them when all they've done is rob us of our land and kill us. Why can't you be a real Irishman?"

"I agree," said James. "Always sitting beside that Protestant Nigel in the bus every morning and talking a load of shite with him, and him as black as the ace of spades."

"He's not a bigot."

"His mother's very nice," Mammy said. "A very decent woman."

James had three deep furrows in his forehead, exactly like Father's when he was angry.

"Daddy's right," James said to me. "You *are* a disgrace."

"Aye, you tell him, son," said Father. "*You're* the sort of Irishman this country needs."

Banging down my fork and knife, I leaped from my chair and stomped outside, where I stood sulking and cursing against the side of the house. I knew I was behaving like a loser, but there was nothing else to do. Half an hour later, Nuala came out and persuaded me to return inside, where things had calmed down. James and Caroline were arguing about whether or not Marc Bolan from T. Rex was effeminate because he wore eyeliner and Father was reading the *News of the World*, getting his fix of sex and scandal from an English newspaper that Mammy had to stuff under the couch when Father McAtamney paid us a visit.

***

My mother and I were traveling in the car and had just finished saying a rosary. We'd been visiting Granny Neeson, who'd been having dizzy spells. The visit had been awkward, because Aunt Peggy was in Scotland visiting Colin, now her fiancé, who was doing a company audit there, and my grandmother, despite her dizziness, had perked up enough to complain to Mammy that Aunt Peggy was wasting her time.

"Taking a vacation to visit the lovely highlands, my backside," she'd said, "as if I'm dying here inside a bubble. What incentive does he have to marry her, I ask you? Two years, she's engaged now. The man's happy enough to stay engaged. She'll never get him to marry her now, as she's over in Scotland already doing her wifely duty, anyway."

An awkward pause had followed, during which my mother, thinking I couldn't see her because I was reading a book, tried frantically to tell Granny Neeson to drop the subject by vigorously shaking her head, though I'd known exactly what she'd meant by "wifely duty."

Granny did indeed drop the subject, by remarking that she was definitely on her deathbed. To ensure that the conversation track had been permanently changed, Mammy began to lament the arrival of the IRA man, which Granny countered by telling her not to bother her with trifles while she was dying. Finally, the two sat in brooding silence until it was time for us to leave.

"I've been meaning to ask you, but it always slips my mind," Mammy said, as the too-close car that had unnerved her finally swung out into the road and passed. "I don't hear you talking too much about the girl you meet up with at the dances. What's this her name is?"

She never forgot names. "Lizzie," I replied.

"That's right."

"She's out of the picture."

I hadn't mentioned Lizzie to my mother until Caroline, angry I wouldn't ask if she could attend another dance, huffed and told Mammy I had a steady girlfriend. In all honesty, I'd dumped Lizzie because she'd outlived her convenience. With her, I didn't have to walk up the wall of women and risk rejection. In addition,

Lizzie helped end the horrible taunting on the school bus, albeit unknowingly. As a result of having a girlfriend, my reputation had improved markedly among the boys, more so when they found out she was older than me.

But Lizzie had grown more and more troublesome. It was nerve-wracking being with her. I felt nothing. My thing never stirred on those rare occasions when I couldn't make any more excuses and Lizzie and I went outside to the back of the Fortress Inn to court in the dark. It remained relentlessly shriveled in her presence. Yet it turned hard as oak whenever Connor touched me. *That* preyed on my mind. I could fool myself that I was thinking about girls when Connor and I were doing things, but my flaccidness when I was alone with Lizzie let me know exactly how things stood.

"Well, I'm glad to hear it," my mother said.

"Why?"

"You're too young to be going steady with girls."

I listened to the low hiss of the car tires on the wet road. Outside, the fields were full of darkness. Rhododendrons shone blackish-green when the headlights struck them as my mother negotiated the curves in the road. At one point, a hare darted from the hedge and stopped abruptly, transfixed by the bright lights until Mother lowered them.

"Are you still thinking about the priesthood?" she asked.

My body stiffened. "I don't know." The tires hissed. I stared out at the pitch-dark fields. "Do you really want me to be a priest?"

She chuckled, the way she always did when she was about to say the exact opposite of what she was thinking. "If you feel it's not for you, then so be it." A pause, and a prickly one. "There's always James, I suppose," she said. "Maybe *he'll* be the one."

"Why is it so important?"

"It's the most wonderful thing for a mother to have a son entering the priesthood. I can think of no greater honor. Think how very proud your Granny is of Brendan."

"Seeing as you mention that . . . " I thought fast and spoke slowly, to make sure nothing I said would set her off. "Granny told me quite a while back that it was Granda far more than she who wanted Brendan to be a priest." I recalled the afternoon I'd visited and came upon her crying sore as she sat on Granda's chair. She called me to her and held me tightly. So tightly, I could hardly breathe. "She said Granda pushed from the first day Uncle Brendan set foot in Saint Malachy's. He wanted a son to become a priest real bad."

Mammy gave me a sidelong glance. "When did she tell you all this?"

"Once, after Uncle Brendan went back to Kenya." I paused. "She also told me I was Uncle's special nephew."

"Why didn't you tell me about this back then?"

"She didn't want me to and made me swear on my future grave not to tell a soul I'd seen her crying about Uncle Brendan." I glanced at Mammy's profile and cleared my throat. "What happened between Uncle Brendan and Granda?"

"Brendan was a young man, like you and James . . ." Mammy stopped talking and I hardly dared breathe, lest the moment be killed.

"No, he was far older than you at the time. There was an argument about something which threatened his becoming a priest, and your grandfather was livid, and—" She fell silent for a moment, then continued, "They were both so headstrong. It happened so long ago, I can't remember the exact details."

"Try."

"It had something to do with his going steady with a girl for a wee while. Your granda felt very threatened by that."

"Was Uncle Brendan serious about her?"

Another short pause ensued. "I don't know."

"Was she nice?"

She cleared her throat, then coughed. "I never met her."

"He became a priest in the end, so why didn't Granda speak to him?"

"People have arguments and stupid pride won't let them back down, I suppose. Now, it's too late for them to make up."

"That seems extreme for a little thing that didn't matter in the end. There must be something else. There *has* to be."

"Extreme behavior or not, that's what happened. That's all there is to it." Again, she peered sidelong at me. "Are you thinking I'm lying or something?"

The directness of her question threw me.

"No."

"I'm glad to hear it."

"It all seems so petty, that's what I mean. Uncle Brendan should have come home to see him when he was dying. That was wrong of him, wasn't it?"

She sighed. "People can be so headstrong . . . pig-stubborn . . . even when it's to their detriment." She looked at me intently now. "Promise me you'll always think well of your father and me. Promise you'll never act so pig-stubborn if something should ever happen and we have a terrible argument one day."

"We'll never argue like that."

"Promise me anyway."

"Mammy, watch out, the *ditch*."

The wheels of the car caught on the grass verge and veered toward the hedge. Mammy shrieked as she turned the steering wheel sharply. The wheels slid and we jackknifed, before the tires caught the road surface again and the vehicle righted itself. We traveled in silence for half a mile.

"Promise me," she repeated.

Her persistence shocked me, especially since I'd assumed she'd been thinking about our narrow escape.

"So long as you don't push me the way Granda pushed Uncle Brendan." I smiled mischievously. "Otherwise, I might have to run away, too."

"May God forgive you for thinking I'm pushing you, Gabriel."

"I was just kidding." I rubbed my chin. "Though I find it difficult to agree with the Church's views on certain subjects."

"We all do," Mammy said, and she laughed, which meant she was relaxed again. "That's normal. I've even had the odd difficulty." She laughed once more and put on the indicator to turn right. A sheep's eyes glittered ghostlike from behind a fence as we swung onto the side road. "What subjects do you not agree with the church on?"

"Minor stuff."

"Like?"

"Take contraception, for example. It's ridiculous to me that the Church won't consider its use."

"Jesus, that's *not* minor stuff. That's major. Using contraceptives is a mortal sin. How can you question that?"

I stared straight ahead. I was taught to question things at school. I was taught to look at all kinds of problems with the honed mind of a Saint Malachy's student. Yet, when I had once dared to question the Church's position on this matter in religious education class, it was taboo—for the priests and for my mother.

"Practicing artificial contraception is a mortal, mortal sin," Mammy insisted.

A mortal, mortal sin. One *mortal* more than an everyday "mortal sin." What Connor and I were doing was also a mortal, mortal sin. Icy chills wracked my body.

"It's killing babies, Gabriel. And very, very selfish."

"What about the poor people in Africa? I don't think God means for those people to have large families and live in poverty, do you?"

"The missionaries teach them about the rhythm method."

"You mean to say Uncle Brendan goes around teaching about the rhythm method as part of his work?"

"Africans have to be taught that the pope forbids contraception, too."

"How would *he* know anything sensible about contraception?"

She didn't respond immediately. At length, she said, "You must always accept what the pope says. You must accept without question. He's God's representative on earth. He understands the divine plan. He knows everything."

She was like a bloody machine gun. Everything spewed out, it was so ingrained.

"Gabriel, never let your Uncle Brendan hear you talk this way. I certainly hope you haven't been putting crazy views like this in the letters you send him."

"What if I have?"

"Craziness like that is enough to give him another nervous breakdown."

"That's ridiculous."

"Here I was thinking I was rearing you the right way, that I was rearing you to be a good Catholic. Now I learn I'm rearing a heathen."

She became a repository of sniffles and tears. My mother did this when she wasn't getting her way.

"Please don't cry anymore."

"Jesus, how can I *not* cry? My heart's broken."

"I'm sure the Church is probably right."

"The Church is infallible. Don't forget it."

Twenty-One

T he IRA man arrived to stay for ten days while arrangements were made to spirit him off to America. Seamus
was in his late twenties and stocky with a boyish face
and tight auburn curls. He didn't fit my image of a vicious IRA
volunteer, though admittedly, I didn't have much information
as to what they were supposed to look like. The world within
which the IRA operated was shadowy, populated with faceless
men who did their deeds in secrecy, and no one dared openly
admit they knew any volunteers.

My feelings toward Seamus and the IRA were ambivalent.
I did not agree with their violent methods, but I was outraged
by the deaths of innocent Catholics in Belfast at the hands of
Protestant paramilitaries. Murder is a mortal sin and I would

have preferred that none of these organizations existed, but my history books demonstrated that peace and justice sometimes don't come about until brutal acts have been committed. The old Knockburn men said things like this, but they also said that the Protestants were stubborn and indifferent to injustice, and maybe the IRA was needed to make them see sense.

Seamus had a hearty laugh, and big hands with spotless nails topped by perfect white crescents because he manicured them regularly. His nails were so at odds with the worrisome life of a man on the run. Although not formally educated, his mind was sharp as a flicked whip. He could help James with his mathematics homework, something I couldn't do, on account of I was so dreadful at it. I had determined to act coolly toward him, but his enthusiasm to join in our games of checkers and talk about books warmed me to him. The man was just so good-humored, you couldn't dislike him.

He read voraciously. He read Protestant, Catholic, and any British newspapers he could lay his hands on. He read my Shakespeare and O'Casey plays, Caroline's poetry books, and Hardy, Austen, and Joyce novels. He sent me to the Ballynure library, two small rooms over a hardware shop, with a list of Russian and American authors that made the old librarian scratch her head.

"You must read Steinbeck's *The Grapes of Wrath* when you find the time," he said to me. "That's what I call a book."

"What's it about?"

"It's about the working man and subjugation. The people in that book were treated the same as the Irish are now. They were forced to leave their land by the enemy—though, granted, it wasn't the Ulster Unionists forcing them to leave." He laughed at his joke. "But their enemies pushed them out of their homes for the same reasons. They pushed them out for greed and power. That's why the Protestants and English are pushing us about, Gabriel. We're disenfranchised, just so the rich Protestant farmers and corporations can make money." He looked at James and me gravely. "Be sure to read that book and tell your friends at school to read it, too."

"Are you on the run because you killed soldiers?" James asked.

Seamus's lips quivered. "It would fit you better if you asked your math teacher questions instead of me."

"Did you kill some, Seamus?" James asked.

Father peered over his newspaper, and I could see he was astounded at my brother's insolence.

"It's bad manners to ask people questions they don't want to answer," Mammy said.

Seamus said, "Let's just say I've done a few wee things I don't crow about. We'll leave it at that."

A murderer was sheltering under our roof. Yet he was so intelligent, so good-natured, and had such beautiful hands, you couldn't help but like him.

My fifth year at Saint Malachy's got even better after Pani bought a car. It was ancient, and he hung two furry yellow dice from the windshield mirror and set a tiger with a scarlet tongue and nodding head on the ledge of the backseat. He parked it in the narrow driveway leading up to the school, near a public housing estate that had been built by the Unionist government in a scurrilous attempt to stop Saint Malachy's from expanding, and we'd sit inside it at lunchtime, listening to pop music on Radio 1.

Martin, Pani, and I also sat together in every class we had in common. We sniggered, whispered, and didn't listen to a word the teachers said. I don't know why, exactly, but I was becoming dead unruly. My troubles on the bus were over, but I was now anxious about not feeling much for girls when I thought about them. I'd also got the stupid idea in my head that I was far smarter than everyone else in my class.

Now that Pani had a car, Martin also convinced him to take us to other dance halls and discos farther afield. My mother didn't object because Caroline and I were spending long hours in my bedroom, supposedly studying, but actually discussing a raft of teenage problems: acne, my fat arse, her crushes, ABBA, and my fat arse again.

With regard to ABBA, I devoured every magazine article I found about them and fantasized regularly about being invited to join the group. Blonde Agnetha with her straw yellow hair and throaty voice became an obsession. I daydreamed about conversing with her, and she was always captivated by my amazing intelligence. At other times, I'd strut about my bedroom, a pair of rolled-up socks serving as a microphone, singing the words to their song "Waterloo" as it belted from the record player.

Acting became another passion of mine at this time. I got a part in our school drama department's production of *Twelfth Night*. I'd tried out for the part of Malvolio, but got Viola.

I'd acted in small plays we'd written in second-year English class with Miss Brown and enjoyed it. But acting in front of class peers is one thing; their parents, quite another. I was shy, but Mr. Casey, the head of drama, believed I had talent and said I'd be very successful in the role.

Father was skeptical of boys donning ladies' clothes for a school play. My mother's theory that the play would look grand on my future university application forms did not persuade him.

"Why did he have to cast you as the woman?" he asked one evening. The entire family and Seamus were gathered in the living room and I was standing on top of a parlor chair in my costume, a polka-dot dress because the production was a contemporary one. Mammy adjusted the dress's length with pins. "Why couldn't he give you a man's part?"

"Because I'm good at the role."

Nuala handed Mammy another pin.

"What will anybody from Knockburn who sees it think?" he asked.

"It's just a play, Harry," said the IRA man, setting down his newspaper.

I sighed exaggeratedly at Father's dank ignorance of Shakespeare. Even Seamus, now in his final two days with us, didn't say a word about the part. I could see he understood, even though he'd had no formal education.

The phone rang in the hallway and Mammy went out to answer it.

"I'm not the only person playing a female role," I said to Father. "I've told you twice that Martin's playing Olivia and he has to wear women's clothing throughout the *entire* play."

Though nothing was said, Father's look spoke volumes.

Mammy returned a few minutes later. "That was Brendan on the phone. He didn't sound like himself. I hope to God he's not relapsing."

"What do you mean?" asked Father.

Seamus was reading his newspaper again, his face was hidden behind it.

"He was vague and rambling," she said. "I asked how the missions were doing and he said, 'Only so-so.' When I asked how he was he said, 'A bit depressed.'" She glanced at Seamus's paper. "He did sound very down."

"Poor Uncle Brendan," said Caroline. She closed her textbook. "I hate to think of him sad."

"Any word of him coming home?" Father said. "Sure, he's long overdue. A gallop home would soon put that depression nonsense out of his head."

"He's coming in May. He didn't say for how long. And then, without as much as pausing for a breath, he asked how your mother's health is. He said he'd been thinking about her a lot." She fell silent for a moment. "Do you think he's had some sort of premonition about her?"

Mammy was very superstitious. It was so bad that she wouldn't allow a pigeon to rest on the roof of our home, just in case it might be a dove, as doves resting on roofs always meant a death in the family. She chased them away with stones. She'd even broken one of the front windows once because she was such a lousy shot.

"Don't be stupid," said Father.

"I didn't want to tell yous, but I woke up in the middle of the night very recently and I heard something wailing," Mammy said. She was, of course, also terrified of hearing the banshee. "I didn't want to say anything to scare yous but now Brendan's asking about your mother's health."

"Don't be crazy," I said.

"I'm telling yous that wailing came from nothing alive on this earth," she said. "May God strike me dead if I'm lying. It was at the corner of the house one second and far away the next. I'm telling yous that's exactly what the banshee does."

Father laughed and Mammy glared at him.

"Brendan also said he has something to share with us, but I couldn't wheedle out of him what was to be shared," she said.

"I hope he's not ill," Nuala said.

"That crossed my mind," Mammy said. "Cancer runs on the Harkin side, Harry. Didn't one of your uncles die of cancer when he was about Brendan's age?" She shivered involuntary, as people do when they're discussing something uncomfortable. Then she answered her own question before Father could reply. "But there's such a paucity of priests for the foreign missions, I'm sure God wouldn't take Brendan in his prime." She regarded me intently, probably to remind me of our conversation about having a priest in the house.

"He said something else very strange," she added. "He told me that he loves us all and asked me to throw in an extra wee prayer for him when we're saying our nightly rosary."

"What's so strange about that?" said Father. "If anybody's got God's ears, it's got to be you. You're hardly ever off your knees."

Seamus chuckled, and immediately crinkled his newspaper noisily to disguise it.

"That's an odd statement for Uncle Brendan to make," Caroline said. "As if we'd dare *not* love a priest."

"All the same, it was a bit peculiar, Harry. And he finished his call very odd, too. Brendan always finishes with a 'May you find peace in Christ's love,' but he just said 'Bye' this time. *Bye.* That was it, honest to God. No, something's up. He never fails to say the 'May you find peace' bit."

Because rehearsals took place after school hours, Auntie Celia and Mammy made arrangements to pick Martin and me up after school. They rotated duties so that every other week I stayed overnight at my aunt's house, which was great because sex was now an important part of my life. I thought about it nearly all the time, just like Fergal, whom I'd criticized for the very same thing just a few years earlier. In addition to doing stuff with Connor, I masturbated two or three times a day, and at least once nightly, too.

"What part of sex do you think about most when you're wanking alone at night?" I said to Connor in bed one night.

"Riding." He reached over and seized my thing. "What do you think about?"

This was my cue to fondle him.

"The same thing."

That was a lie. The truth was I could not get a hard-on when I thought about a girl, not even if I gave her huge breasts. No matter how much I concentrated, my thing wouldn't respond. I couldn't get it beyond a soft firmness and had to think about a man to get it stiff. Once it was up, however, everything worked fine. It was just that the means employed to get it to that point felt false. More and more, this preyed on my mind.

"I've often wondered how a woman feels when it's being done to her," Connor said.

"You have?"

"You know the way teachers tell us that if you do something rather than just read about it, how it helps you understand the thing even better? Let's take you and tennis, for example. Because you play it, you understand what's going on at Wimbledon far better than if you just read the rules. Isn't that right?"

"What does this have to do with riding?"

"Think about it. If a man does it once, don't you think he'd know better how the woman feels? Don't you think he'd be able to satisfy her better? He'd know exactly what she's feeling and be able to please her brilliantly as a result."

"Aye, I see what you're getting at."

"How about you try doing it to me?" he said. "Only this one time, mind."

"Ride you? I don't know. I think it would . . . I'm not sure."

"If it makes us better at riding girls, why not?"

Connor rolled over on his tummy and stretched out his legs like a toad in mid-leap, and I climbed on top of him. Seconds later, I yelped and leaped out of bed.

"My thing's hurt." I pulled back the curtain and examined it in the dusky orange glow of the street lamp.

"What are you talking about?" he asked.

"Jesus, switch on the light, quick." I saw blood. "I'll bleed to death. What'll I do? *What the fuck* will I do?"

"Shush, shush. You'll wake everybody."

"It's full of blood vessels down there and we won't be able to tell Auntie Celia what happened." I looked at my thing again. "Connor, what'll I do? *What the fuck* will I do?"

He seized his school pants off the floor, pulled out a tissue and wiped my thing. A car with a broken exhaust passed noisily down the street and my roiling imagination conjured up images of wailing ambulances, peering doctors, and hot-faced explanations.

"It's almost stopped bleeding," said Connor.

The bleeding had slowed, but my foreskin was torn. "That's the last of this sort of carry-on," I said. "We shouldn't have tried to do that in the first place. It's not fucking right."

"It's time we stopped the whole caper," he said. "I've been thinking it for a while now."

"Never do anything again?"

"I'm sixteen. We should be concentrating on girls full-time. If we don't, we might turn ourselves into queers."

I felt queasy. "You said it didn't matter, provided we thought about girls."

"I'm older than you and it could begin to take over if I'm not careful."

"Do you think so?"

"Definitely."

"Connor, I want to ask you something. Have . . . have you ever thought about boys when you're wanking? You know . . . just for a wee change . . . when you're tired of thinking about girls, maybe?"

"Only homos do that. Are you calling me a fucking homo?"

"No."

"Have you thought that way when you wank?" he asked.

"Jesus, no way. Only homos think that sort of stuff."

"We're both all right, then."

We climbed into bed. Connor switched off the light and I lay cold and wooden beside him. The clock's tick in the hallway began to accuse me. *Tick-tock, tick-tock, tick-tock. Ho-mo, ho-mo, ho-mo.* Sporadic traffic passed up and down the streets. Happy girlfriends and boyfriends driving by in cars. My world was ripped and torn.

Tick-tock, ho-mo, ho-mo, tick-tock, ho-mo, ho-mo, ho-mo.

Connor's breathing settled into rhythmic slumber. I wanted to stop the clock but I couldn't—Auntie Celia would hear me try to open its casing.

Ho-mo, ho-mo, ho-mo, ho-mo.

I'm not a homosexual, my mind screamed. I turned on my side and stared at the dusky glow of the wallpaper, its sheen like ice. I'd never initiated things. Connor was the one who always started things between us.

Ho-mo, ho-mo.

Now he didn't want to do it anymore because he was scared he'd be homosexual.

HO-MO, HO-MO.

I lay on my back and passed my fingers over the cold sweat on my chest. I took a deep breath. Another surge of warmth swept over my body.

I experienced a fierce urge to bang my head against the wall. I wanted to cry and bang my head hard to stop the thoughts. But banging my head was useless and crying was feminine and I'd still have to get up in the morning and go on.

I sat up and watched Connor's contented breathing. Up and down, pause, up and down. *How can he be so selfish?* I wondered.

Nothing would be changed in the morning, except he and I would arise and never touch each other again. I could stand it no longer. I had to get up.

I rose very gently, but still felt dizzy; I thought I'd faint. With my hand on the wall, I took a few slow breaths and went into the hallway, now silent and dark as mortal, mortal sin. I felt my way along the wall, passing the clock, passing Auntie Celia's room, where I could hear Uncle Frank snoring. I went into the bathroom.

Switching on the light, I looked in the mirror. I despised the image gawking back at me in the stark brightness. Falling on my knees before the toilet bowl, I knelt and prayed and beseeched God to come and help me. I prayed and beseeched for ten minutes, making up the prayers and pleas as I went along.

And He came, just like He'd come to me so long ago. He was my maker, my one true friend. His soothingly masculine voice spoke inside my head. He stopped the whirling thoughts. He told me I was good, that I was not to be so hard on myself, that I was His child.

Twenty-Two

s I came up the lane toward Granny's yard, I saw her laughing and blinked rapidly to make sure my eyes weren't deceiving me. She stood by her turf stack with a bunch of soldiers. One of them removed pieces of turf from the stack and placed them in the cardboard box she used to carry them. Another soldier saw me and set his mug of tea down fast. He grabbed his rifle off the ground, pointed it at me, and ordered me to put my hands in the air.

"It's okay, Corporal Ingham," Granny said. "Gabriel's my grandson."

The man's shoulders relaxed and he set the rifle back down on the ground. "Nice to meet you," he said, and extended his hand when I drew up to them.

I shook it weakly and stared at Granny, who had a plate of homemade tea scones slathered in rhubarb jam in her hand.

"The boys were hungry from patrolling in the mountain," she said, with a shrug.

A squawking sound filled the air as three of Granny's hens ran out of the coop.

"Jesus, I mustn't have closed the damned door properly," she said. "If they get out, I'll never catch them."

The soldier placing turf into the box sprinted across the yard and slammed the henhouse door shut. He chased one of the two escaped hens, catching it as it was about to dart underneath Uncle John's car.

"Help him, Gabriel," said Granny.

I ran to the coop and opened the door. About five-ten, like me, with broad shoulders and cropped sandy colored hair, the soldier had no rank stripes on his uniform, which meant he was a private. His skin was tanned and he looked as if he should still be attending school.

A plump, speckled hen drew closer. I grabbed it when it started pecking the earth and put it back in the coop.

"The other one's gone around the side of the house," said Granny.

We walked across the yard and I let the private take the lead when we reached the corner of the house.

"Where do you think it is, mate?" he asked.

His eyes were turquoise and sparkled in the sun. I found it hard to look away.

"Let's check by the haystack," I said, pointing to a large one in the middle of the first field. "There's always plenty of insects near hay."

We climbed the barbed wire fence and walked across the field.

"My name's Richie," he said, and held out his hand.

I didn't want to shake a British soldier's hand, but I couldn't stop myself. His grip was firm. Tingles ran up my spine. I couldn't stop those, either.

"I'm Gabriel. Are you a private?"

"You're sharp as a glass shard, mate," he said.

"You look too young to be in the army."

"I'll soon be eighteen," he said, glancing toward the house. "I fudged a wee bit on the form." He winked. "Only by a few months."

I'd never met anyone who'd lied on an official government form.

"Your gran's a nice lady," he said. "Mine lives in Wales."

"You're Welsh?"

"Mum was. My Dad's English and I grew up in London. You ever been there?"

I shook my head.

"You should go. I think you'd love it." He smiled so mischievously, I couldn't help smiling back.

The hen came around the haystack and Richie dove toward it. He missed and two feathers billowed in the air. His forehand had white-gray hen shite on it. I couldn't stop laughing at his disgusted face as he wiped his hand on the grass. He laughed, too. The hen ran, its wings flapping, across the field. When it reached the hedge separating the field from the bog, it flew over and disappeared.

"Mr. Fox will dine well tonight," said Richie.

"We'd best not tell Granny."

"You got that right, mate." He winked. "Our secret, right?"

Father drove up as Granny and I watched the soldiers walk in single file across the heather. After climbing out of the car, his eyes followed Granny's toward the departing soldiers. He watched for a long moment and then his gaze fell on the empty tea mugs in my hands and the plate with one uneaten scone in Granny's.

"You made tea for those bastards?" he asked, glaring at Granny.

"What of it?" she said.

His eyes widened. "Making tea for English scum isn't on—it could also get you shot."

Granny started toward the house. But then she stopped abruptly and turned back to Father.

"Those lads don't want to be in Ireland any more than we want them here," she said.

"They're scum."

Granny shook her head and took two steps toward Father.

"Harry, darlin', you're confused. Our enemies are the Unionists. *They're* the ones discriminating."

I nodded vigorously.

"You know that wee lad who helped you catch my hens?" Granny said, looking at me.

"Richie?"

"Aye, him. He's a Catholic." Granny turned from me to look at Father. "So put that in your pipe and smoke it, Harry."

Darkness encroached on the silvery sky as I held the sides of the ladder Father had propped against a telephone pole alongside the public road, about fifty yards from our house. Standing at the top of the ladder, Father fastened the Irish tricolor flag to the pole. There was no breeze and he stretched it out and admired the bars of green, white, and orange.

"That'll show them soldiers the sort of people who live 'round here," he said.

Father Cornelius raised his bushy eyebrows behind the heavy, black-framed glasses as he stood near my desk and regarded me. He held my term paper high in the air for a moment before opening his fingers and allowing it to drop on my desk like a piece of garbage.

"Your essay hinted at promise in the first few paragraphs, but, as usual, didn't deliver by the end. You really are going to have to pick up your socks."

Next, he addressed Martin, who sat beside me. "This shows promise, though I'm cognizant of the fact you've had the benefit of a repeat year to reach the passing standard."

"Fucking homo," I muttered, as the priest walked away.

My cousin was too busy salivating over the juicy comments to reply. Pani heard and sniggered as the priest approached Paddy Flanagan.

Father Cornelius was vice-head and we'd had him for English literature for three months now. The British Army had arrested Mr. McGovern, our regular teacher. He was imprisoned on a ship on Belfast Lough, accused without a shred of evidence of being a member of the Official IRA.

"Nice effort," the priest said to Paddy, who grinned dead cheesy.

It stung like hellfire that someone like Paddy Flanagan was getting more "nice efforts" in English literature than me, but I knew I'd show everyone what I was made of when I took the O level examinations. I'd cram like hell, pass every subject, and show everyone I was both a terrific actor and student.

Father Cornelius knew I was a good actor already. Sometimes he came in to watch the evening rehearsals, and he hadn't been reticent about coming up on the stage afterward on two occasions to tell me that I made a very convincing Viola. I'd acted dead cool while he'd praised me in front of the other cast members, but inside I'd basked in the glow.

"I really think I'll become an actor," I said, after I'd finished my last bite of sausage. It was a week and a half before opening night and I was mostly happy with my performance. The only glitches were a few lines that wouldn't stick, no matter how many times I went over them. "They've got the Lyric Players in Belfast and I think I'll apply to them instead of university."

"As if they'd take you," James said. He rose from the table and laid his plate in the sink. "They only want good-looking people."

Caroline and Nuala giggled. James examined his face in a mirror that our mother kept on the windowsill. He squeezed a creamy pimple. Since puberty struck, my brother was obsessed with his oily facial skin. I'd even caught him sneaking into Caroline's bedroom behind her back to slather her astringent lotion on it, though he might as well not have bothered.

"You couldn't be an actor with those horrible pus spots," I said.

He looked over his shoulder at me. "Daddy, what do you think of our Gabriel becoming an actor?"

"I'll 'actor' him." Father wiped milk from his mouth with the edge of his hand. "Fit you better you were helping me. Luksee, if you want pocket money this summer, you'll have to work for it. I'm not dishing out cash for you to go dancing or run 'round the country with that clown of a cousin of yours and get nothing in return. I've got a job starting this summer and you can help out. Why should I take on another man and pay him when you're available?"

"Gabriel will go gladly," said my mother.

There was no point protesting when both parents agreed on something.

"You can hire Martin, too," she said. "They'll be company for each other." She nodded at me. "Yous'll have more money for spending when yous go on holiday with Tommy in Bundoran." She chuckled. "Martin will be glad to work alongside you. I'm sure Celia pays him very little when he helps out in her shop."

That was true. Martin was forever complaining she paid him peanuts.

"Martin and his flat feet and stumpy legs is no use to me on a building site," said Father. "I need strapping men."

"Try him out," she said.

"How much will you pay?" I asked.

"After deduction of living expenses, I'll give you twenty pounds."

"I don't have to pay living expenses—though if I must, then you'll have to pay me the same rate as you're paying your other employees."

Father laughed before taking a gulp of milk. The manner in which he drank tea or milk at home infuriated me. It was uncouth.

"You drive a hard bargain, Gabriel. Aye, we'll make a businessman out of you yet." He laughed at his wit. "I'll tell you what, I'll pay you twenty-five pounds a week."

"Mammy, I want twenty-five pounds a week for doing chores," Caroline said.

"Harry, that's far too much," said my mother. "What would our Gabriel need so much money for?"

"I'll be doing men's work," I said.

"I'll give it to them." Father took another noisy slurp, then wiped his mouth. "But I want a decent day's work, and there'll be no boss's son favors. You'll be treated the same as my other men."

After being excused from the table, Caroline and I went to my bedroom where, instead of studying, she complained about the wages issue for a while, and then agreed to listen to the lines of the play that I was having difficulty with. This time, I recited them perfectly. Thereafter, I crept out to the hallway and phoned Martin to learn if he had any interest in working for Father. At first he was very hesitant, grilling me about whether the work would be hard or dirty and if the workmen were friendly—until I told him what our wages would be. He hung immediately up to tell Auntie Celia he was quitting work at her shop.

Twenty-Three

As I watched Martin and Pani file out of the room, I didn't feel cocky like I had minutes earlier, when I'd nudged Pani and we'd sniggered aloud at a double entendre in the Shakespeare text a boy had been reading aloud. Father Cornelius, seated at his desk, kept me waiting while he read something. I wished there was another class lining up at the door, but the stairwell was as noiseless as inside the room. Downstairs, a door banged shut. Father Cornelius walked to the door, closed it rudely, and returned to his desk, where he continued reading. Teachers were masters of creating horrible silences.

"Come here, Harkin," he said, after two excruciating minutes.

I rose from my desk and went over to him.

"Why are you trying to ruin yourself?"

"I'm not, Father."

"Don't think I haven't observed your fondness for crudity in class. You're obsessed with baseness." He looked fiercely into my eyes and I looked away like an admonished dog. "I've checked into your overall performance and, aside from a favorable comment from your drama teacher, it appears your grades are as bad as your sense of humor. Judging by how you performed in your mock exams, you're going to fail your O levels. You're going to fail, just like your cousin. Do you really want that, boy?"

"No, Father."

I'd done badly in my mocks and the priest was probably one of seven teachers who'd wanted to speak to my mother at a parent-teacher meeting held a few weeks ago. Thankfully, she hadn't attended. She and Father argued when he refused to accompany her and, accusing him of shirking his responsibility, Mammy decided to retaliate by not going, either.

"Stand erect! Spread your feet and place your hands by your sides." His black-brown eyes ran with searing deliberateness up and down my body. "Every cell of my being wants to send you to Father Rafferty, *boy*." He paused until the echo of the emphasized word was devoured by the silence. "Do you know what that means?"

"Yes, Father."

"What does it mean if I march you to his office now, *boy*?"

Priests at Saint Malachy's addressed us as "boy" at such moments in order to ram home their absolute power. His stressed use of that word rendered me insignificant faster than any stinging whack with a strap on my hand could.

"That I'll be thoroughly punished, Father."

"Perhaps suspended, too. Do you know why? I'll tell you why. I'll tell you exactly. Other teachers have written in the Burgundy

Book that you've been troublesome all year. Troublesome and impertinent." He paused again, to let it sink in that he'd been checking the Burgundy Book. "Is there a reason for this disruptive behavior, Gabriel?"

Gabriel! Suddenly I was Gabriel again. He'd terrified me, but the second chance was now coming. Immediately, I transported myself outside the classroom. I imagined running down the stairs toward my next class.

"I've been a bit silly and I'm sorry, Father." I made sure my tone dripped with apologetic meekness.

"When good boys of your age behave badly, there's usually something behind it. Do you have problems or confusions?"

A hot body flash culminated in my face; I could feel it. "I . . . I haven't got problems or confusions."

He sighed. "As I said, the only people with good words to say about you are Mr. Casey and your physics teacher. The former said you were an excellent Viola. However, that's an extracurricular activity. I don't have to tell you the Examination Board doesn't take prowess as a budding thespian into consideration." His brows rose and he looked at me quizzically while placing his pale hand on the table. The black hairs on its back stood out in relief. I was struck by the hand's largeness. For no logical reason, I thought his hands more resembled a farmer's than a priest's.

"I will apply myself diligently from now on, Father Cornelius. Now if I could—"

"How did it feel to play the part of Viola?"

"It was a challenge."

"I've often wondered what effect it has on our boys to be compelled to play female roles. Did it feel strange in any way?"

"It was just a role."

"Of course, of course. But how did it feel to dress in women's clothing?"

My eyes moved reflexively to his flowing soutane, but I held my tongue. "Father, I'm late for my next class."

"Miss King has you now, does she not?"

"Yes."

"I notice she's also entered comments in the Burgundy Book." He paused. "You're quite right to worry about tardiness. I'll have a word with her. She'll understand."

He began stroking the side of my buttock with the velvety gentleness of a baby's touch. The hairs on my leg started crawling.

"Father Rafferty is a most unforgiving priest, isn't he?" he said. "Will you promise to apply yourself from now on, Gabriel? I'm very concerned about you." The strokes became firmer.

"I shall, Father."

My voice sounded girly. His hand arced toward my fly. I stepped back.

"Come here," he said.

"Father, I need to—"

"Stand here." He pointed to the spot.

I obeyed. The fumbling recommenced.

"Father Cornelius, someone might come in and catch us doing this."

The words I'd used didn't sound right. They were words I should never have needed to say to a priest. Priests didn't do wicked things. The stuff boys said about Father Cornelius were jokes. Everybody understood that was so at the end of the day. These words I'd used sounded like collusion. My mind played with the words, flinging some away and fitting in different, better ones that I should have used. The air in the classroom chilled a part of my skin that never should have been exposed in the first place. The word "boy" echoed in my head and mixed with the dough of different, better words I should have used. Chair legs scraped.

He eased to his knees as he said, "No one will come." I stared at the cresting waves of gray hair running across the back of his head, waves almost like Father's and Uncle Brendan's. I stared at the waves until my parched eyes stung. I turned away and gazed out the window where the defined images of boys playing football became gray and blurred.

After he'd finished, Father Cornelius put me back in order, zipping up my fly and smoothing my trousers. He sat in his chair again.

"I lost my self-control just now," he said. "This shouldn't have happened. You can leave."

My feet would not move.

"Go to your next class," Father Cornelius said, insistent.

"Why did you ask if I was confused?" My voice was flat and distant, like I was outside the window looking in. "Is there something about me that told you I'm not normal?"

"There's no such thing as 'not normal' in God's eyes."

Father Cornelius cast his eyes to his lap and massaged his left temple with the hand that had touched me.

"Something about me must have showed I'm maybe not normal. What is it?"

"You're a bright young man, Gabriel. You'll grow up and find yourself a lovely girl one day. Don't ever think you're not normal. Don't even consider such a thing. The only thing is you're too sensitive behind all the belligerence." He paused. "Let's not give another thought about what happened. It *must* be forgotten. It was the devil at work."

I was too sensitive. It oozed from me like a stinking perfume.

"You must stop acting the class clown. Do you hear?" Father Cornelius sprang from the chair unexpectedly and raked his hair as he strode up to a window. He thrust it open and took a deep breath. For a moment, the terrible deafening silence returned as he stood gazing out at the football field. "Look here, *boy*. This incident's to be forgotten immediately." He swung around and stared at me. "Do you understand?"

I didn't speak.

"I said, do you understand?"

"Yes, Father."

He returned to his desk. "Let's say an Act of Contrition together and receive forgiveness from the Higher Power." He fished a purple stole out of the pocket in his soutane and sat. "Kneel before me." His big farmer's hand trembled as he laid it upon my shoulder.

I moved my lips as he recited the long version of the Act of Contrition. At its conclusion, he made a large sign of the cross in the space between us.

"You may now leave. I'll speak to Miss King."

I returned to my desk, eased my satchel off the floor and started down the room. I was different. The boys were right all along. Henry had known I was different. Aunt Peggy had known and warned my mother. Noel had known I'd allow him to do things with me. So had Connor. But he was now normal, like every other boy. He and I acted as if nothing physical had ever occurred between us, yet I wanted it to happen again.

"Oh, boy," Father called as I reached the door.

I stopped and waited without turning to look at him. I waited for the final words. There were always final words in awkward situations.

"No more fooling in class. Study hard and maybe, *just maybe*, you'll scrape through. Otherwise, you and I will pay a visit to Father Rafferty with *all* that that implies."

The velvet-dressed threat. The guilt wrapped in compassion. Angry heat surged through my body. Every cell sweated at his overriding power.

Pani and Martin were dying to know what had transpired. We sat in Pani's car at lunchtime, but I didn't feel like listening to ABBA. I wanted to be alone and replay, analyze, work out other endings that could have been, had I only said different, better words. I needed to sort out my thoughts before the end of recess, so I could go to my next class and forget everything that had happened.

"I'm on a warning." I rolled my eyes toward the padded ceiling, when what I really wanted to do was let them plummet to the floor. "Next time, it'll be Father Rafferty's office and possibly suspension."

Pani looked hard into my eyes. I couldn't take his scrutiny and turned away to look beyond the boxwood hedge to a small crabapple tree.

"Bastard," he said.

"You're lucky he likes blondes," Martin said. "Maybe you should settle down a bit, Gabriel. It is getting close to exams, and you know what happened to Pani and me last year."

Pani guffawed as he reached out with his long middle finger to turn on the tape player. I shivered as Agnetha's dulcet voice snaked out from the cassette. For the first time, I took no pleasure in her singing. As her voice was chased and finally engulfed by heavy synthesized rhythms, I felt suffocated and needed to leave the car.

For a while, I strolled aimlessly. I came to near the line of arborvitae flanking the football pitch, my obliviousness pierced by the sound of boys talking as they smoked furtively. The cigarette stink reminded me of my failures with Lizzie. I walked the corridors, passing the tuck shop where junior boys were trying to buy goodies. A red-faced, blonde boy, a first- or second-year, fought his way up to the counter, shoving larger boys who could have flattened him. The boy saw me and instantly stopped pushing, fearing perhaps that I'd pull him out of the line and lecture him because I was older. He wasn't sensitive. I was his superior, but he was stronger. His will wouldn't allow Father Cornelius to do what I'd just allowed him to do. I was made of paper in comparison to this steely junior.

I continued on quickly. I retreated to an empty art room. I stared out the large windows at senior boys filing past an orderly line of juniors waiting to go into the school dining room. A row of pretty watercolors, bunches of foxgloves, seashells, and gnarly driftwood, lay drying on the long bench running the length of the room. God made delicate foxgloves and pretty seashells with smooth, pearly interiors, and He also made me.

"Why the hell are you doing this to me, God? What have I done to you?" I howled. I gripped the edge of the bench. "Why have You made me *different* from the other boys? Is it some kind of sport? *Am I just a fucking sport to You?"*

The art room resumed its indifferent quiet. I felt like ripping apart one of the seashell paintings. "Jesus and Mary, why can't you intercede for me? Why can't you make Him make me just like the other boys? Do you want me to fucking well hate and spurn you, too?"

But God knew I would never spurn Him. He knew He was in every molecule of my being. He was my life force. Moreover, fear wouldn't allow me to turn away from Him. I was too frightened. Without Him, I'd really have nothing.

For the next few weeks, attending Father Cornelius's classes was purgatory. Out of the corner of my eye, I saw him watching me.

I wouldn't look at him directly unless it could not be avoided. When he asked someone to read aloud and everyone bent their heads to their texts, I caught him watching me and my heart froze thicker than a fort's walls with hate. I could not hate God, but I could hate Father Cornelius.

When he watched me, I wondered if the devil was inside him, if he'd try to get me alone again. I wished him dead. I wished him dead when he directed his stupid, clever questions at me in class to force my participation, while he sat in a soutane and dog collar, his white farmer's hands resting on the desk. I wished him dead as I pushed the words from my throat, keeping my tone pancake flat so the other boys would never suspect anything bad had ever happened.

He did succeed in quelling my boisterous streak, but still I didn't feel like studying. I didn't study and I tried to turn back the homosexual thoughts. But the more I bridled and spurned, the more the deviant yearnings clung to me. Worst of all was nighttime. I would lie in bed after saying my prayers and the image of a handsome sixth-former would come to mind, followed by another, sometimes even a teacher or a passerby I'd seen on the street that day, and I'd fantasize a little and then pray them away. But the deviancy was patient and lurked 'til I was prayed out, and then it stormed back until, broken and loathsomely willing, I'd seize upon one favorite image and my fevered hand would become a piston, working and working until the moments of ecstasy came, followed always by oily, black, despairing guilt, guilt spliced with *Why me, God?* shrieked repeatedly into the downy pillow.

I'd curse Father Cornelius, but deep within I knew he wasn't the only one to blame. What he'd done was sinful, but my desires had their own poisonous roots. I'd also try to bargain with God. I'd make desperate promises, promises to lead a good Catholic life if He'd just see His way to spare me, just see His way to turn me normal. If He'd just allow me to get aroused around girls so I could marry and have children one day, I'd be utterly His.

He must have partially heard my bargaining, because my old English teacher was released from the prison ship a few weeks later and Father Cornelius was gone from my sight. There were no more daily reminders. Now, I had to see him only from afar, and bear him if we chanced to meet in the corridor when, as a well-bred Saint Malachy's boy, I was required to greet him courteously.

As time passed, I also developed a solution to the nighttime yearnings that assuaged my guilt and fears. It was a powerfully simple solution. As I performed the night act, I'd allow myself to think about a man right until the cusp of orgasm, whereupon I'd substitute him for thoughts of a naked girl whose face I could never see but whose breasts were always succulent and firm. In that way, I was thinking about a woman as I carried myself through, which meant everything was normal. I also convinced myself this was a great test that God set and wished me to pass. He was testing me, making me go through this painful phase, and all I had to do was struggle and pass and all would be fine.

Twenty-Four

I n the midst of all my fictitious fornication, Uncle Brendan
arrived. Auntie Celia had arranged to pick my mother up
on the afternoon of his arrival, as she wanted someone to
accompany her to the airport. Apparently, Uncle Brendan had
informed her that he didn't wish Granny to be present, which
Mammy found extremely strange.

When James and I arrived home from school that evening, I
found Mammy seated rigid on the living room sofa beside Uncle
Brendan. Auntie Celia, despite her wide hips, was squeezed in a
narrow parlor chair, staring out the window. The curly horns of
what looked like a carved ebony antelope, presumably a present
for my mother, protruded from its brown paper wrapping.

"We've just got in a little while ago," Mammy said. "Your uncle's plane was late."

"James, I wouldn't recognize you," Uncle Brendan said. He rose, shook my brother's hand, and then peered at me. "Gabriel . . . my God, you're as tall as me. You're a man now."

Auntie Celia watched intently as he embraced me. I felt embarrassed as the hug dragged on. Men, much less women, never hugged in Northern Ireland, and I kept patting his back while I waited for him to withdraw. When he did, his eyes were misty.

The shyness I'd felt when I'd met him first so many years ago returned. I also felt terribly shabby in my uniform: my blazer was worn and the pants gleamed from two years of sitting on wooden school chairs. My skin looked anemic in comparison to Uncle's nutmeg tan. He was even more handsome than I'd remembered, his frame lean, with no tiny paunch like Father had. Instead of clerical garb, he wore jeans, a wine-red T-shirt, and sneakers.

"I've football practice in fifteen minutes," said James. "What's to eat?"

"Make toast and scrambled eggs," said Mammy, and she glanced at me. "The rest of you will have to make do with Chinese takeout. I haven't had time to cook."

Uncle Brendan's eyes followed James as he left the room.

"God, Eileen, I've been in Kenya far too long. Your children are no longer children."

Mother sniffed as she pushed a wayward strand of graying hair behind her ear.

Auntie Celia emitted a mournful sigh. "Gabriel's in the same class as Martin and Connor now," she said.

It was as if she'd forced herself to speak, and what she'd said sounded wrong. It sounded as if I, not Martin, was the intruder in my class. Uncle Brendan smiled wanly.

The intervening years had been good to him and I'd never have guessed he'd been ill, not that I knew what to look for— I'd never met anyone who'd had a nervous breakdown. Uncle was about thirty-five and better preserved than any man of similar age in Knockburn. Here, most men over thirty looked much older, their faces weather-beaten from tough farm work or manual labor in all kinds of rain and wind. Silver wings adorning his hair made him noble of appearance. The idea of silver wings appealed to me greatly, and I wished I could sprout them then and there, until I remembered my hair was brown and flat, not black and wavy like his or Father's. Black, curly hair also peeped from Uncle's open collar, much denser than Father's, and I hoped to acquire this Harkin attribute, though, as I slipped a finger discreetly into the gap between two shirt buttons, things didn't feel promising.

"Martin's older than Gabriel," Uncle said. "How can they be in the same class?"

"Don't you remember I wrote you saying Martin didn't pass his exams?" Auntie Celia's tongue flicked out and moistened her upper lip. "Your prayers and masses didn't work too well in Martin's case . . . though now we know why."

"That's right, I forgot," said Uncle.

"Your prayers didn't work." Auntie's eyes narrowed, as if to reinforce her blame.

"The problems with my calling took over everything, Celia."

Mammy coughed. "Gabriel, you might as well know your uncle's left his vocation."

I stared at her incredulously. No one left the priesthood. I didn't even know it was possible to reverse Holy Orders.

"Why?" My mind raced all over: I saw Granny Harkin crying as she talked about him; I saw him administering last rites to the old woman with cancer; I saw myself serving Mass on the night he'd said it in our home. Leaving the priesthood was the ultimate disgrace to visit on a decent family.

"Why must you leave, Uncle Brendan?"

Auntie Celia stared out the window.

"It's a long question to answer, but, basically, I'm being called to do other things with my life. The priesthood's not for me. It's wrong. It's been wrong from the beginning. I've been fooling myself."

His eyes burrowed into mine. I saw his pain, and saw immediately that it was important for me to understand.

"I see, Uncle Brendan," I said, careful not to allow my tone to reveal my lingering shock.

Auntie Celia's chair creaked shrilly as she rose. "This will kill Mother, Brendan."

I was sure she was dead wrong there.

"For God's sake, Celia, don't say that," Uncle said. "I have to be honest with myself."

"Honest, indeed." Her tongue flicked over her lip again. "You should have made sure you'd a call in the first place. Priests don't get made in a day. You had plenty of time to change your mind at that seminary in Rome you ran off to."

My mother nodded at Auntie Celia, but Auntie didn't see because she was trapped in Uncle Brendan's stare. He was giving her one of those brother-and-sister stares that meant nothing to Mammy, yet communicated a thousand messages between them. I recognized the penetrating, frozen eye lock. I used it on Caroline, James, and Nuala when I needed to rebuke or communicate with them in a stranger's presence.

I thought about the money my mother had sent him over the years for masses. Masses for two deceased grandfathers. Two pounds when she was taking her driving test for the fourth time. Masses when Father was starting his business. I'd even sent him a pound for a secret petition. He'd never asked in his subsequent letter what my petition was for. He'd simply written and said he'd received the money and would say three masses, even though a pound only paid for one. I considered whether his leaving the priesthood might have diluted its effects.

"It's God's will and we'll just have to hold up our heads and learn to deal with it," said Mammy.

"Are you getting married to a girl from Kenya?" I asked.

Uncle Brendan laughed grimly. "Nothing like that."

"Thank God for *that* small mercy," said Auntie Celia. "Yes, indeed, thank God for that. If a darkie woman had been in the picture, I'd definitely have to pack my bags and go to live in Belfast, where nobody knows me." She walked up to the fireplace and rested her hands on the mantel, very mannishly. "Brendan, you are very misfortunate and the terrible thing is, it always comes home to roost with us. It comes home to roost with your poor family." She spun around to face him. "Daddy's dead and gone, but you can be sure he's spinning circles in his grave after you add the effects of this to the results of your first charade."

"Celia, that's enough," my mother said.

I didn't understand what charade she was talking about, but it seemed bad. The electric tension between the three of them was palpable.

"The hurt Brendan's already caused our poor family before becoming a priest," Auntie Celia lamented.

A decent cough would have floored me. Now, I understood. In one utterance, Auntie Celia had transported us back to the time when Uncle Brendan had gone out with a girl and upset Granda, who'd badly wanted a priest in his family.

"I said that's enough, Celia. You'll get over it."

"Fine for you to say, Eileen, but you don't understand things from the Harkin perspective," Auntie Celia continued. She shook her head and laughed falsely, speaking as if Uncle Brendan wasn't present. "You can't understand, because you're not his sister. You're not a Harkin. You won't have to face the people knowing they're laughing because one of the Harkin's has left the priesthood."

"*I'm* married to a Harkin," said Mammy. "I sign checks using the Harkin name. I believe that makes me one of yous in people's eyes." She laughed shrilly. "Yes, that's more than sufficient to cover me when the muck starts to fly."

"If I'd known it was going to cause this amount of trouble," said Uncle Brendan, "I'd have stayed away for good. Then, you'd all have been none the wiser."

Auntie Celia's mouth opened for a moment and then closed.

"I know you're upset, Celia. You're my only sister and have every right to be. I'm so sorry to inflict such pain on the family." He turned his head from her as if it were too painful to look at her. "There's no woman involved and I'll stay single for life. The simple truth is I should never have entered the priesthood."

Uncle Brendan paused, then continued, "When I took Holy Orders, I thought I had a vocation, but I was fooling myself. I was trying to please someone else. That was wrong." Uncle rose, walked over to the sideboard, and began to stroke the reddish breast of one of the shiny bird ornaments I'd always liked. He emitted an odd little chuckle as he picked it up and examined it. "Why, Eileen, I remember these pretty birds! I remember Mother and I spent a whole day searching china shop after china shop to find just the right wedding gift. She said I was being too pernickety, because Harry wouldn't look at them more than once, anyway." He chuckled again. "I'll bet she was right, too."

Mammy's eyes showed her confusion, but her tongue activated quickly. "I could see you took care in picking them." Her eyes cut to Auntie Celia. "I'm very fond of my wee budgies. Harry is as well, but you know how men are about such things. Men never pass remarks on an ornament, whether its quality or not."

"Cockatoos," Uncle Brendan said.

"Pardon!" Mammy's eyes crinkled.

"They're cockatoos," said Uncle Brendan.

Mammy gazed at the birds as if seeing them for the first time. "I see . . . very good."

There was an awkward silence, as all eyes focused on the glittering ornament.

"I was just as careful about deciding to leave the priesthood," Uncle said. He set the ornament down carefully. "It's taken me a long time to leave, precisely because I didn't want to disgrace the family. But the truth is, it's been gnawing at me since the second year of my ordination. At first, it was doubt I fought against. I reckoned every priest has doubts at some point, so I just put my shoulder to the wheel and worked harder. But doubt was replaced by the certainty I'd made a grave mistake. I'd gone into the priesthood because I felt guilty about letting everyone down. I'd gone in because Father wished it and I thought it would make everything right between us again."

Auntie Celia sat tight-lipped, eyes still riveted on the glittering cockatoo.

"I didn't have these feelings in the seminary. I don't know why I didn't have them. Maybe I was suppressing the thing . . . or maybe I was in denial. I already knew I'd made a mistake during my last visit to Ireland, but I'd resolved to continue serving and do the right thing. I knew I wasn't the first priest who'd made a huge mistake.

"Celia, believe me when I tell you that I've fought against leaving. I've fought it and fought it every hour of every day, until my mind knew only frustration. And despair. And *still* I had to go on, for the sake of my pupils. I was in despair so deep and shapeless, I'd never known it could exist in the human condition. I honestly don't know how I got out of bed in the morning, or how I made it back to bed at night. I prayed and prayed, until even that failed and God abandoned me completely."

Uncle Brendan fell silent for a moment or two. I couldn't breathe. He'd endured the same pain as me.

"I even thought it'd be better if I just ended—" The corners of Uncle's mouth trembled. "I had the breakdown instead."

The air was viscous as my mother toyed with the collar of her blouse and Auntie Celia stared at Uncle, her mouth agape. I pondered which would have been the bigger disgrace to her. Would it have been his leaving the priesthood, the going out with a darkie girl, or the big unmentionable? None of them probably thought I knew about the last. My heart beat faster as it tried to pump blood that was surely as viscous as the air in the room. The thought of Uncle Brendan far away in his sun-filled mission, rising and praying and pushing away the despair, filled me with a curious mixture of pity and selfish relief. I felt a burst of immeasurable closeness to him and would have crossed to him and put my arm around him, if I'd been brave.

"We have to deal with it," he said, taking a handkerchief from his pocket and wiping his brow. "I've come through a breakdown and I'm *not* going to allow it to happen again. Life for me is outside the priesthood. I know it will be difficult for all of you for a while, but I must move on. I'd like you to accept my decision, or at least stay silent if you don't." He returned to the sofa and stared into the dark hearth.

"Brendan, I knew you had a breakdown, but this other thing . . . I had no idea." Auntie Celia went over to him. "I didn't know you were having thoughts of that nature. Listen, I've been very selfish. You're my little brother. We'll deal with it. We'll work through this." She shook her head at my mother. "I had no idea it was so bad."

"We'll pray and stick together," my mother said.

"You're family and we'll support you, no matter what," Auntie Celia said. "My God, just let anybody dare say a word against you or give you so much as a sidelong glance when I'm around. I'll throttle them. You're a Harkin. We'll get through the scandal. Why, we'll laugh and wonder what all the fuss was about a year hence. By then, people will be busy feasting on some other scandal, please be to Jesus. Aye, this scandal will be dropped by then, like a dog drops an old soup bone for a fresher one."

She placed her hand on top of his, and they looked into each other's eyes, seeming to forget about Mammy and me for an instant. "Are you all right now, Brendan? You're not having dark thoughts anymore, are you?"

Uncle shook his head slowly.

Mammy asked if he had any plans for the future and Uncle said he wanted to do a social work course in America. Neither Auntie Celia nor she knew anything about social work and listened intently as he explained it in detail. After he finished, Auntie Celia looked at the clock and suggested she and Uncle Brendan start doing the rounds to inform the rest of the family, as everyone would now be home from work. Twice, my mother offered to accompany them while they debated their itinerary. There was no response until my aunt muttered it wasn't necessary, at which point Mammy insisted on going. Auntie Celia and Uncle Brendan went out to the car and my mother whipped on her coat.

"Get your father to take Caroline to the Chinese restaurant when they get home," she said, opening her purse.

"Might it be best for Uncle Brendan and Auntie Celia to go alone?" I said. "They'll be better able to talk as brother and sister in the car without you."

"They *don't* want to be alone." She ceased rummaging in her purse for a moment. "You heard her ask for my support."

"Only to tell the neighbors. Now, it's only family."

"Don't be ridiculous. And don't say a word about this to your father. Not one word until I get back, so he can be informed properly."

Auntie Celia's car revved up, prompting Mammy to root furiously in her purse and complain about my aunt's lack of consideration. Finally, panicked by the sound of the reversing car, she thrust the purse in my hand and raced out the door.

They returned after nine o'clock. Caroline, James, and I ceased studying and ran from our bedrooms to the living room, where Father was watching TV. My mother peered at him and then at me, trying to determine whether I'd said anything. Father and Uncle Brendan hugged and then Uncle asked if he'd heard the news. Mammy's face softened at the sight of Father's blank look and she commenced telling the story, though an abbreviated version this time.

Uncle finished where she left off, and when it was done, my mother asked, "Aren't you going to say something, Harry?"

"It's not as if it's the end of the world." Father looked at Uncle Brendan. "Whatever makes you happy is all that matters. If you weren't happy, then you did the right thing." He studied the TV screen for a moment before turning back to him. "You have to do what's right for yourself, and to hell with what the neighbors say."

"It'll be hard, because of all the gloating our neighbors will do," said Auntie Celia.

"The neighbors be damned," said Father.

Auntie Celia solicited Father's opinion on the best way to break the news to Granny Harkin, but Uncle Brendan insisted he tell her on his own.

"Granny will take it well, Uncle Brendan," I said. "I know."

He smiled and pressed his hand gently on my shoulder. The subject was dropped as Father chatted to Uncle Brendan about his business. He launched into the usual litany about how useless his workers were, and how some of them wanted to work and collect the dole on the sly at the same time.

Before Uncle left, Father took him outside to see a large shed he'd built to store his equipment in, as well as the gleaming new track excavator he'd purchased. It was my first time to see it, too. James, anxious to show off, climbed into the cab, started it, and moved the boom about until Father told him to stop. I hung by the big doors and watched, observing by their easy manner that the two brothers had a great deal of love for one another, although Father's was disguised by machismo.

"I can't stop that one from driving my machinery," Father said. He jingled coins in his pockets. "James is a character."

Uncle Brendan turned to me. "Can you operate it?"

"He's just like you, Brendan," said Father. "Gabriel's better at the books and has no time for diggers."

"It takes all types to run a world, Harry."

We watched the taillights of Auntie Celia's car streak out the gate.

"Poor Brendan, this is going to be such a hard cross for him to bear," Mammy said after we went into the living room.

Father sat and picked up the newspaper.

"Let's talk no more about it. Sure there's not much scandal in that nowadays, with the way the world's turning."

"Tell *that* to Celia. She squawked like a half-shot crow this afternoon and said he should never have entered the priesthood to begin with." Mammy paused to await Father's response, but he offered none. "Did he talk much about being a priest when he was Gabriel's age?"

"I don't remember."

"It was your father's pushing," she said, clearly displeased by his unwillingness to be drawn into conversation. "Pushing never works. It's either in them to be priests, or it's not."

"Quit your talking."

"Your father pushed and now the cock's come home to roost. He should have accepted that Brendan wasn't meant to be a priest. Brendan started associating with that girl and *that* was a sign for your father to stop pushing him." Mammy looked about fleetingly, taking in what we were each doing: Caroline and James had settled down to watch the news and Nuala and I were setting up the checkers board. She must have suspected I was listening, because her eyes returned quickly to me and caught me watching her.

"I'm glad you told Auntie Celia to forget the past," I said. "It was disgraceful, making such a big deal about the fact Uncle Brendan disgraced her and the others just because he had a fling before he went to the priesthood."

"Your auntie was raving herself to distraction," said my mother. "It was the shock talking. I thought she'd been far too quiet on the journey down from the airport."

"She overreacted," I said, "just like Granda overreacted, right?"

"Don't speak ill of the dead, Gabriel."

"I think Granda was very uncharitable. He got what he wanted in the end."

"Your granda saw it as a threat. The woman was pretty, with big, sparkly eyes and a smile to match. Always clad in the latest fashion."

"You told me once that you never met her."

Mammy's face reddened. "Once or twice, but not for long."

Father glanced up from the newspaper.

"Was she from around here?" Caroline asked, and she moved closer to Nuala and me.

"No."

"Do you think Uncle Brendan regrets letting her go?" she asked.

"That's your uncle's business and not our concern."

"Things don't add up," I said. "Granda's deep bitterness makes no sense. I told you that before."

"You've been told already that your Granda was pig-stubborn. Isn't that right, Harry? Look, tomorrow's a school day, so off yous go to bed. It's been a long afternoon and I need a bit of peace. Besides, you should be studying instead of trying to play Sherlock Holmes. It doesn't take much detective work to investigate the shambles you made of your mock exams."

The cut silenced me.

"Nuala, you go to bed," Mammy said. "The rest of yous to your rooms and study, now."

As I sat at my desk, I knew Mammy was raking up Uncle Brendan's past with Father. It proved too great a temptation. I sneaked down the hall and stood by the living room door. Indeed, Father was talking, but the TV volume was turned up. I couldn't hear a thing. I put my palms on the door and pressed my ear closer. Suddenly, it burst open and I spilled inside.

"What the hell do you think you're doing?" my mother said. "Are you snooping? That's the only thing you're good at these days, in addition to failing exams."

I gawked idiotically at her as Caroline's door opened in the background.

Mammy turned her head to look at Caroline. "Take a good look at your sneaky brother. He's nothing but a good-for-nothing snoop." She looked back at me. "Go to your room this bloody instant and get that nosy beak of yours into a textbook. Don't let me see it again until you're at the breakfast table."

Twenty-Five

The scandal washed into every Knockburn home and surrounding Catholic town. My mother reported daily how she noticed people whispering as they came out of shops, or while they stood in line for confession and behind graveyard headstones, how they became silent or suddenly began talking about the weather as she passed by.

Auntie Celia said her shop sales were up, though only for ices, fruit, and vegetables. Farmers' wives who'd always gossiped behind her back that her china selection was limited and daylight robbery had the gall to come in now under the pretext of shopping for wedding gifts. When they finished asking their pointedly indirect questions and saw they were to get no information, all but the most brazen felt obliged to buy a carrot or a couple of pears in order to save face.

"You're fine about what Uncle Brendan's done, aren't you?" I asked Granny Harkin during a visit not long after Uncle Brendan's return. He'd gone to visit an old school friend.

In response, Granny placed a large slice of warm, home-baked rhubarb tart on a plate and set it before me.

"I'm full, Granny, but thanks."

Her rhubarb tarts had become a long-standing grievance between us. I'd once forgotten myself in her presence at a wake and accepted a slice of her neighbor's rhubarb tart. It hadn't mitigated matters when I informed her the offending slice contained much more strawberry than rhubarb, or that I'd taken just two small bites and set it aside as soon as she reminded me I detested rhubarb.

"Brendan must do with it whatever God intended," Granny continued. "If that means social work, he's got my blessing."

"You're educated, Gabriel," said Uncle John. He wiped crumbs off his lips with his gnarled fingers. "I can't make heads or tails of what Brendan says about this social work business and I didn't want to appear ignorant probing him about it. He says it's some kinda counseling. He says people get counseled when they have mental problems, or lose limbs in an accident, or when they have problems of . . . well, you know, of an intimate nature." He paused. "Jimmy Kelly didn't get counseling when he had his arm yanked off by the combine harvester last year. He got nothing from the government."

Granny, who had the pie dish in her hand and was about to rise, set it down on the table again. "Exactly what is social work, Gabriel? More to the point, will he be able to make a living at it?"

"It's done more in the big cities." I didn't wish to appear ignorant about the subject, either. "There's lots of counseling in Belfast and people do make a living at it."

"What's the world coming to?" asked Granny. "City people always were peculiar. Imagine running around airing problems of an intimate nature to strangers. If things like that need airing, they should be aired behind a closed bedroom door." She shook her head like a sage. "Did anybody's limb ever grow back as a result of this counseling, is the question I want answered?"

"He'll have to stay in America after he's finished his schooling if he wants to make a living at it," said Uncle John. He slapped his tummy twice. "Only the Yanks would pay good money for a stranger's advice."

Uncle Brendan and I were standing in the meadow beneath a solitary beech tree near the grave of Granda's old carthorse. He'd asked me to join him for a walk because he was leaving soon for America to speak to university contacts and other people about courses and places to live.

"I hope you're not disappointed in me, Gabriel." It was the first time he'd spoken to me directly about his leaving the priesthood.

"It's your life."

"You're fine with my decision, then?"

"I think Auntie Celia was out of order when she said Granda would be spinning in his grave."

"If you're thinking even slightly about the religious life, I trust I haven't put you off."

"That was a long time ago."

"A long time ago?" He laughed softly. "Next, you'll be telling me you're very old. I remember you telling Father McAtamney once you were going to be a hairdresser *and* a priest. It seems like it was only yesterday." He fell silent. "Of course, you wouldn't remember that."

"I remember. I've always had a good memory. Sometimes, I wish I didn't." I placed my foot on the mound of fieldstones I'd erected years ago as a marker for the old horse's grave. "Many things have happened since then to change my mind about the religious life."

"What sort of things?"

"Girls, for a start."

That sounded false. It was false. A heavy pressure built inside my head and a tear popped from the corner of my right eye and began to trickle. I could feel it trace down my cheek and wheeled around quickly to look in the direction of a cluster of old farm buildings in the distance.

"What's the matter?" he asked.

I focused on the sagging roof of the barn as I willed myself into control. "Nothing . . . nothing's the—"

"Are you thinking about your granda?"

"I want so much to be involved with a girl and get married and have children someday." I turned back to Uncle Brendan. "I want that so much."

He appeared surprised. "There isn't anything to prevent you."

"Don't you want to marry and be a father one day, now that you've left the priesthood?"

Uncle stared at the grave for a long moment. His Adam's apple rose and fell as he swallowed. "I'm sure it must be wonderful to bring up a child." His voice wavered. "I'm sure there's nothing more wonderful than to watch part of your flesh and blood grow up to become successes."

He walked up to the stone wall behind the tree, laid his hands on its top, and stared beyond to a twenty-foot-wide band of tall firs marching like soldiers up the side of the hill. "I was about eight years old when the forestry commission planted those trees yonder. They were so small and delicate, and your father and I used to jump over them. Now, they're almost full-grown. I never got to see their in-between stages." He peered at me. "Were they beautiful in their in-between stage, Gabriel?"

"All the times I've come here, I've never given those trees a second thought. They've just always been." I walked up to him and observed them, too.

"It's true," he said. "We take everything for granted. We don't notice changes in things because we see them every day." Uncle laughed, then looked sidelong at me. "I bet it's the same with your school things, too. You probably haven't even noticed how much you've learned since you first started Saint Malachy's, because you've been doing it incrementally every day."

"Uncle Brendan, may I . . . ? I'd like to ask you something."

"Sure."

"Did Father Cornelius teach you when you were at Saint Malachy's?"

"Isn't he the vice-head?"

"Yes."

"Is he one of the strict priests?" Uncle chuckled.

"He taught me English for a while." My mouth quivered. The pressure in my head returned. I let out a long gasp and then became a mass of heaves and sobs.

"Son, what's wrong?"

He draped his arms around my shoulders and drew me to him. My forehead touched his solid chest and it felt wonderful. He stroked my crown until the hacked sobs softened and died. His heart beat fast. Another burst of sobs threatened and I steeled myself into a semblance of control and withdrew from him. His gaze remained fixed on me as I hung my head and sniffed myself back to composure.

"It's better to get a problem off your chest. Believe me, I know all about things like that."

"If I tell, will you promise not to say a word to anyone?"

He remained silent as he considered the request. "It depends on what it is."

"I must have your word, or I can't tell."

"You can trust me to do the right thing, Gabriel." He patted the top of the wall. "Tell me."

I hoisted myself on the wall, feeling the corky dryness of the lichen underneath my moist palms. The stones were warm from the afternoon sun. Heat radiated into the seat of my jeans as I told him about Father Cornelius and how I was too sensitive and how the priest had detected this and somehow knew he could do wicked things to me. Throughout, he made no attempt to interrupt me. I suppose years of teaching taught him not to do that, but his face was pale by the time I reached the end.

"Don't you believe me?" I said. My one overwhelming concern was that he wouldn't, because this was a priest and a teacher I'd just told him about.

"Of course, I believe you," Uncle Brendan said. "I'm amazed you haven't told your parents. They could have done something."

"Mammy believes priests can't do any wrong. She can't even watch a man and woman kissing on TV. She changes the channels. And Daddy would never understand a man doing things to another man, much less a priest." I shook my head. "When I was younger, he couldn't understand why I allowed boys to bully me. So how could he deal with this?"

"They would understand because this is a serious matter. I know Knockburn's a small place and people live very sheltered lives here, but what happened to you is abuse, Gabriel. Your parents would understand that."

"What if . . . if I'm homosexual?"

Uncle fell into a reverie as he looked away to the marching firs. Finally, he looked back at me. "What makes you think so?"

I couldn't bring myself to tell him about Connor. That was real. That had happened.

"I . . . I think about men a lot."

He didn't speak for a long moment. "Do you think about girls, too?"

"A bit. Not much."

A bird trilled in the silence. A cold sweat broke out over my body. Sweat dripped from my underarms.

"I'm frightened, Uncle Brendan."

He laid his arm on my shoulders and gently squeezed the back of my neck. "You might be homosexual, or it might be a phase you're going through."

"Do you think so?"

"Sure."

"Which?"

Uncle cleared his throat. "There are many types of people in the world, Gabriel. Some people are smart. Some not. Some people are handsome. Some not. Some people are naturally fat. Some not. Some people are heterosexual. Some are homosexual." He shrugged. "Regardless of how we are, we're all God's children and He loves us."

I bit the inside of my lower lip hard. "Have you ever felt this way?"

His eyes narrowed for a moment. "God will still love you even if you are."

"I can still be a good Catholic?"

He laughed softly. "I consider myself a good Catholic and I left the priesthood."

"It's a phase, Uncle Brendan. Let's forget we talked about this."

"We have to tell your parents."

I leaped off the wall. "I don't want them knowing about this. No way. They'd—"

"I mean about Father Cornelius."

"I don't want them told about that, either."

Uncle Brendan came to me. "He abused you sexually."

"No . . . no. I know my father better than you know him. And you promised me."

"I promised to do the right thing and telling them is the right thing."

"Then treat me like an adult," I said. "Treat me the same way you did when you told me you'd left the priesthood."

Uncle's head jerked back slightly. "This involves great wrong-doing on Father Cornelius's part."

"I need it to go no farther. I didn't even plan to tell you. It just came out. But now it's out, I'm feeling better. There's no need to do anything more."

"I know this is painful for you, but he must be stopped."

"I expect you to understand how I feel because you know about pain."

His head jerked back again like I'd punched him in the face.

"I'm sorry," I said quickly. "I didn't mean to say it like that."

He sighed as he placed his hand on my shoulder. "I'll agree, on one condition. You must consent to my speaking to Father Cornelius."

"No, Uncle. No, please."

"You have to trust me. I'll respect your wishes, but you must agree to this. You can be sure he's abusing other boys and it needs to stop. Father Cornelius is very sick and needs treatment."

I was in the biology laboratory when the school secretary came in and informed my teacher that I had to report to Father Cornelius's room. The door was open when I got there and the priest was seated at his desk, white-faced and white-knuckled. Uncle Brendan stood over him.

"Gabriel, Father Cornelius has something important to say to you."

He waited until I drew up beside them before nodding gravely at the priest. My furiously beating heart echoed in my ears.

"Please accept my apologies for what I have done," Father Cornelius said. "I've acted disgracefully. I'm sorry for the pain I've caused. May God forgive me for this terrible act." Lowering his head, he stared at the top of his desk. "Will you accept my apology and forgive me for my weakness?"

"You're *sick*, Father Cornelius," Uncle Brendan said. "We've discussed this and you've recognized you are ill. Doing this to young boys is an illness and *must* be acknowledged."

"I'm ill."

"Do you accept this man's apology, Gabriel?"

"Yes."

"Father Cornelius has agreed to resign his position here at the end of the year. He'll then travel to England, where he'll seek treatment for his illness. I don't believe they'd understand the nature of this condition in Ireland, so it's for the best he travels across the water and remains there for a while. Not another word shall pass our lips about what transpired here today. Not a soul shall be any the wiser and Father's otherwise exemplary teaching record will not be tarnished."

Father Cornelius raised his head slightly.

"When his treatment is over," Uncle Brendan continued, "he'll come back to Ireland, if he so desires, and that'll be the end of the affair."

"Thank you, Brendan."

"It's Gabriel, you thank."

Now that I'd told someone about what had happened and there'd been a resolution, I felt much better. I discovered that I'd also lost the hate I had for Father Cornelius.

A few weeks later, Uncle Brendan left for America and I began studying in earnest. The number of things to review was endless: novels had to be reread, quotes learned from poems and plays, German and French vocabulary expanded (Latin and Irish I gave up on, figuring they were dead languages, anyway), and the Books of Genesis and Luke reviewed for religious education. Subjects like mathematics and the sciences couldn't be crammed, so I left those to luck and my mother's novenas. A pass in math was mandatory. It was one of four core subjects that had to be passed, failure in any one translating to automatic rejection by all universities and relegation to the inferior polytechnics.

A warm, sunny third day of June heralded examination month. Throughout the three weeks and two days of examinations, I surprised myself, raising my hand often to request extra writing paper in a number of subjects. I felt extremely confident after it was all over. Only in Latin, Irish, one part of a physics paper (calculation of velocities), and two chemistry questions (inorganic and one reaction equation) had I had nothing to contribute.

Twenty-Six

D ressed in a faded T-shirt and old jeans with a gaping hole in the right knee, I joined Father's workforce at six-thirty one morning. I sat in the back of his transport van, its musty stench of oil reminding me of his lorry cab on the trip to the Larne harbor many years ago. On the way into Duncarlow to fetch Martin, we stopped to pick up Father's workers. When we arrived in the town, my cousin was already waiting outside Auntie Celia's shop, a bright orange lunchbox tucked under his arm.

"Does gentleman Jim think he'll be working in the site manager's office?" Father asked.

Martin was dressed in a pair of gorgeous, immaculately pressed parallels with one-inch cuffs, a matching college sweater with narrow, twin maroon bands on each arm, and wedge-heeled shoes just like the Bay City Rollers wore on "Top of the Pops."

"Aye, that'll be management, Harry," said Dessie, one of Father's longest-serving excavator drivers.

The other men sniggered. As there wasn't much room in the van, Martin had to squeeze beside two hefty, dozing laborers. One of them grunted irritably when Martin trod on his foot.

"Didn't Gabriel tell you to wear your old clothes?" Father asked, stretching his head back to hear Martin's response as we sped along the main road.

"These are my old clothes, Uncle Harry."

"Dessie, it must be great to live in a town," said Father. "You never have clothes with holes because you never get a chance to wear them out."

"One half of the world doesn't know what the other's up to," said Dessie.

Martin and I exchanged confirmatory glances that these men were beneath us and of no consequence.

When we arrived at the factory site, as Father had previously pointed out, we were given no special treatment. Our duties consisted of raking and gathering fieldstone in the long expanses of raw earth that they were transforming into lawns running along the factory building. Father sent Martin to work with a crew at one end of the factory, me to the other.

A sour stink wafted up from the soil and grew increasingly unbearable as the sun grew warmer. Flies buzzed about my face and sweat trickled into the corners of my eyes and stung. My lower back ached. I kept checking my watch, but its hands never seemed to advance. After what seemed like an entire day of work, the first break—a mere fifteen minutes—came around, and I left my position to locate Martin. I found him cranky, but managed to get him in a better mood before the break ended.

But at lunchtime, his arms and short legs barreled down the site toward me.

"You said this would be an easy job," he said. "Your father's working me to death." His face and neck were redder than Vesuvius in eruption.

"It is a bit tough, isn't it?"

He ranted as we walked down the road toward the only tree providing any shade in the entire site. Martin didn't even lower his voice when other workers passed by. My blood heated up. We sat underneath the tree, where Martin whipped the lid off his lunchbox and tossed it on the grass. He took out a sandwich, cut daintily into a triangle and with its crust removed, as if he were on a picnic. After a bite, he put the sandwich down and savagely thrust his curled fingers in front of my face.

"Look at my nails," he said. "They're *black*. My hands are blistered. Look at my sandwich. It's black! And I'm sunburned."

"The sun is strong. Pity you didn't bring some lemon juice for your hair."

That shut him up for a long moment.

"This is just plain ridiculous," he said. "My body's not designed to endure this torture. It's not worth twenty-five pounds a week. It's not even worth a hundred."

In all honesty, I was seething at Father, too, and Martin's words only made me angrier. "It's not my fault. I just didn't understand how lawns get made. I didn't realize stones and rocks had to be gathered, or that the damned soil is leveled by hand."

"Why hasn't he got machines to do it? If Uncle Harry's making so much money, why hasn't he got machines to perform the slave work?" Martin shook his head. "I can't be expected to do this the entire summer. It's not on. You must tell him I want to do something else."

"You're acting like an old woman. It's only for six weeks and we'll have lots of money for the holiday."

"There won't be a holiday if this slavery continues, because I'll be in the hospital."

We fell into a broody silence, during which I ate and watched three shirtless men erect guttering on the factory roof. I tried to avoid looking at them, even turned my head away a few times. It didn't work. No matter how hard I tried, I kept taking furtive peeks. I was pleased when they finally left—but disappointed, too.

"I didn't mean that, Martin," I said. "I'm sorry."

"You should be."

Another flash of temper charged from my brain, demanding articulation, but I managed to keep my tongue in check. Martin could be just as sharp as his mother on occasions and, also like her, didn't mean it. He dusted his trousers and scraped acrid clumps of reddish-brown soil off his shoes with a twig, which I found hilariously idiotic. He was going back to do more filthy work.

"I really am, Martin."

"Accepted." He wiped his sweaty bangs and swatted at a fly, but missed. "I am, as well. I realize it's not your fault."

All too soon, the lunch break was over. I went back to my area and didn't see him again for the rest of the afternoon. Later, in the van on the way home, Father asked my cousin how he'd enjoyed his first day doing real work as he winked conspiratorially at Dessie.

"I'm sure I know every kind of rock and stone that's to be found in Ireland, Uncle Harry."

Father and Dessie roared like idiots. Martin's lips tightened.

Next morning, Auntie Celia stood alone on the street outside her shop.

"Harry, he's resigned," she said. "What did you do to him?" She giggled, then thought better and killed it. "He told me last night he wasn't going back to work, but I didn't ring you because I thought he was tired and would change his mind. This morning, he was grafted to the bed. I couldn't get him to budge."

"That's quite all right, Celia," Father said.

Auntie Celia stuck her head halfway inside the side window and smiled at me. "Gabriel's hardier. Martin says it's his allergies." She withdrew her head. "Between you and me, Harry, I think he doesn't want to admit the work's too much for him." She smiled. "Would you take Connor in his place? That chap's breaking his father's and my hearts."

"What's he done?" Father asked.

"He's hanging out with the wrong sort and won't listen to us." Auntie looked up and down the street, and then put her head closer to the car window. "Somebody told me they saw him with chaps who're suspected of being in the IRA," she said, her voice lowered. "They broke the windows of the Orange Hall with stones."

"Can't blame them for that," said Father. "The bastards can use their sashes to plug the window holes."

Auntie Celia's eyes widened. "Jesus, the police could catch him. He'll be accused of being in the IRA and jailed."

"Young fellas like Connor get up to a bit of mischief," said Father. "He won't get into real trouble."

"Harry, that's easy for you to say. Gabriel doesn't gallivant with the wrong sort."

Father's face was inscrutable as he regarded me and then looked back at Auntie Celia. "I must be going. Lost time is lost money. If I need Connor, I'll let you know."

My luck changed two weeks later. Father began a road repair project on the outskirts of Castlebenem, a pretty Protestant village in the heart of rolling countryside, and I was sent there to labor. Castlebenem was also horse country. Girls and boys my age, smartly dressed in jodhpurs and white shirts, rode by with poker-straight backs and upturned chins.

It didn't trouble Father's workers that these people looked down on us. They didn't know any better. But it irked me something fierce. I didn't want to be seen in that light, so I made a point of trying to befriend one girl who usually smiled as she rode by. Of medium build, she had straw-yellow hair like ABBA's Agnetha, but she wasn't as good-looking. Her hair framed an oval, country-red face. Her feet looked mannishly large in the stirrups, too.

Indeed, when Father's workers first saw her approach, the girl garnered much admiration and wolf-whistles, until she drew closer, whereupon they picked up their shovels and began working again.

The next morning as she approached, I braced myself to speak. "That's a lovely horse you're riding."

The horse's chestnut thighs came to a halt.

"Pardon?"

"That's a lovely horse. What's its name?"

"Stroller."

The horse's velvety flanks quivered for no reason other than its progress had been impeded.

"Isn't that the name of a famous show jumper? I've seen him jumping on TV shows."

"I named mine after him." The girl's eyes narrowed for a moment, undoubtedly because she was surprised a laborer would know anything about show jumping. "I'm Fiona McFarland. Who are you?" After introducing myself, she stood on her stirrups and swept her eyes over the gawking workers. "This seems like awfully hard work."

Her accent was English, like that of a BBC announcer, and she didn't look so plain to me anymore. At the same time, I wondered if there is an unwritten rule that horsy girls resemble their horses, in the same way many dog owners resemble their dogs.

The beast's flanks stopped quivering and he chaffed at the bit and snorted. I was sure he sensed my nervousness. When he began to reverse, she yanked the reins.

"I'm only doing this work for the summer," I said, and upped the ante. "I'm still at school. My father has the contract to do this job."

The horse continued reversing. While I took several discreet steps farther into the ditch in case it lunged forward, I considered if I should repeat what I'd said in case she hadn't heard.

"He's a trifle frisky this morning," she said, in reference to the horse. "I'm a student, too."

"Where?"

"Granderson College."

Granderson was a prestigious coeducational Protestant school about four miles from mine. The Saint Malachy's junior and senior rugby teams played there, but because we specialized in Gaelic football and rugby was a Protestant game, they were superior and always thrashed us soundly.

"You sound English."

"I went to boarding school in England for a time. But I beseeched Mummy to persuade Father to let me come back home. Last year, he relented."

Only filthy rich Protestants attended boarding schools in England.

"Are you boarding at Granderson?"

"Not for much longer. I hate it. I can't ride every day." She looked over her left shoulder as someone started up the steamroller. "I've told Mummy I'll take A levels there, but only if they agree to my commuting daily." She laughed, and the rich tinkle was instantly absorbed by the screech of the great rollers crushing and flattening the road's surface. "I've had enough of cold dorms and bossy monitors."

I laughed to indicate agreement, wondering at the same time why the hell I was, as I knew nothing about cold dorms and monitors. "So, you're starting A levels next term, too?"

"No, I'm sitting O levels this coming year, but you've got to work on parents a few years in advance, don't you think?" She glanced over her shoulder again.

Out of the corner of my eye, I saw Father approaching. I stepped from the ditch with alacrity, thrust my shovel into a pile of gravel, and began spreading it about. Fiona kicked the horse gently in its sides and started away.

"I see the boss is coming," she said, not looking back. "Cheerio for now."

"Talking to a horsy lady, eh?" Father asked. He watched as the horse broke into a canter.

"What of it?"

"Who's her people?"

"McFarland."

"Jasus, you go straight for the top drawer. The McFarlands are big people 'round here. Her father owns every blade of grass you set your eyes on hereabouts." He laughed. "Well, get back to your work. Lost time is lost money."

I loathed the way Father referred to rich people as "big." Knockburn people were always referring to wealthy people as "big" people; in so doing, they subconsciously categorized themselves as little people.

From that morning, if Father was not in the area or was at another job site, Fiona stopped when she rode by and we'd chat snatches at a time. Father asked Connor to help out for two days, as one of his laborers was ill, and I even introduced him to Fiona on the first day.

"She's dead ugly, Gabriel," he said, after she rode away. "The horse is a beauty, though."

"Fuck off," I said.

The day was hot and sunny and our arms and necks glistened with sweat as we smoothed the roadbed in preparation for tarring. During the lunch break, Connor went down to a narrow river surrounded by tall gorse. Five minutes later, he called out that I should join him. I found him scooping water and splashing it over his face and bare chest. His dark pink nipples were stiff from the cold water. Off in the mid-distance, Father's workers talked and guffawed as they ate their lunch.

Sitting beside Connor on the smooth rock, I took off my T-shirt and splashed water over my torso.

Without warning, Connor reached over and momentarily squeezed my crotch.

"Hot weather makes me so fucking randy," he said, touching his own crotch. He touched me briefly again and chuckled. "You as well, eh?"

My entire body tingled with excitement.

"Come on, Gabriel." His voice was husky. "Let's fool around like we used to do."

Connor was a fake. He still had the same desires. Just as I was about to comply, I thought about him rejecting me that night and about Fiona.

"We mustn't do this," I said, rising but still not really wanting to leave.

"For fuck's sake, it's just a bit of fun. You're feeling as randy as me. What's the harm?"

"We ended that caper." I hopped off the rock and started back to the worksite. He caught up with me as I reached the fence.

"Are you suggesting I'm a homo?" he asked.

I shook my head.

"I'm no fucking homo. Understood?"

"We're both not homos," I said.

He didn't return to work the next day.

Road repairs progressed quickly due to the long stretch of excellent weather. By the beginning of the fourth week of July, the crew had moved three miles outside the village. Late one Tuesday morning, Father arrived in a great hurry from his factory site and informed me that he was running late and had to take our foreman to a meeting with the Department of the Environment in Belfast.

"I want you to keep an eye on the men," he said. "If you see them skiving, don't be afraid to tell them to get back to work." He winked to reinforce we were bound in a secret conspiracy. "You're the boss's son, so keep 'em hard at it. Lost time is lost money."

I didn't want to be in charge. As it was, the men were already suspicious of me because of who I was. Often, conversation stopped abruptly if I came into the vicinity, and the recently employed or more nervous workers would scatter like town pigeons. I needn't have worried, though, as all that was required to keep the spades and picks busy were periodic walks about the construction site. But I was very self-conscious about doing so and always pretended I was looking for something.

By four-thirty, Father still hadn't returned. Already two of his laziest workers were consulting their watches, traces of fret already on their grimy faces. I wasn't worried. He always got back from meetings before knocking-off time.

At five o'clock, as I was about to make one final patrol, a girl called out my name. Fiona waved as she cantered across the field and entered a paddock containing red and white horse jumps. I watched her for several minutes and then scrambled down the low bank, climbed over the barbed-wire fence, and ran up to her.

I drew up to Stroller and patted his sweaty neck. "I didn't know you practiced around here."

"This is our home farm," she said. "Our house is over there." Following the direction of her extended arm, I saw the red-brick chimneys and slate roof of a house rising above a copse of trees in the near distance. "I'm practicing for a gymkhana outside Londonderry next week."

Even though she was Protestant and I knew Protestants said "Londonderry" instead of "Derry," it riled me. I avoided asking where exactly the show-jumping event was taking place because I'd have to say "Derry" and she might get annoyed at me for the opposite reason.

"Could I have a go on the horse?" I said.

"Your father must be away." She grinned as she dismounted.

"There's only half an hour of work time left and I've always wanted to try riding him."

Fiona took off her riding hat and placed it on my head. It fit perfectly. For the first time, I realized we were exactly the same height and, now we were eye to eye, I also noticed her nose was a fraction off-center and her irises were far more green than blue.

"You've got an audience," she said.

Five of father's employees leaned on shovels by the roadside watching us.

"Give her a good, hard riding," one of them shouted.

The others laughed coarsely.

"The amazing thing about double entendre is these people think it's only they who get it," she said. "What shallow lives those men lead."

I sniffed. "Very shallow."

After struggling in a most undignified fashion into the saddle, I adjusted the riding hat and peered down at her. It was surprising how high I was, and more than a bit frightening. Fiona took the slack of the reins and led me around the paddock.

"Could I try on my own?" I asked after a bit.

"Well, okay—just grip the reins and dig your heels into his sides gently. He'll start walking."

It was a treat, one of those occasions where I felt like a god. I was in supreme control, though admittedly my feet wouldn't stay in the stirrups. The combination of the creaking saddle, the horse's docile power, and the coarse, oily touch of its mane was exhilarating. After five minutes, I tried a canter, but my buttocks slammed into the saddle until Fiona showed me how to move in rhythm with the horse's pace. Every time I thought I'd finally mastered it, I'd suddenly forget the rhythm and be back to arse-slamming.

"You catch on quickly," she said, after I finally succeeded.

"I want to try one jump."

"That's not such a good idea, Gabriel. It requires a lot of skill. The next step is usually to try galloping."

"Just one jump."

"I don't know."

"A really wee one."

She walked up to a jump and regarded it for a moment. She removed two crossbars so that it stood only eighteen inches high and looked at it again.

"What exactly must I do?"

"Just canter toward it and the horse will know. Remember, your buttocks will rise up off the saddle as you go into the jump."

After lining up the horse, I sized up the jump and then smacked my heels into his rubbery sides a few times until he broke into a canter. On the approach, I imagined I was in a major competition and the jump was four-feet high. Because I knew the men were watching, my body tingled with pride. It didn't matter that the horse was definitely in charge. I clutched the reins and watched the clumps of chocolate mane rising and falling on his bobbing neck. The horse began to ascend; I saw white cotton clouds; my arse rose up off the saddle. And then all became tangled confusion. My foot slipped out of one stirrup, my torso swayed backward and then listed to the side, and I began to fall. Somehow, I cleared the jump with one foot fully in its stirrup. I slid some more, finally hit the ground, and was dragged across the grass.

The horse stopped abruptly. Looking toward the beast's front, I saw Fiona had grabbed the reins. I set about freeing myself with as much dignity as I could muster.

"Are you all right?" she asked.

Father shouted from the roadside. Like an idiot, I jumped up and started brushing grass stains off my dirty jeans.

"Not a scratch."

"I really shouldn't have let you jump. You're very persuasive. I was awfully silly."

"Don't think anything of it. It's me who's foolish trying to be Eddie Macken on my first try."

"*Come here*," Father called.

"I was left in charge of his men." I started away quickly. "Thanks for everything. I'll see you again."

Father's fury gave strength to my legs and I sprinted out of the paddock and across the field.

"This is what you do when my back is turned?" he said. "Get into that bloody van."

"Aye, you'll not be representing Ireland any time soon wey a performance like that," one of the men said. "What do you say, Harry?"

Father didn't reply. I was getting the silent treatment.

As I sat at the dinner table that night, Father said to my mother, "What do you think I caught him doing this afternoon?"

Nuala was already seated and Mammy was setting down a lamb casserole.

"I go off to Belfast and leave him in charge, only to come back and catch him on top of a bloody horse." He regarded me murderously. "Aye, we're making money when he's acting the gentleman and all my workmen are leaning on shovels watching him."

"Don't be so dramatic," I said. "It was almost quitting time."

My mother's face remained impassive for a moment longer, and then she laughed.

"What the hell are you laughing at?" Father pulled a chair out roughly and sat. "He's fucking useless."

"I'm not useless and you're overreacting. I've been doing a damned good job. All *you* want me to do is watch over the men and snitch on them when they're not working. That's no job and I'm not a bloody snitch."

His eyes widened simultaneously with his mouth. "I'll take James to work instead. I'll ask him when he comes home from football practice. That's exactly what I'll do. *He's* sensible."

"Harry!" Mammy said. "He made a mistake."

"Why don't you take James? You've always made it clear you prefer him, anyway. You've always treated us differently." I leaped off my chair, jabbing my index finger at him. "I've never been good enough in your eyes."

"That's enough of your backchat," Mammy said. "Don't talk back to your father."

"I'm *not* talking back to him. I'm telling him how things are. It needs to change. Uncle Brendan understands me far better and he was in Kenya when I was growing up. He listened and knew what to do when I needed help."

As soon as the words were out, I knew I'd gone too far. My mother's gape confirmed it. The momentary silence filled with enough energy to light up every home in Knockburn.

"What are you talking about?" she asked.

Father's chair squealed, and he lunged at me. "Don't you fucking well talk to me like that. Who do you fucking well take me for?"

I dodged his grasp and ran around the table He gave chase. It was surreal. Caroline watched from the sink, her hands covered in soapy bubbles. Nuala grasped a gold crucifix around her neck that I'd bought for her at a church mission. The chain had turned a dull orange within two weeks of its purchase and Mammy said it was made of cheap tin, but Nuala never took it off. I dashed toward the door and somehow Father's foot connected with my arse before I reached it. It didn't hurt and I didn't stop.

"Clear off to America and let him feed you, if that's how you feel," he called after me.

I hung about the yard muttering curses as I kicked stones and invented ways to make him pay. After I'd calmed down, I sat on the trunk of the curved climbing tree. It was now dying. Diesel oil from his machinery had seeped into the soil and poisoned its roots.

Half an hour later, Caroline came out. "He's calmed down, but the things you said in there were a bit strong. He makes no difference between James and you."

"How'd you know?"

"Oh, stop."

"To hell with him."

"Mammy told him you're anxious because the exam results will soon be out." She paused. "That's it, isn't it?" She laid her hand fleetingly on my shoulder.

"I don't know what it is, Caroline. I'm just so angry at him all the time."

"Don't. He says you're to come in."

When I went in, Father said I wasn't fired and the matter was over, as far as he was concerned. He didn't speak to me for the remainder of the evening, though, which meant he was still disappointed in what I'd done. Mammy kept biting her lower lip and sighing every so often, stuff she did when she was excessively tense. I caught her looking under her eyes at me a few times, too.

Next morning, I got up, but never felt less like going to work. At the breakfast table, Father was back to his old self. He told me the jobs I had to do on the site that day, even joked I should stay away from the horses. It was as if nothing had happened. I still harbored a grudge, but I had to admit his attitude was a quality I admired. Father never allowed anything to fester; he forgot unpleasant incidents quickly and always forgave readily.

That evening, Mammy maneuvered until she got me alone after supper and grilled me about what I'd meant when I'd said Uncle Brendan once helped me. I was fully prepared. I concocted the excuse that I'd wanted to hurt Father at the time and had made the whole thing up.

"Well, you hurt your father very much when you said it. His skin's not as thick as you think. Granted, he doesn't show his feelings much, but that doesn't mean he doesn't have any. And, son, if you hurt him, you hurt me, too. You'd do well to remember that."

"I'm sorry."

"You promised me a long time ago you'd never turn on your father or me." She paused. "Do you remember? It was in the car one evening. We discussed how pigheaded your granda had been about Uncle Brendan?"

"You mean the night you lied and told me you'd never met his girlfriend?"

She ignored the provocation. "You won't do this again, will you?"

I clenched my teeth as I nodded and she said the whole affair should be forgotten, the quicker the better. However, she didn't mean it. When I got my paycheck on Friday, I discovered an entire afternoon's pay had been docked. When I asked about it, she said I shouldn't be gallivanting about on horses belonging to Protestant girls on my father's time and the deduction was to teach me about responsibility.

Twenty-Seven

As soon as I laid down the receiver after talking to the headmaster's secretary, I felt Father had a point when he'd said I was useless. I passed down the hall to my mother's bedroom where she waited, Nuala perched on the edge of the bed beside her.

"I passed four subjects."

"This isn't the time for jokes," Mammy said. "What did you really get?"

"An A in religious education and Cs in English, chemistry, and German. The rest were Es and Us."

"How many unclassifieds?" Nuala asked.

"Five."

All those days I'd raised my hand in the examination hall to request extra writing sheets flashed before me. The essay booklets provided by the Examination Board hadn't been enough. I'd needed more paper, and for what? A bunch of unclassified grades.

"This is an absolute catastrophe," said Mammy. "What am I going to tell your father?" Mother's face twisted into the shape of a Notre Dame gargoyle. "By Christ, if that Fergal or Connor passes, he'll have some choice words for you."

The stirrings of acidic criticism, right on cue. She was so predictable. I said nothing, continued to regard her snarling face as I tried to decide whether to repeat the year or die. Dying seemed preferable. She was still ranting five minutes later when the phone rang. Caroline called out that Auntie Celia was on the line. My mother started from the room, though not before taking a second shot.

"She's phoning to boast about how well your cousins have done, I've no doubt."

Martin passed, but Connor didn't. I felt relieved, though not completely, because there was still Fergal to go. Poor Martin hadn't passed math this time either, which meant the universities would not accept him and he was doomed to attend an inferior institute of higher education, no matter how well he did in his final exams two years from now.

However, the news mitigated my catastrophe in Mammy's eyes and she decided to call Fergal's mother. Caroline, Nuala, and I listened, scarcely a breath exhaled between us, until my mother's voice rose from dejected to animated. It transpired that Fergal had done worse: only three passes, though no unclassified grades. In comparing mediocrity to atrociousness, she'd found solace, though she continued to fret about what our neighbors would say.

Her incessant fear of telling the neighbors about my failure was ridiculous. It infuriated me. I felt no sympathy for her self-inflicted predicament and had to leave. I walked to the twin-arched bridge, where I hopped up on its wall and dangled my legs over it. Halfway down its stone façade, a sturdy sycamore protruded from a fissure, its roots clinging with silent tenaciousness to the caked limestone binding, defying both gravity and oblivion in its need to survive. It seemed at once admirable and pathetic.

I left the bridge and strolled along the riverbank before returning to the house. Father was already home when I got there and reacted surprisingly civilly. There were no banged fists on tables or *I saw it coming*s. He simply looked me squarely in the eyes as he gave me a backhanded compliment, saying I'd have to do better next time because I had the brains.

Uncle Tommy, Auntie Bernie, and their two children, Philip and Anna, were already at their summer bungalow on the north side of Bundoran town in County Donegal when Martin and I arrived for our visit. After supper, Martin and I changed to go out for the night. Auntie Bernie summoned us into the living room when we returned downstairs and laid down the house rules, chief of which were that we were not to eat in cafés that looked suspect or use public lavatories. Philip caught practically every illness going around and my aunt, already neurotic about her own health, was terrified of infection. Satisfied with our promises to obey the rules, she skimmed her gaze over Martin's clothes.

"Those will get filthy," she said.

We planned to go to the amusement arcade. Martin wore white jeans and a matching balloon-sleeved shirt, open to his sternum to show off his tan. His body was in reality boiled-lobster red, except for his orangey-brown face, the result of countless applications of fake suntan lotion. Martin's skin didn't tan like mine; it was too fair. But he refused to accept defeat. He swallowed great quantities of pills meant to kick-start melanin production, but which succeeded only in making his insides loud as a baby's rattle when he walked.

"Don't talk to those bold hussies I see hanging around the arcades," Auntie Bernie said, as we edged toward the front door.

"Bernie, they're fellas wanting a bit of fun, for Christ's sake," said Uncle Tommy, winking at me.

"Boys, I'm all for you having fun," she said, "but fun doesn't entail experimentation of any kind. Not on my watch. You hear that, Martin? No experimentation and no alcohol, either. You're seventeen and have another year before you can drink beer."

We discovered the larger amusement arcade situated on the north end of the town was the most fun. It had a dizzyingly high helter-skelter, a decent ghost train ride, and dodgems. Martin and I got into a dodgem and were soon pursued by two girls. The driver, an olive-skinned girl with a long neck swathed in love beads, teased my cousin good-naturedly every time she crashed headlong into us and then outmaneuvered him deftly when he tried to retaliate. After the second ride, as we were exiting the car, she and her friend approached.

"Hope I didn't cause too many bruises," she said. "If I did, I'm a nurse and I'll be delighted to help bandage you up."

"You can help by driving me to the local hospital," Martin said.

"I'm Sheila, and this is my friend Bridget."

The girl was stocky and had a purplish-red blister on her chin that she'd tried to conceal with makeup. Her prominent front teeth sank into the fleshy inner lining of her jutting bottom lip.

"Are you lads game for a go on the helter-skelter?" asked Sheila.

I declined, and Bridget wasn't keen. She and I opted to take a ride on the electric swing boats, but that was a mistake. The cars crisscrossed at increasingly ferocious speed and seemed to miss one another by a hair's breadth, judging by the rush of air in my face at the swing's extremity. During the initially sedate part of the ride, I learned the girls were nursing auxiliaries who intended to become nurses one day and this was the last evening of their vacation. Bridget had a soft-spoken Donegal accent and asked lots of questions while touching my arm.

Martin and Sheila were already waiting when the ride ended. They'd decided in our absence we'd eat fish and chips at a nearby café and then go to the dance at the Astoria ballroom afterward. As it had been a long time since I'd been with a girl, I found it enjoyable dancing and smooching on the dance floor. The only unease occurred when I found myself looking at attractive men. One in particular, a tall football player type with proud, square shoulders, caught my eye and I kept sneaking peeks. If he was dancing, I watched to see if the girl would stay with him, hoped she wouldn't, and felt genuine relief when she walked away at the end of the set. It was ridiculous to wish like this, I knew, but I just couldn't stop myself.

"As it's my last night here, why don't you come back to my B&B for a while?" Bridget asked at the end of the dance. "Our landlady's a witch, but she'll be in bed by now."

"I think . . . ahm, let me see what Martin wants to do."

Sheila had already asked Martin and I could see he was also hesitant. However, the girls insisted it'd be fun.

The terraced house lay two streets from the seafront and the heavy salt air eclipsed the fragrance of crimson and white roses growing in rusty metal urns by the front door. No sooner had we passed inside the dim hallway than the girls took charge. Placing a skinny finger on her lips, Sheila removed her shoes, signaled to Martin to take off his as well, and then led him up the creaking stairs. Bridget guided me into a damp-smelling living room. She switched on a lamp perched on a small doily-covered table next to a bay window. A matted sheepskin rug lay before the hearth and two armchairs and a crushed-velvet maroon sofa were pushed against walls awash in photographs and a Sacred Heart picture with its de rigueur flickering lamp.

After settling me on the sofa, Bridget went upstairs. On her return, I saw she'd retouched the makeup around her blister and opened her blouse one more button. She sidled close to me.

"Don't worry," she said. "The old dragon won't hear us now."

"She doesn't allow male visitors?"

Her mouth puckered and she glanced at the Sacred Heart picture. "If we hadn't already paid the old bitch, we'd have left after the first night."

Bridget drew her face close for a kiss, but its application proved difficult because my tongue kept curling around her jutting teeth. It became quickly apparent nursing auxiliaries on their last night's vacation could be very randy. Growing impatient with my reticence to explore, she took my hand and guided it inside her blouse as we negotiated kisses. Her skin was warm and interestingly firm. Curiosity competed with my reluctance. She swung up her legs and eased back on the sofa. I eased on top of her, cupped my hands around her breasts, and squeezed. They felt mouthwateringly ripe, like soft oranges. The alternating soft pliability of her breast and rough hardness of the nipple were the most exciting things my hands had ever touched. I explored the textures with my fingertips. I'd never known a woman's body could have such manly roughness amid its feminine softness.

She sighed and my body was suddenly ablaze. I sped my lips voraciously from one rough nipple to the other, back and forth, back and forth, spurred on by her groans of pleasure. I grew stiffer and stiffer as each touch and moan merged to become unfathomable ecstasy. But she wasn't yet done with her womanly tricks. Emitting another charged sigh, she thrust her pelvis hard against my pulsating cock.

The front door opened. Someone stumbled into the hallway, softly singing. Bridget ceased raking my hair and her neck and shoulders stiffened. The drunken stranger passed by our door and started up the stairs. We kissed again, more passionately as my incited fingers reached underneath her skirt, dipping inside her knickers and plunging into unfamiliar liquid warmth. Never had I felt such a thing. I kissed, feasted, probed.

The singing recommenced, aggressively intrusive now, piercing our fragile intimacy. The melody transformed to hoarse yells when the fellow couldn't get his key into the door lock. A woman shouted at him to stop the racket, followed by a deathly silence, during which Bridget shoved me to the floor.

"That's the second night in a row, you drunken cur," the woman said. "Get out of my house. You're waking the household with your cat screeching. Get out or I'll summon the *Gardai* to haul you to jail."

Footsteps thumped down the stairs. The front door flung open. Bridget and I adjusted our clothing at a ferocious speed.

"Jesus, I can't get my blouse buttoned properly," she said.

The door slammed shut.

"Who's got the light on in there at this hour of the morning?" the woman said.

Neither of us spoke. We focused on the door, which was slightly ajar. It opened wider. A severe-featured woman entered clad in an electric-blue satin nightgown, her hair tucked into a hairnet.

"*You*, again. I might have known."

Rapid footsteps started down the stairs. The landlady spun 'round and peered out into the hallway. "Halt! You, in the white. Halt, I said." She tore out of the room.

"I'm just leaving," Martin said.

The sound of male laughter rushed in from the street as the door opened. I scooped up my shoes and dashed out of the room.

"Donegal trollops bringing Derry tramps in here," the woman shouted from the threshold. "Next time I catch curs like—" I swept by at enormous speed and almost sent her careening into the street, "Ah, Jesus, what the—"

I found Martin pacing back and forth at the end of the street.

"I dropped my fucking shoe on the stairs," he said. "What'll I do?" He ran his fingers rapidly through his hair. "Go back and fetch my shoe."

"No bloody way."

"You must."

As I tied my laces, he paced and cursed. We walked back to the B&B in hopes the woman might have thrown it out into the street. The upstairs lights burned and Sheila, Bridget, and the woman screamed at one another.

"It's gone, Martin. She called us 'Derry tramps.' You won't get it back now."

My cousin raised his hand to the bell, but couldn't bring himself to ring it.

Despite such a precipitous ending to my first true sexual adventure with a woman, I knew exactly what people in love meant when they compared it to walking on cotton clouds. The next six days in Bundoran were beautiful. I'd touched a girl's private parts and my body had responded as it was supposed to. I was the same as other boys. I wasn't a homosexual. Every afternoon, I sunbathed on the beach, fantasizing about touching Bridget's hard nipples, and I'd grow excited and have to roll over on my belly in case Auntie Bernie noticed.

On the final night, the cotton clouds dispersed when I spied the attractive football player type with the great shoulders at the dance hall again. I couldn't take my eyes off him as before and I didn't have Bridget to distract me from myself. I spent the entire evening watching him from a discreet distance. Later in bed, after Martin was sound asleep, I self-abused myself near witless thinking about him. The last-minute substitution of Bridget's soft breasts and rough nipples didn't alleviate the guilt this time. Homosexuality stalked me still. It would not be denied. I could never let down my guard.

A letter from Uncle Brendan awaited me on my return home. He was beginning studies at the University of California, Berkeley, in September. After expressing commiseration about my poor academic showing, he said it was understandable on account of my ordeal concerning "sick Father Cornelius." Fearing my mother might come across the letter as she cleaned my room, I took it outside and burned it, watching the edges of its feathery, gray-white ashes glow scarlet as they ascended to die in the breeze.

Twenty-Eight

Humbled by my examination debacle and extremely grateful to Father Rafferty for permitting me to return to Saint Malachy's, I set about working diligently at the college from the first day of the new school year. Pani and Martin had moved on to the sixth form and I was lonely in my classes now, although we continued to meet up at lunchtime.

Early in the new term, my bruised ego took an additional knock when the issue of my fat arse reemerged. As is usually the case when someone joins a new class, a bully must be reckoned with, and Roland set about making my life a misery. A skinny youth with body odor and badly cut hair, he taunted me unmercifully about my arse.

We were three months into the year and I was at my desk, rechecking math homework during the first short break, when Roland said, "Hey, poof, come here, I need to speak to you right now."

Five other classmates were present and, as was my usual response, I ignored him.

"Fucking yellabelly," he said.

I watched under my eyes as he strutted up to the blackboard, picked up a stick of chalk, and began writing.

After he'd finished, the boys laughed. I looked at the blackboard. The words *Harkin is a fat-arsed queer* confronted me.

"That stays on 'til the teacher wipes it off," he said. "Otherwise, I'll have to give you a good hiding."

The boys laughed again. The hoarse resonance of their laughter was unbearably humiliating. It mocked my years of docility in front of Mickey and all the others who'd taunted me. A keg of resentment, my mind exploded and I bounded toward him, cursing like a washerwoman.

"You fucking-well remove that, *now.*"

My hands clenched to fists and Roland's eyes dropped to them. Curiosity tinged with doubt flashed in his eyes.

"Fuck you." He threw back his head contemptuously and turned to walk away.

I spun him around and punched him in the chest. The punch was so violent, it propelled Roland through three rows of desks, his arms rising and legs buckling as he sped backward. He landed on his skinny arse in the middle of the room, and he picked himself up quickly and made no attempt to approach me.

"I'm leaving this room for exactly one minute, you bastard," I said. "If those words aren't off the board by the time I get back, I'm going to make you *lick* them off."

I walked hurriedly around the perimeter of the football field. The boys fell silent when I reentered the classroom. The words and Roland were gone. Without acknowledging the removal, I sat and recommenced my work.

A sea change occurred and the boys accepted me. Even Roland, once his bruised ego recovered, tried to befriend me. I thought about what a few old Knockburn men said about political violence, how sometimes it was necessary in order to focus an enemy's mind. The strategy worked in a school environment, too.

My repeat year at St. Malachy's passed without further incident. When the exam results published, mine were astounding—a coveted string of A and B grades. Even Father Rafferty deigned to congratulate me personally, something I'd never known him to do. Connor and Fergal were marginally successful and left school, Fergal to help his father on the farm and Connor to take a job at a local bank in Duncarlow.

Moving into the sixth form to begin the first of my final two years at Saint Malachy's, I chose to specialize in history, English literature, and economics. Becoming a sixth-former was an unofficial rite of passage: we had our own common room, replete with a careers reference library, plump sofas, magazines, and newspapers; and teachers treated us as adults. No longer was it assumed we were present in class against our will. We were now proven young men bound for universities throughout the United Kingdom and Ireland.

A few weeks before the end of the first term, Uncle Brendan, who was coming home for Christmas, informed me he was arriving a little earlier so he could attend the annual prize-giving at school, where I was to be presented with an award for my turnaround. I greeted his news with mixed emotions. I looked forward to seeing my uncle, but didn't relish the prospect of receiving such a prize in front of him. The award, a new category at Saint Malachy's, recognized the "Best Improved Pupil of the Year" and reminded me of a raw period I wanted to forget.

On the actual night, I stepped across the stage to enthusiastic applause and received my prize, a gilded goddess of Grecian style atop a plinth of polished Connemara marble. The irony that she was yet another woman whom I didn't wholeheartedly desire did not elude me.

"It's quite an honor to have a new category created just for you," Uncle Brendan said, after I turned back from receiving congratulations from a woman seated on my other side. "Once your name's inscribed and she's set in the trophy cabinet, you're immortalized in the school's annals."

I peered at my twenty-three-inch-high goddess. "A dubious honor, is it not?"

"An honor, notwithstanding."

A few days later, in the privacy of Granny's home, he reiterated how proud he was of me and told me that I was a survivor and how very fortunate I was, because what had happened with Father Cornelius could have wreaked havoc on my impressionable young mind. He paused and peered at me, obviously trying to gauge if I wanted or needed to discuss the matter further.

I remained utterly impassive.

"I'm here if you need to discuss Father Cornelius or your feelings for boys, Gabriel," he concluded.

A shiver whipped through me. "Everything's fine now," I said. "What we spoke about in the field that day is water under the bridge."

His lips curled into a feeble smile. "I'm here if you need to talk."

The idea occurred to me that if he was bringing up my uncomfortable past then I could jolly well bring up his. "By the same token, I'd like to know something about the woman you dated before entering the priesthood, Uncle Brendan. No one seems to want to talk about her, or why there was friction between you and Granda about it. You can tell me about it. I'm an adult now."

He reddened and didn't reply immediately. "It was a painful stretch in my life and, while some good things came out of it—"

Uncle paused when Granny came in to collect the empty teacups. She lingered, clucking as she fluffed up and adjusted the sofa cushions. She looked at Uncle Brendan intently as she passed by him on her way out again.

"It's a period of my life I'd rather forget," he said.

"Why don't you want to tell me?"

"I don't want to discuss my past with you or anyone else."

That God had helped Uncle Brendan overcome his unhappiness with the priesthood and move on with his life compounded the glimmer of hope I harbored within myself with regard to the war raging inside me. Indeed, the hope that Bridget's ripe breasts and liquid warmth had stirred within me that night at the B&B grew with the passage of time. There were days of optimism and days of denial. That she'd aroused my blood signaled the certainty I'd turn out normal on optimistic days. But there were more denial days, days when doubt as black as a winter midnight crammed inside my head, days when my obsessing alter ego convinced me that I had to be a homosexual because I hadn't tried to repeat the experience. It feasted on my doubt, filled me with angst born of the certainty that it had indeed all been a fluke, that I wouldn't get aroused if I tried with another girl, and thereby assured its utter accuracy. I avoided further contact lest this prove to be the case.

It was also becoming increasingly difficult to ignore or reason away the terrible desires. I was seventeen and they were relentless.

No matter how much I swept them away, they returned seconds later to beat me down, corrupting my every thought, even in the sanctity of the classroom. There were two of me: good Catholic Gabriel, who wanted to be normal and lead an exemplary life, and dark, degenerate Gabriel, who lived only to lust. Sometimes, in the common room, I'd look out the window and watch the sun disappear behind a wooly, navy blue cloud, and the cloud's core would stay dark while its ragged edges were gilded like my unwanted goddess. I was the gilt-edged cloud with a core of darkness.

The only way to vanquish dark Gabriel was to submit to his degeneracy. I'd masturbate and a temporary, reassuring calm always came afterwards. Then, a day arrived when, as I conjured up the habitual, last minute figment of Bridget's breasts, I found myself unable to climax. I tried again and failed. It happened the following day. And the next. I wanted to talk to someone desperately, but I couldn't, not even Uncle Brendan. Sometimes, my insides felt so hot with panic, I wanted to run about the house, hurling china and upturning furniture. That was impossible, of course, so I'd run to the secluded spot by the river where we used to bathe as children and scream away my terror at the bemused cows chewing on the lip of the high red bank.

Toward the end of the year, I passed my driving test, though my parents would not allow me to borrow the car to attend dances yet. But another perk of being a sixth-former was that we got invites to parties at other schools called "sixth form socials." With Martin and Pani, now in their final year, I went to my first social at Saint Clare's College in a coastal resort town ten miles from our school. It was a cheerful event, monitored scrupulously by glowering nuns in off-white habits, who, circling the dance floor perimeter like beneficent tigresses, were ready to pounce should a dirty-minded schoolboy attempt to kiss one of their precious charges.

An unexpected invitation came to attend the Granderson College social. It was the first time Saint Malachy's boys had been invited to a Protestant social. Schools of different denominations rarely socialized, and when they did, it was always at athletic and debating competitions. We'd no doubt been invited because our senior rugby team was doing surprisingly well and gaining respect in the hallowed circles of Protestant school sports departments. Father Rafferty was delighted. In his eyes, we'd crossed some invisible barrier. He swooped into the Common Room to strongly recommend a contingent of us attend, and that we behave in exemplary fashion when we did.

"I'm not going," Pani said, after I'd told him I knew a pupil there. I spiced it up by adding she'd spent the entire summer teaching me how to ride, though omitted to say it was on a horse.

"We should go," Martin said, turning down the volume of the Neil Sedaka tape playing in Pani's car. "It'd be an education."

Pani adjusted the rearview mirror so he could check his pimples. "Education, my arse," he said. "No way am I going there." He squeezed a pimple on his chin.

"You can park your car in a dark corner of the school car park so nobody'll see it," Martin said.

He'd articulated exactly what I'd been thinking, both of us having chalked Pani's reticence down to embarrassment about his old car with its noisy exhaust and a fresh dent on the passenger door, which also screeched unmercifully when opened.

"It's got nothing to do with my car," Pani said, looking savagely at Martin. "I can't abide the thought of hanging around snotty Prods."

Martin worked on Pani and got him to change his mind. On the night of the social, as we drove up the winding drive, Pani's car headlights struck the enormous pale-gray girths of beech trees and miles of sprawling rhododendrons. The hedge was endless. Just as we were beginning to think the drive would never terminate, he turned a curve and a rambling Georgian mansion with ivy-covered gables confronted us.

Pani emitted a great rush of air through his teeth. "It's just like Queen's University."

We thundered into the half-full car park. Martin peered around the car park frantically. "Park over there." He jabbed his finger excitedly in the direction of a less well-lit area. Pani drove toward an empty bay next to four girls climbing out of an orange BMW 2002.

"Not *here*," I said, through gritted teeth.

"Both of you go to hell."

Pani reversed into the bay so fast, he caused the driver exiting the BMW to whip her leg back inside and shut the door.

Martin lowered his head. "I'm *not* getting out of this tin can until they go inside." He pretended to search for something at his feet. "I'd never survive the screech of that fucking door."

The driver glared in at Pani before joining her friends, who were adjusting their hair and patting wrinkles out of their skirts. All the girls turned to look at Pani's car and then started toward the entrance. Martin waited until they'd disappeared inside before opening the car door, its screech especially monstrous given the school's regal setting.

"How many times have I told you to do something about this?" Martin said. Placing his hands at the back of his neck, he flung out his hair so the ends flowed evenly over his shirt collar. A car entered the parking lot. "Jesus, somebody's coming. Let's split, Gabriel." My cousin didn't wait for me. He spirited across the car park in his bottle-green flared pants, slowing to a walk only when he'd reached the narrow path sweeping to the entrance.

I hurried after him. "You could have waited," I said as I joined him.

"That car's a fucking disgrace."

"Well, hurry up and pass the driving test and borrow Uncle Frank's car."

His face went splotchy. Martin had already taken the test—twice. He was a good driver, but he couldn't handle the conditions of the driving test. The pressure made him forget to signal when turning and he could never execute a three-point turn. It took him five maneuvers.

We checked our reflections in the glass panes of the entrance door. "Is my hair still nice at the back, Gabriel?"

"It's fine."

The school social, like others we'd attended, was set up in the gymnasium. Within a minute of entering, Fiona, whom I hadn't seen for almost two years, called out to me from across the room. She wore a checked midi-skirt and a dazzlingly white blouse with abundant ruffles that set off a hunter green twinset. A single strand of pearls was her only adornment. Her hair was ABBA-blonde, though now boyishly short, and her cheeks were as ruddy as I remembered. She wore no makeup. I was excited she'd even remembered my name. Pani arrived and I made the introductions.

"How's old Stroller?" I asked.

"He's turned into a fine jumper. And I've got a gray now, too."

Martin's eyes lit up. He loved horses.

"Mind if I try him out some time?" I asked.

She laughed and affectionately smacked my arm. I could see Pani, despite his vitriol about mixing with Protestants, was suitably impressed.

"Sure, but no jumping this time." Fiona chortled.

So did Martin. Indeed, he buzzed around her like a bumblebee around a flower. He remarked on her elegant necklace and asked if she wanted to dance. Fiona seemed surprised, as it was still very early, but she accepted and led him away to join circle of ladies dancing in a dusky corner. Within two minutes, she returned with the girls in tow. After introductions, we chatted until, as always happens in such situations, people begin engaging in side conversations.

"Have you decided which universities you'll apply to next year?" she asked me.

"Whoever'll accept me."

"I'm serious."

"I'm thinking of reading law at Trinity or Queens."

"No English universities?"

The idea of attending an English university both terrified and attracted me. My adventurous side longed to quit Ulster and leave all the petty bigotry behind, but the quiet side felt sure that strange men in England might take advantage of me. I'd read of such things in the English press, how perverts sought out "Dilly Boys" who sat on the steps of the Eros fountain at Piccadilly Circus. Such reports filled me with dread. It was impossible to share this with Fiona though. She'd been to school in England and would probably laugh at my foolishness.

"Shall we dance?" I asked.

She nodded and we went out on the floor.

"So, you haven't applied to an English university, then?" she persisted.

It struck me she might think I was just a narrow-minded Catholic. "Someone I know goes to university in Cardiff and likes it a lot. Maybe I'll apply there . . . perhaps Durham, also." Our eyes locked, and she smiled. The more I looked at her, the more I began to forget about the disturbingly boyish hair. "And you?"

"I'm planning to read economics anywhere but here. The older I get, the sicker I get of all the fighting and bigotry. I'm leaning toward Cambridge, Bristol, or the London School of Economics."

I admired her directness in alluding to the quagmire of Northern Irish politics so assertively. Not once during that summer when we'd first met had we mentioned politics. We'd talked only horses and school.

"All good schools," I said.

"If I end up in Bristol, and you in Cardiff, then we'll likely bump into each other. There'll only be the Severn Bridge and a few miles separating us." She grinned mischievously.

"I didn't know that."

The set came to an end and I stood beside her, utterly unsure what to do. I was intrigued to know more about her, but the fact that she was a girl, as well as the fact that I hadn't experienced any reassuring surge of physical attraction to her, weighed on my mind. Before I could decide or take my cue from her, a thin girl in an emerald satin dress brayed Fiona's name from across the gym and slithered toward us. This was probably a secret arrangement they had to aid one another in awkward situations with boys. Caroline told me girls did this sort of thing.

But Fiona made no attempt to leave. About ten feet to my right, Pani looked similarly perplexed. He stood by a girl's side, thrusting his head back every now and again to adjust his mop of unruly hair, a habit of his when he was dead unsure. Fiona introduced the girl in green, Heather, and we chatted politely for half a minute or so. No signal came forth to call Fiona away and, after an *absolutely lovely to meet you*, Heather slithered away. Heart pounding, I slipped my arm around

Fiona's waist and couldn't believe it when she immediately sidled up to me.

All the barriers fell. It was as if we'd seen each other every day since that summer we'd first met. We danced, helped ourselves to food from the buffet table, chatted, and danced some more. Toward the end of the evening, after learning she'd traveled to the social with Heather and another friend, I asked slyly if I could see her home. I knew she'd decline. She was an impeccably bred Protestant and would most likely suggest we make another date.

She accepted without hesitation, which put me in a terrible pickle. I hadn't asked Pani. There was also the dreadful matter of his car. I excused myself and walked frantically around the gym looking for him, all the while cursing myself for my damned stupidity. I found him near the coffee urns. He was chatting to the girl I'd seen him dancing with earlier. As soon as propriety permitted, I butted in and pulled him aside.

"We're taking Fiona home. I'll do the same for you when my parents let me borrow the car."

"You sly dog."

I was relieved the first obstacle had been so easily overcome. I glanced about. "Ahm, Pani, what excuse should we use about your car when she hears it?"

Its hideousness couldn't be ignored, especially when Fiona had told me as casually as if she were talking about the weather that she was having both horses shipped to England when she went over to university. That's how damned rich her father was, and now I was seeing his daughter home in a cacophonous deathtrap.

"Don't push it," Pani said.

"I didn't think she'd accept a ride home on the first night." His girl was now looking quizzically at us.

"Come to think of it," he said, "where does Fiona live, exactly?"

"Castlebenem."

"Are you out of your fucking mind?" Pani turned away and looked over at the girl, mouthing he'd be right over and sealing his commitment with a honeyed smile. When he turned back to me, I got a bulge-eyed snarl. "We'll have to go through a bad Protestant area to get there." His voice had lowered precipitously when he uttered the word "Protestant," on account of where we were. "It's late. We could end up with cut throats if the UDA have set up an illegal checkpoint to try and snare Catholics."

"Don't be silly." I laughed to disguise my own sudden unease. "We won't get snared."

While Fiona chatted to some friends after the social ended, Pani, my cousin, and I discussed the problem clandestinely. Martin sided with me and Pani eventually gave in.

Outside, Fiona's glance at the dented car door hinted strongly that I'd been right to be concerned. Its tooth-aching screech, notwithstanding Martin's burst of fake coughs as he whipped it open, confirmed it. We roared our way across the car park to join the line of exiting cars.

"Sorry about the noise," I whispered. "Giles says the body shop did a horrible repair job on his exhaust."

"Sorry, Gabriel, I didn't hear that," she said. "What did you say?"

Boys and girls gawked in as they crossed in front of the car or walked alongside it. The line moved slowly and then came to an eventual halt. Unable to fake it any longer, Martin said something about searching the dial to find Radio Luxembourg and lowered his head toward the radio.

"You know damned well it's pre-programmed," Pani said.

He pressed the button and the Radio Luxembourg jingle came on to accompany the metallic snort of his muffler, thus obliging Martin to continue staring ridiculously at the radio or lift his head and look out the window again. He chose to lift his head and look out. After what seemed like hours, the traffic started moving and the muffler's whine grew to a roar as we sped toward Fiona's home.

⊗

As our liking was mutual, Fiona and I started dating, but I didn't tell my parents about it. She was a Protestant and they wouldn't accept her.

To my surprise, Father bought a new car, a gorgeous fire-engine red Mercedes, and added me to the insurance policy so I could borrow it at night, despite Mammy's high-pitched objections. I took Fiona to other Catholic school socials along with Pani and the girl he'd met at Granderson College that evening. Occasionally, we went to a disco by the seaside that was attended by both Catholics and Protestants.

Caroline and Connor, the latter now dating a twenty-year-old bank teller, came as well. Sometimes Martin joined us, although not often, as he didn't have a steady girlfriend. Unfortunately, the fruit of deceit being ultimate discovery, my sister forgot herself one evening in my mother's presence and let it slip that Fiona came from Castlebenem. It didn't matter to Mammy that Fiona was a pupil at exclusive Granderson College, that she owned two horses being shipped to England in the near future, or that her father owned every blade of grass around the village. All that mattered was that Fiona was of the wrong religion.

"Harry, put your foot down and stop this craziness," she said, as I was about to leave for a dance. "Take back the car keys."

"He's only young once," Father said, "and has more sense than to get serious with a Protestant lassie."

"These things get serious." Shallow lines had formed recently above my mother's eyes and mouth, and they deepened to fissures as she squinted and clamped her lips shut to a fraction just below the point of bloodlessness. She twisted her torso around sharply toward the television with not the slightest intention of watching it.

"We'll have no Protestant hussies about this house," she said to the television. Then she whipped 'round to me again. "There's more than enough of your own kind to date."

"I'm not bloody-well marrying her."

"I'm not allowing her to darken my doorstep."

"Her people's very big," Father said, "with pots of money."

"I don't give two hoots of a tawny owl who or what her people are. She could be royalty, and she's still not coming about here."

Father's eyebrows arched and he peered over to indicate he sympathized with me.

"I'm not giving her up," I said.

"Jesus Christ, you're as pigheaded as Brendan," she said. "The damned same as him. Every bit as determined to bring people trouble. Is that what you're planning to do? To follow his example and disgrace yourself, and us, into the bargain?"

"You're overreacting, Eileen," Daddy said.

I smiled brightly at Father. Sometimes, he really surprised me.

"You can just go to hell, Gabriel," Mammy said. "I'm washing my hands of you."

As she left the room, she slammed the door so hard the windowpanes vibrated. I couldn't believe she'd invoked Uncle Brendan's name to suit her own selfish needs, especially since she'd been so understanding when he'd left the priesthood. It was infuriating. Didn't she see that she was as bigoted as those women she'd challenged years ago at the bacon counter in the supermarket? Moreover, Fiona was fun. I wasn't giving her up. Of course,

Mammy didn't—couldn't—understand that Fiona was also proof I couldn't be gay.

For the first time, I felt hatred toward my mother. I resolved not to back down, no matter the cost. A moral stand had to be taken against her bigotry.

I stopped talking to her. It lasted for weeks, becoming so bad, a room would literally grow tense as soon as one of us entered and saw the other was present. Only Father didn't notice, or if he did, he did a good job pretending he didn't. The silence was poisonous—but so was her intolerance.

Matters came to a head during the seventh week, when she burst into tears at the supper table.

"You're destroying me," she said. "You'll drive me into a mental institution."

"I would like to speak to you," I said, "but I can't accept your attitude about Fiona."

My delivery was dry and awkward, as if my tongue needed oiling. She and I started talking again and she abandoned any further attempt to sanction me. I was permitted to see Fiona, on the condition I wouldn't get serious and eventually marry her. This condition, together with a promise I would not bring her home, concluded the issue. My mother felt she, too, had won.

Twenty-Nine

W ake up, Gabriel." A callused hand shook my shoulder briskly. Standing at the side of my bed, dressed in jeans and a sweater, Father stopped shaking me only after I lifted my head off the pillow.

"What time is it?" I asked, rubbing my eyes.

"Four in the morning. I need you to come with me."

Five minutes later, we climbed into one of his dump trucks, with the logo, HARRY HARKIN, LTD, KNOCKBURN, and telephone number written on the passenger door. As we traveled along the road in the darkness, Father explained that the IRA planned to disrupt all traffic between Derry and Belfast as a protest against the internment of seven local men who'd been taken by the British Army the previous week. Accused of being in the IRA and participating in shootings and bombings, the men were being held at the Ballykelly police barracks without due process, interrogated under the Emergency Powers Act that the British government used as a weapon against only the Catholic community. As the owner of a construction company and a Catholic, the IRA had approached Father—along with a few other construction company owners—and told him to drive to a quarry near Duncarlow, where his lorry would be loaded with gravel. He was then to drive to the bottom of the town and dump it across the main road leading from Derry to Belfast. I was his alibi, in case the police stopped him. They'd never believe a middle-aged father would take such a risk and break the law in the presence of his young son.

Under the guard of two hooded men brandishing rifles, we waited as an excavator dumped gravel into the bed of the first dump truck, and then Father pulled up for his to be loaded. When we arrived in Duncarlow, three more men wearing dark green jackets and black balaclavas also stood guard, one armed with a Thompson machine gun. One of the IRA men watched me intently, a revolver handle peeking from his right jacket pocket. In a cacophony of squealing air brakes and roaring engines, each driver raised the beds of their trucks in turn. Gravel and stones spilled out to form mountains across the road. Now almost five o'clock, there was still no traffic on the road.

Presently, the man with the revolver lit a cigarette and walked over to one of his colleagues. My heart stopped and then began racing. The man walked and smoked his cigarette like my cousin Connor.

"Pity we can't hang around to see the look on the police and soldiers' faces when they see this mess," said Father, and he laughed as we drove away. "They'll have a lot of digging to clear this away and open the road for a bunch of angry people who'll be late for work in Belfast."

My mind dumped information into my consciousness as fast as Father's truck had dumped the gravel and I couldn't form the words to reply. Surely the man could not have been Connor; many other smokers held their cigarettes with the burning end cupped inside their hand. I was imagining it. My cousin didn't know how to fire guns. He was a respectable banker now.

Now beginning my final year at Saint Malachy's, I had a major decision to make. University applications had to be completed by early November. The process, administered from England, allowed five university choices in descending order of preference, and one was obligated to attend one's first choice upon acceptance by that institution. I felt enormous pressure. Martin was now studying at a fashion institute in London and loving it, and Fiona and Pani (who was repeating because he'd only passed one exam and not even a mediocre institution would accept him) couldn't wait to quit Ulster. They tried frequently to persuade me to leave, too. Fiona, knowing I hated Ulster politics just as much as she, couldn't understand my hesitancy.

But Belfast beckoned as a violent refuge. Going to university amid its bombs and shootings appeared to be my safest option. There weren't homosexuals lurking on its street corners, like there were over in England, as that sort of activity was illegal in Ulster.

At school, Father Rafferty made me head boy and I was in charge of the prefects, the dispensing of fairness and compassion now truly mine. The tiny apricot shield, that varnished symbol of power I'd first seen on Finbar's lapel years ago, was now affixed to my blazer.

During lunchtime, Pani and I drank frothy cappuccinos in a new café in town that welcomed students, or we drove around town in his car. Unfortunately, our jaunts in his old motor terminated abruptly one morning. As Father Rafferty recited the Angelus at assembly, an enormous bang rocked the gymnasium. Dust and plaster rained down upon us and windows shattered. Father Shaw, the vice-head, barged through one of the gymnasium doors, mounted the stage, and conferred with the headmaster.

We were informed that a bomb had gone off in the council housing estate abutting the school's west wing. The estate was a sore point with Father Rafferty; it challenged his priestly obligation to turn the other cheek. It had been hastily constructed by the Protestant-dominated borough with the sole purpose of preventing Saint Malachy's from purchasing the land for expansion. Part of the estate's surrounding lawn ran alongside the school's driveway where Pani parked his car.

After assembly ended, we ran to the driveway and saw that his vehicle was damaged beyond repair. Bedlam existed at the driveway entrance. It was akin to watching a war film: Pani wailed the loss of his car, policemen shoveled debris into trash bags, soldiers crouched pointing guns, and ambulances screamed their hurried approach. Later, I learned a part-time Protestant policeman (who was also our government-appointed truant officer), his Catholic wife, and their four-year-old child had been blown to pieces by the massive car bomb. It was body parts I'd seen the police shovel into the trash bags.

This man may or may not have been bigoted. But he was married to a Catholic and had walked our corridors in the execution of his duty to monitor Catholic school truancy. The hideous reality of Ulster life confronted me starkly.

I told Uncle Brendan about what I'd witnessed when he called the following weekend. There was a silence after I'd finished and I thought we'd been cut off.

"No, I'm still here," he said. "I was just thinking about all the horseshit young people have to put up with over there."

If the carnage hadn't been so heavy on my heart, I would have laughed and teased him about using such a Yankee term.

"Someone should take a stick to the politicians and beat them about the head until they agree to work together and reach a solution so everyone can live in peace over there," he added.

"That's easy for you to say, Uncle Brendan. You're gone from here."

"Get out of that cesspit. The only thing it's good for is sucking the souls out of the youth. I don't want to see that happen to you. You've got a good soul." Uncle Brendan paused. "You're dear to me, Gabriel."

Though it made me feel good, I didn't know how to respond to his last statement. My parents never said things like this to me.

"Go to university in England," he continued. "Get away from this evil. You'll eventually settle down with Fiona, or some other nice girl, and have those children you want."

Shocked by the bombing and influenced by what Uncle Brendan had said, I began giving more serious weight to going to an English university. However, his advice had been a double-edged sword, as his aside about my marrying and having children had stoked the flames of my anxieties further.

Fiona and I had progressed to the petting stage, but it gave me no pleasure. The lusty urgency I'd experienced with Bridget in the living room of the Bundoran B&B had never repeated.

Granted, I got erect, but it wilted quickly and I would not allow her to touch me. Luckily, Fiona didn't appear eager to touch my thing, or to have me touch her. She spared me anguish in that regard when, feeling it my manly obligation to probe her body further, I slipped an unenthusiastic hand underneath her skirt one night.

"I'd rather not, if you don't mind," she said, clamping her hand around my wrist.

We'd been cuddling in the car, following a night of celebrating the fact that she'd come second in a horse show, and I drew my face from her breasts and gazed at her in feigned annoyance.

"That's for committed relationships." She bit her lip. "I hope you don't think I'm prudish."

"I always thought Protestant girls were easier than Catholic girls."

Fiona didn't laugh.

"It's a joke."

"You're okay about us not . . . you know . . . going all the way?"

"I respect you, Fiona."

Flashing strobe lights roamed like searchlights around the room. Along one side of the dance floor was the elevated disc jockey's kiosk, where a young bearded man sifted through records. Fiona, Caroline, and I were at Tramp's, a large seaside resort disco frequented by Protestants and Catholics. We'd met up with Connor, too, who was here with a new girlfriend whose name I didn't bother to memorize. He discarded girls more often than underwear.

The track ended and Middle of the Road's "Chirpy Chirpy Cheep Cheep" started playing.

"Let's get a drink," I hollered to Fiona, peeling my damp shirt off my sweaty chest.

"We've just arrived," she said, and she turned in a circle holding her hands high in the air. "I want to dance. You go."

I walked off the floor and stood at the perimeter for a minute, watching her and Caroline dancing together. Threading my way through a dense forest of people, I reached the bar and ordered a beer. Tramp's management turned a blind eye to underage drinking.

"Hey there, mate." A hand tapped my right shoulder. "Long time, no see."

A young man with cropped hair pushed into the tight space beside me. Dressed in a blue T-shirt and faded jeans, I recognized his intense blue eyes instantly, though I didn't remember his name.

"How's your Granny doing?" he said.

"She's fine."

"Any more hens escape since?"

The bartender placed a pint of beer before me on the counter. The soldier's eyes flicked from mine to the beer.

"I'll pay for it . . . a pint for me, too." As we waited for the bartender to return, the soldier must have spotted my confusion. "Richie," he offered. "Gabriel, isn't it?"

"How'd you remember my name?"

He flashed me a beautiful smile. My heart and belly lurched. As he leaned over to settle with the bartender, I couldn't stop my eyes running up and down his strong chest and defined forearms that were the color of caramel. He clinked my glass and we sipped our beers.

"Great place this, isn't it?" he said.

I nodded, knowing I had to leave but unable to command my feet to move.

"I can enjoy a night out here without worrying about getting shot." He grinned at my half-open mouth. "I've got a black sense of humor."

All the men in the place, including the male bar staff, wore their hair fashionably long and sported heavy sideburns. Richie stood out like a beacon. Afraid Connor would catch me talking to a soldier, I glanced hastily around the room.

"There's more of us around." Richie pointed to his left, where a group of short-haired men sat at a table with a group of women. "Your lot would blow my head off if I showed up at one of your dance halls." He laughed. "Even if I'm also a Catholic."

When I didn't reply, he looked around the disco. The silence lengthened and made me feel awkward.

"Thanks for the beer," I said, and started to leave.

"Why don't we go out to the foyer for a minute?" he asked.

Again, my heart reared and started racing. I looked beyond a group of people to the dance floor and could see Fiona and Caroline still dancing. I agreed.

A long line of people waited to check their bags and coats into the cloakroom when we reached the foyer. The place roared with conversation and laughter. I followed Richie to the top of the room, where we stood near an oversized window.

"Why'd you become a soldier?" I asked.

"Long story," he said, and winked. "You got all night?"

Unsure how to respond, I didn't speak.

"My old man and I didn't get along," he said, "so I signed up three years ago." Richie looked at me. "It was a big mistake. I found out too late that it's us and them in the army."

"What do you mean?"

"There's the officers and there's the cannon fodder." He took a sip of beer. "One more year and I'm out."

Pounding rhythms from the disco punctuated our silence. Our eyes met and lingered. My body sizzled with electricity. I looked away. My hand trembled so much as I lifted the glass to my mouth that the beer fizzed up.

"I'm going out on a limb here." Richie waited until I looked at him. "Has anybody ever told you that you're an attractive bloke?"

People milling about the place turned fuzzy and the room became wavy. The din sounded hollow, protracted. I stared out the black windows until everything returned to normal.

"So are you," I said.

The air between us grew ferociously charged. I could scarcely breathe.

"A mate of mine's got a holiday rental nearby," said Richie. "You want to see it?"

Looking about the foyer, I thought I saw Connor exiting from the men's lavatories and hastened toward the exit door before he saw me.

A silver moon gleamed as I followed Richie across the parking lot toward a caravan park. In the distance, the sea shimmered. Frothy waves crashed soundlessly against rugged black cliffs. We entered the park and walked along a narrow path flanked on either side by caravans resting on top of concrete blocks. Halfway along, Richie tugged me toward the entrance door of one of them. A pure white seagull was perched at one end of its roof. My breaths shortened. As if in a dream, I watched him insert the key in the lock and open the door.

The interior smelled of the sea and was bathed in yellowish light from a weak lamp in one corner. Richie's hands reached out and I felt my body pulled gently toward him. Our chests and bellies pressed together. His lips touched mine. They felt soft and mobile. It felt no different than when Fiona and I kissed. And yet it was—very. He was a man and I was a man and men's lips were never supposed to touch like this.

I pushed him away and wiped my mouth with the back of my hand.

"You liked it," Richie said. He put his arms around my waist and his face loomed closer and closer. I trembled so violently I thought I'd faint.

"You've never kissed a man before, have you?"

I shook my head.

He stroked my back for a moment and then kissed me again. A dam burst inside me and I was flooded with sensations and needs I'd never experienced before. We embraced tighter and tighter, our tongues exploring every gap in our teeth and fold in the lining of our mouths. Richie unbuttoned my shirt and his hot tongue explored my nipples. They were on fire. The tip of his tongue skimmed over my chest next. His was defined, like men I'd seen in cowboy films on the television, and covered in wiry brown hair. His body had a nutty, masculine smell. My cock was rigid, so rigid I thought it would bust through my fly. His hand passed over it, squeezing, prodding.

He steered me toward the bedroom at the back of the caravan and we fell on the rumpled bed. We got naked. Every part of his body was rock hard and beautiful. We kissed passionately as we writhed on the bed. He inserted his tongue in my ear and I experienced hot and cold pleasure as he wiggled and thrust it about. Then his head moved down and down until his mouth found my cock. He sucked me and I had to stop him very quickly, because I was close.

"Do you prefer to top or bottom?" he said softly, at the end of a long French kiss. "I'm easy."

"What do you mean?"

He guided me on top of him.

A minute later, when I climaxed, I thought I was dying. Never had I experienced such intensity. It didn't seem possible to recover from such an enveloping sensation. We lay on the bed, drenched in sweat, Richie running his fingers through my hair.

"How'd you know I was homosexual and that I'd come here with you?" I asked.

Richie's fingers stopped massaging my scalp. "It's nicer to say 'gay,' Gabriel. Homosexual is harsh. Clinical." He looked at me earnestly. "My sixth sense told me." He chuckled and added, "You need it in the army. They hate gays."

I thought about this for a moment and then rose. Though I'd been here just fifteen minutes, it felt like I'd been away from Fiona for hours. Richie sat up and watched me dress.

"I'm off duty again in three weeks," he said.

I stopped buttoning up my shirt. "You're a British soldier. I can't."

"Nobody knows us around here."

I zipped my fly.

"We like each other." Richie stroked my arm. "I liked you the moment I saw you."

I finished buttoning my shirt and kissed him. "I've got to go."

The seagull resting on the caravan's roof lifted into the night air when I got outside, its sharply sculpted wings flashing white in the streetlight as it rose. I sprinted out of the caravan park and slowed to a brisk walk as I neared the hotel entrance.

"Where've you been?" Connor asked, stepping out from behind a sycamore tree.

"Getting fresh air. It's smoky inside."

His eyes lowered to my chest. "What's up with your shirt?"

Looking down, I saw it was lopsided.

"Buttoned it wrong at home." I walked quickly away and redid the buttons before entering the hotel.

I found Fiona standing in front of the bar and told her the same lie I'd told Connor, but added that I'd felt nauseous. She bought it. Later, as I drove home, I relived my experience with Richie and became so distracted I almost smacked into a car in front of me that stopped for a changing traffic light.

"I'm so happy to be out with you tonight," I said, laying my hand on Fiona's knee.

"Even though you almost killed us just now," she said.

"Yes, watch where you're going," Caroline said, from the back.

"It's wonderful to be together," I said, not caring if my sister overheard. "Don't you think?"

"It is. I'm just surprised you pick this moment to say so."

Three weeks later, I lied to Fiona for a second time and made an excuse not to see her. I met Richie instead. He and I met outside the disco but couldn't go to the caravan as his friend, the owner, was entertaining his girlfriend. We walked along the deserted beach hand-in-hand, stopping frequently to kiss. It was so romantic, so right. Before leaving, we went into the nearest dunes. Despite my open shirt and pants bunched at my shoes, I didn't feel the early fall chill blowing in from the water.

More lies to Fiona followed as Richie and I met again, including twice at the caravan, where we made love, and once at a bar in another town, where he informed me the manager was gay and allowed people like us to drink there, provided we behaved discreetly. Discretion means different things to different people, apparently, and the effeminate behavior exhibited by some of these men disgusted me, the way they limply drooped their hands or touched one another when they talked. Richie didn't like it, either.

During this period, I also met with Fiona, but things had changed. I thought only of Richie when I kissed her.

I entered the London School of Economics as my first choice of university on my application form and Queens University in Belfast became my safety school, the choice made for no other reason than Richie came from there and I held a secret hope we might continue to see each other when he left the army. I hadn't even spoken to him about this, though, for fear he'd think I was clingy and dump me.

On one of our walks along the beach, I told him that I didn't want to hear about his work in the army. It made me uncomfortable to listen to his stories about what he and the other soldiers did. I also felt guilty—entirely for dating a British soldier and not for being gay. Quite frankly, I'd used up all my reserves of guilt on this supposed sin and, intellectually, I figured God had made me this way. How could something that felt right be sinful in His eyes? The one thing Richie and I agreed on was that if I ever drove up to a checkpoint and saw him, I was to ignore him. I wasn't even to smile, as soldiers were on high alert at those stops and noticed everything.

Unable to reconcile my happiness and lying to Fiona, I arranged to meet her at the café near Saint Malachy's where Pani and I drank cappuccinos. I arrived early and secured a booth at the end of the room where we could have privacy. I watched from the window as she parked her car on the street. She fixed her bangs in the rearview mirror and adjusted her slate-gray skirt and navy school blazer after exiting her car.

Her smile when she came up the stairs made me feel even shittier.

"So, what's so important, you needed to see me on a school day?" Fiona asked, after the waitress set a mug of coffee and chocolate éclair in front of her. "Not that I mind."

"I picked the LSE as my first choice."

"That's fantastic, Gabriel." She put her hand on top of mine. "Both of us over in England. Wow."

She'd applied to Cambridge, and University College London was her safety school.

"I . . . I . . . we need to slow down things between us, Fiona. Final exams are around the corner and—"

"They're six months away." She whipped her hand away. "What are you talking about?"

I wanted to tell her the real reason, but she'd never understand. Anyway, it would be impossible to tell her the truth. I couldn't bear to think of her seeing me as a queer. Better she hated me than that.

"My parents told me I have to stop seeing you. They're afraid we're getting too serious and it could affect my studying." I leaned across the table. "They're not allowing me to borrow the car anymore."

"I'll fetch you."

"We're too young to be serious. They've got a point."

Tears welled in her eyes. The natural red of her face deepened. I shifted in my seat.

"You want to end us?"

I stared out the window, watching a woman and her child enter a pharmacy across the street.

"Is there someone else? Is that why? Have you found a Catholic girl and you're dumping me?"

I turned back to her. "There's no other girl."

We sat in silence, me staring at her untouched éclair and Fiona dabbing her tears with a tissue. Upper sixth Saint Malachy's students laughed gruffly in the other booths. The cappuccino machine hissed violently as the waitress prepared another coffee, steam rising from it in eddied puffs.

Fiona let out a sudden cry and rose. Students in the next booth looked over their shoulders as she rushed out of the café. I'm not proud of it, but I'd figured Fiona wouldn't make a scene when surrounded by other students, and I was right.

※

"You did the right thing," Richie said. "It always best to be honest, even when it's hard. Fiona'll get over it."

We stood inside the Mussenden Temple, a circular structure made of Roman columns about fifteen feet in diameter. It was part of the Downhill demesne built by Frederick, Fourth Earl of Bristol, in the early eighteenth century. The estate was now a ruin, but the temple was still intact and stood on a cliff looking down on a beautiful sandy cove.

"We have to meet in secret," I said. "We sneak around. What's honest about us?"

He took his hand off a pillar and pulled me to him.

"It's how things are for gay people."

"Forever?"

"Not in London. We have a future now that you'll study there." He squeezed me tightly. "You and Fiona had no future."

Blood pumped furiously through my body and made me lightheaded.

"Only if I get the grades the LSE want," I reminded him.

"You'd better."

A middle-aged couple entered the temple and Richie and I parted. We weren't fast enough. The disgust on the man's face shocked me. I felt dirty.

Thirty

I found my mother hanging laundry in the small lawn behind our house. She stood with three clothes pegs in her mouth as she stretched a bedsheet over the line. A spring breeze ruffled her hair, blowing strands away from her ears.

"I thought you were studying," she said, as she pegged the sheet.

I watched her for a moment, the only sound coming from the transistor radio in her laundry basket. She enjoyed listening to political discussions on Radio Ulster and BBC Northern Ireland.

"I have to tell you something," I said, after she tossed another sheet on the clothesline. I cleared my throat. "I'm gay."

"If you help me, I'll be gay, too."

"I'm a homosexual, Mammy. I can't handle keeping it a secret anymore."

The muscles in Mammy's face stretched and slackened as she fought to regain her composure.

"What makes you think you're like that?"

"I am."

She dropped the pegs on the grass and came over to me. "Homosexuality isn't normal, Gabriel."

"It's normal for me . . . and other people who are."

Mammy laughed sharply. A part of me felt sorry for her. First, she'd hoped I'd become a priest, but had stopped pushing after Uncle Brendan quit his vocation. Now, I was telling her I liked men.

"I wasn't attracted to Fiona," I pressed. "That's a sign."

"That just means she wasn't the right one." She rubbed her neck. "Try courting a dark-haired girl and you'll see."

"God created me gay, Mammy. Uncle Brendan said it's okay."

"You talked to him?"

"I struggled to accept myself and couldn't talk to you or Daddy."

"He said it's acceptable to be with other men?" She shivered, like a wind passed through her. "He shouldn't have said that. It's a mortal sin."

"I'll have to live with that, won't I?"

"You can't receive Holy Communion."

I shrugged.

"You're confused. I've heard about this. It's a phase. Some sensitive boys go through a period like that. It'll pass."

She laid her hand on my forearm. I could feel the vibrations of her desperation.

"Let's talk to the doctor. He'll explain that it's a phase."

I met her gaze. "If you love me, I need you to accept me."

"How . . . what must . . . I . . ." Mammy regarded the limp bedsheets, tears sparkling in her eyes. Finally, she looked back at me.

A car rattled over the cattle grid at the entrance to the driveway.

"Jesus Christ, your daddy's home."

"I'm telling him."

She clamped her hand over her mouth and looked at me with bulging eyes.

I recalled what Richie had said about honesty, words I'd pondered for weeks now. He'd also said people like us had to be careful in public and I remembered the disgust on the man's face when he'd seen Richie and I kissing at Mussenden Temple. But being honest with the people you loved, with the people who were your flesh and blood, was very important.

"He needs to know, Mammy"

She grabbed my arm. "It's best I tell him."

Feeling I owed her that small favor, I nodded my consent.

As we ate dinner, Mammy kept looking over the kitchen table at me, hoping perhaps I'd changed my mind and would give her some kind of signal.

"Mammy, why do you keep staring at Gabriel?" Caroline asked.

Father glanced at Mammy and then at me.

"I'm *not* staring at him." Mammy took her plate of uneaten food and scraped it into the trash.

Setting the utensils down nosily on the plate, Daddy rubbed his belly as he rose. Instead of heading into the living room like he always did after eating, he walked to the back door.

"Where are you going?" Mammy asked, shooting me a glance.

"One of the lorries sprung an oil leak and I need to fix it for tomorrow."

He left.

Ordering James and my sisters to their bedrooms to start their homework, Mammy approached the window by the kitchen sink. I joined her. Light raindrops trickled down the pane and distorted Father's body as he crossed the yard and went into the huge shed he'd built for truck repairs. Mammy washed a dish and handed it to me to dry. She sighed heavily and shook her head when our eyes met. When we were done, she dried her soapy hands and went outside. I watched her cross the yard. After she went inside the shed, I counted sixty seconds and followed.

Parked about twenty feet inside the entrance to the shed, I could hear Father tinkering with something metallic inside the hood of the truck. John Denver's "Take Me Home Country Roads" played on the dump truck's radio. Father loved country music, a passion he shared with James. I found the lyrics sappy. Cans of engine oil and black grease lay on the floor. I still couldn't see my parents as I crept closer.

"He can't help being that way, Harry. This is normal for him."

"*Normal.* Do you hear yourself?"

There was a silence.

"God accepts him."

"He might, but no fuckin' way am I."

There was a high-pitched screech of metal against metal.

"I tried to make a man of him." Father hammered something. "Him going off to university in London will make it worse. The English are all poofs."

My body went cold as alabaster.

"Brendan told him it's okay."

"Why am I not surprised? Aye, he's got Brendan in him, doesn't he?"

"Brendan's not a homosexual."

"I mean the way he made people's life miserable." Father coughed. "Well, I didn't take that fella under my roof only to find out I've raised a queer."

I shook my head like a dog with an ear itch to clear the ringing in my ears.

"It's as much my roof as yours, Harry. And you were glad to take Gabriel in at the time."

"We should never have adopted him."

The ringing grew intense. My parent's voices melded into the background. I staggered away from the truck, overturning the can of engine oil.

Mammy emitted a stifled cry, like a wounded fox, as she stared at me from the front of the lorry. "Gabriel!"

"What's this stunt you're pulling?" Father asked, cleaning his hands with a rag.

"Uncle Brendan's my father?"

Mammy let out another wounded cry. The rag dropped out of Father's hand. I ran out, rushing past Caroline and James, who were walking toward the shed.

Raindrops bounced on my head as I sprinted across the hayfield. Tears streamed from my face. A herd of grazing cattle scattered in terror. Leaping over a barbed-wire fence, I entered another field containing stacked bales of hay. I raced up to a stack and hurled myself against it, pushing my face into the prickly hay. The bristles stabbed my cheeks and forehead and it felt good. I kicked and beat at the hay wildly with my fists. Bales tumbled. I scratched my skin and didn't care. Ropes securing three bales split open and the hay scattered on the grass and over my school uniform.

"Gabriel!" Caroline shouted. "Where are you? Come back!"

I raced to the road and then kept running. At the church, I darted into the telephone box, jammed coins into the slot, and dialed. The air was stale and forbidding, as if warning me I shouldn't call. I knew I shouldn't, but didn't care.

I'd been sitting on the church wall for two hours, darting back and forth between the wall and a laurel hedge when cars drove by, in case people wondered what the hell I was doing.

"Hiya, Gabriel."

I looked up to see Mr. Kelly, clad in a rubber mackintosh, approaching on a bike.

His gaze went immediately to my swollen, red eyes. Just then, Richie pulled up in a red car. I sprang off the wall. Mr. Kelly peered inside, making me suddenly conscious of the shortness of Richie's hair. The only times you saw hair that short were on the American GIs who ran a communication base on top of mountain near Duncarlow, the local policemen, and British soldiers. I ran over and got in the car.

"Drive," I said, slamming the door.

"Are you alright?" Richie asked, squeezing my knee.

"I hope I didn't get you in trouble calling the barracks."

"It's okay. Sorry about the wait." His eyes scanned the road and hedgerows. "I was out on patrol."

"Were they suspicious a fella with an Irish accent was calling you?"

"I said you're a bloke who finds me cheap music in Belfast."

The rain had stopped by the time we got to an isolated mountain road Richie knew. Walking across the heather and spongy earth, we reached the top of the hill and trekked along the crest until we came to an outcrop. The lights of a small town twinkled in the heart of the valley. Beyond, the gray water of Lough Foyle lay heavy against the backdrop of the Donegal hills across the Irish Republic's border. Richie put his arm around my shoulder.

"They lied to me all these years," I said, after I finished telling him everything that happened. "I'm not their son."

"Technically, they didn't lie," said Richie. "They just didn't say anything . . . like you didn't say anything about being gay 'til tonight."

I jerked back my head.

"Finding out you're adopted isn't like finding out you've got terminal cancer, is it?" He smiled grimly. "Let's be real."

"You can't understand."

He massaged the back of my neck. It felt good, lessening the resentment I felt towards him.

"I'm not belittling it, but seems to me you've still got parents." Richie shrugged. "I don't. Mum's dead and I never see my old man anymore."

Wrenching a stalk of grass from the rocky soil, I twisted its wiry stem around my finger.

"A chap I messed about with once told him I was gay. Dad confronted me and then threw me out on the street."

I mulled this for a moment. "My father . . . fuck, he's isn't that anymore." I glanced at Richie. "What is he now?"

"He's still your old man. He'll probably work his head around the gay thing, in time." Richie tousled my hair. "You'll have to do the same about them. You're a man now."

"So many bloody secrets. Their shitty secret." I looked hard at Richie. "Our secret."

"I'm up with honesty, like I told you," he said, "but our secret, you have to keep from them." He smiled. "'Til we're together in London."

⁂

Despite Richie's words, I sat numb in my bedroom as Mammy explained how Uncle Brendan had helped Granda on the farm before he went off to the seminary and how, during that period, he'd met a girl at a dance and gone out with her.

"It was against your granda's will, as you already know. He used to say, 'All decent Knockburn families have a priest and the

Harkins aren't going to be any different.' Brendan was his last hope, until he got the girl into trouble."

"I'm a bastard." I'd never pondered the true meaning of that word. It was used ubiquitously, the first word rolling off boys' tongues at school when they hurled insults. Now, it sounded so harsh and clinical.

"Don't *say* that, Gabriel." She sat on the bed beside me and laid her hands on my shoulders.

"My father is my uncle, and my uncle is my father. And you? Who are you to me?"

She opened her mouth to reply, her eyes mirroring the hurt I'd just administered.

"Who are you to me?" I asked again.

The hideous reality swept through me again and I shrugged her hands off my shoulders, rose impetuously, and crossed to the window, where I stared vacuously out at the landscape.

"I'm a family disgrace," I said, watching my words turn to mist on the pane.

Mammy came quickly to me and turned me around. "I'm your mother. That's who I am. Nothing can change that." She embraced me. "Not your being gay or adopted. It's love and a lifetime of experiences that make us mother and son, not an act of intercourse and a birthing."

"Where's my real mother?" I willed her to keep holding me, even though I'd just knifed her heart again.

"She's dead," Mammy said. "You were born prematurely by Caesarean section and the operation went wrong. The anesthetic went to her brain. They didn't know until it was too late. Your . . . your mother wasn't a local girl, and she wouldn't marry Brendan. She said getting pregnant was a big mistake and that she wasn't going to make it any bigger by marrying a man she didn't truly love. She planned from the start to give you up for adoption, and your father and I had been married a year and . . ." Her eyes focused on my face. "Gabriel, don't think for one moment you weren't wanted. I wanted you." The fight was back in her eyes. I hadn't vanquished her. "I wanted you from the first moment I set eyes on you."

I didn't speak.

"It was all planned when the family found out she wanted to give you up," Mammy continued. "Brendan wouldn't hear of you being adopted by strangers. He put down his foot, so your granda suggested Daddy and I adopt you, because we were married." She laughed mirthlessly. "The neighbors were already wondering why I wasn't yet pregnant. You know how they expect it within a year of marrying around here, otherwise the gossip starts up there's something wrong, that the wife's barren. Your granda said I should wear maternity clothes and nobody would bat an eyelid. He said that way the whole thing could be resolved, because nobody would find out and Brendan's disgrace would be kept inside the family."

She squeezed me and then let go. "Gabriel, it took me a while to agree to that. And I'll be honest and say I didn't want to do it at the beginning. But then I thought about the baby . . . I thought about you, and how you had a right to have a loving family. Your father was all for it, too."

"Granda asked you to do this?"

"I told you, your granda was a very determined man. He thought only to save the Harkin name. He ruled the roost; everyone did his bidding. And for all his praying and holiness, he went to his grave never forgiving Brendan for what he'd done. That's why Brendan didn't come home for years, even for his father's funeral. Your granda was full of useless Harkin pride and Brendan was bitter. They never made up."

"I'm responsible for all this bad blood. I'm responsible for the disgrace." Scenes from my childhood and youth flashed before me. Now, I understood why Granny had compared me to Uncle Brendan so often in my youth. Now, I understood why they'd been evasive when I'd asked about the circumstances of Uncle Brendan's leaving, and why Mammy had been so furious that night when she'd caught me eavesdropping at the door. "I'm a disgrace."

"I'm your real mother and I want you to understand something: you're no disgrace. You're my son." She touched my cheeks. "You were part of me from the moment I saw your cheeky little face in the pram. You had the plumpest little hands, which you kept making into fists like a boxer." Mammy laughed, but her eyes were focused inward. "I loved you from that moment. It was as if I'd carried you. I felt no different when I had Caroline." She squeezed my shoulders. "That's the truth."

Mammy's gaze was now in the present. She regarded me without flinching. "Everyone agreed that the whole thing was to be forgotten and never discussed. You'd become your daddy's and mine. When anyone official needed a birth certificate and could see you were adopted, your father and I would explain the inconsistencies to them and that you didn't know about it and weren't to be told—unless you found out." Mammy paused. "And now your daddy's let it out. I feared Caroline might, but it was your daddy."

"Caroline knows?"

"She discovered the birth certificate two years ago. She brought it to me and demanded an explanation. You know how she is, Gabriel. At first, she was very sad and cried, but then she saw the right thing had been done and agreed not to say a word."

My sister knew about me. My knees trembled so uncontrollably that they threatened to buckle.

"Your father doesn't even know Caroline found out."

My sister had known something about me for ages that I hadn't. I felt violated. "Mammy, I need to be alone."

"We've made a terrible mistake. Please forgive us."

"I had a right to know." My voice shook. "Caroline knew."

Mammy left, and I threw myself on the bed. My mind fizzed with a thousand thoughts. Granny Harkin was still my grandmother. But what were Granny Neeson and Aunt Peggy to me? Did James and Nuala know and my mother just wasn't saying? Had she told them and sworn them to secrecy, as she had Caroline?

I felt hopeless, adrift. My past was a lie. No matter what Mammy had said about her love for me, I was not of her blood. The bonds of love between a mother and offspring, unquestioned because they form inside the womb, had had to be formed externally between her and me. And Father? The bonds between he and I had never developed, and now I knew that it was because I wasn't his natural son. Now I understood why he preferred James, why he didn't love me like he had him. I was different. I was an obligation. He kept me at a distance because I was not of him.

I went to the window and stood for ages watching the dusk methodically paint the clouds to oblivion. I continued to stare at the nothingness until a knock on my door brought me back to the present. My mother entered, hands clasped.

"Come out to the living room," she said. "James is just home from football practice . . . I've told him and Nuala."

I didn't feel like talking or listening, but I knew she needed me to go out with her and I'd have to do it soon, anyway. The meeting—for that's what it was—was indescribable. The best way to express how I felt is that the walls, sofa, armchairs, even the ornamental birds I'd always loved, were transmuted. Physically, they were the same items, but the way I related to them was radically different. I'd always related to them as an integral member of the family, as a natural son, as the oldest and head of my siblings, and now I was an outsider. The items were still inside and I was out.

It was apparent that Nuala and James hadn't known until that evening. I could see that Nuala had been crying, and she never cried. She spoke first, albeit hesitantly, and that trait was out of character, too.

"Gabriel, this makes no difference, just like your not liking girls as much as boys doesn't make a difference."

Apparently, Mammy had told them about that, as well.

Thankfully, everyone agreed. The platitudes commenced, just as they always do in arduous situations: how it didn't matter one single bit; how we were still brothers and sisters and nothing would change; how we always stuck together, through thick and thin, how this would be no different. My mother started sobbing. Caroline and Nuala turned to comfort her while James and I watched. After Mammy recovered, a stream of collective memories and family jokes ensued. It was like a grotesque wake, and I the living corpse.

"You always were different," said James. He chuckled. "Remember how you ran away when Ciaran came to fetch you for the football match and Daddy wanted to send me in your place?"

I remembered that Saturday as if it had been yesterday. I'd run off to the pigsty and tried to read the dirty magazines Noel had shown me. It hurt to think of it, because it had shown even then that I really was different—immeasurably different.

More joking reminiscences ensued about how independent I'd always been. During each anecdote came a stinging reminder of how I'd never been the person I'd thought I was. I'd never been a real son, a real sibling. My mind wouldn't stop flicking through the past. It examined scenes I hadn't thought of for years: family conversations around the supper table about local scandals and neighbors; my parents laughing about something funny I'd done or said; their concern when I told them I felt responsible for Henry's drowning; their fury when I'd failed my first exams at Saint Malachy's; and the subsequent pats on the back about later successes. It was as if I was compelled to scrutinize and revalidate each memory in light of this new knowledge. Through every experience, during every moment, my parents had known. This knowing that I was not their flesh and blood made my head throb with cold realization.

Nuala bounded over, wrapped her arms tightly around my neck, and kissed me fully on the lips. We never kissed on the lips. It was always on the cheek. I heard the hideous strangled gasps before realizing they came from me.

"I'm sorry," I said. "I don't know what to do. It's not the same. You don't know how I feel; you can't know. None of you can. I'm adopted. Things are changed forever."

"Stop," Nuala said. "You hurt me when you say that. You're still my brother, and that will never change."

"Son, Nuala's right," Mammy said, her voice very shrill. "We're still a family. Things have changed, but it's still the same. We're all feeling awkward, but that'll pass. We'll go on as before."

My gaze moved from Nuala to the gleaming ornamental birds.

"Mammy's right, Gabriel," added James. "It's new and awkward for all of us, but tomorrow's another day." He looked at Caroline, who nodded vigorously.

"Only one thing has changed, and that thing is knowledge," my mother said. "The actual circumstances have been the same since the day you were born, and the only thing that's changed is your knowledge. Everything else remains just as it was. Your relationships with your father and me haven't changed. Your relationships with your brother and sisters aren't any different because of what you've learned today.

Those things remain the same, and the passage of time will help you see that. Time heals all wounds, Gabriel."

I slide my eyes from the birds and locked them on hers. She held my gaze for a while, and then her mouth opened and her lips trembled into a smile.

I waited alone in the living room for Father. As his car drew into the driveway, I went to the kitchen and sat at the table. It was nearly eleven-thirty. I'd banked up years of grudges for such a time as this, but instead I was tense. Earlier, Mammy had offered to tell him that I knew all about my past. I'd agreed, initially, but it was something I had to do. I was no longer a boy.

"What are you doing up so late?" he asked when he came in.

I could see that he was surprised to see me. He opened the fridge door, took out a bottle of milk, and raised it to his lips. I watched his throat muscles rise and fall behind skin irritated and flaky from shaving. His habit of drinking straight from the bottle had always disgusted me. Tonight, I didn't care.

I forced myself to keep my eyes on his face. "I understand now why you've always preferred James to me." My voice trembled. "You've always wanted me to be just like you, and I could never be. I tried and tried, but I could never be like you. It makes sense now."

He regarded his big, oil-stained hands for a moment. I felt my skin tingle. Was he thinking about how I was a homosexual, or how I wasn't his son?

"It makes no difference," he said. "You know that, don't you?"

"Granny always said I was more like Uncle Brendan. I liked the things he liked and I didn't care about your lorries and—"

"Brendan played with machinery when he was younger," Father interrupted. "He was always riding our neighbor's tractor. I don't think that explains why you and I like different things."

I said nothing.

"Fathers and sons don't always like the same things." He cleared his throat. "Let's get one thing straight, Gabriel. You've brought this up before, but I've never preferred James over you . . . or any of the rest of them, for that matter."

"When I was younger, you always picked on me. You always made me do all the work about the house."

He laughed. "Aye, because you're the eldest. It's how I was reared. That's how your granda treated me. I just did the same as a father."

"I tried to do well in my studies to make up for it, but it was never enough. You never viewed my successes as being equal to James's."

"I'm not educated." Father regarded his hands again. "What do I know about books? I know about football and tinkering with machines because I've always been around them. I was never one for studying. You know that, son."

He paused and lifted his eyes. Mine wanted to flee.

"I've always been proud of you," he said. "You were the scholar in the family. You're like Brendan that way. I was very proud of you, just as I'm very proud of James when he does well at his activities. Luksee, it was a great day for me when you made it into Saint Malachy's."

I remembered his pride, and how he'd boasted to our neighbors. I'd overlooked that.

"I made no difference between any of you," he said. "If I did, I wasn't aware of it."

"I've always felt a failure in your eyes. And now I know I am because I'm . . ." My tongue froze. It was still hard to say the word "homosexual" to a man who'd never thought of such a thing. I back-pedaled fast to try and put him on the defensive again. "I resented you. I didn't even want to travel alone in the car with you. I didn't want to talk to you."

"There were times when I knew you were acting strange. I chalked it down to you being more sensitive, or puberty, or something." He was silent for a moment. "Maybe I should have given all of you more attention, but it wasn't in my nature. I was never one to hug or say nice things. I was reared that it was womanly, that men don't go in for that." His eyes swept from my face to focus on a nearby cupboard latch. "Don't think I'm disappointed in you because of this homosexual business."

My heart leaped.

"Your mother says you're made that way and you can't change it. I've thought about it tonight and I can accept it. I won't lie and say I understand it. But there are lots of things I don't understand in the world. And yes, you're adopted. That can't be changed either, but you're mine as much as James and the rest of them."

My head pained with the thrust and retreat of thoughts: I was adopted and I was gay and he accepted me. He wasn't my natural father, no pieces of his blood were in mine, and I loved him completely.

Thirty-One

My cousin Martin telephoned from England to say several of his friends at the Fashion Institute were gay and he supported me fully. That really helped. Uncle Brendan also called, wanting to talk about my birth and adoption, but I wouldn't be drawn, and told him bluntly I didn't want to discuss it. He'd once been a priest and, as such, charged with a duty to be truthful at all times. I felt betrayed. I'd exposed my soul to him at the horse's grave in the meadow and he'd had the opportunity to expose his that day, too. He'd also had the opportunity when he'd asked me if I wanted to talk about Father Cornelius and I'd asked him to tell me about the girlfriend he'd had before he went off to the priesthood. Now everything was in the open, he wanted the whole thing aired and put to bed.

He offered to come over from America, but I wouldn't hear of that, either. He tried to insist, and I reminded him in a steely voice that he hadn't wanted to see his family for years after he'd fled to the missions and, more specifically, during his nervous breakdown. Why should it be any different now? I knew it was a slap in the face, but I also knew his soul-exposing could wait until I was ready, just like he'd made me wait.

A raw fear that I wouldn't get the required examination grades and the London School of Economics would reject me ensured that I settled down to my studies. Five weeks after the revelation, Richie went on leave to London for a month. We didn't even see each before he flew out, as my father needed the car unexpectedly on the night we'd scheduled to meet. He telephoned to say goodbye, faking his accent when my mother picked up the phone and pretending he was a school friend ringing to ask about a homework problem.

The month Richie was away dragged like a year. I forced myself to concentrate on my school work, telling myself repeatedly as I learned Shakespeare quotes and macro- and microeconomic theory that my doing brilliantly in the A level examinations was the only way I'd get to join him in London, where he would live after his tour ended in September and he quit the army. But inside I felt empty, as if a part of me as vital as an arm or leg was missing, knowing he was across the water. I daydreamed in class and at my desk in the bedroom at night, wondering what he was doing as I outlined an essay, whether he was meeting friends for dinner or going to a pop concert in Hammersmith.

He'd also told me there were gay bars and a nightclub in a part of West London called Earl's Court where he wanted to take me when I moved there. As I lay in bed, especially on Friday and Saturday nights, I'd break out in a cold sweat thinking he was at the disco and might meet another man better looking than me. Though only eighteen months older, Richie knew much more about the world than I did. London was full of beautiful men and I was just an eighteen-year-old who'd never been out of Ireland.

When we met up at his friend's caravan two weeks after his return, I felt I'd throw up as I scoured his eyes for the smallest tell that he'd met someone else. He didn't avert his gaze, grabbed me fiercely, and forced his tongue deep inside my mouth. We tossed our clothes every which way on our path to the tiny bedroom, really just a double bed surrounded by four walls. I was on fire. His beautiful, familiar smell dissipated the remains of my anxiety.

"You don't know how much I missed you," he said, as we lay tightly together despite our body heat. "One night, I said 'fuck it' and almost flew back to Ulster early." He raised his right arm high in the air, formed a plane with his hand and I watched it cross the ceiling. "But I couldn't have gone back to the barracks without raising questions."

He fetched his rucksack from the living room and took out a brown paper bag, which he gave to me. "Sorry it's not wrapped."

Inside was a long scarf with black, purple, and yellow stripes and embroidered with the words "London School of Economics."

I squealed.

"You've got to get the grades now," he said. "It cost a fortune."

No Christmas present from my parents had been as beautiful, not even the beloved farmyard set I'd begged Santa Claus to bring me when I was ten that still sat, fully intact, in the attic. Every hope I had for Richie and I was woven into the tight weave of that scarf.

I kept thinking about my birth mother and one day informed Mammy that I was going to visit her grave in the churchyard thirty miles from my home. Mammy offered to come and help me search for it. We located the grave in the shadow of an ostentatious granite monument whose inscription declared that interred inside was the body of a man who'd emigrated to New Orleans in 1814. We knelt on the black granite coping at right angles to each other, the sharp edge digging uncomfortably into the space below my kneecaps. Directly beneath my birth mother's name, etched in tarnished gold, were the names and birth and death dates of two older people who'd died in their seventies, within six months of each other. The man's name had been Gabriel.

I looked at my mother who was whispering prayers. She nodded twice, her eyes shiny with tears. After blessing herself, she rose. The edge of the coping had left deep impressions in her tender flesh.

"I'll leave you for a while," she said. "I'll wait back in the car."

I watched her recede, saw her pause and look back after she reached the entrance gates. It felt so peculiar, being alone, looking down at the white marble-chipped grave of a woman who'd taken her last breath giving me my first. After a minute, I rose and placed a bunch of bright pink roses I'd brought in the middle of her snowy marble bed. I approached the headstone, where I was compelled to trace the first letter of her name. The coldness of the polished granite stirred something within me and made me incredibly sad. It wasn't the sadness of losing a loved one, rather the sadness of never knowing if she'd have come back to claim me had she lived.

"I'm sorry I never knew you," I murmured. I lingered a few moments longer, regarding the pristine bed of chips and the pink roses, then turned away.

On the drive home, Mammy was unusually quiet.

"I'm not feeling strange or anything," I said, after five minutes. "Like you said, time heals wounds, Mammy."

She squeezed my forearm.

Thirty-Two

Squealing brakes, shouts, and loud banging awakened me abruptly.

"Open the door," a man yelled, in an English accent. "Open up, *now.*"

I glanced at the clock. It was three-fifteen in the morning.

"*Open,* or we're breaking the door down!"

"Who is it?" Mammy called back.

"British Army."

She emitted a clipped shriek. "What do yous want at this time of the night?"

"*Open the fucking door.*"

I ran into the hall as Mammy opened it. Soldiers with faces painted green and black and brandishing rifles swept inside. Two went into my father's bedroom.

"You've got one minute to get dressed," a soldier said.

"What the hell's going on?" Father said.

A sergeant pointed his gun at me. "Hands up."

He prodded me in the back with the barrel and ordered me to follow a policeman into the living room, where James was already lined up against a wall.

"Face the wall with your hands up," he said.

"Leave my children alone," Mammy said. "They're only schoolboys."

She was struggling to stay calm, but her voice trembled. Her cheeks were bloodless. Two soldiers pushed my father into the room and told him to stand facing the wall. Nuala ran from her bedroom in her pajamas, followed by Caroline, who clutched her dressing gown tightly at the throat.

"There's a soldier searching under our beds," Nuala said. She started crying.

"There's nothing of interest to you in this house," Father said.

Pots crashed on the kitchen floor.

"Rip the place apart," the sergeant called out. "We'll find the guns."

"Yous damage anything in this house and we'll set the law on yous," my mother said, her voice much firmer now. Blood surged back to her face and neck. "Where's your warrant?"

"We don't need one." The policeman laughed coarsely. "Your husband have a warrant to tip gravel over the Londonderry to Belfast road a while back?" He guffawed.

"What are you talking about?" Father asked.

"You think we didn't know you helped out the IRA?" the policeman said. "Are you in the IRA?"

A soldier came in from the hallway. Despite his painted face, when we locked eyes, the room started turning like I'd a fever. I crumpled on the floor.

"Get the fuck up," the sergeant barked. "Get him on his feet."

Richie's hand grabbed my shoulders. I didn't feel his touch. He dragged me up and swept my feet apart with his foot.

"Face the fucking wall," he said. "*Now.*"

"Frisk him," the sergeant ordered.

His hands ran along the insides of my legs and up my sides. In the background, glass shattered. The sound seemed miles away. Dust rained down in a corner of the ceiling as heavy feet trod across the attic. The bones of the house shook. Seconds later, floorboards splinted above my head.

"Nothing in the rooms, Sarge," a soldier said, as he came into the living room. "Found fuck-all."

"That's because there's *fucking* nothing to find," James said.

"Quiet, James," my mother said, then turned to the soldier. "Tell your men to stop cursing in front of my children, Sergeant."

"Nothing in the attic," someone yelled.

"Get him into the wagon," the sergeant said.

"Let go of me," Father roared. "You're hurting my fucking arms."

I turned my face to look. Richie didn't stop me. Putting their hands under his arms, the soldiers hoisted Father above the floor. He struggled and swore as they moved toward the front door. He clawed at the doorjamb, but the soldiers had momentum on their side and whisked him outside. It was astonishing to see my father, a man always in charge, who never asked for advice, carried in such an undignified manner.

"Those two as well," the sergeant said, indicating my brother and me.

"You're *not* taking my children," Mammy said. "Over my dead body."

Richie's eyes met mine. I turned back to the wall.

"She said they're in school, Sarge," Richie said. He prodded me gently on the small of my back with his knuckles. "Where do you go to school?"

I didn't answer. Even if I'd wanted to, the lump in my throat wouldn't allow me. My eyes stung something fierce.

"I asked where you go to school, mate," Richie asked.

"They go to Saint Malachy's," Mammy said. "You can call the headmaster. He'll verify it."

"It's true," the policeman said. "Our intelligence confirms they've four kids at school."

"Where are yous taking my husband?" Mammy asked.

"Ballykelly barracks."

"What for?"

"For questioning, missus," said the sergeant.

"If there's as much as a scratch on him when he comes home, yous'll have me to answer to," she said.

My mother had come from nervousness to ferocious defiance in the space of mere minutes. But it was all show. She knew as well as I did her threats had no bite. The Ulster government consistently covered the army's blunders when it came to harassing Catholic families like mine.

"Let's get out of here," the sergeant said, and he walked toward the door.

Richie gripped my right shoulder and squeezed. I stiffened. He patted me twice and left.

The next twenty-four hours were an accumulation of foggy occurrences. The phone rang nonstop as visiting relatives and neighbors offered long faces and sighs. Mammy's moods swung like a wrecker's ball, laughter and jokes one moment, frets and wails the next. I was also worried for Father, especially after some of our visitors' narrated secondhand stories— in detail—about the torture of prisoners at army barracks throughout the province. And this time I was the one holding a huge secret.

Twice, Richie rang, pretending to be a friend wanting to talk to me about an economics problem, but I told Mammy I didn't want to talk to anyone from school. Next afternoon, I drove to Duncarlow to fetch an apple tart and cake Auntie Celia had baked for Mammy. I'd just put them in the back of the car and was about to get into the driver's seat when Richie pulled up alongside me in a dark blue car.

"You planning to arrest me now?"

"Please, Gabriel."

"Fuck off."

Connor came out of Auntie's shop and stooped slightly, trying to see whom I'd yelled at. I jumped into the car and drove away in a cloud of smoke and pebbles. All the way home, I checked in my rearview mirror to see if Richie was following.

He reappeared in a different car the next evening as I was walking home from Granny Harkin's.

"Get in the car a minute."

"I don't want to see you again."

I continued walking and he drove alongside me.

"I'd no choice," he said.

I walked faster. He swung his car onto the verge and opened the door. Leaping across the narrow ditch, I climbed over a rusty barbed wire fence and sprinted across the field. He gave chase. A circle of sheep scattered as I ran. I charged into a copse of sloe-bushes and pines, crashing through the underbrush and zigzagging as I made my way down the slope toward the river, burbling in the background.

Richie grabbed me as I ran into a clearing ringed with blazing gorse. I spun around and rammed my fist in his nose. Blood spurted from his nostrils. His eyes opened wide, but he didn't let go. I suppose years of military training prepared him for attacks like this. As he dragged me to the ground, I lashed out again and struck him on the jaw. He climbed on top of me, pinned my arms with his knees and held down my shoulders.

"Bastard, get off me," I said. "I fucking *hate* you."

"I told you, I'm the cannon fodder." His grip was hard as steel. "I follow orders. That's how the army works."

I struggled a little more and then let my body go slack. We didn't look at one another or speak. A bird trilled in a nearby holly tree. The river murmured. In the distance, a cow lowed three times.

He took his knees off my arms but stayed on top of me, his butt bearing down on my chest and his thighs tight against my sides. He raised his hands in faux surrender.

"I had to act like you were the enemy," he said.

"*Act?*"

"The sarge would have been suspicious if I'd treated you soft." He wiped blood from his upper lip with his hand. "You know that's true."

"I want to sit up."

Our eyes met for a long moment and then he rolled off me. I sat up and wiped dirt off my shirt.

"I'd no idea we were lifting your old man 'til it was too late." He crossed his heart. "What would you have done in my position?"

"I wouldn't be in the fucking British Army. Full stop. End of story." I rose and adjusted the waist of my jeans. Folding my arms, I stared at the holly tree and asked, "When will they release him?"

"Forty-eight hours, if they can't pin anything on him."

I considered my next words. "It's over between us."

"Don't say that."

"What was I thinking? You're the enemy!"

He grabbed my hands. "Look me in the eye and say that."

Belligerent, I looked into his unblinking turquoise eyes. He was not my enemy. He was cannon fodder.

My eyes watered. My head felt it would explode there was so much pressure. "What are we going to do, Richie?"

"It'll be over soon." He put his arms around my waist, pulled me against him, and kissed me. I could taste his blood. English blood tasted the same as Irish.

As Richie predicted, the government released Father the following day. Wan and tired, he limped into the living room.

"Jesus, I'm stiff," he said. "The bastards made me stand eighteen inches from a wall. They had me spread-eagled and leaning into it with just two fingers for support." He laughed. "But they couldn't break me. They got no admission from me."

Mammy went to him and he kissed her on the mouth. Nuala, Caroline, and I looked at one another, so unusual was it to see a public display of affection between our parents. Nuala ran up and kissed him.

I went to him. "I'm happy you're home, Daddy."

He embraced me and patted the back of my head. "So am I, son. So am I."

Classes at school were now finished and the A level examinations were due to begin in fourteen days. I'd been studying at home ever since, but it was now Friday evening and I was taking a break. Richie and I were on the beach. We couldn't use his friend's caravan as a couple from England was using it for the weekend. We'd bought sandwiches, apples, and sodas at a grocery and picnicked on the sand, sitting on towels he'd brought while listening to pop music on his transistor radio. Though after nine o'clock, the weather was unseasonably hot and we peeled off our clothes on a whim and went swimming in our underpants in the brisk water. It was magical, the sun a crimson ball sliding slowly toward the distant horizon, the sky swatches of indigo and burnished copper, the sea grass on the dunes swaying lazily in the breeze. A short distance away, a man stood admiring the seascape from the dune nearest the public road, undoubtedly also surprised to see people bathing in late May when the Atlantic water wasn't yet warm.

After we came out of the surf, the water droplets gleamed on Richie's tanned skin and reminded me of the beautiful man I'd watched changing years ago on the beach as a kid. I wondered if he'd married the girl who'd scolded me for rolling beneath the towel to peek at her boyfriend's privates. Even as a six-year-old I'd known I was a different. Noticing me watching him, Richie leaned over and kissed me.

"Stop. That man on—"

"He's gone." He laughed. "You think I've got a death wish?"

A low rumble commenced, like the sound of far distant thunder. A man and woman riding two sleek horses, one dappled gray and the other black, galloped toward the water. We watched them skirt along the water's edge, jets of water kicked up by the horse's hoofs, and finally merge with the gathering dusk.

We collected our things and headed back toward our cars. At the foot of the last dune, we embraced. This would be the last time we saw one another until exams were over.

"Nothing less than As, mind," he said, as we started up the dune hand-in-hand.

"Understood, taskmaster."

He'd have left the army and would be living in London by the time my results were posted in mid-August. Though I could live with him in his one-bedroom apartment in London and travel to the LSE from there by the Tube, we'd decided I should live in the University Halls of Residence for the first year, as all freshmen did. That way, I'd make friends and enjoy a fuller university life. In the second and third year, I'd live with Richie in Chiswick.

Richie tossed the damp towels into the back seat of his car. Though the curtains were drawn in the houses on both sides of the quiet street and no one was around, we didn't want to take chances, so we pretended we were two buddies taking our leave.

"Good luck," he said, and we shook hands.

"Thanks."

"See you at the caravan last Friday in June." He climbed into the driver's seat. "I'll have some ice-cold beers ready to celebrate, so make an excuse to your parents and stay overnight."

"Easier said than done."

He started the car. After checking up and down the street, I leaned my head in through the car window and kissed him quickly.

I watched until the taillights of his car disappeared around the corner before driving off.

During the ride back to Knockburn, I thought about my future with him in London and the exams and how so much depended on getting the required grades. About a mile from home, the headlights of an approaching vehicle blinded me and forced me to slow down. I reached up to adjust the rear view mirror as a white van overtook me. It came to an abrupt stop thirty yards ahead, forcing me to brake sharply to avoid crashing into it.

Two men in black masks ran toward me. They opened my door and dragged me out.

"What's going on?" I said.

They didn't speak. I knew from stories I'd heard that this was the IRA. The taller man twisted my arm behind my back and frog-marched me to the van. The doors opened and they pushed me inside, where another man was waiting. The shorter man who'd helped take me to the van climbed inside. His companion, also masked, bound my hands behind my back.

"My father's car . . ." My mouth was dry with panic. "What are you going to do to me?"

Visions of my bloodied body lying in a ditch crowded my mind.

The van took off at high speed. Still, no one spoke.

"Please . . . tell me. My parents will—"

"They'll be told where to find you."

The last thing I remembered was the looming butt of a rifle and then the crack as it crashed against my face.

When I came to, my head was pounding and I felt a scalding sensation inside my nose. They removed my hood. I sat on a parlor chair, my torso bound to it with a rope tied so tight I could scarcely breathe. A Tilley lamp lit the bulging whitewashed walls. An ancient dresser with broken drawers stood in one corner. Scraps of newspaper and feathers littered the wooden floor. Dampness as thick as butter permeated the air. A star twinkled through a hole in the roof. It was clear that no one had lived in this cottage for years.

I could hear men talking in another room. In front of me, the taller of the men who'd kidnapped me, still hooded, sat on a chair. He screwed the top on a small brown bottle and placed it in the pocket of his green parka jacket.

"Where am I?" I asked, moving my arm to try and rub the side of my aching head.

He didn't answer.

"Are you the IRA?" I swallowed hard but my mouth was still dry. "I've done nothing wrong."

"I've never had to deal with a queer before," said the man. "First time for everything, I guess."

"I want to go home."

"Aye, in a brown box after we're done with ye." He coughed. "You're disgusting. How can you have sex with men?" He spat on the floor. "Real Irishmen don't do that."

"Please let me go."

"Did you tout on your own father and the other men?"

"I'm no informer. I'd never do that."

The man hit me hard on the cheek with his big hand. "Don't fucking lie. Tell the truth and we'll finish you off mercifully."

A shiver ran up my spine. "I didn't inform on anybody. I swear."

"You've been doing the dirty with a fucking British soldier."

My mouth opened, but I couldn't speak.

"How much does the army pay for a tout? Or is him fucking you pay enough?"

"Please, I beg you . . . we never talk about what's going on. It's a rule we have."

"You think I was born yesterday?"

A door opened behind me. The floorboards creaked as someone walked up the room. The person drew up behind me. I turned to look. Though also masked, I recognized his hands first, and then the way he cupped the cigarette so the lighted end faced toward his palm. He'd been smoking that way since he was a teenager, the way the so-called "hard men" smoked when we'd been at Saint Malachy's.

"Connor!"

He didn't speak.

"Connor, tell him I'm not a tout."

His hand hesitated and then he put the cigarette to the mouth hole of the mask and took a long drag.

"I know it's you," I said. "Please tell him."

"Give me a minute with him," Connor said to the man. "I'll get it."

The man rose, spat at the floor in front of me again, and walked out. Connor sat and took off his mask. We looked at one another without speaking for a long time.

"What is it you're to get?"

"A confession."

"I've no information. You've known me my whole life, Connor. You know I'd never inform on anybody."

"I thought I knew you'd never screw with British soldiers."

"I'm *not* screwing. We're together. He's leaving the army soon. And he's a Catholic. Granny made him tea once."

A car door slammed and the engine started. Lights shone through the small window as it drove away. Connor walked over to the window and looked out at the darkness.

"There's only one way you can make this right," he said, lighting a fresh cigarette with the old one as he made his way back to me. He took a long puff. "You have to find out when the soldier's unit next patrols around here and let me know."

"So you can kill him?"

Connor shrugged.

"We never talk about his work. And I wouldn't do it even if we did." My voice cracked. "He and I are together and I'm no tout." I met Connor's frigid stare. It used to be my cousin couldn't look you in the eye. Had the IRA trained him to hold a person's stare? "After what we've done together . . . you know exactly who I am, Connor."

His eyes flitted toward the door. "What's that supposed to mean?"

"You know exactly."

"Why'd you tell Uncle Harry and Auntie Eileen what you are?" He shook his head. "Some things you keep to yourself."

"I didn't want to live a lie."

"You're talking crazy."

"I can help you, Connor. Auntie Celia will understand. And Martin supports me."

"What the fuck are you trying to say?" He fumbled in his jacket pocket, took out a revolver, and put its icy snout to my temple. His hand shook. It was surreal. I shut my eyes.

The door opened. "You get it?" the tall man asked, as he strode up the room.

"He's not a tout." Connor jammed the revolver back in his pocket. "He's a fucking poof, but no tout."

"He's been having it off with a British soldier," the man said. "That's punishable. He pays the same price any Catholic woman fucking a soldier pays when she's caught."

"I'm not getting involved in that," said Connor. "Our orders were to get a confession and he's got nothing to confess." He walked away.

The man yelled for someone to come and help him. Grabbing my hair, he pulled back my head so fiercely I thought he was trying to tear my scalp off. Someone rushed up the room and hands started cutting my hair. The scissors were blunt; the ends of the blades dug into my scalp. After the man finished, they bundled me into the van again. We drove for twenty minutes or so and then the driver must have pulled into a ditch as the van went slightly lopsided. The doors opened from the outside and I was pulled out and tied to the same telephone pole where I'd helped Daddy hoist the Irish flag a year ago. The flag was tattered now. One of the men poured a bucket of thick black paint over my head and shoulders. Seconds later, a blizzard of white and brown feathers enveloped me. The men jumped into the van, blared the horn five times and drove off at high speed.

Everything was deathly silent and then I heard running footsteps.

"Oh, sweet Jesus," Mammy cried.

She, Caroline, Nuala, and Granny ran up.

"What have they done?' Granny said, as she tried to untie the rope around my chest.

She couldn't do it and Nuala took over, biting at it with her teeth to loosen the knots when she couldn't succeed with her fingers.

"You poor thing," Mammy said. "What possessed you to consort with a soldier, Gabriel?"

"Now isn't the time," Granny said. "We need to get him cleaned up before Harry gets home."

Daddy was in the living room when I came in after bathing. I was too tired to be nervous. My dark, glossy hair was ruined. The only thing Mammy could do to make me look respectable was shave off what tufts remained with an electric razor, which she had. There were abundant cuts and scratches where the scissors had punctured my scalp. My forehead was swollen and my cheeks blazed from scrubbing off the tar-like paint.

"A fuckin' soldier?" Daddy said.

"I didn't tout on you to the British soldiers like they accused me of doing."

His mouth pursed in disgust.

"I want you gone from here by tomorrow." He smashed his fist down on the arm of his chair. "You have no home here."

Mammy rose off the sofa and stood before me. "He's not going anywhere. His exams begin—"

"He's out," said Father, looking from face to face.

"Daddy, please," Caroline said.

"It's not his fault he likes a soldier," Nuala said.

James watched from the door, his face also contorted. How alike he and Father looked when angry.

"His being homosexual is one thing," said Father. "I could live with that. But sharing a bed with the fucking British enemy . . . !"

"Dead right, Daddy," said James. "He might as well shoot Catholics."

"You're angry and I understand that," said Mammy. "But Gabriel's not a murderer."

"He's *out*," said Father, looking at me with murder in his eyes. I'd never seen such hatred in his face. "How can you go with a soldier, the people that shot those innocent people dead in Derry?"

"He's not a paratrooper," I said.

"They're all murderers. Every fucking one." He tucked his fingers into his palm and formed a tight fist. "I want you gone by tomorrow evening."

"He's got nowhere to go," Mammy said.

"You can leave with him if you want, Eileen," Father said. "He's *not* in this family anymore. He and I are finished."

Mammy, Caroline, and Nuala started crying.

"That's enough, Harry," said Granny.

"Have yous lost your wits?" Daddy said, and banged the arm of the chair again. "He's bedding a fucking English soldier—*scum*."

Granny leaped up. "Come on, darlin'." She crossed the room and pulled me out of the chair. "You'll stay with me until your daddy comes to his senses."

For a woman of eighty-three, her grip was astonishingly firm as she led me out the door.

⚭

Despite Granny's hopes and Mammy's pleas, Father did not relent. Granny said I would stay with her until I left for England. I reviewed for my exams at her home and ate lunch and dinner with Mammy, but always took care to leave the house before Father returned from work. My brother tolerated my presence, but my dating Richie was something he could not condone.

In a weird way, I understood both my father's and brother's anger. Many Catholics were dying and suffering at the hands of the police and army, including the fourteen murdered victims of Bloody Sunday. My parents had attended the protest against internment in Derry that day and had had to crawl on their hands and knees along the streets when the soldiers started firing live bullets. I still remembered Mammy's bloodied knees. Richie was Father's and my brother's enemy. They despised him more than they despised my homosexuality. They'd never understand how Richie was just a cog in the British Army, that he didn't make decisions. They'd never understand that he was cannon fodder.

It also proved impossible to see Richie anymore. It was too dangerous. I was sure the IRA watched my every move. We'd spoken on the phone and I'd told him what had happened, though I didn't disclose the incident with the paint and feathers. What was the point in causing him unnecessary distress? We resolved to meet again in London in early October, when I would arrive to attend Fresher's Week at the LSE.

382

Thirty-Three

T he person I called first after the exam results posted
two months later was Richie. He was now finished with
the army and living on the three years of wages he'd
saved during his Ulster tour as he decided whether he wanted
to go to night school or find a job. I urged him to attend night
school to take A level courses and then go on to university. He
was too intelligent to work in an electronics store selling TVs,
or something of that ilk.

Within two weeks of the results, I received a letter from the
LSE confirming I was accepted to study law. Neighbors, friends,
and my family congratulated me—even James, albeit begrudg-
ingly. I took it.

My joy was doused only by Father's refusal to acknowledge my success, never mind my existence. It wasn't extinguished entirely by his response, because I knew I was not responsible for his bigotry. Though I wasn't sure Mammy's maxim that time healed all wounds would apply to my father.

Before I left for England, Uncle Brendan sent me three thousand pounds and promised to send more throughout the year. Granny gave me four thousand.

"It's your lifetime supply of lambs for market," she said, "now I know you'll never be a farmer." My mind flashed back to my lamb, Bonnie, and how innocent a time childhood was, how so much had happened in my life since then.

At the docks while awaiting the ferry to England a week later, Mother embraced me so tightly the pressure on my upper arms lingered after she pulled away.

"I'm very proud of you, son," she said. "Work hard, and don't take any drugs. There's a lot of that going on in England and people will tempt you."

"I won't, Mammy."

Her eyes ran over my short hair and moustache. She didn't like it, but I'd refused to shave it off.

"Say your prayers and go to mass on Sundays. Don't miss any."

I nodded, the irony that she considered me devout despite my having had sex with a man foremost in my mind. The ferry's thunderous horn blared. After a final embrace, I picked up my suitcases and walked up the gangplank.

It seemed to take forever for the ship to travel along Belfast Lough and finally enter the choppy Irish Sea. The crossing to Liverpool and train to London took the guts of a day. I felt grimy and tired when I finally entered the Euston station concourse at noon the next day. The place was enormous, built of massive naked girders and ribs of steel, with rows of plate glass forming the high roof overhead. I felt as important as an ant. People bustled about the concourse with a knowledgeable air. These people were part of London, knew the city intimately and their roles in it. Would I ever feel like them?

I made my way to the information kiosk, my arms aching as the suitcases were so heavy. Richie wasn't there. I scanned the milling crowd. After ten minutes, I panicked. We'd planned that I'd spend the weekend at his apartment in Chiswick before I moved into the University Hall of Residence. Horrible thoughts crowded my head. What if he'd changed his mind? What if he'd gotten cold feet? What if it had all been my imagination and he really didn't care for me as much as I thought he did?

"Gabriel!"

He came to me with his arms outstretched, his amazing blue eyes flashing in the shafts of sunlight spilling down on the concourse. He wore a red plaid shirt, faded jeans, and a pair of Doc Martens he'd told me about. We hugged. I expected it to be brief, but he made no attempt to end it.

"The moustache suits you," he said. "All you need now is some faded jeans and a plaid shirt and you're a clone, too."

I laughed. Richie had told me about the clone fashion among gays.

He picked up the largest of my suitcases and we headed up the steps and out the exit. When we reached the street, he summoned a black taxi and we bundled inside. Our driver wore a purple turban and took off at high speed after Richie told him where to take us. Richie sat much closer to me in the cab than I expected. London really was going to be different.

"Welcome to your new life." He squeezed my thigh and kissed me quickly on the cheek. "I've so much to show you."

In the rearview mirror, the driver's almond-shaped, dark eyes locked briefly on mine. A woman's rapid voice rattled over the walkie-talkie, telling other cab drivers in a cockney accent I recognized from TV to pick up fares. I was in a new world. My new life had begun.

Afterword

As *A Son Called Gabriel* is republished by Pegasus Books, some readers may wonder why I decided to change parts of the novel as originally published.

While Gabriel's story is not mine, his family is not my family, and the novel explores universal themes like love and sectarianism, there is some truth in the parts of the narrative depicting his growing up gay in a religiously conservative neighborhood and in the personal and external torments he endured. In the 1960s and 70s, Northern Ireland's Protestant and Roman Catholic communities were very homophobic and the Reverend Ian Paisley, a Free Presbyterian, spearheaded an assault on the latent LGBT community with his "Save Ulster from Sodomy" campaign after the parliament in London decriminalized homosexuality. His efforts were ultimately unsuccessful, but Northern Ireland still remains quite homophobic. The Democratic Unionist Party (DUP), the majority political party forming the government in Northern Ireland and founded by the late Dr. Paisley, refuses to allow same-sex marriage, despite it now being legal throughout the rest of the United Kingdom.

As I wrote *A Son Called Gabriel*, there were several nights when, after I read a scene I'd written, I'd break down because it brought back bewildering and painful memories of my own experiences as a sixteen-, seventeen-, and eighteen-year-old. A few years after the book's first publication, I began to feel I had not been as true to Gabriel as I should have been. I wondered if I'd interwoven too many of my personal feelings with Gabriel's and, as a consequence, had shortchanged this budding young man. Had I constrained his growth, denying him both happy as well as painful opportunities and experiences? Had I left him in a sort of limbo, neither fish nor fowl, heading into his future still somewhat troubled?

As more time passed and I became increasingly perturbed about the injustice sustained by the LGBT community, my community, the wise words of the late Harvey Milk in his "That's What America Is" speech sounded louder inside my head:

> Gay brothers and sisters, . . . You must come out. Come out . . . to your parents . . . I know that it is hard and will hurt them but think about how they will hurt you in the voting booth! Come out to your relatives . . . come out to your friends . . . if indeed they are your friends. Come out to your neighbors . . . to your fellow workers . . . to the people who work where you eat and shop . . . come out only to the people you know, and who know you. Not to anyone else. But

once and for all, break down the myths, destroy the
lies and distortions . . .

As the community asserted itself increasingly, the world
indeed moved haltingly forward regarding LGBT issues, as
Milk had predicted. People began to understand that men and
women who identified as gay, bisexual, or transgender were
indeed not the threat to society that religious zealots and bigots
portrayed them as, that they could form relationships as loving,
committed, and important as their own, that they were indeed
their brothers and sisters, mothers and fathers, cousins, uncles,
and aunts, friends and co-workers, and, admittedly rather shock-
ingly to many, even their wives and husbands. My own long-term
relationship, which has brought joy, burdens, and responsibili-
ties equal to any heterosexual union and that demands the same
recognition and respect, is further proof of Milk's hypothesis
now crystallized into undisputable fact.

With the advent of legal same-sex marriage in the US,
I knew I had to rewrite a fundamental part of the novel.
While no marriage other than heterosexual marriage crosses
Gabriel's mind throughout the narrative, I felt compelled
to acknowledge the silent gay men and women who grew
up in the same era as he did, who were as reconciled and
happy with the newly minted adults they'd become as most
LGBT people are today, but who also understood they had to
escape the homophobia and sectarianism of rural Northern
Ireland and live their dignified truth in England's cities and
beyond. For Gabriel, though the rigid political and religious
milieu conspired to deny him equality (because he was both
a member of the population's religious minority and a young
gay man), I needed to depict scenes of hope and happiness,
even if his happy relationship had to remain secret due to the

omnipresent threat of exposure and the dire consequences that would surely follow.

I feel unburdened now that I've done Gabriel justice and sincerely hope those readers who've enjoyed the earlier version of the novel will agree.

—Damian McNicholl
Pennsylvania, 2017

Acknowledgments

Thanks to my editor, Katie McGuire, Claiborne Hancock, Iris Blasi, cover designer Derek Thornton, interior designer Maria Fernandez, the sales people, and everyone else at Pegasus Books who worked on the novel. And to Margaret O'Connor, my agent and friend.